SHAMAN WINTER

"Anaya jumps headlong into magic . . . with elements of time travel, sorcery, and confrontation between good and evil . . . unravels at a fast pace . . . entertaining." —*Sunday Denver Post*

"Baca immerses himself in New Mexico's history and culture, and it is a real pleasure to follow his tour of contemporary New Mexico and the same sixteenth-century land during the Spanish entrada. . . . It's another pleasure to read a novel written by one of the greatest contemporary novelists—a mark of the maturity of the Chicano novel."—*Hispanic* magazine

"Vivid . . . woven into the plot is a bit of history, mysticism, and danger." —*Naples Daily News* (FL)

"Enthralling . . . Anaya is a master."
—*Riverside Press-Enterprise* (CA)

"Enjoy the author's extensive use of symbolism, the Spanish language, and deft blending of cultures. . . . Anaya's books always have much to offer readers. SHAMAN WINTER is no exception."
—*Fort Worth Star-Telegram*

"As always, the veiled past and the rich traditions Anaya grew up with continue to beat at the heart of his stories." —*Weekly Alibi*

more . . .

"Fast paced . . . fascinating and absolutely eerie . . . a vivid picture of the spirituality of another culture. . . . Anyone who enjoys a brilliant tale that is a bit different needs to try the Baca novels or for that matter any of the works of Mr. Anaya."

—*Midwest Book Review*

"Anaya's blend of mysticism and fact makes the book a fascinating read." —*Shelf Life*

"With elements of love, loss, and spirituality, Anaya has yet again woven a multifaceted and richly textured tale." —*El Paso Times*

"Wrapped in mysticism . . . A tangle of conspiracies, high-speed chases, murders, and chaos unravels at a fast pace." —*Arizona Republic*

RIO GRANDE FALL

"High-flying mystery . . . a refreshing piece of literary work." —*San Antonio Express-News*

"Complex and richly drawn."

—*Albuquerque Sunday Journal*

"Blends magical realism with the earthiness of good crime fiction." —*Houston Chronicle*

"A fascinating hybrid of detective story, adventure yarn, and shamanistic magic." —*Kirkus Reviews*

"A thrilling adventure." —*Library Journal*

"Ambitious. . . . There are stories within stories in this narrative. Some of them are ancient and mystical, others are contemporary and realistic. In Mr. Anaya's incantatory voice, they are all magical."
—Marilyn Stasio, *New York Times Book Review*

"Splendid."

—*Rocky Mountain News*

"Memorable."

—*Publishers Weekly*

"Something new under the sun . . . puts a cultural spin on the classic murder mystery."
—*Arizona Republic*

"Anaya has created an easygoing and amiable detective in Sonny Baca, a fellow we should see more of in future books."
—*Washington Post*

"A rhapsodic journey. . . . Magical, mystical, and often poetic."

—*Buffalo News*

"His most ambitious novel. . . . He is the leading storyteller of the Nuevo Mexicanos."
—*Houston Chronicle*

Also By Rudolfo Anaya

Bless Me, Ultima
Bendíceme, Ultima
Alburquerque
The Anaya Reader
Zia Summer
Jalamanta
Rio Grande Fall

RUDOLFO ANAYA

SHAMAN WINTER

WARNER BOOKS

A Time Warner Company

WARNER BOOKS EDITION

Copyright © 1999 by Rudolfo Anaya

Cover design by Andrew Newman

Warner Books, Inc.
1271 Avenue of the Americas
New York, NY 10020

Visit our Web site at
www.twbookmark.com

A Time Warner Company

Printed in the United States of America

Originally published in hardcover by Warner Books.
First Paperback Printing: April 2000

10 9 8 7 6 5 4 3 2 1

To the ancestors,
who brought their dreams
to New Mexico

SHAMAN WINTER

Part I

The Shaman Dreams

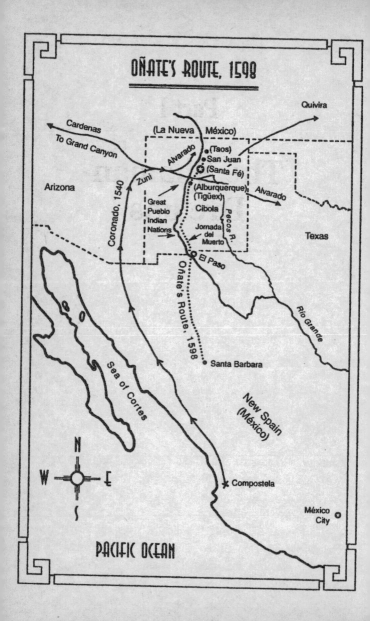

1

Sonny awakened with a cry tearing from his throat. "Aaaowl Woooman!"

He reached for her, feeling she was within his reach, just beyond the luminous light of the doorway, but the dream was already fading.

"Híjola," he muttered, rubbing his eyes and struggling to sit up. A dream, but it seemed so real.

He shivered. His bedroom was cold.

He looked around, half expecting to see the desert scene of the dream; instead, he was enveloped in the soft aura of a December dawn flooding through his window. He had startled Chica. She peered from the blankets where she lay snuggled, looking at him with an understanding expression.

"Qué pasa?" her seal-like eyes seemed to ask.

"It's okay, Chica, just a dream," he said, petted her, and lay back into his pillow.

Chica was the red dachshund that had appeared in the neighborhood. Don Eliseo, Sonny's neighbor, took her in and fed her, but she insisted on making her home with Sonny.

"She's lost," the old man said. "I fed her, but she keeps coming to your door."

"Let her stay," Sonny said. Don Eliseo had set up a box for her to sleep in, but every night she jumped on the bed and burrowed beneath the blankets.

Sonny reached for the notebook on the bedstand. During the past few months his dreams had been very real, and don Eliseo had suggested that he record them. The old man was teaching Sonny how to construct his dreams.

"A person can actually be in charge of their dreams," the old man said.

Sonny doubted him at first. Dreams were supposed to be incoherent, random images that came out of nowhere. Symbols that needed to be interpreted. How could one order one's dreams?

"When you enter the dream, you leave this world," don Eliseo replied. "The two worlds are connected by a luminous door. You are the master of your life in this world, so you can be the master of your dreams."

Sonny followed his instructions, and he had become adept at it. Dreams that used to come as jumbled images now came as stories that somehow Sonny began to manipulate even as he dreamed.

"Let's see," he whispered, wetting the tip of the pencil with his tongue, and then began to record the dream.

In the dream I was a Spanish soldier named Andres Vaca. I was with Oñate on the banks of the Río Grande just before he started his march into New Mexico in 1598. . . .

He paused and saw himself again, standing on the sandy banks of the river, staring across the slow-moving, muddy waters. To the north lay the unknown province, that huge expanse of land the earlier Spanish explorers referred to as la Nueva México.

Oñate's expedition had come north from México to the banks of the Río Bravo, as it was called on some of the early maps, near a place called el Paso del Norte. From the valley of San Bartolomé in Nueva Viscaya, they had traveled, journeying north to the promised land, la tierra adentro, the land of Cabeza de Vaca, Coronado, and the other earlier Spanish explorers. Behind them lay the desert of Chihuahua.

Andres stood looking north, Sonny wrote, wearing a white shirt and black pantaloons, and the helmet and breastplate of a soldier. For the soldiers and families who had come with don Juan, this was more than a new adventure, it was a chance for a new life. They realized there were many more dangers to be faced as they crossed the desert called la Jornada del Muerto, but the explorers were eager and expectant.

The vision of what la Nueva México promised was a constant inducement for the weary members of the expedition. For the men the possibility of finding gold meant they could be hidalgos, hijos de algo. They could acquire land and a proper title, something they could never hope for in Spain or México. Yes, the life of a landed gentleman was worth risking one's life for. Even the Adelantado Oñate dreamed of finding rich mines to rival those of Zacatecas.

On the other hand, the goal of the Franciscan friars who accompanied the expedition was to save pagan souls, the souls of the many Indian tribes described by Cabeza de Vaca, Fray Niza, and Coronado. Already the friars had been busy preparing the natives of the region for baptism.

Andres sniffed the clean desert air and smiled. Let the friars do their work, he had other things on his mind. Behind him, in the camp, he heard the sounds of the men preparing for the wedding ceremony. A smile lingered on his lips and lit his brown eyes. This evening he would marry a young

woman, the one the tribe called Owl Woman. The friars
would baptize her, give her a Christian name, and she and
Andres would be married. He felt rejuvenated in his purpose
for going north. Now he would have a wife by his side, and
he would raise a family in those unknown lands.

Sons and daughters to populate the land. Sons and daughters to build villages and make peace with the Pueblo Indians of the north. He had had enough of the gold-induced
carnage that had swept over México like a plague. He was a
soldier, and he had done his share of murdering, but an apparition had come to him one day on the field of battle. A
woman dressed in blue appeared and told him to go north to
meet his destiny. He was to put away the sword and become
a farmer. Andres resisted the apparition's words, and the
next day he was wounded in battle. Near death's door he
again saw the woman, and she repeated her message: Go
north into the new land, put away your sword, and turn to
the earth for your sustenance.

He had heard the stories of the great Coronado, and he
knew that in the northern mountains lay meadows where
cattle and sheep would thrive. Fields of corn and vineyards
would fill the valleys. The woman's voice induced these images, and Andres Vaca said, Yes, I will follow this path. It is
meant to be.

The horses in the remuda whinnied. Perhaps they sensed
a desert coyote moving in the sandhills. A cool breeze
drifted across the river, and on the branches of a cottonwood
tree a large raven landed.

"In the dream I was Andres Vaca," Sonny said to Chica.

Don Eliseo had said, "Dreams are a journey into the
world of spirits. Since it is your journey, you must construct
the dream. Do not be at the mercy of other forces that come
to tamper with your dream. With practice, it may be that

someday you may become master of your dream. Many are masters of this material world and learn to manipulate it to their desire. But few become masters of their dreams."

The old man knows about dreams, Sonny thought and returned to his notes.

Someone approached Andres Vaca.

Buenas tardes, Capitán Vaca, the man called.

Buenas tardes, General, Andres Vaca replied, turning to greet Juan Pérez de Oñate, the newly appointed governor of New Mexico.

Forgive me for interrupting your reverie, Andres, Oñate said, addressing the young man informally.

Not at all, Andres Vaca replied. In my contemplation I was merely enjoying these last moments as a single man.

Oñate smiled. You are marrying an exceptional woman. With her at your side, I am sure destiny will treat you kindly.

I was looking to the north and imagining the great adventure that awaits us, Andres replied.

Yes, Oñate said. On an evening like this I also am filled with the desire to see the northern mountains. Following the Great River of the North, this Río Bravo, we will find a mountain range called the Sangre de Cristo. There in those valleys we will settle.

Andres nodded.

The journey has been long and difficult, Oñate continued. Now we stand on the banks of this river, the same river described by Coronado. To the north lies the province of la Nueva México. Land that His Royal Highness has commanded us to conquer and settle. We are to pacify and christianize los indios. The Crusaders who saved Jerusalem from the heathen Muslim could not have had a greater purpose.

The Spaniards' relationship to God was imbued with such a purpose. With the help of God only a century before, they had driven the Moors out of Spain, driven out the Jews, and in the few decades that followed, they had conquered the New World. Surely there was divine intervention in those historical events. The finger of God stirring the history of man. This faith in divine guidance had become part of the Spanish character, a driving force that pushed them recklessly and ruthlessly across the New World.

The Spanish crown now claimed the lands from Tierra del Fuego to this newly established interior province of New Mexico. Riches beyond the imagination flowed to Spain, and the crown thanked God. This belief that God approved their right to reap the rewards of ancient civilizations and to save the souls of los indios had become the manifest destiny of Spain.

This land to the north has been called the kingdom of the fabled Seven Cities of Cíbola, Oñate continued. I feel in my blood the gold and silver mines of Cíbola will make us all rich beyond expectation. And just as important, thousands of native souls will be baptized and saved.

He turned to look at Andres. The young woman you marry will be the first native baptized. All bodes well for our adventure.

I am glad you are pleased, Andres replied.

He knew other Spanish soldiers had taken Indian women for their wives in México, but the love affair that had developed between Andres and the Indian girl was a surprise to all. The woman was not an Aztec princess, she had no rich father or uncles to provide a dowry, she was a native of the new region, a people the Spaniards had just met.

Yes, I am pleased, Oñate said. You are one of my finest soldiers, Andres, and if you permit me to say, you have been like a son to me. I have been able to confide in you while we waited for the expedition to be under way, and you have been loyal.

You do me an honor, Andres replied. My loyalty and my love for you is as deep as my vision to settle in la Nueva México.

Oñate smiled and placed his hand on Andres' shoulder.

It is our vision that brings us to this land, Andres. You are the first of many who will marry the Indian women. I suppose if we could bring more of our women from Spain, it would be different, but if we are to survive, we need to raise families. We need sons who will make good soldiers. And we need to be mindful of our purpose, to baptize the natives. As Father Bartolomé de las Casas has pointed out in his treatises, the Indians do have souls.

I never doubted that, Andres replied, thinking that in thousands of masses he had attended as a good Catholic, he had never felt his soul come alive as it did when he was with Owl Woman.

The captain general nodded. We also will need farmers. Men who can feed our colony. This is the beginning, and it is a stroke of luck. You gain a wife, and I cement friendly relations with these people. Our caravans returning to México with the gold of la Nueva México will have a friendly outpost here.

They were interrupted by someone hurrying toward them and calling Andres. They turned to see a soldier, one of the guards stationed at the Indian camp.

Someone has stolen the girl, he cried in Castilian Spanish.

Qué dices? Oñate responded.

It's true, General. Owl Woman is gone!

Worry clouded Andres' forehead. He realized why he had shivered in the river breeze. Evil was in the air, something that had haunted him in the tranquil village of Alburquerque in Spain long before he had decided to sail to the New World. Even in the pristine desert, at the edge of this new province to the north, the evil presence had finally caught up with him.

Stolen the woman? Oñate questioned. He looked at Andres. It's a game. Perhaps some of your friends have stolen the bride as is the custom. Or perhaps it's part of the Indian ceremony of marriage?

No! the soldier replied. The Indian women came out of the jacal where they had been all day with the girl. They were crying in the most terrible way, and when I went into the hut, the girl wasn't there! The fear in the eyes of the women assures me it's no joke.

We must go, quickly, Oñate commanded, and he and Andres hurried after the guard toward the Indian camp.

In his heart, Andres felt his dreams collapsing.

The expedition from Nueva Viscaya had come this far. Here they were met by a friendly tribe of Indians, men who appeared with bows, long hair cut to resemble little Milan caps, and colored with red paint. Manxo, they said, greeting the Spaniards in peace.

Here, while the expedition rested and reorganized itself for the final trek northward, Capitán Andres Vaca had fallen in love with a young woman of the tribe. He had admired the beauty of the Aztec women in México-Tenochtitlán, and like the other soldiers he had bedded with his share. But he had never felt the certainty of true love.

That's what he had felt when he saw the young woman the elders called Owl Woman. He had gone with Oñate to negotiate with the Indians; Owl Woman sat with the chiefs and the shaman. It was clear that even at her young age she was their equal. They turned to her for advice, and she interpreted for them. She had returned Andres' gaze, letting him know that she was interested in him.

He was surprised at the affection he felt, and more surprised when he realized she was returning the interest. But he knew the young woman was special. She was the daughter of a shaman, and she had been sent to the land of the Aztecs to study. While in México-Tenochtitlán, she had learned the language of the Spaniards. The elders treated her with great respect, for about her were whispered the stories of a special destiny.

Andres learned from the tribal warriors that she was called a person of peace, one who carries dreams. She had in her possession a beautiful black bowl that was carved from obsidian.

One evening while the camp was finishing its supper, Andres had walked upriver to bathe. He entered the cool water and quickly and vigorously washed away the day's sweat and dust. When he looked up, he saw three women on the sandy riverbank. Two older women and Owl Woman. The older women spread a blanket on the sand, then disappeared. The young woman disrobed and entered the water.

Andres stood transfixed by her beauty. The women had seen him bathing, which meant they had chosen to be there. She was coming to him, her full beauty revealed in her nakedness, holding in her hands the black bowl he had seen.

Instinctively he covered himself. He felt like Adam looking at Eve in the Garden of Eden. Yes, this was truly Eden. This great river that flowed from el norte was the holy river that flowed through the garden. The pristine desert around them was still warm with the heat of the day. Birds warbled in the mesquite bushes and sang joyously in the cottonwoods along the riverbank.

Eden, Andres Vaca thought, I have come to the gate of Eden.

Owl Woman walked calmly to him, and they stood looking at each other without fear or guilt. In her eyes Andres saw an innocence he had never seen before. That attraction in his heart mixed with the sweet desert perfume of the evening dusk and blossomed into love.

Me llamo Mujer del Tecolote, she said. Her Spanish was faltering but understandable. She dipped the bowl in the water and raised it above her head, then let the water wash over her jet-black hair.

Baptism? Andres thought. She calls herself Owl Woman.

Me llamo Andres Vaca, he replied, and she dipped the bowl again and stepped forward to raise it over his head. She stood so close to him he could feel the curves of her breasts touch his chest. When the water splashed on his head, he felt a shudder go through him.

Dios mío, he thought, this must be a dream. No joy on earth could equal what I feel.

Three more times she filled the bowl and washed him, and he stood still, enraptured by her touch, hardly daring to breathe for fear of breaking the spell.

Con esta agua bendita, tu eres mi esposo, she said as she washed him.

It was more than a baptism, it was a marriage ceremony! She was becoming his wife, he her husband.

She handed the bowl to him. Los días del sueño nuevo, she said.

Sí, Andres replied, taking the bowl and filling it with water. He washed her as she had washed him, four times, allowing the water to splash over her head.

Tu eres mi mujer, he said, whispering the words, believing any moment the bubble of the dream would burst, his hands shaking from the silkiness of her skin.

When the ceremony was over, she took his hand and he went with her to the blanket on the bank.

Andres shivered, not from the water evaporating on his skin, but from the incredible lightness he felt from the young woman's touch.

She beckoned him to lie by her, encouraging him to touch her, smiling when he kissed her. She drew him close, and he entered her, feeling a consummation of the marriage bed in the warmth of her embrace. Her moans of love blended into the murmur of the river, the drone of insects in the bushes, the swirl of the end of day.

He felt fulfillment. The woman had given herself freely to him, picking time and place. He remembered the woman in his vision who told him to go north, and now he knew why.

Here on the bank of the river at the start of a great adventure, thousands of miles from his home in Spain, he had met his destiny, and it brought great clarity of purpose.

Voy con usted, Andres, she said.

Sí, he replied, accepting her. Te vas conmigo.

She smiled. Mi amor. Tu corazón.

She was giving her heart to him.

Niños, she said.

Sí. He nodded. Suddenly the thought of children was natural. It was part of her plan, and she was sharing it with him.

Aquí, she said, and reached for the dark tripod bowl and handed it to him.

He took the bowl and held it up in the light of dusk. It was the kind of bowl he remembered seeing somewhere, perhaps in one of the many mercados he had wandered through in México. Ah, but this bowl was special. He felt the energy of life pulse in the black bowl. She was saying it held their children, their future.

Sí, niños.

Nuestro destino. She nodded, searching for the words to convey the meaning of the gift.

Sí, nuestro destino. He smiled. Ah, the bowl held the dream. Their dream. Dreams of things to come.

She pointed north. Nuestra tierra.

Sí. La Nueva México.

Then she pointed south. Tula.

Ah, Tula, he repeated. He had been to Tula a few years earlier. It was the sacred city of the Toltecs, that civilization of ancient México that preceded the Aztecs. In dreams he often saw the ruins of Tula, and now he had met and fallen in love with a woman who carried a sacred bowl from there.

He looked at the symbols engraved on the outside of the bowl. There was a pattern there, he was sure, but he couldn't read the glyphs. He was sure that it must be a bowl the priests of Tula had once used in their ceremonies. A peaceful feeling emanated from the bowl.

He gazed on Owl Woman's lovely face, a classic face of Indian beauty. Was real love between a man and woman always like this? He felt he had entered her and remained in her. Perhaps it was the blood, the seed deposited, the soul of him already growing into hers. Now both were contained in this magic bowl. Perhaps it was her magic, the sureness in the way she had come to him and given herself to him. The way she spoke of their life together as if they had known each other a long time.

Mujer del Tecolote, he said. Owl Woman. The bird of wisdom of the ancient Greeks. For the Indians of México, the owl was the bird of the shaman. Only the shaman dared speak to the owl. The shaman could take the form of a coyote, jaguar, or owl. This is the way they traveled, the way they came to power. The owl crying in the bosque could be a shaman.

Sí, she replied and pointed at the glyph of an owl on the side of the bowl. She moved her finger. Next to the owl, the horns of a bull.

Tu eres Vaca.

Andres laughed. Sí, Vaca! This was incredible!

Long before the Spaniards reached the New World the Toltec priests who carved this bowl had known he would come to join his blood to the blood of this woman. The bowl held their dream and destiny. Andres Vaca was destined to be here in 1598 on the banks of the Río del Norte, waiting with the expedition of don Juan de Oñate to travel north, joining his destiny to that of Owl Woman's.

But there were no bulls or cows in the New World before the Spaniards came, he thought. How could the priests, the ancient carvers of this calendar of dreams, have known?

Es un sueño, she said, reading his thoughts.

La vida es un sueño, he repeated.

Dónde aprendiste hablar español? he asked her.

Hablo sueños. I speak dreams, she replied, smiling and leaning close to him, touching her forehead to his. A current passed through them, a current as exciting as the physical love they had just shared.

What a gifted woman, Capitán Andres marveled as Owl Woman rose and slipped into her soft buckskin dress.

Calendario de Sueños y de Paz, she said. Together they held the bowl, their fingers touching.

She spoke dreams, she passed the dream to him, she was the keeper of the Bowl of Dreams, visions of the peace to come over the land and its people.

Her dark eyes carried a message of love as she leaned and

kissed his lips softly, a kiss as warm and sweet as the juice of ripe prickly pears.

The bowl spoke, a silent language from the past, a dream of the ancients. Its artistry was as complete as the story it held. The finely polished Calendar of Dreams was a heart throbbing in his hands, a new time being born.

Then a vision of the vast land to the north swept over him. He saw the weary colonists following the Río Grande to la Nueva México, and he saw himself, a sad and disillusioned man riding across the vast desert, alone. Why alone? he thought, and clung to Owl Woman.

No me dejes, he whispered, sensing something wrong.

Voy a preparar, she replied.

She was going to her people to prepare. The marriage ceremony had to be completed within the circle of her people.

Esta Olla de Sueños es nuestra, she said, and disappeared into the brush of the river, taking the bowl with her, the bowl holding the seed and promise of their dreams.

Andres felt a shiver as the sun set. A warning cry from a coyote cut the air. But he shook off the bad feeling. This was a time for celebrating. He had met and made love to a beautiful young woman, an enchanting woman. Something magical had happened between them.

I have a wife! he shouted. Niños to raise in la Nueva México! He dressed quickly and hurried back to the camp.

Early the next morning Andres Vaca sought out one of the Tarascan guides who had come with them from México. Juan Diego knew many of the languages of the Valley of México, and he had quickly added Spanish to his repertoire. He could converse with these natives of el Paso del Norte.

Juan Diego would help interpret for him. Together they went to the girl's pueblo, and Andres Vaca spoke through the guide to the girl's parents. There was no need to explain, the pueblo had already begun preparations for the wedding feast. All knew that Owl Woman had chosen the young captain as her husband.

The elders told Andres Owl Woman's story. When she was only a girl, Owl Woman had journeyed south with a shaman to the land of the Aztecs. She had visited Tula, the ancestral holy place. When she returned, she brought with her the bowl the ancients called the Calendar of Dreams.

The priests of Tula knew their time on earth was coming to an end and that their way of life would be ruthlessly obliterated. Their temples were desecrated, the ceremonies abolished by the Spanish friars.

The dream of peace was dying, but the elders of Tula knew a new dream could be born. Owl Woman was chosen to carry the Calendar of Dreams north. She was instructed to wait for the man who could take her north to the old pueblos. There among the descendants of the Anasazis a new dream was to flourish. There she would give birth to a new people, and she would deliver the bowl to the priests of the pueblos.

So Andres Vaca learned that his destiny became part of Owl Woman's fate, and the two in turn were part of a greater destiny yet to be fulfilled in la Nueva México.

When he reported the proposed marriage between him and the young woman to Oñate, the entire Spanish expedition was glad to have something to celebrate. The journey to the banks of the Río Grande had been long and tiring. The Chihuahua desert especially had been cruel to man and beast. Already the colonists complained of the suffering they had endured, and there was still la Jornada del Muerto to cross before they arrived in the northern mountains.

Now we have allies! Oñate told his soldiers. Guides to

lead us, men of this tribe to speak to the northern tribes on our behalf. Capitán Andres Vaca has done us all a great service. We will prepare a feast to celebrate his wedding. Like Cortés before him, he will wed an Indian woman and deliver sons and daughters to the lands of the north.

The wedding plans rippled like a fresh breeze across the tired camp. The women warmed water and bathed, and they removed gowns and shoes from their trunks.

Somewhere a fiddler tuned his fiddle, and the excitement of the coming fiesta filled the air.

The men went upriver to bathe and wash their clothes in the river. The barber trimmed beards, and the cooks baked corn tortillas from the corn flour the Indians brought as a gift. Even the blacksmith sang as he replaced worn-out horseshoes.

In the afternoon the Spaniards hunted along the river, and with their harquebuses they killed many ducks, geese, and cranes. The Indians brought large fish they caught in the deep pools of the river, and a feast was prepared. Cooked in mesquite wood, the fish and fowl were savory, and the Spaniards gorged themselves.

The Indians also brought honey, piñon nuts, and bread made from the paste of a desert plant. The cautiously guarded store of Spanish wine was consumed in great quantities.

All day the food arrived, delivered by the Indian women, and all day the Spaniards ate, sang, and danced. At the evening wedding they would give thanks to the Almighty for having delivered them to this kind people who lived on the banks of the river.

Oñate had given a speech during the meal. He asked the friars to bless the momentous event, then he spoke.

This is a day of thanksgiving, he said. We who come

north to settle the kingdom of la Nueva México have endured a long journey. Our provisions are low, our feet are sore from walking. Some have allowed their spirits to sag, and I have heard there is talk of turning back. And yet the good Lord has answered our prayers and brought us to these natives who live on the banks of this great river. They plant corn, which they have shared with us. They fish the river for these succulent fish and feed us. In a few days we will leave this blessed spot that we call los Puertos, el Paso del Norte, for here indeed we take our first step into la Nueva México. But we will never forget these vecinos, los Manxos, who, though they are heathens, have shared the bounty of their land with us. Some will travel north with us and guide us, for they know the land. And the young woman who is to wed Capitán Vaca will also come with us. For this we give thanks.

A great cheer went up from the men; and the natives, sensing something important had been said by the bearded leader of the barbarians, also cheered. The first meeting of the Oñate expedition with the natives of the kingdom of la Nueva México had gone well. No blood had been spilled on either side.

But the celebration was short-lived. Now Owl Woman was missing, and Capitán Andres Vaca was hurrying to the Indian village. A stately bridal house had been erected from poles of the desert mesquite and covered with the green branches of the river cottonwood. A pine tree had been brought down from the mountains as soon as the wedding was announced, and the men from one of the clans peeled the bark from the tree and planted it in front of the jacal. From crossbeams at top of the pole hung sacks of gifts for the wedding guests, food in the form of bread, dry corn, vegetables. Even one of the Spaniards' slaughtered sheep hung there. During the ceremony the men the Spaniards called clowns would dance and frolic and finally shimmy up the tree to cut loose the gifts to distribute to the pueblo.

The women had tended Owl Woman all day, bathing her and covering her body with the luxuriant oil of the sunflower. They washed her hair with yucca roots and yerba de la negra, then tied the long, black glistening hair into the braids of marriage. Under their care and in the secrecy of the bride's house, the young woman had been transformed.

Now as Oñate and Andres Vaca approached the jacal, they found the women outside the hut, crying and filling the air with their keening.

Where is Owl Woman? Andres shouted. He didn't understand the cacophony of voices that answered him.

Andres entered the jacal and was met by Juan Diego. What has happened?

They say a spirit came, Juan Diego replied. They say an evil spirit came from the sky and stole her away.

What do you mean a spirit from the sky? Andres asked.

The shaman who stood by Juan Diego raised his hand. As he spoke, Juan Diego translated.

It is the one we call the Bringer of Curses. He came for Owl Woman, claiming her as his own. He came and he left his sign.

He pointed at the soft-tanned buckskin that lay on the ground.

Andres drew closer to the marriage bed and spied four black feathers on it. He bent to pick them up, but the shaman stopped him.

No, do not touch the feathers. The Bringer of Curses has taken the woman who was to be your wife. Now you must go in search of her and bring her back. She carries your children. If you do not find her, there will be no future for your children.

Who is this Bringer of Curses? Have you searched the village? She can't disappear into thin air! Perhaps she went to the river.

No, the shaman replied. She is not here. The Bringer of Curses has taken her soul to the land of misty dreams, there where we cannot see clearly.

Where is this land of misty dreams? he asked the shaman.

It is the underworld, the place of spirits. The Bringer of Curses came for the girl because he wishes to destroy you. Long ago you fought a battle with him. You have fought many battles with him, and now he has found a way to kill you.

Andres drew back. There it was, the evil that had followed him from Spain now came to steal away the woman he loved. He shuddered, feeling defeat in his blood.

Yes, he mumbled, I have fought many battles with him.

Owl Woman came to bring you the dreams of peace, the shaman continued. This river is the center of our world, and from here in four sacred directions live the people. We have made peace with the earth and the universe. We have vowed to respect all life, for we are the children of the dream. She was to give birth to your children, so the great violence you have done to our world can be forgiven. Together you were to deliver the Calendar of Dreams to the north, and there your sons and daughters would learn to live in peace with the earth. But without the knowledge of the dreams, you are nothing.

Nothing, Andres repeated. Only last night he had dreamed the curse of violence that had followed him to the Americas had lifted. He had awakened with renewed energy, his heart singing. Suddenly the dreams of finding gold and becoming rich and prosperous seemed unimportant. It was not gold he desired. What he wanted was the dream of a new home in la Nueva México, of family, of the love Owl Woman brought. He was part of that dream, and it could come true.

There had been too much violence and death in the conquest of México. If that could be averted in la Nueva México, then the colonization of the region would not be written in blood, and the future would be one of peace and harmony.

Where do I search for her? Andres asked the shaman.

There! The shaman pointed at the opening of the bridal house. A luminous light filled the entry way. Andres Vaca squinted. Shading his eyes with his hand, he walked through the entry and its blinding light.

The shaman had said that he and the Bringer of Curses had fought this battle before. Now the future was at stake. If he didn't find Owl Woman, there would be no future.

2

Sonny laid down his pen and glanced at the clock. It was nearly seven. Over the Sandia Mountains Venus, Sun-bringer, was as dull as a pea in the eastern sky.

"Incredible," he said to Chica.

December 18 he dated his dream.

He had seen city workers putting up Christmas decorations in the downtown streets when Rita drove him to physical therapy. The radio played Christmas carols, and along North Fourth Street once-empty lots were suddenly covered with small piñon and pine trees. But the season aroused little emotion in Sonny.

Each morning he got up, showered, dressed, and got into his wheelchair to go to therapy. When Rita brought him home, he sat in his chair and looked out the window or read. Don Eliseo visited him daily, usually at lunchtime to fix Sonny something to eat.

"Gotta keep your strength up," the old man said, meaning Sonny had to overcome the waves of depression that swept over him.

Don Eliseo's close friends, don Toto and doña Concha, also visited once a week. Don Toto's lowrider Chevy needed a battery, so they showed up less frequently. When they came, don Toto brought a bottle of his homemade wine and they drank and told stories.

The three elders were in their eighties, and they knew enough stories to fill a book. Sonny's brightest part of the day was spent listening to his old friends. Don Eliseo brought a bag full of piñones and Concha baked biscochitos, filling the kitchen with the aroma of the sugar cookies, cinnamon, and anise. They spoke about their lives, how it was when they were young, the neighbors they knew in the ranchitos up and down the North Valley, vecinos they went to visit in the Indian pueblos, the vast gardens and vineyards that dotted the valley.

"Now it's all commercial," Concha said. "If you don't got money, nobody pays attention to you."

"We've got more than that," don Eliseo reminded them. "We have our spirit. The way of our ancestors."

"Our herencia." Toto nodded.

They told stories about witches, brujas and brujos who could fly in the form of an owl or other birds, old stories the Hispanos and Mexicanos of the Río Grande had forgotten. Stories about Navajo witchcraft their grandparents had told.

"The brujo is as old as Adam," don Eliseo said. "They fly to capture your soul in their circle of evil. A good brujo, a shaman, he flies to set the soul free."

They looked at Sonny.

"The spirit is powerful, it does not die," Concha said. "It flies around. I still hear the old people. . . ."

On and on they went, telling about spring planting, the cleaning of the acequias, the summer milpas that needed constant care, the harvest of the fields under a moon so full it was a sun that embraced the Río Grande valley, filling it with a light so bright it cast shadows.

"We worked in peace with our neighbors."

"We slept in peace."

"Now it's gone. What will come in its place?"

Sonny listened.

In the afternoon Rita came with food. An enchilada dinner with beans and rice, hot tortillas, coffee, natillas for dessert. She saw to it that he ate well. Throughout his convalescence, she had cared for him. Without her he would not have survived the depression that came with the paralysis.

So he thrived on food for the soul and body. Don Eliseo's lessons and the mouthwatering, hot chile that smothered the beans, meat, and potatoes sustained his spirit. Listening to the old man, Sonny discovered that don Eliseo knew how to enter the world of dreams. During the long December afternoons he was sharing his knowledge with Sonny.

His mother came often, to bring freshly laundered sheets and make his bed, and like Rita to bring food to fill his refrigerator.

"You have to eat," she coaxed him, bringing hot menudo spiced with red chile from the Barelas Coffeehouse. They made the menudo the way he liked it.

When he was alone, Sonny read. In the afternoons he returned to reading as a solace. New Mexico history books he had accumulated since he finished college and was always too busy to read, he now devoured. He read beneath the dates and historical events, trying to understand the underpinnings of the Indohispano culture of New Mexico, the culture of his ancestors, which seemed to flare into life at odd moments. Then came the sudden illumination. The dreams he was having were related to the history he was reading.

"You have a gift," don Eliseo had said. "A dream is a way to enter the world of spirits. It is also a way to enter history. If you want to return to a place and a time in which your ancestors lived, you must dream about that place. The dream takes you there."

Create the place you want to visit in a dream? Sonny wondered. Was it possible?

That's what happened last night, he thought, slapping his thigh. I was reading about the Oñate expedition. I created the time and place, and my dream took me there.

"I'm learning to create my dream!" he said to Chica, rubbing her. "Don Eliseo's going to be proud of me."

He had become, in one way or another, the capitán in the expedition of Juan de Oñate, and the woman he loved had been kidnapped.

Why did he feel he knew the Indian woman so intimately? In the dream he had made love to her, and she had assured him she would bear his children. The marriage was planned, then the Bringer of Curses struck.

Chica scratched eagerly at his arm, rising to lick his face. It was all right, he was awake and a new day was starting.

"Sí, buenos días to you," he said.

Soon after Sonny returned home from the hospital Chica had shown up, as if she understood the man sitting in the wheelchair needed her. Rita placed an ad in the paper advertising the found dog, and she called the local vets, but nobody claimed her.

"Keep her," don Eliseo said. "She has come for a reason. She has magic, look."

Sonny looked into her eyes, and the understanding he saw there surprised him. A few years ago he had sold his mare, Stella, to a girl named Kristan. The closeness he had felt for the mare was the same he felt for Chica, the same spirit shone in her eyes. He vowed to go by Sondra's North Valley stable and check on Stella as soon as he felt better.

"Animals adopt people," don Eliseo had said, and he cut

a dog door into the kitchen door so Sonny wouldn't have to climb into his wheelchair every time Chica needed to be let in or out of the house. When she needed to, she would go outside, bark to announce to the world that she was now watching over Sonny's house, stake out her territory, and then rush back to sit patiently by his side.

Something of her spirit began to rub off on Sonny. He took an interest in her, and a bond grew between them. He secretly hoped no one would call and claim her.

"You're a great friend, Chica," he said.

She barked, jumped out of bed, and ran out of the bedroom. In seconds he could hear her outside, barking. She would explore for a few minutes, then the cold would drive her back inside.

Sonny rubbed his legs, still weak from the paralysis he had suffered when Dr. Stammer placed two paddles from the defibrillator machine to his head and shot a jolt of electricity into his skull. He had lived through it, but it had jumbled his nervous system. Those first few days he could barely talk, couldn't move, but slowly he recovered his speech and the use of his hands and arms.

Using the strength in his arms, he lifted himself out of bed and into his wheelchair. He wrapped a blanket around his cold legs, and on the way to the bathroom he pushed the thermostat up to warm the house. In the bathroom he heaved himself up and stood clumsily, clutching the cabinet, to use the toilet.

Damn Dr. Stammer! The sonofabitch nearly killed me. Early October, the most beautiful time of the year, during the balloon fiesta. I chased a shipment of dope right into Stammer's lab.

"Tamara saved my life."

The blood of the doctor splashed through the image, and Sonny shook his head.

He remembered very little. For weeks he lay in bed, a near vegetable. Rita fed him. His mother came every day and bathed him. Don Eliseo lifted him onto the bedpan. He was helpless. Anger coursed through his blood, invaded his thoughts.

Don Eliseo spoke to him.

"This will not last," he assured Sonny as he sat with him in the afternoon. "You are being born again. Think how lucky you are, you can be born again as Sonny Baca. Here in this place, now. Keep that in mind. Only a brujo is born again."

A born-again shaman, Sonny thought. "Why is this place so important?" he asked the old man.

"Because you need to center your soul," don Eliseo explained. "The shock has scattered your soul. This valley is the place of your ancestors. They are here to help bring your soul together."

"My ancestors are here?"

"All around you."

Sonny listened. Voices spoke to him.

For don Eliseo the spirits of the ancestors hovered in the breezes that swept over the valley, the wind of the universe. He honored them with prayer, and they lent strength and guidance. All was alive, nothing was lost.

Sonny had nearly given up hope those first few days he was paralyzed. When he realized he couldn't move, he entered the underworld, a helpless bag of flesh, and for a while he gave up on returning.

But those that loved him wouldn't let him remain in the darkness that engulfed him. They pulled at him, cared for him, spoke to him. They wouldn't let him give up. They fanned the lone ember that was his soul.

His mother helped bring him back from the world of the dead. Rita forced him to eat to regain his strength, whispering her love in the frozen nights. Lorenza the curandera massaged his limbs, made muscle and nerves spring back into action, worked to make the scattered energy harmonious.

I owe them so much, he thought as he entered the shower, clutching the towel rack for support.

"I am here, now. I'm not dead," he said as he turned on the hot water and scrubbed. He had to shower quickly. Even with him leaning against the shower wall, his legs would support him for only a few minutes.

Living with a jumbled brain these past months was hardly what he'd call being alive. For weeks his speech was slurred. Something in the circuitry of the brain had been screwed up. He couldn't grip anything with his fingers, and when he told his right arm to move, his left one did, but slowly the shorted circuits returned to normal. The strength in the arms returned, and the leg muscles were beginning to respond.

At first, when he realized how bad off he was, he wanted to die. Better dead than a cripple, he thought. The first few weeks had been especially tough. Rita bought him a computer with a board he could hold on his lap to spell out messages.

"Where is Tamara?" he had asked Rita when he could punch the letters on the laptop computer board.

"No one knows."

"And Raven?"

"Disappeared."

"Madge?"

"In jail."

Don Eliseo appeared. The old man sat by his side during the long, empty days of November. The old man told stories, long involved stories that wove the history of New Mexico into his personal life. He interpreted his dreams, told him of the seven paths into the dream world. Sometimes the old man brought a book and read from it. He was especially fond of the Frank Waters novels.

Sonny listened, slept, and the adventures in the books filtered into his dreams. Sometimes he awakened to find don Eliseo had fallen asleep in the chair, and then Sonny wondered if he was awake or dreaming, or simply a character in the novel lying on the old man's lap.

With the recovery also came depression; memory returned and he realized how bad off he was. Would he remain a cripple? No one knew. The young neurologist who checked him weekly couldn't promise anything. "It's a matter of time," he kept saying.

"I can't do it," Sonny had confessed one night to Rita. "Better to die."

"No!" Rita replied. "I'm not letting you go!"

She slipped under the covers with him and lay next to him, saying nothing, caressing his chest, then slowly down to his stomach, his thighs, fondling him. He sniffed the dark air and smelled the fragrance of her body, the spice of her flesh and sweat. "Ah," he responded, his desire for her breaking through the dead weight he felt in his soul.

She made love to him and the soul-sickness lifted, a springlike night filled the valley, and the sense of wonder returned to Sonny's heart.

"I can finally smell you, taste you," he whispered, and she laughed. They lay together in the aromas their bodies gave to the November night.

Rita talked about the future, what she needed to do to fix up her restaurant, how he could help, and they could be married on Christmas day, and how many children she wanted to have, talking into the night as if nothing had ever happened.

"How can you be so sure?" He hesitated.

"I am."

Her love and direction, which he always knew was strong as a hundred-year-old cottonwood, surprised even Sonny. She was planning marriage and family. The future. So the darkness lifted, memories and patterns returned, his strength returned. Rita's love brought hope. He figured he would have to learn something of patience.

The neurologist was pleased with Sonny's steady improvement. Each time Rita drove Sonny in for an office visit the young doctor poked pins into Sonny's arms, legs, hands, feet, then nodded and said, "He's coming along, he's coming along. Whatever you're doing, keep it up. Don't need to see you but once a week. Keep up with the therapy. Good day."

Lorenza came often. As she massaged him, she reminded him of his guardian animal spirits, the coyotes. Survivors. He was a coyote, he would survive.

"Become coyote," she whispered.

He turned himself into a rough, gruff coyote, using the strength of the coyote spirit, and a new energy filled him. He opened the door and howled at the moon, and down the dirt road that was La Paz Lane dogs answered his cry.

Thank God for good friends, Sonny thought as he finished his shower and dried himself quickly. His legs were trembling, ready to collapse. Sitting on the toilet seat, he pulled on a pair of jeans and a black turtleneck, then lifted himself into his wheelchair. He turned to look into a hand mirror and comb his long, thick hair.

"Ah, if I could just walk," he said to the image in the mirror. "Go dancing again."

Brown, intense eyes stared back at him, eyes he didn't remember. Was this the Sonny Baca he once knew, or was this another man?

He ran his fingers through his black beard. Rita had asked him if he wanted a shave weeks after the incident, and he said no. "Let it grow."

Now he had almost three months' growth. "Like the bearded Andres Vaca in the dream," he whispered. "The spitting image."

Pushing a lever, he quickly maneuvered the electric wheelchair back into the bedroom. Hanging on the mirror over the chest was the Zia medallion. Gold engraved with the sign of the Zia sun.

The medallion had belonged to Raven. Sonny had first seen it on him in June, the summer the people of Alburquerque now called Zia summer. Raven and his cult had murdered Gloria Dominic and tried to blow up a DOE truck carrying high-level nuclear waste to the Waste Isolation Pilot Project site near Carlsbad.

Sonny looked closely at the medallion. The round sun had four radiating lines projecting in the four sacred directions of the universe. Simple in its execution, but the artist who engraved it had carved the energy of the sun into the medallion, a mystical flow that connected Sonny to the world of spirits.

Raven used the medallion to create chaos. For a few days in October he had held Rita and Diego's daughter captive, until one dark night in the Sandia Mountains Sonny found them. They met, Sonny as the coyote and Raven as the dark bird of the forest. Using Sonny's pistol, Lorenza saved Sonny by shooting at Raven. The bullet hit the medallion, and now as Sonny felt the indentation the bullet had made, he saw again the images of the struggle that had taken place in Raven's circle of evil.

Had it not been for Lorenza he would be dead. And Rita would have become Raven's cohort through an initiation that would have dragged her into his world of evil.

That's the last time he had seen Raven. After that Sonny ran into Dr. Stammer.

But now Raven had returned in the dream. The four feathers Andres Vaca saw were Raven's calling card. Raven was the Bringer of Curses.

What was it the shaman told Andres? That he had been fighting the evil power for a long time. Was Vaca a prior reincarnation of Sonny? Had he fought Raven in that small village in Spain only to discover that Raven had followed him to the banks of the Río Grande? Followed him to steal away Owl Woman and continue the chaos and disruption on which he thrived.

"You and Raven are old souls," Tamara Dubronsky had told Sonny. "You are like brothers, and there is no peace between you. You have been enemies in prior lifetimes. The Zia medallion changes hands. You use it for good, Raven uses it for destruction."

Where did the medallion originate? Sonny wondered.

He rubbed the gold with his fingers. Egypt, Lorenza had suggested. Probably cast by priests of the sun. For those ancient dynasties, the Zia sun was the god Ra, the shining power in the medallion.

"How would they know?" Sonny had asked her.

"They could see into the future," she replied.

There in the Nile Valley the priests had looked into the

future and had seen a river like theirs, not as big and powerful as the Nile, but a river that formed a sacred corridor in the desert. An oasis of power, a green serpent winding from northern mountains, through desert, to the sea. The Río Grande. There the people would pray to the sun, pray for its blessing and that its cycles and seasons be preserved, pray for rain to nurture their crops. In an Egyptian temple, millennia ago, they had cast the sign of the Zia sun into the gold of the medallion.

Sonny shook his head. Lorenza knew. He put the medallion around his neck, then wheeled into the kitchen to make coffee. Chica came bounding in through the little door, seeking the heat of the furnace vent.

"Cold out there, isn't it?" Sonny smiled. The thermometer outside his window read twenty degrees.

"Maybe I am cursed," Sonny said to Chica as he filled the coffeepot. "Like the captain in the dream."

That's what Andres Vaca had said. A curse had followed him all his life.

He looked out the kitchen window across the dirt road to don Eliseo's house. The old man had come out of the front door, shuffling toward the withered cornfield. There he would pray to the rising sun.

Outside Sonny's window the water in the coffee can he kept for the birds was frozen solid. A couple of sparrows pecked at the edges. Along the sides of the dirt road, puddles of water left from last week's winter rain wore laces of ice.

The sun came over the southern crest of the Sandia Mountains, and in the frozen field of corn don Eliseo raised his arms in prayer, greeting the light. Sonny knew the days of the winter solstice were upon them. In three days the sun would rest at the most precarious point of its yearly journey. In the religion of the indigenous people, this was the most important day of the year, for if the prayers were not strong enough, the sun would not return, it would sink into the southern horizon forever.

Exceedingly holy days. Days of preparation, ceremony, attentiveness, prayer, expectation. Don Eliseo's prayers must be strong and good.

The old man believed every cell in the universe was connected, all was energy and light, and that clarity of light filled one's soul if only one was attentive, receptive. But as sure as there was clarity, there was darkness. Evil in the universe. Hidden in the very germ of creation was the inherent chaos.

"The Bringer of Curses is Raven," Sonny said to Chica. He wanted to tell the old man his dream, but as he was about to open the door to call out, the phone rang. He reached for it.

"Are you Sonny Baca?" the woman's tremulous voice asked.

"Yes."

"Are you the detective?"

Sonny smiled. I used to be, he thought. Now I'm in a wheelchair, learning to walk, trying to learn to live again.

"Yes, but—"

"Our daughter disappeared last night," the woman said. "Please help us. She's gone. We don't know—"

"Wait, wait," Sonny cut in. "Did you call the police?"

"Yes. The police came. They were just here. Oh, Mr. Baca, you have to help us. We read about you in the paper. You're our last hope."

"I can't get around very well," Sonny tried to explain. "I'm sure the police will do everything they can."

"They don't understand this."

Understand? Sonny wondered. Missing teenagers were

common. The cops usually tracked them down, or they got hungry and came home. That is, those that didn't get sucked into drugs, the pornography business, or prostitution. They might be found if their rebellion didn't propel them out of their neighborhood into the mean streets of distant cities.

"Did your daughter leave a note?"

"No, she just disappeared."

"Last night?"

"Yes."

"How old is she?"

"Sixteen."

"Has she ever left home before? Have you checked with her friends?"

"Mr. Baca, she was here, in her bedroom. She just disappeared."

Nobody just disappears, Sonny thought. But he had chased enough teenagers to know they got into all sorts of emotional tangles: boyfriends, girlfriends, gangs, parental restrictions. They just flew, and tracking them was not his favorite job. Once the kid came home, the parents usually forgot to pay the investigator they hired.

"What's your name?" Sonny asked. He reached for a notepad and a pencil.

"Eloisa Romero. My husband is Arturo. Our daughter's name is Consuelo. We have only one daughter, Mr. Baca. Now this. We don't know what to do. Who to turn to."

The woman's voice was near breaking.

"Did the police search the house, her room?"

"Yes."

"Did they find anything?"

"On her bed, four feathers. . . ."

"Oh, no," Sonny groaned. Raven. But why? Who were Eloisa and Arturo Romero?

"They asked us if the feathers came from one of her toys," Eloisa continued. "She still keeps all her toys in her room. But no, there are no black-feathered toys. It's something evil, Mr. Baca, that's what I think. But why us? Oh, God, why us?"

"Has anyone called you, saying they have information, or they want money?"

"No. The police said this was possible—"

Ah, Sonny's memory bank clicked. Arturo Romero was the mayor of Santa Fé. He had made a fortune in the recent real estate boom and by selling cheap santero art to tourists. All along he paid his dues to the party machine. It sounded like a classic kidnap/ransom case. But why Raven?

First the dream and the kidnapped Owl Woman, now the missing Consuelo. Unrelated? No. On both empty beds lay Raven's black feathers.

"Let me have your address and phone number," Sonny said, and scribbled down the information. "I can't promise anything, but I'll try."

The woman thanked him tearfully. Sonny hung up the phone and called Rita. There was a message for him on her machine. "Sonny, buenos días. I didn't want to call and wake you, but if you call, we're on our way to see you. With breakfast, so don't eat anything. Un beso, mi amor."

He thought of calling Diego, the compañero who had helped him in October, but he knew Diego was very busy working on the house he was building. The Hot Air Balloon Fiesta board had given Sonny enough money to get a house going for the homeless Diego and his family.

He dialed his brother Armando, a used-car dealer.

A very seductive, gravelly voice greeted him. "Mornin', y'all. This is Marlene. How can I help you?"

Marlene? I thought it was Jeanine? Ah, my bro has a new

woman, Sonny thought. Women slipped through Armando's fingers as fast as used cars.

"Hi, Marlene, this is Sonny. Mando's brother."

"Oh, hi, Sonny. How are you feeling?"

"I'm fine."

"I'm so glad. I think that's marvelous. Simply marvelous," she said in a syrupy West Texas drawl. "But why are you calling so early?" she asked in a sleepy voice. "Is something wrong?"

"No, nothing wrong. I need to talk to Mando."

Sonny smiled when he heard her trying to rouse Mando from sleep. Mando had been trying to set up a used-car business for the past few years. He bought one, sold it, went on to the next, just keeping his head above water.

"Hey, Bro, how you doing?" Mando's sleepy voice came on line.

"Great, you?" Sonny greeted him.

"Fine as wine, Hermano. What's up? You okay?"

"Yeah, fine. I need a van."

"Wheels? Hey, the only car sitting in Mando's Used Cars is a fifty-seven Chevy. Cherry, but the generator's out."

"I need a van with a lift for my wheelchair. Can you lease one for me?"

"No problem, if you got the credit. I'm so short—"

"Call Sheila García. Here's my MasterCard number." He read his card number to Armando.

"Ten-four. Anything else?"

"I need a mobile phone in the van. That should do it."

"No sweat. How soon?"

"Right away."

"Hey, Bro, it's midnight."

"It's not midnight, the sun's up. I need it now."

"Hey, only for you would I get up this early, leave this warm bed and the loveliest Texas blue bonnet."

Sonny heard Marlene squeal, then a purr and whispering: "You are so good. . . ."

"Ay te watcho, Bro!" Mando cried, disappearing, Sonny guessed, under the warm sheets with Marlene.

"Gracias," Sonny said, and hung up the phone.

His brother Armando was as reliable as wind in spring, always there with a smile, always broke, always with a big, nice-looking mamasota hanging on his arm. A lovable guy intent on making it big in the used-car business, but he, too, seemed cursed. He just couldn't seem to get beyond a couple of bombed-out heaps that he called Mando's Used Cars.

"If I get the van by Christmas, I'll be thankful," Sonny said.

A knock at the front door meant Rita and Lorenza had arrived. Sonny guided his motorized chair to the door, followed by a barking Chica. Rita, Lorenza, and don Eliseo were already letting themselves in. Santa's elves were delivering a hot breakfast. Sonny smelled the aroma of the food Lorenza carried.

"Amor," Rita greeted him, and leaned to kiss him. "Cómo 'stás? Why up so early? I thought we'd find you snoozing. Look who we found in the cornfield."

"Buenos días le de Dios, don Eliseo," Sonny greeted the old man.

"Buenos días, Hijo," don Eliseo said, patting Sonny on the shoulder and bending to pick up an eager Chica. "Buenos días, Chica."

"Hi, Sonny," Lorenza greeted him and leaned to kiss his cheek.

"Why up so early?"

"Strange dreams. And you two?"

"Huevos rancheros con chile verde for our birthday boy," Rita explained.

"Birthday?" His birthday had come and gone in October.

"Happy thirty-one anyway."

"Estas son las mañanitas, que cantaba el Rey David," she sang as they all headed into the kitchen. "Hoy por ser día de tu santo, te las cantamos a tí. Despierta, mi bien, despierta, mira que y'amaneció. Ya los pajarillos cantan, la luna ya se metió."

"Feliz compleaños!" Rita kissed him again.

"Feliz compleaños," don Eliseo joined in.

"Ay, you shouldn't have." Sonny winked. "But thanks."

The aroma of hot tortillas and chile filled the kitchen as Lorenza unwrapped the packages of food. Rita owned Rita's Cocina, the best Mexican food restaurant in the North Valley. Huevos rancheros were a specialty, and his favorite morning meal. Over easy, with refried beans and fried potatoes on the side, lots of green chile, and flour tortillas with which to scoop up the food.

"We celebrated in October," Rita said as she set the table, "your mom brought a cake, but you don't remember. You were incommunicado. Good, you started the coffee. Look, a low-fat chicken taco for Chica." She served the dog the taco, and Chica vacuumed it up.

"Nothing dainty about her eating habits," Sonny said.

"Or yours," Rita kidded him. Sonny loved to eat, and when he sat down in front of one of her Mexican meals, he ate with gusto.

While they ate, he told them about the dream, knowing that the more details he could retain, the more clues it would provide. The three people in the kitchen knew about the world of spirits, they knew about dreams. At the end he told them about the phone call from Eloisa Romero, and the missing daughter, Consuelo.

Rita looked at Lorenza. The feathers were obvious: Raven.

"Why in my dream?" Sonny asked, holding Chica in his lap when he was finished eating. He looked at don Eliseo. "And the dream is about an event that took place in 1598. I've been reading that part of the New Mexico history book. Oñate crossed the Río Grande and camped near present-day El Paso, ready for his grand entrada into New Mexico. Crazy Spaniards. Why in the hell didn't they just stay home."

"You wouldn't be here if they had stayed home," Lorenza said.

Yeah, Sonny acknowledged. The Españoles and Mexicanos had come up the Río Grande, settled beside the Indian pueblos, intermarried and created la raza cósmica de Nuevo México, the mestizos of el Río Grande del Norte. Those Nuevos Méxicanos, los manitos, were Sonny's ancestors.

"What was the captain's name in the dream?"

"Andres Vaca. With a *V*."

"How did you know?" Rita asked.

He shrugged.

"It's possible you're related," Lorenza said.

"He looked like me."

"We have to know for sure," Lorenza insisted.

"Why?"

Lorenza looked at don Eliseo. The old man had sat quietly, listening attentively to Sonny recounting his dream, sipping his coffee. The history of the people flowed in his blood and was cradled in his memory. He didn't invent meaning for the symbols and signposts in the dreams, he knew them intimately. And don Eliseo's soul was as clear as morning light. In his own soul resided the communal dream of the people.

"Been there, done that," the old man had a right to say, but he was not the kind to brag.

"Andres Vaca is one of your ancestors," don Eliseo said. "Raven, disguised as the Bringer of Curses, was there. He's back."

"But he didn't attack Andres in the dream," Sonny said. "He took Owl Woman."

Don Eliseo leaned forward, his voice trembling. "Raven has found a way to get into your dreams."

"Get into my dreams?"

"This summer he tried to get you in his evil circle up in the mountain. He thought that in his nagual, as a raven spirit, he could destroy you. You met him with the power of your coyote spirit and took the Zia medallion from him. If he can't kill you in this world, he will try to kill you in your dreams."

"I don't get it," Sonny said. So Raven was the Bringer of Curses and so he had kidnapped Owl Woman. It was only a dream.

"Andres Vaca is one of your grandfathers. Owl Woman is one of your grandmothers. She is one of the original abuelas of what will come to be your line of the Vaca family of Nueva México. Andres and Owl Woman are the progenitors of your bloodline. Raven has found a way to kidnap the grandmothers. Without them, you cease to be."

Sonny felt the fine hairs on his back and arms rise. Raven had stolen the grandmother, and if he kept her in the underworld long enough, there would be no sons and daughters for Andres Vaca and Owl Woman, and thus no bloodline leading to Sonny.

"It can't be," Sonny said, looking from the old man to

Lorenza then to Rita. "I'm here. Now. Do you mean if he kills Owl Woman, I would just disappear?"

The old man nodded, and Sonny knew better than to laugh. He wasn't kidding, he was serious.

"Haven't I taught you," the old man replied, "that the dreams of your ancestors are yours. The most power any person can acquire is to be master of his dreams, for that means he can travel in time to the world of spirits. That is the great power a man can have on earth. By entering your dream, Raven can travel to your past and destroy it."

"And thus destroy me?" Sonny whistled softly. He looked at Lorenza. She nodded. She agreed with don Eliseo. The world of spirits was the world of dreams, and Raven knew it well. Sonny had not yet mastered that world, so he was vulnerable.

"But if he captured Owl Woman, if he took her away from Andres Vaca, and thus kept their child from being born, why am I still here?"

"There are four roots to a man's history," don Eliseo said. "As there are four sacred directions from the Center. Four quadrants of the universe. He needs to take four grandmothers in order to kill your spirit."

Sonny looked at Rita. Her worried look told him to listen to the old man. He knew Raven's ways.

"Four roots, four grandmothers," Sonny thought aloud. "How can I be sure I'm related to the Andres Vaca of my dream?"

"If you need to be convinced, trace your ancestry back to 1598," don Eliseo said. "If Andres Vaca and the Indian woman are listed in church records as your ancestors, then it is so."

Time bending, mind bending. Sonny shook his head. What the hell was the old man getting at?

"I don't have a genealogy. I know my Baca grandparents from Socorro, and the Jaramillos from La Joya. That's it. How do I trace back to 1598?"

"The archives in Santa Fé," Rita suggested. "The library there has records dating back to 1598. Or Zimmerman Library." She had taken don Eliseo's interpretation of Sonny's dream to heart. Sonny was in danger! She stood behind him, softly massaging his shoulders.

"Yes, the University of New Mexico library has special collections on New Mexico history," he agreed.

He had spent time in the archives when he was a student. He had concentrated on a teaching certificate, but history and literature were his real loves. He had spent as much time as he could browsing through the stacks, letting his instincts lead him into old volumes in the archives.

Sonny looked at the old man. "It will help you to know," don Eliseo said.

He wasn't kidding. He was warning Sonny. His life was in jeopardy. He had revealed the meaning in the dream, a prophetic and possibly dangerous meaning. It was up to Sonny to use the interpretation, wild as it seemed.

Lorenza's look also told Sonny she too agreed.

"Is the kidnapping in the dream connected to the missing girl in Santa Fé?" Sonny asked.

"Probably," don Eliseo replied.

"How?"

"Are you related to the Romeros?"

"Not that I know of," Sonny replied.

"There has to be a relationship, even if distant," don Eliseo said. "So he kidnaps a young girl here, living flesh. A complement, after all these centuries, of the ancient grandmothers. You see, if Raven can kill four maternal grandmothers, he kills you by killing your history. But he needs these young girls for his own purpose."

He stood up and looked out the window. "In three days the sun is at the solstice. It will either be born again and return to bless us, or it will sink beyond the horizon. When the sun is at the weakest point of its cycle, Raven will strike. He will bring down the sun and set up his kingdom of night that follows. He needs four women, one spirit for each quadrant of the universe."

"His new kingdom," Lorenza said. "He kidnaps four of Sonny's grandmothers, and four girls. Four old spirits, four new."

Don Eliseo nodded. "In this way he controls you in this time, and in the world of spirits."

"He has taken a grandmother in my dream," Sonny said. "And one young woman. Three to go—" He shook his head. "Andres Vaca and Owl Woman lived four centuries ago. It just doesn't make sense."

"It does make sense!" the old man interrupted, his tone irritated. "I have been teaching you about dreams to protect you from Raven."

"You knew that's how he would come?" Sonny asked.

"Dreams are the way of all curanderos," don Eliseo replied. "We fly in dreams. The dream connects us to the history. Raven knows this. But go. Go to the library and see if Andres Vaca is written in the records. Then you will believe! Buenos días," he said, and walked out the kitchen door.

"Buenos días," they replied.

"I guess I pissed him off," Sonny said as he watched the old man hobble across the road. It was the first time in their two-year relationship that he had doubted don Eliseo, and the first time the old man had stalked away.

"Why not satisfy yourself," Rita whispered in his ear.

"Okay, let's do research," Sonny said.

"Zimmerman Library?" Rita asked.

"It's the closest."

"I can drive you," Lorenza offered.

"I called Armando this morning to rent me a van I can drive. Going up to Santa Fé to help the Romeros may be the best way to find out if don Eliseo is right about my ancestors. Raven took Consuelo. I have to stop Raven."

"But you're not strong enough to drive," Rita protested.

She touched Sonny. Like him, she sensed Sonny's dream and the disappearance of Consuelo were connected.

"I can drive you," Lorenza volunteered.

"You sure you have the time?" Sonny asked.

"I always keep the solstice week free. These are the most important days on my calendar. Now your life is connected to the time. . . ."

"Yeah." Sonny knew Raven worked around the equinoxes and solstices.

"You'll have to be careful," Rita said.

"I will," Sonny replied, holding her hand for reassurance. "If Raven shows up, I've got my trusty forty-five."

He looked up at the single-action Colt .45 that hung in its holster on a hook at the door. His bisabuelo's pistol, the one Elfego Baca had carried into many a fight. Sonny had never fired it at a person.

3

To Sonny's surprise, his brother showed up with a van in record time. Rita helped Sonny with his leather jacket, gloves, a scarf, and his black cowboy hat. "So you won't catch cold," she said. "With your black beard and hat you look like one of those old-timers from las Gorras Blancas."

"Then I better go armed like them." Sonny indicated his pistol, and Rita, with a slight frown on her face, reached for the holster and handed it to Sonny.

"Do you think—"

"No, I won't need it, amor, but just in case." He said no more, and they went outside.

"Hey, Bro," Armando greeted Sonny. "You're looking great." He slapped Sonny on the back. Plumes of frozen breath laced the frigid morning air.

"Feeling great," Sonny answered. "Pretty chilly." He shivered.

"Thank you, señor." Armando winked. "Hey, no wonder you're doing great. Two gorgeous women like these to take care of you. Hello, Rita." He smiled, giving both her and Lorenza an abrazo.

"I'm not complaining," Sonny said. He looked at his

brother, and the thought struck him: If what don Eliseo believed was true, Armando's existence would also be threatened. They were twins. Could history unravel from the past to the present? How many ancestors would disappear? The entire line of Bacas from New Mexico? How many others?

Don Eliseo's interpretation of the dream, not the cold air, made him shiver.

"Hi, wiener dog." Armando bent to pet Chica, but she growled. "Okay, okay, be nice. I'm not going to eat you."

"Used-car salesmen aren't her style," Sonny said.

"Hey, a lot of people don't like us," Armando replied. "But we play an important role in society. We take used cars off your hands. Now that you've got a van, want to sell your troca?"

Sonny's truck stood parked in the driveway. It looked abandoned, dusty. He really hadn't thought about his truck, but he knew don Eliseo had been starting it each morning to keep the battery alive.

"No," he answered, thinking one day he was going to drive again.

"Old cowboys never part with their trucks." Armando smiled and opened the van's side door and pushed the button to let down the wheelchair lift. "This thing runs as smooth as one of those cowgirls at the Fiesta Lounge on Saturday night. An artist was using it, so there's a few tarps and canvases in the back. I can take them out."

"That's okay," Sonny said as he drove his chair onto the lift.

"I picked this one because the lift works like a charm, and it's got a counter, like a desk. It's like a little office. Here's the control. Real easy to work. See?"

Sonny took the control Armando handed him. "Elfego Baca rides again," he said, and sniffed the cold air, identifying the piñon aroma in the morning haze. Some of his neighbors were burning wood in a fireplace or a wood-burning stove. Mingled with it was the faint rotting smell of cottonwood leaves.

Weatherman Morgan had predicted a low-pressure weather front approaching from the northwest. There would be snow by nightfall in the Taos mountains, but in the calm before the storm, the fragrances of winter blossomed. The cold morning would give way to a sunny day in the fifties before the front arrived.

"Ready."

"Vamos," Lorenza said. She turned, embraced Rita, and whispered, "Take care of yourself, promise?"

"I promise," Rita replied. She leaned and kissed Sonny. "Cuidado," she whispered.

"For sure," he replied, and patted the pistol on his lap.

"You still carrying the old man's pistol around? Have you ever shot anyone?" Armando asked.

When their father had given the pistol to Sonny, Armando had been jealous. He thought it should belong to him, and he tried to talk Sonny out of it, but Sonny wouldn't budge. Armando finally gave up trying to own the pistol. He just wasn't into history like Sonny.

"Not yet," Sonny replied. He had never fired the pistol at anyone. But Lorenza had.

"Would you?" Armando persisted.

"I guess if I had to save my skin."

The sunlight glistened on the shiny pistol.

"Hope you don't have to, Bro."

"Me, too." Sonny handed Chica to Rita and pushed the control buttons that effortlessly and quietly lifted the chair into the van. "Not bad. Gracias."

"Anytime." Armando shut the door.

"Be careful!" Rita blew him a kiss.

"Ten-four," Sonny called back.

Lorenza got into the driver's seat and started the van. She gave a thumbs-up signal and they were off, heading—if don Eliseo was right—to a meeting with Sonny's destiny.

The University of New Mexico campus spread across the hill just east of downtown. Pueblo on the Mesa it was called, a pueblo of learning. The library, a stunning example of New Mexican pueblo-style revival architecture, sat in the middle of campus. The stuccoed walls, vigas, and wood interior gave the sanctuary of books a warm, intimate feeling, something felt as New Mexican in character. Something close to home.

Lorenza parked on the north side in a handicapped zone, thanking the artist who had rented the van before Sonny. He had left a blue handicapped parking sticker on the dash.

"The place looks deserted," Sonny said as they headed for the door. Only a student or two had crossed the duck pond knoll as they drove in, and the library itself was not buzzing with the usual student activity.

"Christmas break," Lorenza said. "The students are gone for the holidays."

"Ah so." He had lost track of time, spent the nights dreaming and the days analyzing the dreams. But last night's dream had been different. Before he fell asleep, he was thinking of Oñate's entry into New Mexico. The Nuevos Mexicanos were born on that date. The son of Andres Vaca was the firstborn. The river flowing from the Garden of Eden. He hadn't counted on Raven showing up. But Raven wasn't the serpent that brought knowledge, he was the ruler of the land of misty dreams, a land without clear thought, chaos.

At the reception desk Sonny asked for Teresa Marquez, a

librarian who had helped him years ago when he was an undergraduate. Since then he had done most of his research and reading at the downtown city library. He was relieved when Teresa appeared, a dark-haired woman with a radiant smile.

"I'm Sonny Baca, this is Lorenza Villa—"

"I know who you are." She took Sonny's hand. "You're getting to be quite a hero. I've saved the newspaper articles on you."

"Me in a file?"

"Do you know the writer Ben Chávez? He's been doing research on your great-grandfather, Elfego Baca. He suggested that I keep a file on you. Said you would become as famous as him."

"I doubt it," Sonny replied. "By the way, what happens if someone steals my file?" Sonny asked.

"I don't think so," Teresa replied, turning to greet Lorenza.

Sonny wondered if being in a file was like being in a dream. Raven the sorcerer could enter the file and wreak havoc. Some of the old traditional natives didn't allow their pictures to be taken, believing that witchcraft could be performed on the photo. The soul could be attacked by witches who possessed the picture.

There was a history not even the file could contain, a soul few could know. Sonny had been reading the Osiris myth. Isis had sewn the pieces of Osiris together after he had been dismembered by his brother. A new Osiris had been born. Technology was moving in that direction, the creation of the hologram man. Cloning from a cell. Pure witchcraft.

"So, what can I do for you today?"

Sonny explained what they were after, and Teresa led

them into the Anderson Room. One sole person sat at a table, hunched over piles of books at the far end of the room.

"It's all here," she said, pointing at the shelves lined with well-worn books and files that held the papers Sonny needed. "The Oñate Collection."

"Can I check out these books?"

"Oh, no, these are special collections. They're not allowed out of the library. But there's dozens of books on Oñate that can be checked out. I can gather some for you if you like, and issue you a library card so you can take them with you."

"Thanks. That would be a great help."

"Be back in a while. In the meantime, help yourselves."

"Where do we start?" Lorenza asked, placing the notebooks and pencils on the table.

"I guess reading anything that has to do with the Oñate expedition," Sonny gestured. "Just start digging."

Lorenza took books from the shelf and spread them on the large, oak table.

"When does the history of New Mexico begin?" Sonny asked.

"It begins with those who write history," Lorenza answered.

"The Spaniards."

Lorenza shrugged. "The Pueblo Indians were living in the Río Grande valley for thousands of years before the Spaniards came, but they kept no written history."

"The petroglyphs don't qualify?"

"They're not in the stacks."

"How about 'Paso por aquí' inscribed on a rock?"

"History belongs to the conquerors."

He knew the history of the state, and of the country, had often left out the native view. He picked up the volume in front of him. "Gaspar Pérez de Villagrá's *Historia de la Nueva México*, 1610, published in Spain. This man wrote the first epic of the region. Never read this when I was doing my undergraduate work."

"History also belongs to those who control it," Lorenza answered. "The Villagrá epic is hardly ever mentioned in textbooks. History is supposed to start at Plymouth Rock."

She pulled up a chair and glanced over his shoulder.

"Raven is trying to control my history," Sonny said.

"Yes. And if he can acquire enough control, he can . . ."

"Destroy me."

"Yes."

"He's an expert marksman. Why doesn't he just stalk and shoot me?"

"He can no longer kill you that way."

"Why?"

"It's not your body he wants to get rid of, it's your soul. Your real struggle is in the world of spirits. Raven knows this."

"But I have the protection of the Zia sign."

"Yes. So he figures out ways to get to you once and for all. He has killed you in prior lives, and maybe sometimes you got lucky and killed him. But you're caught up in an eternal battle. That's the meaning behind don Eliseo's interpretation of your dream."

Sonny shook his head. He knew Raven liked to play games. Ancient games. Taking Owl Woman was such a game. Now it was Sonny's move.

"We've been at this for a long time?" Sonny pondered.

"Yes."

"He's getting closer," Sonny whispered, feeling a worry in the gut, like a llano whirlwind enveloping a person in its fury even though the person had crossed his fingers and held up the sign to fend off the evil in the dust devil. Raven's evil could not be turned away as easily.

Under his shirt the Zia medallion sat on his chest like an ancient heart beating its own rhythm. Sonny had tried to return the medallion to Tamara, and she had refused it, calling Sonny the new Raven. Sonny and Raven, the flip sides of the medallion, the light of the sun on one side, chaos of darkness on the other. Yin and yang brothers engaged in eternal battle, growing older and wiser, until the resolution of their struggle acquired cosmic proportions.

Sonny rubbed his forehead to clear his thoughts.

"You okay?" Lorenza asked.

"Sometimes I feel like getting rid of the medallion—"

"You can't. The Zia sun symbol is the most life-affirming sign we have," Lorenza said. "If you give up, Raven takes over."

Yeah, Sonny knew. A responsibility had been given to him, and a lot depended on what he did.

He flipped through the pages until he found the date he was looking for. "Here it is. Fifteen ninety-eight, the year Oñate entered New Mexico. Don Juan de Oñate, born 1552 in Zacatecas, México. Fought the Chichimecs, spent twenty years as a soldier, married Isabel Cortés Tolosa, a descendant of Hernán Cortés. She died in the 1580s. Some say he led the colonization to escape the sadness of her death."

"Fifteen ninety-eight, date of origins. . . ." She nodded.

Sonny trusted Lorenza implicitly, he respected her powers. She had taken him into his guardian world of spirits where he found his coyote spirit.

"Owl Woman, bathed in the river of the garden. . . ."

"She keeps the Calendar of Dreams, the bowl. Could you recognize it if you saw it?"

"Yup. I held it in my hands, clear as daylight."

"We know when we disrupt a person's dream we cause psychological injury. But each person's dream is connected to the collective dream, and so to kill one dreamer threatens us all. The dream is history, it is continuous. The dream contains the past and future. Raven knows he can cause incredible harm."

"And he picked me."

"You're point man," she replied softly.

Her voice was vibrant with a knowledge he would never find in the books before him.

"Some Pueblo legends say that even at the time of creation, a germ existed in the ear of corn. Some evil planted there by sorcerers. The corn that feeds us carries a germ— Another way of saying we all come to earth with a positive and negative energy."

"The same plus and minus that vibrate through the universe," Sonny said. "Soul energy, don Eliseo says. One part seeks clarity, the other wants to return to chaos. Each one of us reflects the universe."

"Time and space curve and come around, everything in the universe reappears somewhere, sometime. The dream curves. Raven, the sorcerer, plots the path. He can enter the dream and destroy the dreamer."

"Bang, and I'm gone. What can the books tell us?" he asked, thumping the book in front of him.

"Names, a map of your past. Your genealogy."

"I'm just part of everyone who ever came up the Río Grande. Puro mestizo."

"Let's see if Andres Vaca's DNA is in you," Lorenza said, and flipped the page.

"Okay." Sonny took up a pen.

NOTES

He wrote it across the top of the first notebook page. He read, then summarized:

—The Oñate expedition starts north for the interior province of New Mexico in early 1598. Six months on the trail. 200 soldiers and their families. Founded the first Spanish town near San Juan de los Caballeros, August 11, 1598. "Ciudad de Nuestro Padre San Francisco." Called San Gabriel or San Juan Bautista. Completed the church by Sept. 7, 1598. Great rejoicing. The men played "Los Cristianos y los Moros," a mock battle between the Catholic Spaniards and the Moors.

Sonny paused. "I haven't taken notes since I was in college." He laughed at his effort.

"We need the list of names of those soldiers. The muster roll," Lorenza said. She stood and went to the shelf to browse through the titles.

Sonny continued making notes.

—1519. Hernán Cortez (or Cortés) calls the New World Nueva España. He destroys Mexico City, the Aztec capital of Tenochtitlán.

—1528, Cabeza de Vaca shipwrecked with the Narvaez expedition off the coast of Texas. Wanders lost through the region for 8 years.

Wonder if this Cabeza de Vaca is one of my long-ago relatives, Sonny mused. C de Vaca was a New Mexican family name he knew. In high school he had dated Tillie C de Baca.

Cabeza de Vaca meant "Head of a Cow." Cow man. Cowboy.

He took off his hat and placed it on the table. He hadn't
been riding since he sold his mare. He was no cowboy, but
a drugstore cowboy. Puro pedo.

—1539, Fray Marcos de Niza and the black man Estevan enter Arizona and New Mexico.

—1540, Francisco Vásquez de Coronado leaves Com-
postela with 300 men, 5 Franciscan friars, and Indian
allies in search of Niza's Seven Cities of Cíbola. A
man called the Turk tells them stories of la Gran
Quivira, so Coronado goes to Kansas. Destroys two
pueblos.

—1546, gold found in Zacatecas.

—1581, Fray Agustín Rodríguez leads party into New
Mexico. He and Fray López remain in the Tigüex
Pueblo of Puaray.

—1582, Antonio de Espejo leads expedition into Arizona and New Mexico. Kills 16 Indians at Puaray.

Not beginning to look good for those who don't write
history, Sonny thought. Owl Woman. Can her Calendar of
Dreams make a difference? What had the Bringer of Curses
done with the shiny black bowl that held the symbols?

—1590, de Sosa's illegal expedition. The king of
Spain doesn't want adventurers screwing up the Indians.

—1593, '94, de Bonilla's illegal expedition.

Then Oñate came along. Sonny read Villagrá's Canto XIV carefully. How el Río del Norte was discovered, and how the expedition stopped there in what is now El Paso to rest and take possession of the province of New Mexico. Oñate spoke to his assembled troops and to the Indians:

And because I wish to take possession of the land today, the day of the Ascension of our Lord, which is counted thirty days in the month of April of this present year of one thousand five hundred and ninety-eight, through the person of Juan Pérez de Donís, Notary of his Majesty and Secretary of the journey . . .

Sonny skipped a few lines.

I say that in the voice and in the name of the most Christian King Don Felipe, our lord, only defender and protector of the Holy Mother Church and its true son, and for the crown of Castile and of the kings who of his glorious stock may reign in it, and for the aforesaid my government I take and seize: once, twice and three times; one, two and three times; one, two and three times, and all those which I can and ought, the Royal tenancy and possession, actual, civil, and criminal, at this aforesaid River of the North. . . .

And on it went. Taking possession of everything. The arrogance! Oñate had pounded the ground with a staff and taken the land, mountains, desert, rivers. Everything! And the scribe wrote it down, thus creating history. History was a map the newcomer laid over the land.

Took everything "which are now founded in the said

kingdoms and provinces of New Mexico, and those neigh-
boring to them. . . ."

Took the whole present-day damn Southwest, all of
northern Mexico. Took the whole enchilada!

Just like that, he raised his staff and pounded the earth,
and what awe must have filled the assembly. For they could
look north and imagine the provinces of New Mexico, a rich
land, theirs for the taking.

The Indians, too, must have been in awe, for if they understood the translator, they must have wondered at the gall
and greed of this man, saying he could possess the earth by
merely pounding on it.

No, the earth did not belong to one person or one tribe.
The earth was the mother for all to have and use.

So the man who could write history could take the land,
and Lordy, Lordy, Sonny thought, the Spaniards were consummate note takers if they were anything. They documented everything. History belonged to those who wrote it.

Sonny drew back from reading and rubbed his eyes. Six
prior expeditions and only Oñate's made a go of it. But,
Lord, how he punished the Indians at Acoma.

"Blood and violence," he whispered.

"Raven's work," Lorenza said, and slipped a book in
front of Sonny. "Bancroft's book has a list of the names in
the Oñate expedition. Under the Vs."

There it was, the name of Andres Vaca! Listed as a single
man and a soldier with five years' experience, he owned his
horse, "una legua que se llama Estrella," a breastplate, and
his own sword.

"I don't believe it," Sonny whispered. How could he
have dreamed a man he knew nothing of? He had never
read, or looked at, this book before.

"It's there," Lorenza whispered.

Sonny scanned the rest of the list. In the *C*s he spotted Roberto Cantú, a family man and scholar from México. He dropped to the *O*s.

Teniente General Cristóbal de Oñate
Capitán General Don Juan de Oñate
Juan de Ortega
Ortiz

And below the *O*s, the *P*s.

Segundo Paladín
Simón de Paz
Juan de Pedraza
Alférez Pereyra
Simón Pérez
Capitán Pinero
Alférez Francisco de Posa y Peñalosa
Antonio Pájaro

Sonny drew a breath and looked up at Lorenza. "Antonio Pájaro. That's one of Raven's aliases. Damn!"

Anthony Pájaro was the name Raven had used in the summer to gather the anti-WIPP people around his cause. When that didn't work, he tried to dynamite the WIPP truck. According to the manifest in the book, he had been with the Oñate expedition.

Raven, the Bringer of Curses, moved back and forth in time, sowing destruction. He was a sorcerer who had existed since the beginning of time, an evil brujo who could fly!

As the Bringer of Curses he had taken Owl Woman. He was destroying Sonny's past. But why had he taken the Romeros' daughter, Consuelo?

"He wrote his name in the history book! It's not possible," Sonny said. "Somebody's playing games."

"Raven likes games, remember," Lorenza said.

"He can't just go back and change history!" Sonny complained.

"He has," Lorenza said, and pointed at the book. Bancroft. One of the premier historians of the West. If the historian's list written years ago could be changed, anything was possible.

4

Are you going to read all these?" Lorenza asked as she finished loading the pile of books into the van.

"Keeps me busy while you drive," Sonny replied, carefully stacking the books on the counter. He could position his chair behind the counter, read and take notes as Lorenza drove. A traveling library. What would the Bard say of this?

"I'm hungry for books," he added. "Will they provide clues?"

"In this case they verified what don Eliseo believes. Raven can enter your dreams, change the history books. He's tying you up."

"Not only me. You said if he can get to me, he also gets at a lot of other people. The collective dream, like ripples spreading outward from the center of his destruction. . . ."

They both knew what was at stake. "Where to?" she asked.

"Santa Fé. It's the only lead we have."

"Vamos," Lorenza said, and headed toward I-25.

Sonny felt frustrated, unsure of his direction. Finding Raven listed as Antonio Pájaro on the list of names that entered New Mexico with Oñate in 1598 was enough to rattle anyone. Antonio Pájaro, a soldier in the Oñate expedition, had been watching Sonny, alias Andres Vaca, during the march from Nueva Viscaya in México to the banks of the Río Grande at El Paso. When Owl Woman appeared, he made his move.

If they dug deeper, Sonny surmised, they would find Raven using one of his many aliases through the history of New Mexico.

And why hold Owl Woman captive? Because she was the first grandmother, the only one who could interpret the Calendar of Dreams.

"Do you think Raven's center is now in Santa Fé?" Lorenza asked.

"I don't think so. He likes 'Burque too much. Wants to be near me. But he's following some kind of historic pattern."

He had been scanning through Fray Angelico Chávez' *New Mexico Families,* tracing the Romero history back to the eighteenth century, where it became entwined with the Bacas through marriage. Eugenio Baca (the name was now spelled with a *B*) married María Romero. Sonny made notes, sketching a tree trunk to illustrate his genealogy. It would take a lot of diligent research and time to do a good job and construct the entire family tree. This would have to do for now.

If Owl Woman was grandmother number one, who were two, three, and four? And would they appear in different centuries? Would all be New Mexicans?

"He appears in every lifetime," he mumbled.

"Yes," Lorenza answered. "So do you."

"Historical events," Sonny whispered, making a note in the notebook. He comes to create chaos where history turns, at those hinges of time when things can go one way or another.

Hinge of time. He should be home writing poetry. Maybe that's all he ever wanted to do. Teach school, write poetry, marry Rita, raise a family. Until he met Raven.

In his next set of notes he began an outline of the history of New Mexico. As the van rocked back and forth, his notes were scrawled. Scrawled history. Jagged maps. The first expeditions of the Spaniards into the vast, unknown territory of el norte. La Nueva México.

—Don Eliseo teaches us this corridor of the Río Grande is a sacred region. He knows the teachings of the Hopis, Navajos, Pueblos. This region is sacred space held together by prayer. That's why the ancient ones settled here. It's all in the origin prayers of the Pueblo Indians and their neighbors. In 1598 a medieval Catholicism was brought here by the Spaniards, adding the Cristo, María, and the santos to the sacred, a circle that holds together, provides harmony. Self is also a circle, so is family, community, earth, universe. Raven seeks to destroy the sacred circle. When the last of the sacred prayers and ceremonies are removed from this region we call our home, our center, it collapses—

He sat back and read what he had written, surprised he could put his thoughts into words. Then he read the paragraph to Lorenza.

"Muy bien." She looked at him in the rearview mirror.

The first migrants onto the land were the Anasazis, the ancient people, ancestors of the Pueblo Indians. They had described the sacred mountains, rivers, springs, hills, caves. Sonny drew a map of the pueblos that existed before the coming of the Spaniards.

Sonny looked up from his notes. "Owl Woman came from the pueblos."

"It's a connection most Nuevos Mexicanos have."

"Los abuelos, grandparents. Don Eliseo is like an abuelo to me."

"He is a kind man. Wise in the old ways."

Sonny could see her face in the mirror. Her dark eyes glanced at him, then back at the road. She was a very attractive woman. Her black hair flowed around her shoulders, framing a warm tan face with high cheekbones, arched eyebrows, full lips. When she smiled, she licked her teeth with the tip of her tongue. But the most attractive thing about her were her eyes. They held mysteries.

Now as Sonny looked at her, he remembered how physically attracted he had been to her when she performed the ceremony that took him into the world of his coyote spirit. He had responded to her as a woman. Hormones moved in his blood, sweet fragrances touched his nostrils. The attraction was something both had learned to keep in check.

Lord, if I didn't have Rita, I'd proposition her. Sonny smiled, and the thought made him feel good. For months he hadn't been interested in the world around him. He clung to Rita because she brought love and food. Women and food came together. Why not. His mother's rich milk was the first food he tasted on earth. She was a good cook, she always saw to it that he and Armando ate well. Later in life he discovered sex, and eating seemed to come with it. He often felt aroused when he ate with Rita, perhaps because they often ate in bed together. Food and sex.

He would marry her, they would eat many meals together, and children would be born not only of sperm and ovum, but also from beans, tortillas, chile verde in the summer, red chile enchiladas, huevos con papas fritas, meat stew. Red chile smothering ham and turkey for Thanksgiving, natillas for dessert, biscochitos for Christmas, lenten food for Semana Santa. Children conceived embodied the food of the people, the food of the season. To make love was to eat, to eat was to make love.

"I'm hungry," he said.

"You're always hungry." Lorenza smiled.

"How do you know?"

"I know a lot about you, Sonny Baca."

"I'd better watch my thoughts."

"Watch your dreams. Rita says you eat everything she serves."

"She's a good cook."

"She's also a very good dish." Lorenza was teasing.

"Yeah, she is."

"I'll feed you as soon as we get to Santa." She winked in the mirror. "Not as good as Rita's, I'm sure. What about the Romeros?"

"I don't think I'm going to be of much help. He's the mayor of Santa Fé, a millionaire. I think it's a kidnap/ransom thing. Anyway, no sense in going hungry to the job."

"You're right about that. Roberto Mondragon used to have a restaurant near the plaza. I'll look for it."

"Bueno."

He looked out at the barren landscape, the rolling hills tawny in the winter, dotted with juniper trees, the Sangre de Cristo Mountains rising blue over Santa Fé, the high peaks covered with blue clouds that presaged a storm. To the west the clouds also gathered around the Jemez peaks. The kachina spirits of rain and snow gathering on the mountains. The place was sacred, divine with the light of the sun that made the hills glow with a biblical light of redemption.

He had seen photographs of the light of the setting sun

shining on Jerusalem, on Toledo, Mecca, Machu Picchu. The light blessed the sacred places, like the light shining across the sage of the Taos llano and its mountains. It was the light of New Mexico that drew the original inhabitants, drew prayers, drew artists, brought holy people and hippies alike searching for the center. Light at the center of the universe, even here on the road to Santa Fé, the light of the approaching winter solstice glowed and brought the winter earth to life. Beneath the frozen earth lay the spirit touched by light, and the spirit responded by absorbing the light and giving it back to the viewer.

Buzz of life, Sonny thought.

"I'll call Rita and tell her where we're headed." He dialed Rita at her restaurant, explained what they had found in the library and how it might just be connected to the Romeros' missing daughter. He gave her their number in Santa Fé and asked her if she could monitor his answering machine at home. Raven, he thought, might be calling. And he told her to be careful.

"Rita says to take care," he said as he clicked off the phone.

"We will," Lorenza replied.

He could smell faint traces of her perfume in the van, and a faint aroma of sweet herbs that clung to her. Ah, yes, he thought, we will.

"Sixteen ten, Governor Peralta moved the capital to Santa Fé," Sonny said, entering the note in his notebook. "Raven was there."

Lorenza nodded. "Probably. It was the beginning of a new era for the manitos."

Sonny read on, making notes as he read.

From 1610 to 1680 a great missionary spirit would fill the Franciscan friars of New Mexico. They wanted souls for

Jesucristo, but in the process they would also teach the Pueblo Indians of New Mexico a great deal of Hispanic culture. Language; use of iron, horse, sheep, and cattle; and the arts of the church, music and the making of santos and retablos. The Pueblos would accept much, even accepting some of the saints of the church into their kachina pantheon. The saints would become guardian ancestral spirits who joined the old kachinas to do good and bring rain to the earth of the Pueblos.

The problem lay not with the Indians; it was the friars' missionary zeal that drove them to destroy the ceremonial kivas and to burn masks, fetishes, and other paraphernalia. Dances and the handling of snakes were prohibited. The Holy Office of the Inquisition, which was headquartered in Santo Domingo Pueblo, commanded the friars to beat and hang those medicine men who resisted conversion from their old ways into the Catholic religion.

"The Bringer of Curses," Sonny thought aloud.

"¿Qué?"

"A rift between the religion of the friars and the religion of the Pueblos. There was even a bitter struggle between the Spanish civil authorities and the church. Greed and pride led them practically to blows. The Pueblo Indians, caught in the middle, suffered. Oñate instituted the encomienda system, so the head of each Indian household had to pay tribute in corn and blankets. With repartimiento the Indians were forced to work the Spaniards' fields."

"Spanish gentlemen didn't like to soil their hands in the earth," Lorenza said. "Repartimiento was another word for slavery."

"Smallpox, measles, cholera, whooping cough decimated the Pueblos. . . . Talk about curses."

Sonny went on recounting the history until they drove

into Santa Fé. Downtown and around the plaza the Christmas decorations were already hung. An overcast sky turned the day chilly; still, tourists wandered around the plaza. Many came from Texas, California, New York to ski, to vacation, to revel in the southwestern atmosphere.

Lorenza circled the plaza once. "Roberto's gone, but we can get French cuisine." The street was lined with coffee shops and delis catering to tourists.

"The tourists want continental," Sonny replied.

"New people, new age. In La Fonda you can get a psychic reading while you drink your margarita. There's little room left for traditional curanderas."

"But you're not traditional," Sonny said.

The *traditional* curandera his mother had taken him to when he was a child was a little old woman dressed in black. She smelled of osha. She did simple healing with prayers, massage, and candles. She didn't practice the kind of craft Lorenza knew; she didn't dream of entering the powerful world of spirits. And she sure didn't look like Lorenza.

Under the portal of the Palace of the Governors, vendors sat on blankets, selling their jewelry. Good-looking gringas dressed to the hilt in the Santa Fé style were shopping. Silver and turquoise made beautiful Christmas gifts for those back home.

"Ah, here's one." Lorenza pointed at the small café on a side street. "You ready for a snack?"

"I'm always ready," Sonny replied. They parked and entered and ate what Sonny described as "some of the best" posole con menudo he ever had, spiced with red chile from Puerto de Luna. The sopaipillas were not crisp enough for his taste, but then only Rita's sopaipillas pleased him. For dessert, sweet rice pudding and coffee.

From the bearded waiter they got directions to the

Romeros' home, a chic place on the eastern foothills. Lorenza parked in the graveled driveway, and Sonny let his chair down on the lift and rolled toward the front door.

Arturo Romero, a stocky man in his forties dressed in blue suit and red tie, answered the door. "Welcome. Please come in. We've been expecting you. I am glad you could come, Mr. Baca. I didn't know—" He indicated Sonny's chair.

"Had a little accident," Sonny replied, and introduced Lorenza.

Arturo led them into a large living room decorated with an enormous Christmas tree and many presents, which, Sonny guessed, might not be opened this Christmas. Chimayó rugs covered the Saltillo tiled floors, and expensive santero pieces filled the nichos. One, a large Muerte in her cart by Patrociño Barela, stood by the fireplace. The mayor had good taste, expensive taste.

One corner contained an altar with the statue of la Virgen de Guadalupe, brightly decorated with lighted votive candles. Eloisa and Arturo had been praying for their daughter's safe return.

Eloisa Romero entered, and her husband introduced Sonny and Lorenza. If Consuelo bears any resemblance to her mother, Sonny thought, then she's a beautiful girl. Even pale and drawn as Eloisa was from worry, her New Mexican beauty shone through. Sonny figured they were in their forties, and Arturo Romero had the Santa Fé business world by the tail, until yesterday.

Eloisa greeted Sonny and Lorenza warmly and thanked them profusely for coming. It was clear she had been crying. When the greetings were over, they sat, and Sonny asked them to recount what had happened.

Arturo took the initiative. "The parishioners from the

Santuario put on *Los Pastores* every year. You know, the play of the shepherds going to the birth of Jesús. Consuelo was going to play the part of Gila, the shepherd girl. She went to the church to practice. There have been a rash of rape cases lately, so I stayed up. When I saw her car lights shine in the driveway, I went to bed. I thought she was home, safe—"

"Nothing like this has ever happened," Eloisa interrupted. "We know everyone. Now this." She touched the crumpled handkerchief to her eyes. Her husband reached out and held her hand.

Sonny glanced at Lorenza. In the play Gila was a virgin on the way to the birth of Christ with other shepherds. Along the way the shepherds are tempted by Satan, until St. Michael gets rid of the devil and the shepherds arrive in time to deliver humble gifts to the baby Jesus.

"Had Consuelo been in the play before?" he asked.

"No," Eloisa continued. "It was her first time. She's wanted to play the part of Gila since she was a little girl. She had memorized her lines. She was so proud."

"Doesn't one of the shepherds try to steal Gila?" Sonny asked.

"Yes, the hermit. He is tempted by the devil, and he thinks Gila loves him. When all are asleep, he tries to steal her, but she screams and awakens the other shepherds and they beat the hermit. He claims the devil made him do it."

"But they continue to the birth of Christ."

"Yes."

"Christ is born, bringing a message of love to the world. The shepherds are there. One more dream of peace is born—"

"I don't understand," Arturo said, puzzled.

Consuelo was playing the role of Gila in *Los Pastores*, Sonny thought. The morality play had been brought by the

Españoles to New Mexico and performed every Christmas since then. With Consuelo gone, there was no Gila to attend the birth of Jesus. Was there a pattern here?

"Tell me about your daughter."

Eloise described her daughter. She was their only child, a junior at the Santa Fé Academy, straight-A student, loved by teachers and classmates. She was happy, planning for the play and Christmas, there was absolutely no reason why she would run away from home. No reason. Everyone at the church that night had been contacted by the police. They had last seen Consuelo leaving the church.

"Do you have enemies?" Sonny asked, looking at Arturo.

He shrugged. "I'm in politics, so one makes enemies. Those who really hate me are those who opposed my company creating the Romero Estates on the ski run road. The conservationists and water rights people fought tooth and nail to keep my company from developing the subdivision. Maybe since they couldn't beat me in the courts, they took what is most precious in my life."

Sonny shook his head.

"No, I don't want to believe it, either. But if you can find our daughter, you can name your price, Mr. Baca."

Unlike the last mayor, who kept a check on the developers who gobbled up land and water, Arturo Romero was pro development. Romero Estates had been in the courts for years, and recently, Sonny remembered, the courts had cleared the subdivision. The road to the ski run was priceless property, and the proposed condos and golf course would take a lot of water from an often thirsty and growing Santa Fé.

Arturo Romero was a classic example of a Chicano entrepreneur who bought into the system whole hog. He was a multimillionaire. Had enough money to buy a lot of votes, as the gente said. That's how the Jack Nicklaus golf course got built.

But I didn't come to judge the man, Sonny reminded himself. I came to see if I can help find the girl.

"She drove home alone?" Sonny asked. "Her car?"

"The blue Accord in the driveway," Arturo replied. "The police say it hasn't been disturbed. In other words, there was no sign of a struggle. She drove home, came in, then disappeared."

"And the black feathers?" Sonny asked.

"They were on her pillow," Eloisa whispered. "They're evil."

"M'ija," her husband cautioned, obviously not agreeing with her interpretation.

"They are!" she insisted. "I took them and put them in a box. They feel evil." She shivered.

"May I see them?"

"Yes, of course."

She went out of the room, returned with a box, and handed it to Sonny. "It's the work of the devil," she said.

Sonny opened the box. Yes, Raven's calling card. "I can get rid of these," he said, glancing at Lorenza, hoping the gesture would bring the parents some relief.

"Yes, thank you," Eloisa said. "It's brujería." She made the sign of the cross. An intelligent, educated woman who together with her husband had made it to the top of the economic and political power of the city, and still she recognized the signs of evil.

"Nonsense," her husband interrupted. "It's people who wish us harm. We've climbed to the top, and now the crabs are pulling us down. Frankly, Mr. Baca, the chief of police knows my enemies. He promised me he's going to find my daughter."

"So why call me?"

"My wife believes in witchcraft," Arturo replied. "It was her desire to call you. You were recommended by the police chief as someone who knows about these things." He looked coldly at Sonny and Lorenza, as if to say he didn't believe, but added, "But as I told you, if you can help, you name your price. I only want to get my daughter back. I don't care who does it or how it's done. I only want it done quickly!"

"We're good Catholics," Eloisa said. "We've worked hard for all we have, and we've tried to help people. Why would anyone want to harm our daughter?"

"To get to me," her husband answered.

"When did your family come to Santa Fé?" Sonny asked.

Arturo raised an eyebrow, then answered haughtily: "According to the old church records my ancestors came with de Vargas. Many of the old families in Santa Fé date back to the reconquest of New Mexico in 1693. In fact, there were Romeros here with Oñate. Fray Angelico writes the same Romero family returned after the Pueblo Revolt of 1680. The Romero who came with de Vargas was a blacksmith. He married a woman from Taos. You see—"

He pointed at the coat of arms over the fireplace.

"I've done quite a bit of research into my family tree. I belong to a genealogical society. The Romeros were among the first Spanish families of Santa Fé. Many of the original families are related. Do you know your genealogy?"

Owl Woman and Andres Vaca, Sonny thought, it began there.

"I found out one of my first great-grandmothers was an Indian woman," Sonny said.

"Really?" Arturo raised an eyebrow. "Is there anything else?" he asked bluntly.

"No, we've seen what we have to see," Sonny answered. "Do you have a picture of Consuelo?"

"Yes." Eloisa went to the altar, took the photograph sitting at the foot of the Virgin, and handed it to Sonny.

He looked at the lovely face of Consuelo. Lord, if he didn't find her, Raven would keep her soul in his hell forever. He would initiate her into his evil circle to do his bidding.

Raven had taken her at a crucial time: just as she was about to take part in the play about the birth of Christ. He would take three more according to don Eliseo. Raven was rebuilding his harem with the four women that represented Sonny's grandmothers!

Dear Virgen de Guadalupe, Sonny thought as he stared at the altar, Madre de Dios, kachinas de los Pueblos, help me find Consuelo.

He turned his chair. "I'll find her," he said.

"Do you really think so?" Arturo said.

"I have to," Sonny replied.

Eloisa took his hand and kissed it. "Thank you, Mr. Baca. Thank you. We will be forever grateful." Tears filled her eyes.

"Yes, we are grateful," Arturo said. "I don't mean to sound so cynical." He cleared his throat and asked the question Sonny had been waiting for. "Do you think she's alive?"

"Yes, I think she's still alive."

At least until Raven abducted three more young women, Consuelo was still alive.

They said good-bye to the Romeros and boarded the van.

"Kind of arrogant, isn't he?" Sonny said as they drove away.

"Self-made man, old family name, knows how to use the Santa Fé políticos, yeah, he is kind of aloof," Lorenza replied. "But he's hurting. It's obvious the daughter means everything to them. What do you think of the political angle?"

Sonny shook his head. "Raven will play any angle. Along the way he might even ask for ransom money. Why not? He needs to pay those who work for him, he needs to get around—but no. It's not Arturo Romero's political enemies who sent Raven. Hey, this is New Mexico, land of many strange political bedfellows, but we're not into kidnapping the winner's daughter."

"Not yet—"

The phone rang and Sonny answered. The speaker on the other end introduced himself as Leif Eric, the director of Los Alamos National Laboratories. He wanted to know if Sonny could come up to Los Alamos Labs right away? No, he couldn't discuss it on the phone. But it was an emergency.

Sonny had never met the man, but he knew of him. After Sonny stopped Raven from blowing up the WIPP truck in June, Eric had written a thank-you letter to Sonny. With all the retooling the labs were doing to convert nuclear research into peacetime uses, Eric was often in the news. The Los Alamos Labs were a big factor in the state's economy. When Leif Eric told the governor to jump, he only asked how high.

"How'd you get my number?" Sonny asked.

"Matt Paiz, the FBI director in Albuquerque. You know Matt, don't you?"

"Yeah, I know Matt. Anyway, I'm not sure I can make it." Sonny hesitated.

"Hold on," Eric said. "I want Matt to talk to you."

The regional director of the FBI, Sonny thought. What the hell was going on?

"Sonny. Matt Paiz here. Listen, we've got a little problem on our hands. We really would appreciate talking to you. I can send someone for you right away. No cause for alarm, but we need to talk to you."

"Can you explain?" Sonny asked.

"Not on the phone. Look, I know you're kinda wiped out from your last meeting with Raven, but this is something you really need to know about."

"It involves Raven?" Sonny said.

"Affirmative."

"Okay," Sonny replied, "I'll be there."

"Come straight to the administration building. I'll be waiting for you." The phone went dead.

"Qué?" Lorenza asked.

"That was the Los Alamos Labs and the FBI," he replied. "Raven is on their mind."

Just what the hell was going on?

5

When they pulled out of the Romeros' drive, they noticed a late-model Ford Explorer following them. They drove north to Pojoaque and turned east, crossing the river at the Otowi Bridge, then began the climb up the seven thousand–foot-high Pajarito Plateau, where the city of Los Alamos sat.

"We're being followed," Lorenza said.

"Yeah," Sonny replied. He had been watching the Ford.

"Who?" Lorenza asked.

"FBI," Sonny answered. He hoped. They knew how to trace and find him easily enough, but so did Raven.

The Ford tailed them all the way to Los Alamos, then disappeared as they drew near the security office that sat in front of the administration building.

"Sonny Baca," Sonny told the armed guard who peered into the van.

"They're waiting for you inside," the guard motioned. "Park right there, next to the Jeep." A few cars were parked right in front of the building. The bigwig Jeeps, Sonny figured as Lorenza parked the van. An armed security guard stood nearby.

They were met at the administration building door by Matt Paiz. Sonny knew Matt, and although he didn't like some of the tactics his agents used, he had found Paiz to be a decent guy.

"Sonny, how are you. I'm damn glad you could come. Sorry to bring you out when you're still recuperating, but—"

"I'm okay," Sonny said. "Lorenza Villa, Matt Paiz."

Paiz took her hand. "Nice to meet you," he said. "Look, we've got clearance for you, but we didn't plan on anyone else being in on the meeting."

"Why not?"

"Lab security," Paiz explained. "It's always tight, but today it's—" He didn't finish.

"I need her," Sonny said. "She's with me or I turn around and go home."

Paiz looked from Lorenza back to Sonny, nodded. "Okay. Let's get you a badge—" He led them to a receptionist's desk, where he called the labs' director and explained the situation. Both had to fill out visitors' forms and were scanned by the computer. Until they were purged when their visiting time expired, their faces would exist in the memory of the computer. The secretary handed them temporary badges. "Wear at all times," she cautioned.

"Is the Ford Explorer yours?" Sonny asked.

"Ford Explorer?"

"Nothing. So what's the deal?"

"I'd rather have Eric explain it," Paiz replied, and led them down the hallway to his office. The hallway was bristling with the labs' internal security guards and FBI agents. Stern-faced men who stared but said nothing.

"By the way, Casey Doyle's here," Paiz whispered.

Casey Doyle, the director of the FBI? This is big, Sonny thought, but what the hell does it have to do with me?

Eric was pacing back and forth when Matt let them into his office, and Doyle sat grimly in an armchair. Something very important had brought Doyle from D.C. and Paiz from Alburquerque, Sonny thought. What?

Paiz introduced Sonny and Lorenza. "Leif Eric," the director replied, shaking their hands. "Damn glad you could come, Sonny. If I may call you Sonny. This is Mr. Doyle, FBI director."

Eric appeared nervous, but congenial. Doyle hardly smiled. His wrinkled face was sour to the core.

"We owe you an explanation," Eric began. "And it involves some very secure data. I think it would be best if Ms. Villa waited outside—"

Sonny shook his head. "She stays."

"But—" Eric glanced at Doyle, who shrugged, then nodded.

"As long as both of you understand that what you're about to learn cannot be discussed outside of this office. Not to the papers, not to the local police, not to a wife or husband, not to anybody."

"Okay," Sonny said, and sat back to listen.

"Fine. I'll get to the point," Eric continued. "We've just intercepted an illegal shipment of plutonium." He paused, as if waiting for Doyle to add something. "Actually, it's a plutonium pit."

"Do you mean the core of a nuclear bomb?" Sonny asked for clarification.

"Affirmative," Eric replied.

Holy tortillas, Sonny thought. Intercepted the core of a nuclear bomb? He knew a black market in plutonium existed. Now that the world was dismantling its nuclear arsenals, the stuff was being bought and sold. He remembered a small amount of plutonium being intercepted at Kennedy Airport a few years ago.

"We believe it came from Ukraine," Eric continued. "Ten kilograms. Enough to make a crude nuclear bomb, if someone were so inclined."

"Taken right from a nuclear bomb?" Sonny asked, just to make sure he was visualizing the right thing.

"A nuclear missile."

"Ah," Sonny whispered. In its machined, metallic form, a plutonium pit could be smuggled across borders in a briefcase. That's what the CIA and other intelligence agencies had been afraid of all along—terrorist groups getting hold of a pit from a dismantled nuke.

"Is it ready to be used?"

Eric cleared his throat. "Yes. It was obviously taken when a nuclear missile was being dismantled. It came into New York City, went through Denver, and was on its way here when it was intercepted."

Damn, Sonny thought, a plutonium pit. A real live core bouncing around the country.

"How'd you find it?" Sonny asked.

"By accident," Paiz explained. "A state cop stopped a car near Raton. Two men. They shot the cop, but not before he got off a shot. Killed one of the smugglers, the other fled."

Yes, the story had been on the radio yesterday. A state cop shot near Raton, but the story said nothing about the plutonium, and being more concerned with his own health, Sonny really hadn't paid attention to it. He figured it was one more dope smuggler stopped by a state cop.

"Besides the people in this room," Eric continued, "only two of my people know we recovered the core. The two I sent to the crime scene to recover it. We haven't even told the state police what we're faced with."

"So why tell us?" Sonny asked.

Doyle stood and spoke for the first time. "The description of the suspect that got away fits the description of a friend of yours."

For being director of the FBI, Doyle was no superhero, only a seventy-year-old man with a stoop and the weight of the world on his back. He was a political appointee hired to try to clean up the agency. The president didn't want the mole scandal that wrecked the CIA a few years back to be duplicated in the FBI.

He stood in front of Sonny, his eyes boring into him. He was a bent old man, but his look was intimidating.

"A friend of mine," Sonny said. "Who?" he asked, but he already knew.

"The guy who tried to blow the WIPP truck," Doyle said, placing his hands behind his back and walking to the big plate-glass window that faced east. From there he could see as far as the Río Grande valley and the Sangre de Cristo Mountains rising above Santa Fé. Threatening storm clouds hung over the Santa Fé peaks.

"The man who uses the Raven alias," Eric said.

Sonny looked at Paiz, Paiz nodded.

Raven smuggling plutonium? To make a bomb? Dr. Stammer's warning rang in Sonny's memory: Raven's going to Russia to buy a nuke. And I believe him.

"We've been after him since he tried to blow the WIPP truck," Paiz said. "You almost caught him during the Balloon Fiesta when he tried to smuggle in the cocaine shipment. He was selling coke to pay for this. Then he disappeared. Now we know he was shopping in Ukraine."

"How much does it cost to buy a plutonium pit?" Sonny asked.

"Millions," Eric said.

"There are plenty of our enemies out there willing to fund this lunatic," Doyle interjected. "North Korea, Iran, Iraq, you name it. We've followed a trail of money funneled through a Swiss bank account. Over twenty million dollars. Now the account is empty. Raven bought the plutonium all right. We were just lucky to intercept it."

So Arturo Romero won't get a ransom note after all, Sonny thought. Raven has other money sources.

"Does he actually think he can build a bomb?" Sonny asked. "Don't you need a lot of equipment?"

Eric nodded. "If he's got the right people, a bomb can be put together almost anywhere. Out-of-work, disgruntled nuclear scientists from the former Soviet Union or Ukraine are selling their services. Ex–nuclear physicists are a dime a dozen. An expert in focused explosives could be bought. Someone with that kind of expertise could build the detonators. Actually, manuals on how to put together a bomb have circulated on the Internet for years now. What's been lacking is the heart of the bomb, the pit."

"But you have the pit," Sonny said, "so what's the problem?"

"This man is dedicated to a world revolution," Doyle said. "We have a dossier on him a foot thick. He failed this time, but we're sure he'll try again." He placed his hands on the desk, and his gaze bore into Sonny. "We need to find him and stop him."

And I need to find him and stop him, Sonny thought.

"National security is afraid he'll try again," Eric said.

Paiz spoke. "When we first met Raven, we thought we were dealing with a crazy activist who opposed the storage of nuclear waste at the WIPP site. But once we pulled a background check on him, as Mr. Doyle has just said, we found aliases a mile long. Turns out Raven is not Raven."

Sonny checked a smile. How many times had he heard that?

"He's not just an ecoterrorist, and his knowledge of explosives is far greater than that picked up by blowing dynamite in the Grant's mines. He's been around the world, from Libya to North Korea. He's left his footprints all over the place."

"Footprints?"

"A faint trail," Paiz continued. "He's here, he's there—"

"But now he's here," Sonny said.

"Yes. He's here, and he has a base of operations."

"Why here?" Sonny tested their knowledge of Raven.

"Because of the labs," Eric replied. "Between us, Sandia Labs, and Kirtland in Albuquerque, we've got the expertise and the nuclear capability—" He paused, pursed his lips, and said no more.

"So how do I fit in?" Sonny asked.

"He left a message. We believe it's for you," Eric said.

"A message?" Sonny was surprised. So this is why they called him in.

"It's a bowl, and actually Matt's the one who figured the message relates to you."

Sonny's hair along the back of his neck stood on end.

"What kind of bowl?"

"It's one of the most beautiful pieces of pre-Columbian art I've ever seen," Eric said. "It resembles the work from Tula. Pre-Toltec obsidian. There are glyphs carved on the outside of the bowl. I've been collecting Indian pottery since I came to New Mexico, and I've never seen anything this beautiful. We think he was carrying the plutonium pit in the bowl. And here's the strange part, the bowl isn't lead lined, but an initial test tells us the plutonium doesn't emit radiation through it."

Sonny felt sweat along his back. The pot Eric was describing was Owl Woman's Calendar of Dreams! He looked at Lorenza and the look on her face told him she, too, was stunned. Is it possible? his look asked, and she nodded.

"Where did you find it?"

"At the Raton incident. The cop shot Raven's accomplice, a second state police car came up, and Raven fled."

"Unbelievable!" Sonny said. Raven had taken the bowl when he kidnapped Owl Woman.

"It's believable all right!" Doyle snapped.

Eric continued. "I recognized a few of the glyphs on the bowl. The ankh sign. A tree. The sign for infinity. And something which reads like an explosion. A sunburst, much like our Zia sun. And near the radiating sun the glyph of a bull. Sonny Baca, Matt figured. He knew you had chased Raven. And perhaps Raven is chasing you."

"What do you think?" Matt Paiz asked Sonny.

"Yes, that's Raven's method. He leaves clues. Where's the bowl now?"

"It's sitting down at TA-2 with the pit."

"Can I see it?"

Eric looked from Paiz to Doyle. "Do you think you can read the glyphs on it?"

"I don't know," Sonny replied.

He did know that the inscribed bowl was the Calendar of Dreams that belonged to Owl Woman. Maybe Raven interpreted the sun symbol as a sign for the apocalypse of time. Time would come to an end unless the Calendar of Dreams was returned to the people, the heirs of the dream of peace. It was just a stroke of luck that a state cop had stopped Raven near Raton and stumbled onto the bowl and the plutonium.

And, Sonny thought, looking out the window at the gathering clouds of the afternoon, the time of the winter solstice is upon us. Raven has it all figured out.

"It's important," Doyle said. "If you can read any part of it, it might give us a clue about Raven and what he's up to. We need to know who funds him."

"That's why we called you," Paiz added.

"I'll try," Sonny nodded. "One stipulation."

"What?"

"The bowl belonged to my grandmother—"

"What?" Eric arched an eyebrow.

He looked at Doyle, who shrugged.

"Then you did know something about this?" Doyle asked.

"It's a long story," Sonny explained, "but I need to return the bowl."

"Do you expect us to believe—" Eric's voice rose in irritation, but Paiz held up a hand.

"Come on, Sonny, level with us. If the bowl really belonged to your grandmother, does that mean you can read the glyphs on it?"

"No."

Eric shook his head. "The bowl doesn't mean anything to us, as long as we have the plutonium. If it belonged to your grandmother, as you claim, you can have it. What's your grandmother's name?"

"Owl Woman."

"Where does she live?"

Here, Sonny thought, in my heart. In me. In my dreams, in Raven's nightmare.

"Here," he said, looking out the window at the plateau that sloped into the valley. Here in la Nueva México, everywhere.

Eric didn't understand, but he reached for his parka. "I

don't care if we believe you or not, Sonny. The important thing is for you to look at the bowl and see if it has clues about Raven. Come, let's go." He walked briskly toward the door.

"I'll drive with Sonny and Lorenza," Paiz said, and took the back handles of Sonny's chair.

Eric glanced at Doyle, nodded, and they headed out the building. They were immediately flanked by security guards armed with automatic weapons, dressed in protective vests and headgear. Outside, Eric and Doyle boarded Eric's Jeep.

"I'll be at TA-2 with these three persons," Eric said to the captain in charge. "Stand by."

The captain saluted and pulled back, as did the guards around him.

"Follow us. Stay close," Eric shouted at Paiz.

TA-2, the nuclear research reactor building, lay at the end of Omega Canyon. Crossing Omega Bridge, making the loop, and driving along the floor of the canyon meant they could be there in five minutes.

On either side the canyon's walls rose as natural protection for the labs, which produced PU-239. For research purposes only, the labs' administration kept telling the public for years, but those who followed the labs' role in the nuclear industry knew better.

"How well do you know the place?" Sonny asked.

"I've been here a few times," Paiz answered.

"Is TA-2 guarded?" Sonny asked.

"Eric has three or four lab security men there, but they don't know they're guarding a plutonium pit. They think they're guarding an Indian bowl just uncovered at one of the construction sites nearby. Eric knows how to lie. Frankly, I'm surprised he let Lorenza in on the meeting. But you have us over a barrel. You know Raven better than anyone."

"So Doyle is hoping I read the bowl and lead him to the nest of the world terrorists who are behind all this," Sonny said.

"Something like that," Paiz agreed. "I understand the chemists from the metallurgy lab won't have a look at the plutonium until tomorrow."

"How dangerous is it?"

"You wouldn't want to hold it on your lap for too long, but it's fairly safe for now. It's either nickel or silver coated. If you held it in your hands, it might feel warm. Right now it's subcritical, as the physicists put it. You can transport the pit easily enough, couriers transport that stuff all the time. You might be sitting in an airplane, taking your family on a vacation to San Francisco and the middle-aged executive sitting next to you might be carrying a nuclear substance in his briefcase. Destination, Livermore."

"But a machined pit is quite a bit more dangerous," Sonny said.

"Yup. You don't want to be around if the thing goes critical."

"How does it go critical?" Sonny asked.

"If you wrap it in plastic, or drop it in water. In other words, if enough neutrons are aimed at the core or if in some way you excite that baby, then you've got trouble."

"You seem well versed."

"The agency has been aware of the problem. We get training."

"The problem?"

"The number one post–Cold War fear is that a terrorist group might smuggle in nuclear material and build a bomb. The movies you see about terrorists stealing missiles or planes armed with nuclear weapons are just that, movies. What we're afraid of is what Raven seems to be up to. You get hold of a pit and 'buy' the services of the right experts, and you can build a bomb in downtown Santa Fé."

"Why not in New York, or San Francisco? A dense population center."

"No one knows why he picked this place. I guess in large metropolitan areas he could hold the public for ransom, and if he actually blew a bomb, he could cause a lot of casualties. Maybe here he can threaten Sandia Labs in 'Burque. *Suppose* the army has dismantled bomb pits stored in the Manzano Mountains, or right on Kirtland base. And further suppose that a nuclear bomb in our midst would set off those pits, create a superbomb."

"The end of the world," Sonny whispered.

"Something like that. Anyway, I don't believe your grandmother story, either, so why do you want the bowl?" Paiz asked.

"Historical continuity," Sonny replied.

Paiz scowled. "What were you doing in Santa Fé?"

"Missing girl. Consuelo Romero, sixteen-year-old daughter of Arturo and Eloisa Romero, disappeared last night."

"The mayor's daughter?"

"Yup."

"You think Raven was involved?"

"Yes."

"So, he's in the vicinity," Paiz murmured, and made a note in the notebook he flipped from his pocket. "I'll follow up on it."

The conversation had broken the ice, Paiz was friendly, but Sonny sensed there was more to be revealed. Why else had he insisted on riding in the van?

"Has Doyle identified any of the so-called terrorist groups that help Raven?" he asked.

"Off the record?" Paiz replied.

"Sure."

"Doyle's story is that Raven has Mideast connections. He has some, but those aren't the groups funding him."

"Then who?" Sonny asked.

"Someone in *this* country wants the bomb built," Paiz replied.

Sonny arched an eyebrow and looked at Lorenza's face in the rearview mirror.

"Someone in this country is behind Raven?"

"Yes. As near as I can tell, it's a far-right group that calls itself the Avengers. They're probably the best-funded, best-organized group in the country."

"A militia group?"

"They have militia chapters in every state. People who hate the federal government, hate income tax, hate the United Nations, and fear the so-called One World Order. These groups also claim the country's being overrun by 'the brown hordes from Latin America, the yellow from Asia.' "

"White supremacists," Sonny said.

"In the worst way."

"What are they going to do, bomb the immigrants who come looking for work!" Sonny exploded. "What the hell ever happened to the American dream! Every white person in this country has immigrant ancestors! What the hell are we doing now, closing the doors!" He caught himself, paused. "Sorry. I just don't understand this entrenchment. What's the fear?"

Paiz shrugged. "You put your finger on it, fear. They're afraid of the exploding population in the Third World. They look south and say Mexico and Latin America will soon overrun the borders. Food and population will force the people north. Hey, my parents came from Zacatecas, worked hard and contributed to society, raised four kids, and we've done all right. I figure without that escape hatch my dad would still be sweeping streets in Juárez, and I'd probably be running dope for the Mafia."

Sonny nodded. For centuries the Mexicanos journeyed north to trade in the land their ancestors had called Aztlán. There were no borders then. The pre-Columbian Indians from Mesa Verde and Chaco Canyon had trade routes into Mexico.

This was the land of the Aztecs' birth, recorded in their legends and codices. Their ancestors were born in the Seven Caves of Aztlán, their sacred birthplace. Aztlán just happened to be the northern Río Grande valley.

Later the Spaniards and Mexican mestizos had traveled north, using the old trade routes. The Españoles called the road El Camino Real. They came in search of gold, and to finally settle down. The people from the south brought their willingness to work hard, their language, music, fiestas, and added their skills and talents to the native cultures of the Southwest.

"Fear of the Other," Sonny nodded. "Except we're not outsiders."

"Yeah, but they continue to make us objects of their fears. They believe the government is protecting the so-called minorities, so their plan is to take over the government."

"A military dictatorship," Sonny said. "Won't work."

"It will if they can create a crisis that will topple the government."

"Like Oklahoma? That didn't work."

"Bigger. They've been waiting for a really bad economic downturn or a catastrophe—any crisis, and they blame the government. But they don't want to wait much longer. They believe the country is ripe for a civil war. The bombings create distrust in the government. If the feds can't protect the public, they preach, then topple the government and let the Avengers run it."

"So they plan to use the bomb to create the crisis," Sonny said, and whistled softly.

"It sounds far-fetched," Paiz said, "but that's the way I read it. They have a lot of explosives stored around the country, so they can set off enough bombs to create havoc. But they know we're on their trail. We've infiltrated some of the groups, we've recovered explosives. The public is now aware of their tactics and is condemning them. So now their plan is to use one big explosion to create the catastrophe they need. And that's a nuclear bomb. It's the way most dictatorships come into being. Frighten the people into submission. Prove the current government can't provide for their security."

"I used to think these people were nuts," Sonny said. "People who want to return to the Garden of Eden. A kind of frontier mentality where every man is his own boss. No feds, no taxes, everyone armed to the teeth to protect his castle. Lord, it was never that simple. To build their castles they destroyed Native America. Don't they see the falsehood of their arguments?"

"No, they don't. That's the scary part," Paiz said. "You see, the Avengers are a core group we've never been able to infiltrate."

"I thought you said—"

"We've gotten into the militia groups, but the government takeover doesn't just involve the state militia groups. Not just the good old boys who will fight for the right to bear arms. Not just the America-first crowd of the love-it-or-leave mentality. The real leaders are in high government posts. In the military, in research labs, in the Pentagon, senators, representatives, you name it."

"You're kidding." Sonny looked at Lorenza. She was listening closely to Paiz.

Paiz shook his head. "Not kidding. The Avenger group is real, and its members are some of the highest officials in government and business in this country."

"If Doyle knows this, why does he keep harping on Middle East terrorists?" Sonny asked.

"Well, the director has to report to Congress," Paiz said, but his cynical look told Sonny something else.

"The director of the FBI?" Sonny shook his head. "But the militia groups hate the FBI."

"It's a game they play. Hate the government and destroy it, and what better way to topple a government than to have your men in key positions. They've been plotting this for thirty years. They don't want to engage in guerrilla warfare in the woods against the U.S. Army. They're right in the center of power. Washington, D.C."

Sonny slumped back in his chair. So they've gotten into high places, and the bomb Raven would build was to be the trigger to bring down the government. Lord, he thought, life under the Avengers would be like living under Nazi Germany. They would allow no dissension. They would close the borders, not just the physical borders, but the forums where ideas were debated. There would be deportations of those who didn't agree with the party line. The radical white supremacists would create a race war. There would be a bloodbath, the Armageddon they had been preaching all along.

Raven was part of it. He was funded and protected by the Avengers. What they didn't know is that he didn't give a damn about creating a new government, he was using them to accomplish his own goals.

"It doesn't look good," Paiz said. "They have a world-wide network. It's not just us targeted."

"But you start at the center," Sonny whispered.

This was one of the remaining spiritual centers in the country. The Pueblo Indians knew that. Here where the covenant with the ancestral kachinas had been made lay a great power for the good of mankind.

"Raven also wants you. You know that."

Sonny nodded. Paiz had been putting it all together since his agents started chasing Raven. In la Nueva México, Raven had found the spiritual center he needed to destroy. They didn't need New York, Chicago, or San Francisco. They wanted to destroy the spiritual heart. They wanted to blast the dream apart. Go right to the heart of thousands of years of ceremonies that sustained life.

"You feel okay?" Paiz asked, reaching out to touch Sonny. He had seen the sheen of sweat on Sonny's forehead.

"Yeah," Sonny replied. "Just a little tired."

"We could turn back," Lorenza said.

"No. I'm all right."

Don Eliseo had told him this era of time was coming to an end, and a struggle would take place between Sonny and Raven. Between those who dreamed the dream of peace and those who put their trust in the violence of chaos.

He looked out the van's front window. They were nearing the building.

"Does TA-2 have an alarm system?" he asked, looking up at the cliffs that rose on either side of the tech laboratory. Someone with training could rappel down the side of the cliff and land practically on the lab's roof.

"They have sensors at the LAMPF gate."

"LAMPF?"

"Los Alamos Meson Physics Facility."

"But none here?"

"No," Paiz answered, suddenly tuning in to Sonny's uneasiness.

Lorenza pulled the van next to Doyle and Eric's Jeep. Sonny let himself out with the lift. Overhead, threatening clouds hung above the Jemez peaks. The wind moaning through the pine trees on the cliffsides blew harsh and cold. High on the cliff Sonny heard the cry of a raven. Then all was quiet.

He's here, Sonny thought, the sonofabitch is here. But where? There were only two other cars in the lot, both marked "Security."

"It's quiet," he said.

"Too quiet," Paiz replied. He had picked up Sonny's anxiety. Automatically his hand went for his pistol.

"What's the matter?" Doyle asked.

Paiz shrugged. "Just go slow."

"This way," Eric called, and they followed him and Doyle to the front door. When Eric pushed the door open, Sonny heard him gasp. Paiz whispered a curse. On the floor, in a pool of blood, lay the lifeless body of a lab security guard.

Paiz went in, felt for the man's pulse, drawing his revolver at the same time.

"He's just been killed."

Eric had instantly reached for his cellular phone. He pushed a code number and spoke. "Eric here! Red alert!" he shouted. "We have a security man down at TA-2! Repeat, we have a guard down. We need backup!"

Almost at the same instant a siren went off. The labs would instantly be shut down, and somewhere in the security station, Sonny knew the lab rapid-response team was scrambling. They'd be at TA-2 in three minutes. At Kirtland Air Force Base in Alburquerque, a SWAT team would be scurrying toward waiting helicopters to fly to Los Alamos.

"He never had a chance," Paiz said, motioning them back, pressing himself against the wall. Whoever had killed the guard could still be in the building.

"How many guards covering this place?" he asked.

"Three," Eric replied.

"Stay put, I'll check it out," Paiz said, and entered the dark hallway. Sonny followed. They were both thinking the same thing: all the guards were dead. Else they would have sounded the alarm.

The next man lay dead where the hallway made a turn toward the old reactor room. Faceup, his eyes staring blankly at the ceiling, he lay in a pool of blood. The wound was a slash across his chest, a machete blow so vicious and deep it opened the sternum, cut through the heart and into the guts. Someone with incredible strength had caught the guard unaware and killed him with one blow.

Sonny looked at Paiz. Sweat beaded on the agent's forehead.

"What the hell?" he gasped, meaning, What kind of an animal kills like this?

"Holy Mother of God," Sonny whispered. Whoever had killed the guard was only minutes ahead of them.

Sonny shivered. The spirits of the dead men raced around him, crying in silent agony, shocked souls suddenly separated from their bodies. Instinctively he made the sign of the cross, an old habit from childhood days, so that the souls should not possess him.

The guard's blood had spurted on the floor from the initial blow, so the footprints of the assassin were red insignias leading down the hallway. Footsteps of the devil.

A cautious, slow-moving Paiz followed the bloody prints, holding his revolver at ready. Sonny followed in his chair, one wheel creaking in the otherwise silent hall.

What was it Oppenheimer had said that fateful day when the first atomic bomb was detonated at Trinity Site? On the northern end of la Jornada del Muerto desert, which Oñate had traveled through centuries before.

The quotation crossed Sonny's mind: "I am become Death, the Destroyer of Worlds." From the *Bhagavad-Gita*, a Sanskrit text Oppenheimer knew well.

July 16, 1945. Five twenty-nine A.M. and the desert had blossomed with a man-made sun. The first atomic bomb, called the Gadget by those who worked on it, had changed the course of history. Man had tampered with the elements, created new elements, completed the secrets of the atomic table while pursuing the nuclear structure of new elements, processed them and finally laid them at the core of a metallic container, then imploded them with detonators. The rest was history.

Then the Destroyer of Worlds was dropped on Hiroshima, and thousands of people died, miles and miles of flattened rubble lay where life had once teemed. Children with burned flesh dropping from their bodies roamed through the streets, crying a lament new to the world. It was the cry of those who saw their world ending in intense heat. Overhead, the mushroom cloud, the new archetype of the age of technology.

Nagasaki followed, where the horror beyond horrors was repeated. Man using the fire inherent in the elements had turned it against man, woman, and child.

Now Raven wanted to take the energy of the sun, the fire

which was once a gift from the gods, and turn it against mankind. Raven, the demented Sun King, knew that to control nuclear power was to control the earth.

Paiz held up his arm and Sonny paused. Paiz entered the reactor room. There was no sound, so Sonny followed him. In the room sat the eight-megawatt reactor that had been used to make small amounts of PU-239 for research. In the room also lay the body of the third guard, slashed as the other two. All three had never had time to draw their revolvers or sound an alarm. After all, they were at ease, they had been told they were guarding a bowl. Whoever came upon them had struck quickly and with precision. They never knew what hit them.

Paiz moved around the large room, checking the shadows, but both he and Sonny knew they had arrived too late. The small table in one corner appeared unceremoniously empty. Moments ago the bowl containing the stolen plutonium sat there. Now it was gone.

"Oh, my God," Sonny heard someone groan, and turned. Eric entered the room, followed by Doyle.

"He's gone," Paiz said, holstering his revolver.

"How in the hell could this have happened?"

"Lorenza?" Sonny asked.

"I instructed her to wait outside—"

Sonny turned and guided his chair back down the long hallway. He pushed past the dead guard, through the door, into the blinding sunlight. No Lorenza. He called her name. The cold wind buffeted his words, but there was no answer.

The first security Jeep came racing down the road toward TA-2, its siren blasting. The entire canyon seemed consumed with the wailing of sirens. Behind it other cars and Jeeps followed.

"Lorenza!" Sonny called again. Damn! He should have

known better. He shouldn't have left her alone, not for an instant.

"Lo-reeeen-za!"

"Here," she replied, coming around the side of the building as SWAT members surrounded them.

"He came down the cliffside," she said, "dropped right into the building. The rope is still there."

Eric came running out, waving the security guards into the building, shouting commands to the captain in charge.

"Do we have shutdown?"

"Yes, sir! All roads are blocked! No one goes in or out without my permission. Checkpoints are in place on all roads coming in. The state police have been alerted, the SWAT team from Kirtland is flying in. What happened here, sir?"

"Three men—" He stopped, drew close to the captain. "Three guards are dead—"

"Dead?"

"I want this building sealed, do you understand?"

"Yes, sir!"

"No state cops allowed in. No Kirtland boys. Seal the building. Anyone asks questions, and we say that we have the robbery of an ancient artifact we were guarding. A bowl. We believe the perpetrator is still on the grounds," Eric exclaimed. "Do understand?"

"Yes, sir!" The captain saluted and turned to give orders to his men. They spread out around the building while he barked orders into his mobile phone.

Eric turned to Sonny and Lorenza. "We have to keep it out of the press. For the meantime."

"Raven's got the plutonium," Sonny said.

Eric nodded. "God almighty, how could this happen?

We've been on alert since we brought in the core, and he gets through our security. Shit!"

Sonny looked at Doyle, who together with Paiz was coming out of the building. Did he bring Raven in? Or did Raven the sorcerer fly in? Yes, the brujo could fly, he could turn himself into a raven, like the mountain ravens that flew among the tall ponderosa pines of the forest.

He shaded his eyes and looked at the sun. In a couple of hours the sun would set over the Jemez Mountains, and the threatening snowstorm would push in.

Eric looked at Doyle and Paiz in exasperation. "The sonofabitch came into the most secure area in the U.S., killed three of my guards, and— How in the hell do I explain this?"

"Dammit, man! How do *I* explain it?" Doyle cursed.

It didn't look good for anyone. The director of the FBI and the regional director were at the labs when a terrorist came in, killed three guards, and stole a plutonium pit. Doyle would have to explain it to the president.

"Whoever attacked them, this Raven character, must be invisible. The guards just didn't even push alarms. Each man was carrying a phone."

"I don't give a holy banana what each man was carrying," Doyle sputtered. "Your security was breached. I'm called in from Washington to view a plutonium pit that's come across our border, and I'm sitting in your office when this happens. I don't like it one bit!"

"I don't like it, either!" Eric shot back, defensively.

Does Doyle think he was set up? Sonny wondered as he watched the two, like hooked fish trying to break free of what was sure to cost one or both their jobs and reputations.

"We have to keep it under wraps!" Doyle said, turning to Sonny and Lorenza.

"Yes." Eric nodded.

"You never saw this happen," Doyle said to Sonny.

Sonny shrugged. Three men were dead, they had families, and he had given his word to keep mum. But that was before Raven had butchered the three guards.

"Draw some plans up, call it a security drill!" Doyle snapped at Eric. "Just don't let the fucking press in!"

"You have three dead men," Sonny reminded him.

"Yeah, you let us deal with that," he grumbled. "We've had other situations before— Look, I have a plane to catch," he reminded Eric. He paused to look at Sonny, the shade of a smile playing in his lips. "I guess you don't get your grandmother's bowl after all. Tough." He walked to the Jeep.

"Hey, before you go," Sonny said to Eric, "we need to get outta here."

"Sure, sure. No need keeping you here. Captain, escort Mr. Baca and his assistant to the gate."

"Yes, sir," the captain replied.

Eric was visibly shaken. He looked after Doyle, then turned to Sonny. "What do you think?"

"He's alone, and he's nearby," Sonny replied. "He knows the mountains, so he'll head into the forest." He looked up at the blue ridge of the Jemez. "You don't have much daylight left."

Eric and Paiz followed Lorenza and Sonny to the van.

"You can't discuss this with anyone," Eric reminded Sonny.

"We know," Sonny said.

"We have a few days before this leaks out, then my hide

will be pinned to a Department of Defense wall," Eric said. He turned and walked to the Jeep, where Doyle waited.

"Follow me," the captain said to Sonny. He pointed to the Jeep they were to follow. "Don't make any false turns or you will be here for the duration. Understand?"

"Ten-four," Sonny replied. The man was stern, nervous. Something had gone very wrong inside TA-2, and the security team was ready to shoot on sight.

"Look, you've got my number," Paiz said. "Anything comes up, call me. This guy is really crazy."

"You're telling me," Sonny replied, and guided his chair onto the lift and inside the van.

"You okay?" he asked Lorenza when she climbed on board.

"I'm okay. You?"

"Tired."

He wanted to tell her he had felt the souls of the dead guards in the building, but he guessed she knew. She had known it was Raven all along; that's why she went around the building, sniffing around and finding the rope he had used to rappel down the side of the cliff. Even now they could sense his evil presence.

"He's nearby," Lorenza said.

"Yeah, and the guards and fences won't stop him."

"Where will he head?"

"South, to 'Burque."

"He has to go through Bandelier," she said.

"Why?" he asked.

"Sacred place," she replied.

The Bandelier National Monument lay south of the large Los Alamos Labs complex. Long ago the ancestors of the present-day Pueblo Indians lived in the caves carved into the volcanic cliffs. They farmed corn and squash along the small stream that ran through the canyon.

The entire plateau was a place of the ancestors, and the peak of the mountain a shrine to their spiritual ancestors. The kachinas, deities of rain, lived on the mountaintop. And because a sacred time in the cycle of the sun was drawing close, it was time to pray to them.

Or in Raven's case, to threaten them with the fire of the plutonium pit.

"Do you really think he'd go through there?"

"He disrupts the sacred circle every chance he gets," Lorenza replied. "Take the Calendar of Dreams and terrorize the gods of the mountain. Taunt them. As long as he has the bowl, he obstructs their power, tries to turn them away from visiting the pueblos. He has the plutonium, his new god, a radioactive core he claims is stronger than the power of the sun."

Sonny nodded. Her intuitions had always been right. "Okay, let's go take a look. Tell our escort we want to go out Highway Five-oh-one to Four."

Lorenza lowered her window and called out to the captain the route they'd like to take. He shrugged okay, boarded his Jeep, and they followed.

Sonny called Rita and told her where they were, explaining it would be late before they got home. He tried to reassure her they were all right, but he could hear the concern in her voice. Then he called Howard and asked him to check on Rita.

He clicked off the phone and rested his head on the desk. He felt exhausted, feverish. The sight of the dead guards had unnerved him, he admitted to himself. Raven had struck with fury, right under the noses of the best security in the world. Or what used to be the best.

Raven's fiendish laughter seemed to echo in the Jemez canyons as the afternoon wind buffeted the van. Dark clouds swirled on the high peaks. A dark power worked its way up the mountain, and taking advantage of the weak winter sun, it threatened even the ancient deities.

6

They drove out on 501 to Highway 4, where they stopped at the checkpoint. The captain Eric had sent to guide them pulled up and cleared the van. Beyond the gate the state cops had received instructions to let them through. Lorenza turned east on 4.

"Can he really build a bomb?" she asked.

"If he can pay experts, yes. As Eric said, Ukrainian and Russian physicists are out of work. The Avengers have enough money to bring them together. Maybe some of the people working in the labs are Avengers."

"And Paiz suspects the FBI protects them."

"A plot to take over the country. They make us suspect North Korean terrorists, militant groups, fundamentalists driven by their desire for a religious state, even the Russkies."

"And all the while they're being funded right here at home. Driven by a political ideology, and fear."

"And we've been too complacent."

Above them the gray clouds of a winter front swirled over the Jemez Mountains, creating an interplay of molten light and shadow as the setting sun lit them up. On the mountaintop the kachinas were gathering to bring snow to the valley, moisture that would slake the earth's thirst. Yes, the ancestral spirits were gathering on the mountaintop, but they could not yet descend.

Raven was out there somewhere, Lorenza had said. She knew him so well. To destroy time, he needed to strike at the ancestors that kept the universe in harmony.

"I wonder if the medicine men still come here to pray."

"Yes," Lorenza replied. "Except now the Park Service charges them a fee."

"A fee to pray on your own land." Sonny shook his head and reached for his pistol. He took the cartridges out, and with his thumbnail he etched a faint cross on the lead. According to the old stories, even a brujo had to die when shot with a bullet with a cross on it.

As he reloaded, he looked in the mirror. Lorenza was watching him. He knew better, her look said. Bullets couldn't kill Raven.

Yes, he knew, and yet he was still trusting the pistol. What else did he have? The power of his nagual, the coyote guardian spirit? The power in the dream?

He wiped the sweat from his forehead and shivered. Was he thinking irrationally? Raven's presence was near, confusing his thoughts. He trusted the pistol even though he knew the battle was one that would take place in the spirit world, the world of dreams.

"Feeling okay?" Lorenza asked.

"Okay," he answered, and tucked the pistol under his belt.

He felt like praying. For Consuelo, for the three guards, for the world, for the sun, which was three days from the solstice. For himself. Lordy, Lordy, he thought, I need some kind of help.

They were driving along a mountain road flanked by ponderosa pines, past a herd of deer grazing along the side of the road. Lorenza was driving as fast as she dared on the winding road. One hard turn and she might plow the van into the tall pines that bordered the road.

Both knew Raven wouldn't go away. He would wait for them, give them plenty of clues, lead them to him. That was his method.

Pray, a voice whispered to Sonny, and he recognized Owl Woman's voice. She too was nearby, watching over him!

This was the home of the kachinas, the deities of the Anasazis, the "Ancient Ones" who so long ago made their homes here in Frijoles Canyon. The cave dwellers, people who carved small homes into the volcanic tufa, the ashy outpouring from long-ago volcanic eruptions that had formed the Jemez Mountains. They climbed up to their caves on the cliffsides to escape the nomadic enemies who swept down like wolves, murdering the farmers who planted corn and squash along the narrow confines of the canyon.

He should have known! It wasn't just Raven haunting his footsteps. Owl Woman was also close by. She was a grandmother, not yet destroyed by Raven, and she could bless his way.

"Yes," he whispered. Give me strength, Owl Woman. Be the tecolote that fights the raven. Be the good ancestral spirit that guides my path.

He wiped tears from his eyes. "Ah, yes."

"We're here," Lorenza said as they drove into the visitor parking lot and stopped.

Above them the southwest sun cast gigantic slanting rays of light through the dark storm clouds. Streaming light that bathed the earth.

Sonny knew Bandelier. As a university student he had

fished the Jemez with his buddy, Dennis Martínez, and he had hiked through the trails of the monument. Just up the canyon lay the Tyuonyi Ruins, a sacred place, full of the spirits. A place for meditation, especially at this time of the year.

He let his chair down on the lift and tucked the pistol under the wool serape Rita had sent.

"Don't let your legs get cold," she had admonished.

There were no other cars in the lot. This time of the year and of the day was not the best for visiting the park.

The lone park ranger in the visitors' center was surprised to see them. "It's almost closing time. A storm's coming in," he informed them. "You sure you want to go up the canyon?" he asked when Lorenza took out her wallet to buy tickets. He looked at Sonny in his chair.

"We're sure," Lorenza said.

"I'll give you an hour, no more. It's closing time," he repeated, pointing at the clock on the wall.

She paid the fee while Sonny went to the bathroom. When he returned, she went. Sonny browsed through pamphlets. A quote from Adolph Bandelier's 1880 journal caught his eye. He read the entry:

About 4 p.m. the border of the almost precipitous descent into the Cañon de los Frijoles was reached, and it took one-half hour to descend—on foot, of course. The grandest thing I ever saw. A magnificent growth of pines, encina, alamos, and towering cliffs, of pumice or volcanic tuff, exceedingly friable. The cliffs are vertical on the north side, and their bases are, for a length as yet unknown to me, used as dwellings both from the inside, and by inserting the roof poles for stories outside. It is of the highest interest. There are some of one, two, and three stories. In most cases the plaster is still in the rooms. Some are walled in; others are mere holes in the rocks. Much pottery of the older, painted sort, but as yet no corrugated ones. I found entire chimneys, metates, manos and a stone-axe.

Bandelier had been the first white man from the East Coast to explore the canyon. Before him the Spaniards from the Río Grande valley had chased after nomadic Indians, and in their search they had discovered the old Indian ruins that dotted the mesas of the piedmont, but they had no time to explore. Later the canyon was visited by Navajos who raided the villages in the valley, stealing sheep, women, and children. The deep canyons of the plateau provided excellent hiding places.

Bandelier had excavated the caves and dwellings, discovered that the Pajaritan Indians had farmed corn, beans, and squash along the banks of the small creek that gurgled through the canyon. Centuries before the Spaniards came into the region, the Anasazis had constructed their pueblos of mud and stone all over the Four Corners region around Mesa Verde.

Around A.D. 1500 the Anasazis begin to move out of the Four Corners region, leaving behind them the great pueblos they had built at Chaco Canyon. At Chaco they had built roads leading out in the four directions, smooth roads that perhaps were used as trade routes. Roads used to run ceremonial races, some anthropologists presumed. Perhaps the roads were used by the deer dancers coming into the pueblo during the ceremonies, or maybe the roads were meant for the kachinas, pathways for the ancestral deities to enter the pueblo during the blessing time.

The Anasazis evolved into the Pajaritan people, who built

small one-family or extended-family structures on the mesas of the Pajarito Plateau. Here they told the legends of their coming into being, stories of the creation of the people and their role in it. Here the medicine men prayed and the people performed their dances so the cosmos might stay in harmony. Here they honored the spirits of their ancestors.

Sonny read on, learning from the brochure that the Pajarito Plateau consisted of a long shelf of compressed volcanic ash and basalt. The lava spilling out of the long-ago active Jemez volcano formed the plateau over a million years ago. Rain and wind sculpted the shelf into long, narrow mesas and deep canyons. Here Folsom man hunted, later seminomadic hunters and gatherers passed through the region, and finally the descendants of the Anasazis came, the Pueblo Indians. Half a century before Coronado arrived in 1541, the plateau was abandoned and the people moved into the Río Grande valley to found the pueblos of Cochiti, Santa Clara, and San Ildefonso.

"Ready?" Lorenza said.

"How far up the canyon can I get in the chair?" Sonny asked the unenthusiastic ranger at the counter.

"The trail is clear, but it ain't easy even for a motorized chair."

"Vamos," Sonny replied. Lorenza opened the door and they started up the trail. The chair easily handled the first part of the asphalt trail, which was handicapped accessible. Where the asphalt gave way to packed earth, they found the ground frozen, so the going wasn't too difficult. They followed the small, clear stream of Frijoles Creek to the first cave dwellings.

A cold wind descended into the canyon, moaning through the pine trees. Two large crows rose from a tall ponderosa pine, circled, and disappeared up the canyon in the direction of Ceremonial Cave.

Sonny shivered. During the day the winter sun had warmed the cliffside. Long ago shamans studied the course of the sun, counting the days of the solstice. Somewhere in the canyon the medicine men had constructed a slit in the rocks, a Calendar of the Sun. All the ancient people had such calendars, for the course of the sun was important to their survival. The sun was the Giver of Life, the Grandfather.

Now the canyon was empty, save for Lorenza and Sonny and the cold wind whipping down from the peaks.

"I'm tired," Sonny said. He drew in a gulp of the cold, clear air. This high the oxygen was thin. Lorenza nodded. They were close to eight thousand feet high. Here was good enough.

Except for the wind swaying the tops of the trees, the silence in the canyon was eerie. They stopped and let it seep into them. The small gurgling brook ran down the canyon floor, its water was winter clear. The wind whispered in the bare cottonwoods that lined the creek and in the pines that clung to the sides of the cliffs. A call and a royal flash of blue announced a blue jay in the alamos; then came the croak of a mountain raven farther up the cliff.

Lorenza took an eagle feather from her bag. She began to sing, softly. To Sonny it sounded familiar. It was the same song she sang during the ceremony when she taught him to take his coyote form, the spirit of the coyote in which he could descend into the spirit world.

He closed his eyes and let the chant work its medicine. Lorenza passed the eagle feather over him, praying to the deities of the place to cleanse away the presence of the guards' souls.

The spirits of the canyon responded; after all, it was a

holy time, a time when the kachinas of the mountain were gathering in the snow clouds, ready to descend on the Río Grande pueblos.

Animal spirits appeared first, the red fox, a doe with a year-old fawn, a buck, skunks and birds, cackling jays, playful squirrels, all gathering to meet the coyote Sonny felt within.

Above them, the mighty kachinas, so colorful in the light of the setting sun that one was blinded by their presence.

Sonny felt the ghosts of the dead guards disappear. He breathed a sigh of relief. Then the chant stopped. He opened his eyes slowly, watching the last of the animal spirits disappear into the forest along the side of the stream.

"They're gone," he murmured.

"Yes," Lorenza said. "Now I go on to the Long House to pray. Feel up to it?"

"You go on," he replied. He was tired, and there was no use testing the chair. Anyway, from where he sat, he could look directly up the narrow canyon to the nearby peaks. The sun shining through the clouds was worth contemplating.

She leaned and kissed his cheek. "Your coyote guardian is still strong. Be alert."

Then she walked on up the path toward the Long House ruins. Sonny watched until she disappeared around a bend. Was she going to pray or to draw Raven out?

He bowed his head. A swiftly moving bank of gray clouds shut out the sun and the canyon grew dark. Pray, Sonny thought. They had just come to pray in the presence of the spirits of the place.

"Let the spirits of the ancestors bless me."

Yes, pray, Owl Woman said. Her whisper was the soft moan of the wind, the gurgling of the stream, the occasional call of a jay. Sonny felt the spiritual power of the earth permeating his body, filling his soul. Owl Woman was guiding him.

The clouds rolled away, and again brilliant rays of sunlight broke through, a shower of fire. Then she appeared, dressed in the soft buckskin the women of the desert had prepared for her wedding ceremony. She held the Calendar of Dreams, the shiny black bowl on which were inscribed the dream symbols, the future.

The golden light shone on her and bathed her in an aura of beauty. Behind her Sonny saw other figures rise and move, giant figures descending from the mountain, the kachinas of rain, the ancestral deities walking down the path along the creek. Dressed in colorful costumes, the figures came in procession toward him.

These were the cloud people, the rain people, bringing the moisture in the snow down from the peaks of the mountain. The spirits of the mountain had risen and were walking down Frijoles Canyon toward the pueblos of the Río Grande. It was the time of ceremony, a time of blessing.

Sonny heard a moan escape his lips, he shuddered. Owl Woman, his grandmother, had brought the vision, as sharp as the vision he had when he attended the peyote ceremony with don Eliseo! Brighter than his dreams in color! So this was the ancient secret the ancestors had guarded. The spirits did live here on this mountaintop! They came to bless the earth of the valley, to bless the people.

In their masks they came, in colorful costumes and feathers and buckskin. Kachinas for rain and bounty. Kachinas for the sick and for the old. Kachinas for the seeds. Kachinas for the water that flowed down the river into the fields. Kachinas that made the sky rumble and the clouds form on the peaks of the Jemez Mountains. Kachinas for every blessing.

In that final burst of light from the winter sun, they came, their rattles sounding like falling rain, their breath the breath of life, cold and invigorating, filling Sonny with so much beauty he felt tears run down his cheeks. These were the Lords and Ladies of the Light that don Eliseo prayed to. The sunlight descended to earth. Sunlight blessed the earth.

They moved past him, leaving in their wake only the swish of their skirts, the rattle of the gourds that contained the seeds, the distant thunder of the drum on the mountain. Each giant figure moving toward the ceremony of thanksgiving, moving down the mountain to bless the pueblos. Around them the rumble of the storm broke and rolled through the peaks. Dark clouds of swirling snow filled the sky. Now the sun dropped behind the canyon wall and instantly the canyon grew dark, and the visions were gone.

"Beware!" Owl Woman cried, and Sonny turned in time to see the Bringer of Curses, the evil spirit who soiled the path of the kachinas. He came tumbling from the sky to strike at him.

"Raven!" Sonny cried, and braced himself to meet Raven's blow. Raven's attack sent Sonny flying out of his chair, and together they rolled down the incline into the cold water of the creek.

Two objects tore loose from Raven as they tumbled into the icy water. One was a nickel-coated sphere, about the size of a large grapefruit, the other was Owl Woman's bowl.

Sonny remembered Paiz's warning. In water the core could go critical. He reached for it, but Raven was quicker. He grabbed the shiny plutonium pit and thrust it at Sonny.

"Fire!" Raven cried, gasping for breath, his scarred face twisted with hate.

"Where's Consuelo?" Sonny cried out, pushing back into

the mud of the creek, holding Raven's wrist to keep the pit from smashing his face.

"The women are mine!" Raven laughed, straddling Sonny and pushing the spherical core down on him. The shiny metal glistened, dripping with water. At any moment Sonny expected the thing to explode.

"This, too, is mine!" Raven shouted, ripping at Sonny's shirt and exposing the gold Zia medallion. He tore it from Sonny's neck and held it up.

He held Sonny pinned, holding the gold medallion high in one hand, the plutonium core in the other. Now he was in complete control. The Zia sun symbol and the plutonium core were his.

"Time's up!" he shouted.

"Not yet," Sonny groaned, and mustering all the strength he could, he struck, sending Raven sprawling into the creek. Both plutonium and gold medallion fell from his hands. Sonny struggled to rise, to continue to fight, but it was no use, his legs wouldn't lift him up.

"Damn you!" Raven cursed as he scooped up the plutonium core. He was fumbling for the medallion when Lorenza's cry ripped through the air.

Sensing Raven, she had returned and scooped up the pistol from where it had fallen by the wheelchair.

"Raven!" she called.

He turned to look at her. "Witch!" he replied.

"Try this," she answered calmly, pointing the pistol and firing.

The bullet tore through Raven's hand, barely missing the plutonium core.

Raven cried in pain, gathered the pit into his body, turned, and disappeared into the thick forest.

The echo of the shot rolled down the canyon, like summer thunder before a rain. Frantically cawing crows rose from a nearby tree and flew away.

Lorenza hurried down the incline to Sonny, who clutched at a cottonwood sapling near him.

"Are you all right?"

"Just barely," he replied. "Cold."

He was wet and shaking from the freezing creek water. She helped him up. Holding on to the tree, he could stand on his wobbly legs.

"Gracias," he said.

"Can you make it to the chair?"

"You hit him," Sonny said, catching his breath.

"He didn't get what he came for," she said, and reached for the Zia medallion in the water. "This is what he wanted."

"The bowl," Sonny said, pointing.

She lifted the black pot from the water and handed it to Sonny. He held it up and whistled softly.

"Owl Woman's bowl, the bowl I saw in my dream!"

He looked at Lorenza, puzzled. Raven *had* been in his dream! And if he could bring something back from the dream, then anything was possible.

"Now it's yours."

"But he has Owl Woman, and the girl."

"Come on. Let's see if we can get you back to the chair. Gotta dry you, get you warm."

Sonny was wet and trembling. She knew hypothermia could set in quickly. Straining under his weight, she helped him up the slope. He struggled, commanding his legs to carry him and not buckle. If he fell, he knew he wouldn't have the strength to get up again.

They got to the chair, and he sat down heavily, exhausted and shivering from the water and cold, clutching the pot.

Flakes of snow began to fall. Large wet snowflakes that quickly turned the ground white.

"You're going to catch cold," she whispered, removing her black leather coat and putting it around him. She turned the chair and pushed him down the trail to the van.

The ranger came out of the visitors' center to meet them. "Heard a shot," he said, looking at a wet and muddy Sonny.

"Sounded like someone shooting a rifle up the canyon," Lorenza said, not bothering to explain as she got Sonny into the van and covered him with the serape.

"Ah, God, don't the natives know better," the ranger complained. "Probably poachers. If I catch those sonsofbitches . . ." He paused, looked up the canyon.

It lay shrouded in an eerie white light created by the falling snow. He knew better than to chase a poacher in the oncoming darkness.

"What happened?" he asked.

"We got too near the creek, the chair slipped. We're okay," Lorenza said, getting into the driver's seat. She gunned the van, hoping the motor would warm quickly. The ranger shrugged and hurried back to the office.

"What would have happened if the bullet had hit the plutonium?" Sonny asked through chattering teeth.

"I guess Bandelier National Monument and the entire top of the mountain would have been blown off the face of the earth," Lorenza replied. "But what do I know?"

7

Lorenza gathered the canvases in the rear of the van and handed them to Sonny.

"Take off the wet clothes," she commanded.

Sonny stripped and pulled the dry canvases around him. They smelled fresh, the way painter's oils smell. Some poor artist in a wheelchair had once driven around the state in the van, stopping here and there to capture the stark beauty of the arid land, the majesty of mountains. Sonny wondered if he had abandoned his efforts or, like many an artist, just ran out of money.

Where is he now? Sonny thought as Lorenza drove out of the parking lot. Sonny was chilled, shivering, but thankful that he was alive. And he had the bowl.

He held it up and looked at it carefully, admiring the symmetry, the shape, and the mysterious glyphs carved in an ancient language, a language whose signs he couldn't decipher.

The Bowl of Dreams, Owl Woman's Calendar of Dreams. At least this much had come from the encounter, the ancient bowl was in his possession. It was an artifact of classical beauty, but more important, it was also a source of power.

"La Nueva México," he muttered, his teeth chattering.

"Need to get you something warm to drink," he heard Lorenza say, but he was concentrating on the bowl.

Sonny turned on the desk lamp. The light shone on the shiny black surface, revealing the finely raised glyphs. Eric said it was a pre-Toltec piece. One obvious engraving was the plumed serpent thrashing upward along the side of the bowl. The Toltecs had made their covenant with Quetzacoatl.

"What do you see?" Lorenza asked. She was studying him out of the rearview mirror, his face illuminated by the soft glow of the lamp, revealing the shaman eyes.

"A few of the symbols are pretty obvious. Quetzacoatl. There's a circle, or spiral, of glyphs from the bottom of the bowl, around the bowl, up to the lip. Like Jacob's ladder."

Or a DNA molecule, he thought as he put his finger on the bowl to trace the route of the glyphs around the belly of the bowl. What he felt shocked him. A magnetic energy coursed through his hand, up his arm, into his chest.

"It feels alive," he said softly.

"Old energies, old dreams," Lorenza replied. "The bowl represents Mother Earth, the woman. You touch the earth with respect and she vibrates with her power. You touch a woman—" She paused and smiled into the mirror. "But why should I tell you about women."

Sonny looked up from the bowl at Lorenza's eyes in the mirror. Sometimes she reminded him of Rita. He had often thought the two could be sisters. Handsome women, with an inner beauty that shone in their dark eyes. Flashing smiles, full lips, high cheekbones. Real Nuevas Mexicanas beauties.

Rita had kept his interest in life alive by caring for him,

feeding him, and one night when he was so low he wanted to die, she slipped under the sheets and made love to him. He found salvation in the warmth of her flesh.

"There's a sun sign, that's obvious. Our Zia sun, the sun god of the Toltecs, Tonatiuh. Could this be a companion piece to the Sun Calendar of the Aztecs in the Museum of Anthropology in Mexico City?"

"You mean the two might complement each other?" Lorenza said. "And the glyphs on one might lead to the meaning of the other? Intriguing."

"Just wild thoughts," Sonny replied. "I don't know when the Sun Calendar was carved, or even how it was used. We know nothing of the origin of this bowl—"

"It originated in your dreams," Lorenza reminded him.

"Yes, the Owl Woman was determined to bring it here. Now it's here, sitting on my lap, and what does it mean?"

"You mentioned the dream of peace."

"If Owl Woman and Andres Vaca did come north, they brought the dream of peace. They raised their family, my ancestors. The bowl has been here all along! Hidden from us!"

Sonny grew excited, then shook his head. He felt feverish, and the thoughts stirred up by the bowl weren't clear. He was grasping for straws, something to explain his dream.

"Hidden from us because we lost the dream," Lorenza added.

"And now it's possible again. The bowl is here. It can be filled with our dream."

"Sounds beautiful to me," Lorenza said, glancing at him, then returning her gaze to the road. In the darkness the thick snow parted as the van sped down the mountain.

"Raven used my dream to go back into time. He knew Owl Woman and the bowl were there. Now he still has Owl

Woman, my great-great Indian grandmother. How do I get her back?"

The drone of the tires on the highway and the heater's fan filled the dark space.

"The answer has to be in the bowl," Lorenza said.

Sonny followed the line of glyphs with his finger. "A tree, the Tree of Life."

"Go on."

"A tiger. Monkey. Bird. Fish. Snake thunder. Wind sign. Around the sun, other figures. Gods or men? An ankh sign? That's Egyptian. What the hell is it doing on a Toltec bowl?"

"Some say three thousand years ago the Egyptians crossed the ocean, landed in the Americas. Who's to say they didn't travel back and forth."

"They both built pyramids," Sonny said.

"They were connected, somehow they were connected. So the ankh sign appears on a Toltec bowl. The sign of life."

"Mesoamerica as Atlantis," Sonny murmured. "I never bought the theory. Sure, many a prehistoric boat might have landed on the shores of México, but it was the indigenous people who created their own civilizations."

"I agree. People tend to look for connections in the sky, aliens from spaceships, or ships from Atlantis. But as don Eliseo teaches, there is a world consciousness. A collective memory. We are connected. The thoughts of one group affect another across time. Did they need to cross the ocean, bodily, to communicate with each other? No. At certain times on earth, perhaps affected by sunspot explosions or lack thereof, the minds of the world think the same thoughts. That's when mankind moves into new levels of consciousness."

"A world dream," Sonny said. "Mind travel, some kind of mental telepathy, long ago. Why not?"

Don Eliseo talked about the interrelatedness of everything. But Sonny had thought only of the material connection, that atoms and molecular structure were connected. Was mind also connected? The Egyptian priests communicated with those of Mesoamerica? A world mind connecting those who could tune into it? You didn't need to explain historical parallelisms through aliens or travelers from Atlantis, it was simply the great minds of men and women communicating across space and time. Space and time became their thoughts, their ideas.

During the summer drought don Eliseo had gone to a prayer meeting with his Indian neighbors. "We prayed for rain," he told Sonny later. "The weatherman said there is great ocean-stream of wind and weather in the sky. The jet stream. It is like a giant snake entwined around the earth, and when it slides south, we receive its energy. We get rain. Now it is too far to the north, above Montana maybe. So together we reached up and grabbed the tail of the jet stream and pulled it down. With prayer we pulled it down."

The next day it rained. A wonderful steady drizzle that broke the drought. Prayer. Minds connecting.

The old man believed the earth was alive, it had a spirit, a consciousness. To cut the Amazon forest meant the entire weather patterns of the earth would change. A philosopher coughing in China created hurricanes in the tropics. Thoughts, memories, dreams curved around the earth, like the glyphs on the bowl, and affected other dreamers.

"We are connected," Sonny murmured. "Not only in body, but in spirit."

Snow driven wild by the wind swirled around the van when Lorenza pulled in front of the Seven-Eleven at White Rock. The earlier feathery stuff had turned into a heavy, wet snow, the kind that would bend the boughs of even the toughest pine trees. Tall ponderosa pines, firs, blue spruces, even the leafless aspens would gather the wet flakes onto their branches and bend with the gift. The trees were old men and women thanking the gods for the gift of snow.

Behind them the Jemez peaks were hidden in the darkness that hovered over Redondo, covering the mountain. Ancient deities were praying over the sacred mountain, praying and then rising to carry the gift of water down to the pueblos.

Lorenza went into the store and came out with a large hot coffee, aspirin, and a fleece jogging sweatshirt and pants.

"Gracias a Dios they stock a few things for campers," she said. "Put these on. I don't want to deliver you to Rita in your birthday suit."

She helped him slip into the warm cotton shirt and pants. Then she covered him again with the canvases. "Take these." She handed him three aspirins and he drank them down with the coffee. "Try to keep awake," she said.

"Why?" Sonny asked, and the minute he asked, the answer flashed in front of him. She was afraid that Raven would come again if he fell asleep.

"Yeah," he mumbled, and she was on the road again, heading down into the Río Grande valley.

The hot coffee warmed him, the shivering stopped. He told her how he had seen the kachinas right before Raven attacked him.

"It's that time of the year," she replied. "The solstice is near, the spirits of the mountains come to visit the pueblos. They come to bring winter rain, snow. Raven knew that, so he waited for us."

Where the angels gather, the Bringer of Curses appears, Sonny thought. Just what don Eliseo said. The devil always comes to the angels' convention.

The snow that minutes ago had covered the road now grew thin. They knew that by the time they descended into the valley, only wisps of the storm would remain. That's the way it was with a front like this, it would drop snow in the high elevations, but merely dust the lowlands. That's why in New Mexico during the winter people could ski and golf in the same day. From Jemez to Taos, the high peaks would get snow, in Alburquerque, nada.

Yes, Sonny thought, the time for the ceremonies was at hand. Already the Matachine dances had been held at Jemez Pueblo on December 12, día de la Virgen de Guadalupe. More dances would be held on Christmas day, and on New Year's day. The people remembered their prayers and ceremonies. They still kept the sacred calendar of their ancestors, still survived in the essence of their original dream.

Sonny hunkered deeper down into the warmth of the canvases and tried to keep his eyes open. But the hum of the motor, the fatigue, and the warmth made it almost impossible. Even the coffee didn't help. Exhaustion and a soreness crept through his bones.

"Stay awake," Lorenza reminded him.

"Tired," he answered. He had done too much the first day out, he knew that now. But he also knew there weren't many days left. Raven would strike on the winter solstice, the day the sun stood still. Like the first atomic bomb exploding at Trinity, forty miles southeast of Socorro. The sun standing still.

His father, who had been raised in Socorro, and his mother who was raised in La Joya just across the river, told him stories of the "day the sun shone at night." They were children then. His father told of getting up at the crack of dawn to milk the cows when, on his way to the barn, the morning lit up. Five twenty-nine A.M. on that fateful day, the demon light of the bomb exploded over the desert before sunrise, lighting up the skies. "The work of the devil," the old people warned.

Now the Bringer of Curses controlled some of that power. Raven hadn't gotten the Zia medallion he came after, but he had the plutonium. Sonny dozed and saw him holding the nickel-coated ball aloft with his bare hand. A burning sun, a power no man dared to touch, the Raven was flirting with it. Invincible, Raven taunted, I am invincible.

Raven was growing in power, growing in the madness Sonny had recognized at their first meeting. Now the FBI had uncovered part of his past. Raven wasn't Raven, that was just one of his many names. Raven was a sorcerer, one of those brujos who could fly. Not fly like the old curanderas to do a healing, to deliver a blessing, but to destroy.

All this went through Sonny's mind as he struggled to stay awake during the long drive home. Lorenza had called Rita, letting her know when they'd get back, so Rita was waiting at Sonny's place when they arrived.

Chica came bounding out of the house ahead of Rita, barking, tail wagging, jumping up on Sonny's lap the minute the lift hit the ground. Tail wagging, whining with a secret message of love, licking his face, and sniffing the strange smells on her master.

"Chica, good dog." Sonny hugged her.

Rita kissed Sonny, then seeing he was pale and shivering, she exclaimed, "Dios mío! What happened? Your clothes?"

"Raven," he tried to explain with one word.

"Let's get you in the house," Rita said, taking charge. They got him into the house and into the bathroom where Rita stripped his clothes off and helped him into a hot bath. She had made a strong lemonade, hot and flavored with osha, an herb she used for colds. She poured two shots of bourbon into the glass, and Sonny drank the soothing mixture.

Then she helped him out of the bath and rubbed him vigorously with a towel from head to toe. The circulation returned to his limbs.

"Ah, great," he kept muttering. How sweet it was to be cared for by the woman he loved. She covered him with mentholatum, wrapped him in a warm terry-cloth robe, and got him into bed. Chica jumped in with him.

"She's been waiting all day," Rita said. "Don Eliseo kept her, tried to feed her, but she wouldn't eat. Imagine a dachshund that doesn't eat? She's been worried."

"Hey, I'm home, safe and sound," Sonny said, rubbing Chica's belly.

"Let's hope you don't catch pneumonia," Rita scolded as she served him hot chicken and rice soup.

He thanked her weakly. "What would I do without you?" He held up a piece of tortilla with butter for Chica.

Lorenza brought the bowl in and set it on the lamp table. Under the light it shone with a mysterious beauty.

Rita gasped. "It's beautiful. The bowl in your dream!"

Sonny ate while Lorenza told of their meeting with Raven.

"What does it mean?" Rita asked when Lorenza finished. "You dream a bowl and it appears?"

"It means what don Eliseo suspects," Lorenza said. "Raven has found a way to get into Sonny's dreams."

"But he needs to sleep."

"I don't know—" Lorenza cautioned.

Rita arched an eyebrow. "Por qué?"

"She's afraid if I sleep, Raven might appear in my dreams," Sonny said weakly. "Or nightmares."

The warm bath and food and fatigue were already more

than he could bear. He was going to sleep regardless. Chica had already burrowed under the blanket.

"He doesn't have a choice, does he?" Rita asked, looking for guidance from Lorenza.

Lorenza shook her head. "He needs the rest. No, he doesn't have a choice."

Sonny's eyelids felt heavy. "Chica will guard my dreams," he mumbled. "Tomorrow I want to—"

Rita placed her fingers over his lips. "He doesn't know when to quit," she said, and kissed his forehead.

"Is there any way *we* can guard his dreams?" he heard Rita ask.

"No," Lorenza replied. "We may be in the dream, but only another shaman can walk with him. He has to learn to be the actor in the dream."

"Is there anything we can do?" Rita was worried.

"Follow don Eliseo's instructions," Lorenza said, leaning to make sure Sonny heard her. "It's very important that you construct the dream. Do you understand?"

"Yes," Sonny mumbled. "I must pick the place, I have to set up the stage. When I pass through the door into the world of spirits, I must be in charge. . . ."

"Who is your guide?" Lorenza asked.

"Coyote."

"Y los santos," Rita whispered, making the sign of the cross. "May they guard your sleep. Your Señores y Señoras de la Luz, may they shine light on your path."

"Buenas noches, amor," Sonny replied, his eyes closing.

What a woman, he thought. He and Rita had been dating a couple of years, dancing on Saturday nights, and sharing his investigating work. She, like his mother, nudged him from time to time to get out of the detective business. Rita's restaurant was booming, business was good, the city and the state were on a roll, and she had suggested more than once that together they could run the café.

"Become a taco pusher. Me?" he often teased her.

"You need to settle down," she said. "Marry me. I'll make you happy."

"Oh, I know. . . ."

He loved her, the way she talked, spoke, the color of her eyes, hair, the fragrance that lingered around her, her magic green thumb that grew flowers and herbs, her business sense, and in a hundred other ways he loved her, but he wasn't sure he was ready for marriage. He had quit teaching literature at Valley High because he found the schedule too restraining. He liked the freedom of private investigating, even though it meant that from one month to the next, he didn't know where his next meal was coming from.

"Yes, I'm ready to settle . . ." he whispered, smiling at the thought. Sleep could be as sensuous as Rita, a wave of pleasure washing over him. The soreness in his body and the fatigue of the day melted into the mattress, and instantly he was breathing in an even, soft rhythm.

"You need this," he heard Lorenza say. She slipped something cold under the covers. The Zia medallion.

Ah, he smiled.

"And this," she said, and slipped another cold object into his hand. He recognized his pistol.

"You said bullets don't hurt Raven," he mumbled.

"They can't hurt him when he has taken the form of his nagual, his guardian spirit," she replied. "But when he's Raven the man, then you draw first."

She moved away, leaving her enticing body aroma in the swirl of the oncoming dream. The door closed and the room was dark and silent again.

He was sure the hammer was on an empty chamber, just

like his father had taught him. An old rule of the West. Billy the Kid always kept his hammer there. That way if you dropped the pistol, you didn't shoot yourself in the foot.

Carry the pistol into sleep? He shivered. Damn, he couldn't stay awake!

Be master of your dream, he heard don Eliseo say.

It was up to him to will the dream into being. Which dream? The next momentous event in the history of la Nueva México was the expulsion of the Spaniards by the Pueblo Indians. He had to go there. According to the rough family tree he had sketched out, that's where the Anaya branch of the family tree joined the Bacas. The only name he had found in his research was the name Caridad de Anaya. Did he have to find her in his dream?

He moved toward the door of dreams and was surprised to see don Eliseo waiting for him.

Don Eliseo?

Who were you expecting? Bugs Bunny?

Sonny laughed. The old man had a sense of humor.

Are you going with me?

No, not this time. You see, to become the master of your dream you must first go alone. I cannot interfere. Not now.

I've got to face Raven on my own?

Walk straight into the dream. Like this.

The old man walked up to the door.

You open the door, and you walk in. The dream must not be foreign to you, it must be part of your history. Something you create. Look closely at everything. Study every image. Don't let the dream be jumbled up. Pretend it is a story, or a good movie, and when you get back home, you have to tell the adventures in the dream.

Adventures, like Odysseus?

Sure, like that Griego. Or like Juan Chicaspatas, or Pedro

de Ordimalas. Any pícaro will do. Remember, this is la Nueva México. It's your homeland, your stage, get it?

Yes.

Where are you going?

Taos. Sixteen eighty. Remember the book of families? The Anayas married the Vacas and became part of the family tree.

Don't allow Raven to fragment your dream! The dream is a story, a vision, and it must make sense to you!

Don Eliseo's final warning echoed as Sonny opened the door. Gracias, don Eliseo.

The wind whispered de nada.

Sonny stepped through the door and entered Taos Pueblo on foot. Instantly the images of the dream scrambled, but Sonny willed them into order. Like a good story.

He saw a pueblo man who cast no shadow sneak into a church and steal a crucifix.

Popé, Sonny said. This is the chief of the Taos Rebellion. I will follow him.

The man stole through the narrow streets of the Indian pueblo, muttering as he went, cursing the Spaniards, whom he blamed for so much misery. He, Popé, would bring destruction on the Españoles, their god, and all their santos.

He entered an underground chamber and Sonny followed. The walls of the kiva were smooth, hand-plastered. Half sunken into the earth, the kiva was accessible only by using the wood ladder that dropped from the small entrance on the roof.

In the middle of the earthen floor, a small fire burned in a pit, and the flickering flames cast dancing light on the designs that decorated the walls.

Around the fire sat other war captains from other pueblos. Sonny remembered the list he had made in his notebook. Now here they were! Luis Tupatu from Picuris; Antonio Malacate from La Cienega de Cochiti; Francisco El Ollita and Nicolas Jonva from San Ildefonso; Domingo Naranjo from Santa Clara; Domingo Romero from Tesuque; Antonio Bolsas, a Tano Indian; Cristobal Yope from San Lazaro; Felipe de Ye from Pecos; Juan El Tano from Galisteo; Alonzo Catiti from Santo Domingo; and Luis Conizu from Jemez.

These war captains and others represented their pueblos, and tonight they met on a very important mission. Tonight they would decide whether war against Spanish rule should be declared.

Popé entered, sat quietly, and smoked the ceremonial tobacco. For a long time all were silent.

Finally Popé spoke. I vow to take the power from the Españoles.

The men in the room looked uneasily at each other.

One spoke. If we are to drive out the Españoles, then we will do it as brave warriors.

The others nodded. The decision before them was momentous. The Españoles had lived on their land since the Capitán Oñate came in 1598. Each man spoke his mind. Should they make war on the Españoles and drive them away?

The oldest of the war captains spoke. These men of iron who ride on horseback, and their medicine men—the ones they call padres—have become harsh rulers. We welcomed them and accepted their kachinas, those they call santos, into our ceremonies, into our kivas. We have accepted the man who dies on the cross, their Cristo, we treated la Virgen as our own mother. But they call our own kachinas devils. The padres do not allow us to pray to the spirits of our ancestors. They have burned our kachina masks, the prayer sticks, the amulets. They have come into our kivas and desecrated everything we hold sacred. It is time to throw off the yoke of the Spaniards.

Silence filled the kiva, the thin smoke from the fire rose and curled upward and out into the night sky. Again the men smoked the pipe. The men had many vecinos in the Spanish pueblo, farmers like them, many who respected their dances and ceremonies. But the rule of the civil authorities and the padres was harsh.

Another captain spoke. It is not good. We have farmed for them, raised their crops, taught them how to use our acequias to take the water from the streams to the fields. We have paid tribute in corn and blankets. They take our women and children to use as slaves. They quarrel among themselves. The governor and the soldiers tell us one thing, and the padres another. A drought has come over the land, and in every pueblo our people are dying. Surely our ancestors are angry that we are praying to these foreign gods. Our kachinas have guided us since we came to this earth. All this must end.

It is time to cleanse the land, another war captain said. It is time to vote.

Popé did not speak. He was deep in meditation. Even though he was a San Juan man, he had been coming to this kiva in Taos Pueblo for many years. He was an old man now, his sons and daughters were married, and now was the time to be a grandfather and teach his grandchildren. But he could not rest or enjoy his old age when his people suffered so much.

A passage in the history book he had been reading flashed through Sonny's mind. Only five years before this fateful meeting, the former governor, Treviño, had led his soldiers against the kivas, prohibiting all the rituals. Forty-seven medicine men were arrested by the governor and taken to prison in Santa Fé. Four of the medicine men were hanged in the plaza, and the others, including Popé, received a public flogging. Popé still nursed the scars of that whipping.

Terror filled the land. The god of the Españoles had brought only war, pestilence, hunger, and drought. Even the Virgin Mother had appeared in a vision and foretold doom for the colony. Now was the time to join together and drive out the Spaniards. For five years Popé had been speaking to the other pueblos, and many of the men had listened and agreed.

I am for war, Popé said in anger. I will not rest until the Españoles are gone from our land, and their homes and churches burned to the ground.

One by one the other war captains nodded.

Set the date for our attack, the oldest captain said with heavy heart. Each had spoken. Now they would act together.

Popé set the date. August 10, 1680, according to the calendar of the Españoles. He tied knotted cords of yucca and sent them to all the pueblos.

Sonny turned and the time of the dream turned with him. The last knot on the yucca cord was untied and cries of war sounded in the juniper-covered hills and echoed across the ravines of northern New Mexico.

The Pueblo Indians swept down on the Spanish settlements, killing everyone in sight and desecrating the churches. Leaving a trail of death, they descended on Santa Fé. There they surrounded the thousand men, women, and children who were left alive. They cut off the water ditch that fed the city, and they fought off the feeble attempts of the Spanish soldiers to open it. They would starve the Spaniards into submission.

Sonny followed the images of his nightmare, ordering them as he went, and though all was clear, he realized he couldn't change the course of history.

From the other pueblos word came to Popé. The pueblos of Acoma, Zuni, and Hopi had joined the revolt. Everywhere the warriors of the pueblos burned churches, killed priests, and marched on Santa Fé.

Tossing and turning away from the carnage, Sonny let out a cry. He opened his eyes, and in the dim light, he saw Rita. She touched a cool cloth to his forehead.

"Murder, murder," he gasped.

"No!" Lorenza pressed him down. "Stay in your dreams! Don't let Raven control it!"

"Have to," Sonny replied. He knew he had lost it. Could he return and face the outcome of the violent nightmare?

"My notes," he whispered. He knew that on Monday, August 12, after two days of siege, Governor Otermin had stepped out of the burning rubble and mud huts to parley with Popé.

Sonny closed his eyes and returned to his dream.

Are you mad? Otermin asked the Indian leader. We have brought the holy faith to you and your people. We have brought our civilization so you might progress. Is this how you thank us?

Since your Oñate came, we have been made to pay tribute and work your fields, Popé answered. You have desecrated our kivas and punished our priests. Now you must leave this land.

This is also our land, Otermin answered. The king himself has sent us to colonize and Christianize this region. This rebellion is against His Most Royal Majesty. If you desist, I will pardon you, but you must return quietly to your homes and be obedient to the law of His Majesty.

Popé laughed. We will no longer be obedient.

Obedience had brought too much suffering. He offered the governor two crosses. One red, one white.

If you choose the white, we will let you leave in peace, Popé said. If you choose the red, we will make war, and all your people will die.

Otermin chose the red, and for three days Popé made war on the beleaguered settlers, who had taken refuge in the Palace of the Governors. A force of two thousand Pueblo men ringed the capital. It was only a matter of time before Santa Fé would fall.

"What can I do?" Sonny cried.

Where was Coyote? Where was the guide he needed to take hold of the dream?

There is only chaos and madness, a voice replied, and the Bringer of Curses appeared. Sonny saw the dark figure walking in the alleys of the besieged capital.

Two soldiers guarding the back gate of the Palace of the Governors challenged him.

Quién pasa?

Un soldado de Su Majestad, Raven replied.

I don't recognize you, said the suspicious sentry, drawing close to Raven.

I came with the new group of soldiers to serve Governor Otermin and defend the Villa de la Santa Fé.

What is your name? the second sentry asked.

Antonio de Cuervo.

No! Sonny heard himself shouting, trying to warn the guards. Don't let him in! But struggle as he would, Sonny could not influence the events of his dream. Raven was controlling the dream.

What are you doing out in the streets? the sentry asked.

I have been scouting, Raven said, drawing closer and lifting his weapon, a curved sword so sharp that when it came down across the first guard, it sliced off his head. Blood spurted and he crumpled to the ground.

Raven struck again, and the second startled guard was disemboweled. Dios mío, he cried as he fell.

Raven walked quickly through the wooden door, leaving it open for the Pueblo warriors.

The smell of death was in the air. Outside the walls of the Palace of the Governors lay the carcasses of dead cows and horses, smoldering in the flames that had spread around the villa. Shrieks of animals and wounded men echoed in the night. The Pueblo men came in the dark and picked up their wounded, and when they found a wounded Spaniard, they took him. Then the cries of the tortured man could be heard far into the night.

Raven moved quickly to the women's quarters, and all Sonny could do was to follow. In this area of the Governors' Palace the women of the city and the vicinity were bunched like chickens in a coop. One small room, a cell, had been reserved for Caridad de Anaya, the young sixteen-year-old daughter of don Cristóbal de Anaya from Alburquerque. She had come to marry Hernán López, a young soldier, but the plans had been interrupted by the rebellion. Now the young bride-to-be huddled in the small room that had been set aside by the governor.

Rest and do not trouble yourself, Governor Otermin had told her. This uprising will be quelled in a matter of hours. Then, as I have promised your father, the marriage plans will continue. I will be the padrino, and your father and mother will be here at your side. This madness of the natives is only a momentary thing.

Sonny knew that in Alburquerque the entire family of don Cristóbal, and many other families in the haciendas south of Santa Fé, had been wiped out. One son survived, the young Cristóbal, and documents would later reveal that he would live with the Indians until de Vargas returned thirteen years later.

Sonny groaned. His nightmare had become a whirlwind of destruction, tame mares became the trampling horses of the Apocalypse, and there was nothing he could do. He had entered the correct time, but he could not twist the events.

Coyote! he cried. Where are you?

He saw other colonists from Río Abajo, fleeing to Isleta Pueblo, where they gathered in terror, thinking Santa Fé had surely fallen, with all inhabitants killed.

He saw Raven flinging a door open and entering Caridad's room. Caridad de Anaya, he called her name. I come to claim you!

No, Sonny shouted again, struggling. But he realized that he was bound by the rules of the dream. If he struggled too much, he would awaken, and there would be nothing he could do to help the girl. Again he looked for Coyote, but he was not to be found.

If he was to stop Raven, he had to be the actor in the dream, not the mere witness. He had to participate *within* the dream, but he didn't know how.

He could only watch as Raven lifted the young girl from her bed and carried her away, past the confusion of the new attack on the palace. The natives, led by Popé and other war captains, had discovered the open back door and entered the Palace of the Governors, and the battle was joined within the last sanctuary of the Spaniards.

Raven, carrying a screaming Caridad, hurried past soldiers and natives locked in hand-to-hand combat. Their shouts and the thunder of cannons and harquebuses filled the air, and the cattle and horses that were locked in the palace patio bolted and howled, adding to the confusion as the battle swept around them.

At the same time Hernán, Caridad's fiancé, entered the cell. Finding her missing, he ran out of the room calling her name. Caridad! Caridad!

Like the Andres Vaca of the earlier dream, Hernán dashed off in search of his bride-to-be. He had come running to protect her when the onslaught began, but he found Caridad's room empty.

Caridad! he cried, running into the melée, drawing his sword to fight off the natives now filling the patio. He pressed into the battle, swinging his blade with rage, blaming the Indians for his loss.

The explosion of a cannon filled the dream, and young Hernán Lopez disappeared in the blinding light.

Another line of Sonny's ancestors were not to consummate their marriage, another ancestral line was cut off.

Sonny stared into the smoke of the battle. The adobe huts of Santa Fé were burning. The fields of corn were burning. An era had come to an end.

The smoke cleared, and Sonny saw Popé standing with the war captains. Governor Otermin lay wounded, two arrows had pierced his face. It was time to abandon Santa Fé.

Eleven days after Popé marched on the capital, the exodus from Santa Fé had begun.

We will kill them when they are out in the open, Popé said.

No, the oldest war captain replied. The bloodletting is done. Let the Españoles leave our land. Let them take their Cristo and his mother with them to their own place, that land across the sea. There let them pray to their Cristo and santos, and to the Lady Divine, who appeared to them and told them the end of their rule was coming. We will remain in our

pueblos and honor our kachinas. We are not warriors who
like the smell of blood. We are farmers. Let us return to our
ways.

Sonny watched as the long line of Españoles, Mexicanos,
and some natives, Indians who sided with the Spaniards,
straggled down the Río Grande, carrying with them the
same yellow silk banner Juan de Oñate had brought with
him when he entered New Mexico.

On either side of the river the Pueblo Indians camped and
watched the sorry exit of the homeless refugees.

Very well, we will let them pass, Popé said. The battle
was won, but even as he watched the pitiful column march
south, a vision appeared.

They saw it in the smoke of the burning villa.

Look! one of their medicine men cried. The Spaniards
will return. In the wisps of smoke they saw the return of the
Españoles.

They had found no gold, no rich mines of silver, only the
hard life in the valleys of the Sangre de Cristo Mountains.
But they would return.

The land will call them, the medicine man said. Already
they had raised their sons and daughters on the land, even on
to the third generation.

Those who saw the vision recognized its truth.

Let us celebrate, Popé said. Destroy the churches, burn
all their holy items as they burned ours. Kill the cows and
horses, for they do not belong to our way. Bury the knives
and pots made of iron. Burn the sacred books they keep in
their churches.

Everything that belonged to the Españoles would be destroyed.

But not forever. The Españoles and the Mexicanos had
buried their parents and grandparents in the earth of la

Nueva México, and so the blood of the land would call them, the spirit of the land would call them to return.

The people who farmed had learned the ways of the pueblos, had also learned the language, the food, and they shared in the dances and ceremonies. Many moved easily from Spanish village to Indian pueblo, some intermarried. A fusion of blood, of memory, of dream. That memory would draw the Españoles back.

Down the Camino Real, Governor Otermin's bedraggled and frightened exodus came to rest near Sandia Pueblo, a few leagues from the scattered farms that would someday be known as la Villa de Alburquerque.

Why did this happen? Otermin asked an old man they found in the pueblo, one who remained friendly to the Spaniards.

Because you dishonored the way of our ancestors. Because you tried to take away our faith, the old man answered.

It is said that Otermin wept at those words. Others say he only grew more bitter, that he had not learned a lesson.

But Sonny's concern was with Caridad. What had become of the girl, the young woman he knew was one of his grandmothers?

Part II

Solstice Time

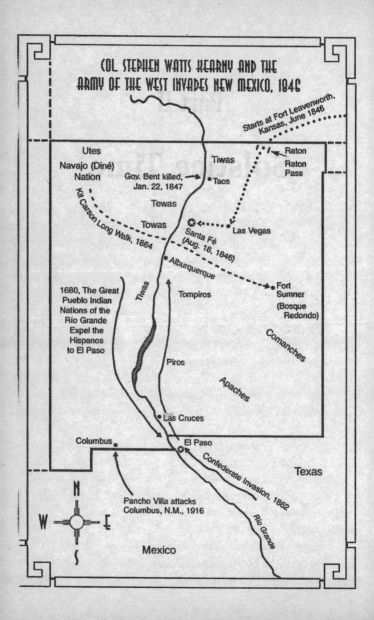

8

Sonny jolted awake, bathed in sweat. The night's fever had passed, but he felt sore and weak. The sense of helplessness he had experienced in the dream permeated every muscle.

He sniffed the air. Even the smell of gunpowder seemed to linger in the room.

"Nothing! There was nothing I could do!" he groaned, awakening Chica, who peered from under the blankets. "Raven took her and I just stood there! So much for being master of my dreams!"

He felt anger, then he breathed deep to let it subside. The New Mexico families were connected. You dug into one family tree and found the roots spreading. His parents often talked of the parentela, the relatives whose roots went back in time and spread across the state. One of the Anayas of la Merced de Atrisco in Alburquerque had married into the Bacas of Taos. Distant relatives. Very distant, but relatives. Familia. Was Caridad the daughter of the Cristóbal Anaya mentioned in Fray Angelico's book?

Congestion filled his sinuses, and Sonny reached for a tissue from the box that lay on his bedside table.

Since when do I have Kleenex next to my bed? he wondered. He looked at the bedspread. A patterned blue comforter, not the old serape he had bought in the Juárez mercado a year ago. He smelled the clean, crinkly sheets. They had felt so good to get into last night, but he had been too tired to notice much more. He looked at the window, where white lace curtains glowed in the light of the morning sun.

Lace curtains he hadn't noticed before. Rita's work, he smiled.

"Gracias, amor," he murmured, and pushed his feet over the side of the bed. Chica crawled out from under the covers, wagging her tail and looking up at him with loving eyes. Seal-pup eyes. Sometimes they reminded him of deer eyes, the brown eyes of a doe he had seen while hunting with Cruz Trujillo high on the Taos Mountains. Other times her eyes were human, so perceptive, understanding, and searching.

"Buenos días, Chica." He rubbed her ears, the scruff of her neck. "Go do your thing."

Chica leaped off the bed and disappeared. Moments later Sonny heard her barking outside. In a few minutes she would be back, ready for breakfast.

Groaning, Sonny tested his legs. Yes, the thigh muscles tensed, the strength was there, it was just something in the brain that was still jumbled, not giving the exact commands to the legs. His calves were weak, his toes cold. The cold dip in Frijoles Creek had been a shock to his system, but maybe for the best.

"It's only a matter of time," he said, trying to psych himself up. "Stronger than yesterday."

He looked at the phone. It was going to ring. He shivered with dread.

Reaching out, he touched the bowl, felt its pulse again. There was no bowl in last night's nightmare, only the carnage of the rebellion.

But he had ordered the dream, the time and place. He just didn't have the power to be the main actor. Raven could come and go as he pleased in Sonny's nightmares.

"But I have the bowl."

Maybe the bowl didn't mean anything to Raven. He was after the women, not the bowl. Maybe the bowl had been returned to him by Owl Woman.

"Who knows." He shook off the lethargy he felt.

Taking hold of the wheelchair handles, he cautiously raised himself. His trembling legs held and he walked slowly to the bathroom, pushing the chair in front of him and testing each footstep for sign of weakness. He didn't want to fall.

He used the toilet, took a shower, and dressed. After his shower Sonny thought of shaving. His beard had grown thick during the past three months. Dark. He had asked Rita not to shave it when she volunteered to shave him. It made him look older. He felt older. With the beard he looked like the men in the dreams. Andres Vaca and Hernán López both sported dark beards.

Because the Catholic Church and the Spanish civil authorities kept such meticulous records, he would be able to trace his genealogy. But his Indian grandmothers remained nameless, in many cases unknown. The Church had baptized them and given them Spanish names, Christian names. Their Indian names were erased, as if in erasing the name of the heathen, the Church could make them over in a new image.

The names of the grandmothers were missing, but their blood simmered there beneath the surface. Their native beauty could not be erased. It was there in the color of the people, in Sonny's brown skin. It was in the beauty he saw in Rita and Lorenza. Dark eyes, flashing smiles, the high cheekbones. It was there in the memory.

"If I keep my Spanish beard," he said to Chica, "I'll be a Spanish soldier, just like Andres and Hernán."

Hell, he didn't want to be a Spanish soldier. He just wanted to be who he was, or like he used to be, a free-wheeling thirty-one-year-old Chicano from the North Valley. He did enough private investigating to pay his rent, take Rita dancing, help some people. Like his great-grandfather Elfego Baca, el bisabuelo, had helped people. He had shot it out with bad-ass Texas cowboys to show them they couldn't push around the poor farmers from the Socorro Valley.

No, he wasn't Spanish, he was Nuevo Mexicano, a mestizo from the earth and blood of the Hispano homeland, which was also the Pueblo Indian homeland. He was a coyote. The history of the northern Río Grande valley had been washed by many currents, and each flood deposited its sediment in the earth of la Nueva México. The earth held the memory no one could deny. All expeditions to the Río Grande had left their imprint. Now new immigrants were filling the valley, Californians fleeing urban living, New Yorkers with their city accents, from everywhere they came seeking the sun and a slower pace of life.

Sonny turned his chair to the window. Pushing the curtains aside, he looked out. La Paz Lane, that narrow dirt road in the North Valley where he lived, was quiet and peaceful. Last night's storm had passed, leaving behind it only a glaze of snow and cold. Enough to blow away the smog that settled into the valley this time of the year. The air inversion trapped car pollution, dust from the dirt roads, and the smoke from chimneys under a blanket of cold air. The occasional weather fronts that swept across the valley pushed the smog out of the valley and dropped a coating of snow on the Sandias.

Probably six inches of new snow on the crest, Sonny thought. Enough to get the skiers excited. By midday the temperature would rise into the forties in the valley.

Across the street sat don Eliseo's old adobe home, a house built by the old man's ancestors. The family had been in the area for generations. Since before the founding of Alburquerque in 1706.

The old man lived alone, his wife had died years before Sonny moved into the village of Ranchitos two years ago. Don Eliseo's sons were too busy to show up very often, and the old man had become like a father to Sonny—no, not only a father, a mentor. The old man's stories helped Sonny connect with his roots, and his philosophy of life revealed the spiritual nature of the people.

There he was now, ambling out of his front door toward his cornfield. Every morning don Eliseo greeted the sun, bowed his head in prayer and asked a blessing for life. He raised his arms and offered the light in the four sacred directions, offering his prayers to the world. Then he stripped off his shirt and bathed his face, arms, and chest with the cold water of his well.

The sun that rose over the southern edge of the Sandias was the sun of the winter solstice. Don Eliseo would pray that the light of the sun not be drowned in the western shore on the last day of its cycle, December twenty-first. He prayed for people. He prayed for peace and clarity.

In the middle of the sere and frozen stalks of corn, don Eliseo raised his arms to the sun and welcomed the new day. It was twenty degrees outside, freezing, and still don Eliseo was there to greet the sun.

"Lord," Sonny whispered, "if he can pray in the cold, I

can surely pray in here." He closed his eyes and raised his arms in the sunlight that poured in through the window.

"Bless all of life," he intoned softly. "Lords and Ladies of the Morning Light, fill me with clarity. Help me find Owl Woman and the missing girls, Consuelo and Caridad—"

He stopped himself and opened his eyes. Caridad? She was only a dream, she wasn't missing. But she would be reported missing today, Sonny frowned. If Raven was acting both in the dream and in waking life, the girls he had taken in the dreams corresponded to girls he took in real life. Any minute now the phone would ring and someone would report a missing girl.

"Damn!" he swore.

Beside him Chica sat up on her hind legs and motioned with her front paws.

"Yes, time to eat," Sonny agreed. He turned to his bed, and retrieving the bowl from the nightstand, he carried it on his lap to the kitchen, where he placed it on the table. Then he started the coffee and filled Chica's bowl.

Raven wanted the Zia medallion and revenge. That summer during their struggle at the rain-swollen arroyo, Raven had fallen in, and the current smashed him against rocks. Now Raven was not the handsome Anthony Pájaro anymore. One side of his face was a swath of scar tissue. The horrible scars became his mask.

Sonny poured himself the first cup of strong coffee and sipped, welcoming the caffeine charge.

Rita had left him a breakfast in the fridge to be warmed when he awakened. And a note. "Amor, it's 2 am and you were sleeping soundly. Lorenza says there is nothing more we can do, and she *really* insists I get some rest. She's sending me home. Warm the bowl of menudo con posole in the microwave. Warm the tortillas in the toaster. Te amo con todo mi corazón. Rita."

"Mi corazón," Sonny repeated. My love. She shouldn't have stayed up that late. She had her restaurant to run. He could kick himself. His actions affected others, and he didn't like it. He didn't want Rita hurt.

He knew she hadn't been feeling well. Not her old energetic self. He asked her how she felt, but she pretended nothing was the matter. "A cold, that's all," she said.

He thought of her as he warmed the posole and menudo. He liked his menudo with diced onions, oregano, and spiced with red chile. She had left all the fixings, ready for him to use. He popped the homemade tortillas in the toaster. The simmering menudo and the toasted aroma of the tortillas quickly filled the kitchen.

Recovery without Rita would have been impossible. She had been there every step of the way, taking time from running her restaurant to be with him. And Lorenza had been there. They were protecting him, helping him along. Could he ever repay them?

The phone rang and startled Sonny. He dropped his coffee cup. "Damn!" He wiped up the coffee. For a moment he hesitated, then picked up the phone.

"Good morning, Sonny. Leif Eric here. Have you seen the paper?"

"No," Sonny replied. Right now wheeling out to bring in the newspaper wasn't a priority.

"It's splattered on page one!"

"What?"

"The media wants to know why we're shut down. They want to know if there was an accident. Did you talk to the press?"

"No, of course not!" Sonny replied angrily. He'd been

too damn busy trying to stay alive to talk to anyone. But he knew who had tipped the press. Raven. He loved his own headlines. But he wasn't ready to tell the newspapers he possessed a plutonium pit. No, that would come when he actually had a bomb built.

"The media wants to know what the hell's going on here. So far we've been able to keep them out, but they're at the gate. Someone called them. I've been on the phone with the secretary of defense. Everyone, from the president on down, agrees we can't tell the public there's a terrorist loose with enough— You know. We don't want an unnecessary panic."

"Unnecessary?"

"I trust Doyle. His boys are going to nail the killer. But they need time."

Nail Raven? Wishful thinking, Sonny thought. "So you're warning me again to keep quiet."

"Yes. In case the papers call. We haven't released your name, so no one knows you were here."

"Fine with me," Sonny replied, "I have no reason to advertise it."

"Matt Paiz says you know Raven better than anyone. Both he and Doyle have assured me that anything you can do to help would be greatly appreciated. We need to find this man, Sonny, and the sooner the better. Paiz will call you. He wants to work with you."

FBI calling me for help? Sonny smiled. That's a change.

"What else?" Sonny asked.

"Security found a Ford Explorer that must have belonged to him. And the rope he used to rappel down the cliffside. They tell me we must have come upon him moments after he killed the guards. FBI figures he's nearby."

Sonny said nothing about meeting Raven at Bandelier

National Monument. And nothing about the dream. Raven was moving fast; they couldn't keep up with him.

"Anyway, the state police are assisting the FBI, and Doyle has a special antiterrorist unit flying in. Coordinating through Paiz, of course. But right now it's only a training exercise in security, you understand?"

"I understand," Sonny answered.

They were covering their asses. Three guards dead at the labs would be big news, but if the media found out a plutonium pit was loose in the state, there would be a panic. Heads would fly in Washington, including Eric's and Doyle's. And if the media discovered the plutonium was in the hands of a terrorist, maybe the Avengers wouldn't have to set it off. The panic would be the catalyst they were looking for.

A stone had been dropped into New Mexico waters, and the ripples were spreading. The waves would wash up on international shores. Terrorists had not yet built a nuclear weapon. Would it happen here first? The Chamber of Commerce will love it, Sonny thought.

"Good, good. I'll keep you posted," Eric said, and hung up.

"Yeah, you do that," Sonny replied, looked at the phone, and clicked it off. He glanced at the clock. Taking a chance, he called Teresa at Zimmerman, but she wasn't in. Next he tried Ruth Jamison at the public library. She and Sonny had attended Rio Grande High together. Years later, when he took on investigating, whenever he needed help at the public library, he went to her. She was good, she didn't gossip, and beneath the surface there was still an attraction.

"Ruth doesn't work here anymore," someone answered.

"Doesn't work there. What do you mean?"

"She's gone."

"Gone? She can't be gone!"

"Look, mister—"

"Okay, okay. How about . . ." He searched his mind for someone he could trust. Vangie.

"Vangie Quintana."

"She's at the Broadway library. I'll connect you."

Sonny waited, then Vangie came on. "Sonny, how are you? What can I do for you?"

"Hi, Vangie, where's Ruth?"

"You haven't heard? She got married. A writer came by in an old Volks bus, on his way to México. He was doing articles on the revolution in Chiapas, so Ruth helped him. He stayed a few days, they fell in love, and he asked her to go with him."

"And she went, kids and all?"

"Yup. I've never seen her so happy. We're still receiving cards from México as they travel south. It's great, Sonny. A new life for her."

"Yes," Sonny agreed. Ruth deserved a new life. But México? Chiapas? "I wish her luck," he said. "Listen, the reason I called is because I need books on Los Alamos. Anything on the building of the first atomic bomb. Also anything on the new director, Leif Eric."

"Can do. What else?"

"Do you have anything on the militia groups here in the state?"

"Not really," Vangie replied. "Maybe a few news clippings."

"I'll take what you have. And I'm still being chauffeured around, so I won't be in till tomorrow."

"No problem."

"Thanks. Soon as I get outta my chair, I'll take you to lunch."

"I'll look forward to it," she said sweetly.

Sonny hung up the phone and turned to greet don Eliseo, who knocked at the kitchen door before he entered.

"Hey, Sonny," don Eliseo said, "buenos días. Como 'stás?"

"Buenos días, don Eliseo. I'm okay. Cold night, huh?"

"Not bad. I had my estufa de leña going all night. So I was warm as a bug. I remember one winter I went as a borreguero up to Wyoming. I was just a kid, and I went with my uncle. Mi tío Santiago. Talk about cold. We had blizzards blowing that kept us in for a week. Al fin, when we could get out, there were frozen sheep all around us. We lost so many we didn't get paid. Not our fault, you know, but the patrón blamed us, so we didn't get paid. Anda, let me pour," the old man volunteered, pouring the coffee and taking the menudo out of the microwave oven. "You're the one that was out in the cold."

"Rita told you."

"I came over last night. You know, to check on things. You were already asleep."

"I appreciate it, don Eliseo."

"What's a vecino for."

"Sit down. Coffee's ready and the menudo is hot."

"The breakfast of champions," don Eliseo said, pouring himself a cup of coffee. He sat and looked at the bowl. "It's a beauty."

"Ever see anything like it?"

"Oh, no, it's not from the pueblos. Not Hopi or Navajo. No," he whispered, "this bowl of dreams is from the Aztecas. From before the Aztecas. Maybe Tolteca."

"Don Eliseo, about yesterday—"

"It's nothing, Sonny."

"I doubted you."

"You have a right to doubt."

"I guess I just couldn't believe Raven can get into my dreams. I couldn't believe he can kill me that way."

"And now?" The old man arched a thick, gray eyebrow and looked at Sonny. His eyes were dark brown, but the irises were flecked with light.

"The bowl was in the dream, and now it's here. How do I explain that?"

"Things fall from dreams."

"Fall from dreams?"

"Yes. Just like the person. You think you're dreaming, then you fall into your bed." He winked.

Sonny forced a wry smile. "I had another dream last night. Raven took another young woman."

"Ah, cabrón! We figured that. I talked to Lorenza and Rita last night. We knew that might happen. But you needed to rest."

"I couldn't stop him."

"It takes time to master the dream," don Eliseo said, and placed his hand on Sonny's.

"Can I do it?"

"You're almost there, Sonny. You're ordering the dream, so you can get into the river of dreams wherever you want. But you need to prepare the stage."

"Prepare the stage? Like in a movie?"

"Sure, why not. The old medicine men used to call those who travel to their dream los Señores del Sueño. Lords of the Dream. I told you the light of the sun comes to earth in the form of Lords and Ladies of the Light. There are also Lords and Ladies of Dreams. If you can travel to your dream, you become such a person. You have the gift, Sonny. Now you have to develop the power. You already learned to make the dream a story, so it's not cluttered. That's the first step. Now you have to be the main character."

"Write myself into the dream—"

"Sure. You like to read. So think of the dream like a story or a movie."

Sonny thought awhile. "Raven has a plutonium pit. He wants to build a bomb."

Don Eliseo nodded. "I read somewhere they named that pluto cosa after Pluto, the god of hell. Raven works there."

"And that's where he holds Owl Woman?"

"He has a corner in the land of the spirits. A corner in every heart."

A corner? Sonny shook his head. Sometimes he didn't understand the old man's metaphors.

He sipped coffee and stared at the Bowl of Dreams. For don Eliseo, the bowl was a religious icon, a sign from the past. It was related to Sonny's dream and therefore to the wider dream of the community. The bowl was the earth, its round shape reflecting the curve of the earth. The glyphs were symbols encoded with a primal message.

"Raven comes to bring chaos. He wears a different costume every time," don Eliseo said. "The universe was created in violence. There in the womb of time the first spark explodes, like the sperm of a man exploding into the egg of the woman. Birth. The spirit of the universe is born. That's good. We see the light of the Universal Spirit, the clarity of the sun. Our alma wants to join the light. We want peace and harmony. But others remain loyal to that emptiness before life. They love violence, they want to destroy the harmony we feel with the creation. We have to fight them."

"We?"

"We," the old man said hoarsely. "We, too, have been on earth a long time. We carry the clarity of the Universal Spirit in our hearts. It is our responsibility not to let the darkness win. Just like the medicine men are praying to give the sun strength, like the Católicos pray at the church for the birth of Cristo, like everyone prays to the birth of light, we pray."

Yes, Sonny nodded. For the old man the struggle was very clear. Evil versus good. Each person was involved. The whole universe was involved. To fight Raven meant not only averting the catastrophe of the moment, it meant keeping the universe in balance.

Slowly, Sonny told don Eliseo the details of last night's dream.

"Yes, he has that power. When he cannot affect the world as we see it, he attacks in the dream. That is why the world is full of so much violence. Raven, and those like him, are destroying the dream of peace. The saints, the kachinas, the old prophets, all the gods of the earth have been fighting this battle for a long time. But now the dream is clouded. The Bringer of Curses is growing stronger."

Chica whined. She heard the call of raucous crows in the cottonwoods along the acequia. Each winter hundreds of crows came to sleep in the trees. In the morning they spread over the city to forage for scraps. Joggers along the bosque trails often came upon them unexpectedly; then the band of the tribal birds rose, cawing stridently into the air.

"Los cuervos are back," don Eliseo said simply. "They come to eat at my cornfield. Chica chases them."

"Go chase," Sonny said to the eager Chica, and she was out the dog door like a streak. Outside, her barking filled the air.

They listened to her enjoying herself for a moment, then Sonny said. "I felt alone last night."

"No Coyote," don Eliseo said.

"No. He didn't come. I couldn't become Coyote, I couldn't see him."

"Try to find Owl Woman. She will give you the power you need to enter your dreams. The women are the keepers of the dream. For a long time they said the prayers to Mother Earth. They, like the earth, guard the egg that gives birth. They also guard the dream."

Sonny wasn't sure he understood. "Rita?"

"Yes, Rita. She dreams of having your children. Once a woman dreams of the child, she will create it, she passes on the dream."

"How does Lorenza fit in?"

"She understands you have the soul of a warrior. She took you to your coyote spirit. You have met your guardian animal and entered the world of spirits. But she can't take you into the world of dreams."

Sonny fell silent. It made sense, and it didn't make sense. But he trusted the old man.

"What does the name Caridad mean?" he asked.

"Caridad? Es nombre místico."

"Nombre místico?"

"Sure. All the names have a mystic power. Caridad is charity and goodwill. A gift we wish for our vecinos. But in this age we are losing that knowledge. The names are losing their power."

"Consuelo means to comfort?"

"Sí."

"I thought there might be a pattern in the names."

"There is a pattern in the names," don Eliseo nodded. "To name is to make sagrado."

Sonny nodded.

"You see, even the days have their names. A day comes with its proper face, just as each cycle of the moon has a name, and the seasons have names. The cycles of time are not measured by a man's life. No, we are but a speck in time.

Our ancestors from México tried to measure time back to its beginning."

"Why?"

"If they could arrive at the beginning of time, they would know the name of God. Perhaps they would see the face of God, the universe being born. Then the memory of the soul would become clear to them. Then life and its suffering would be attached to the dream, to la memoria. It is fragmented now, you see. Too many realities. But we know they are all one, so we have been seeking that unity since we could first dream."

"Did they get there?"

"We don't know, Hijo. The stories are lost. The dream is shattered. They named the cycles of time, the ages of man on earth, and they counted five to the present time. Each cycle of time lives and dies, like the universe lives and dies. Who is to say how many times the universe has been born, taken billions of years to grow and die, like a tree grows and dies. It becomes a seed again, and it is born from that seed. Seed, birth, death. Our lives are like that."

The old man's words made Sonny reflect. All those tribes of the past in all the disguises called spirituality or religion had one goal, to achieve the most sacred moment.

"And we know so little," he sighed. "La vida es un sueño."

"We fly from dream to dream," don Eliseo said with deep satisfaction in his voice. "Those who don't understand the flight of the soul, fear it. Or they say the power of the soul to fly and visit other worlds comes from the gods. Some say the gift is from outer space." He laughed. "Que pendejos. The gift is inside. Aquí." He pointed at his chest. "The flight of the soul is a gift. Imagine, flying between worlds, between dreams. Imagine being connected to the memory of our ancestors. What peace would fill our hearts. We are here to use our gift, to seek clarity. By filling our souls with light we can be one with the universe. The soul of the universe."

"Pay attention," Sonny said.

"Yes."

"Pray."

"Open your soul to the light, that is prayer."

"There are signs on the path." Sonny looked at the bowl.

Don Eliseo leaned forward and pointed at the first glyph. "Here. An explosion of the sun, the birth. Later the same sun will be held between the horns of a bull, like the Egyptian sun. Then water covers the earth. See here, lightning, the first fire. The sun again, giver of life. The moon, cycles of the woman. But the bowl belongs to this earth. See the tree, it is not the cross of the Cristo, but the Tree of Life of our ancestors. This is the Bowl of Dreams of the Americas."

"Why the Americas?"

"Because our human dream needed to be born again," don Eliseo replied, growing excited. "The time was ripe, and there was hope in the hearts of those who watched the progression of time. Here in the Americas, it was thought, the dream could be planted again."

"Yes," Sonny whispered. He was following the old man's dark, gnarled finger as it pointed to the glyphs along the bottom of the bowl. In the beginning of time, the story said.

"Male and female in one God," don Eliseo continued. "See the signs. Male and female in one burst of light. The creation. The seed of time, the egg being penetrated. Thus the divine imagination penetrates the egg. Then it begins to tell the story in the Tolteca way. Why? Because this bowl was fashioned there in their land. See here."

Sonny peered intently.

"See the tiger. That is the Tiger Sun of their legends. The ending of the first world. One Reed is the name of the year.

The people are incomplete, they do not yet carry the dream within, and so they are eaten by the tiger gods. See here. Four Wind. The second coming into consciousness of our ancestors, and still they are ill formed. So the wind carries them away. They become monkeys."

"A story of evolution," Sonny interjected. "But you call it a 'coming into consciousness.' "

"Yes, evolution is not only of our bodies and our civilizations, but of our spirits. We are the dream people. We must learn to carry the dream. At that time our ancestors were not yet ready to receive the dream of the Universal Spirit, so the wind of the universe came to cleanse the earth. Even the sun was destroyed. Imagine the fear of our ancestors when the sun itself was blown away, and darkness fell again."

"The sun up there is destroyed?" Sonny pointed.

"No," don Eliseo said. "The sun within! The light within us is destroyed. The essence is being cleansed to create a new spirit. It is an evolution of our consciousness. The date is Twelve Serpent. Even in the Bible written by the prophets across the sea, the serpent appears. The earth energy comes winding like a snake to give us wisdom. When we take it inside, we are connected to the energy of the earth. But that is not enough. The spirit within must grow. Each one of us must open ourselves to the light of the Universal Spirit."

Sonny nodded. He knew the old man read a lot, that the bookshelves of his home were filled with dusty volumes, but this wisdom came from the heart.

"But it was not yet time. So a new age appears. The Toltecas called it Four Rain. In this third age of time, the sun was consumed by fire. The people were like birds who flew here and there. They thought they were now connected to the spirit of the universe. Not true. To fly is not just to go from tree to tree gathering fruit, it means to allow the soul to fly into the clarity of light. We could fly, but we did not make the Great Tree of Life our home. And so all had to burn in the great cleansing fire of the creation."

"Like the fire of a supernova," Sonny murmured. The universe was reflected in each person's personal struggle for inner clarity, for growth of spirit. Man and woman on earth created their own ages of birth, destruction, rebirth.

"Yes. And so our ancestors are eaten by tigers."

"Why tigers?"

"The Tolteca priests could have used any animal, but the tiger is the animal of the jungle. The jaguar hunts in the darkness. At night the people heard the roaring tigers who came to eat the flesh so the spirit could be set free."

"Our own animal spirit," Sonny said. He was listening and staring at the glyphs. The Mesoamerican myth of creation. It could have been any myth of creation handed to a community of people, one for the Navajos, the Pueblo world, the Comanches, Lakotas, Cheyennes, Utes, on and on, from Inuit in the frozen north to Machu Picchu to Tierra del Fuego at the southern tip. The myths were revealed by the gods, the covenants were made, and a dream was born.

"See here. This is the sun of Four Water, and the new people formed are drowned. Like the flood in the Bible. The entire world and all its humans are transformed. The spirit grows within, but it was not easy. To acquire the clarity of the light of the Universal Spirit is never easy. Some resisted. Some wished to return to chaos. They preferred no future time. They did not want to see the soul grow."

Sonny let the old man's words sink in. Finally he spoke.

"So Raven wants to end time because he realizes that in time we are perfecting our souls. We are being filled with light until we are one with the universal consciousness?"

"Yes," don Eliseo said eagerly. "You see, it's that desire to resist the light that is evil."

"Those ancestral spirits who refused clarity, are they still around?"

"Yes."

"They speak to Raven?"

"Yes."

"I see." Sonny nodded. The dream of the Americas was destroyed by those who caused violence and destruction. They disrupted the prayers and meditations of those who sought the peace and joy of the universal consciousness.

"The glyphs move in a spiral around the bowl," he said.

"Bringing us to the present age. This sun is called Four Movement. El quinto sol, Tonatiuh. Our Grandfather Sun."

Don Eliseo leaned back in his chair. He looked tired.

Sonny looked into the eyes of the old man. They held secrets, a knowledge Sonny would never in a lifetime even begin to fathom. Under the graying eyebrows and in a sea of crow's-feet, the eyes were sad.

"And this sun, too, will die," Sonny said, sinking back into his chair, filled, like the old man, with a weight of an immutable law that they could not affect or change.

"Yes, the time of the fifth sun will end in violence." Don Eliseo nodded.

"The dreams will die?"

"If Raven wins."

"But if there have been five suns, five ages of time, doesn't it follow there will be a sixth sun?" Sonny asked. "And a seventh. Cycles come and go."

Don Eliseo smiled. "Yes. One universe dies to give birth to another, one cycle of time ends on earth to give birth to the next. But now we have traveled the Path of the Sun for a long time. We know our responsibility."

"And that is?"

"To create the new era of time," don Eliseo replied. "Evolution is in our hands. The old stories told of the desire of our ancestors to end their time on earth."

"You mean they *desired* the end of time? I don't get it," Sonny said. The old man was leading him down a new path. The end of time as sketched out in don Eliseo's stories had been cataclysmic, and life on earth had ended. Why would humans desire the end of time?

"When our ancestors gathered to destroy a prior cycle of time, they were really gathering to destroy a level of consciousness they had achieved. In order to give birth to a new awareness, they had to destroy the old. Don't you see, gathering at the temples or pyramids was a time of celebration! The people knew that an old way of thinking would die, but from the ashes of the old fire a new consciousness would be born. So an era ended, they were creating a new one."

"That's a beautiful way to put it," Sonny whispered. Chica appeared and leaped on his lap. He stroked the dog gently, and she sat silently, looking at don Eliseo as a friend.

"But many of those ceremonies are not held anymore. Those who fear the light of the Center fear the illumination."

"Fear the dream of what we can become."

"Yes," don Eliseo said. "The dreams also have names. See here along the top of the bowl. These are the names of the dreams. Sueño de creación, sueño de la luz, sueño de los dioses, sueño de paz, sueño de los sueños. The dreams are difficult to read. You have to go into each one to understand it."

"I have to learn to read the glyphs of the dreams if I'm to stop Raven."

"Owl Woman," don Eliseo replied.

"Yes." Sonny needed to find Owl Woman, rescue her

from Raven's claws, take the bowl to her so that the dream of the people could be known.

"Gracias," Sonny said, and leaned forward to embrace the old man.

"Estamos aquí para servir," the old man replied, and touched his forehead to Sonny's. This was the kiss of life he had taught Sonny. The kiss of friendship. When their foreheads met, he shared the clarity of his soul with Sonny.

Don Eliseo stood and looked out the window. Sonny understood why the old man prayed every morning for clarity. He, like other priests and medicine men, had been keeping the universe in balance. Their prayers offset the evil loose on the land. But they were old men, ready to die and pass into the mysterious winds of the universe. Those left, the young people, no longer apprenticed to learn the prayers.

"I feel old and tired," don Eliseo said.

Sonny had never heard the old man confess to being tired. He was up by sunrise, working in his garden in the summer and always cleaning up around his house in winter. He visited the Indian pueblos and talked to the medicine men there. He took food to the poor. He was active and vigorous, but now the struggle was proving to be too much.

Sonny understood that it was time for someone younger to begin to take don Eliseo's place.

"I'll wash the dishes before I go."

"No, no. I can get these done. I stand at the sink and it helps my legs get strong. Go on," Sonny insisted.

"Bueno. I got to go take some sopa to Concha. She's got a bad cold and not getting around too good."

"Give her an abrazo for me."

"I will. Adiós. Adiós, Chica. Come and see me."

Sonny watched the old man leave, walking across the dirt road to his home.

Lord, Sonny thought, so many things I don't know, don't understand.

The phone rang and startled him. He felt his hand tremble as he reached for it.

"Mr. Baca?" the voice of a man said.

"Yes."

"Sonny Baca? They told us you're a detective. You find missing persons."

"Who are you?" Sonny asked.

"Alberto García. I live in Taos. Ranchos de Taos. I need to talk to you."

"Your daughter is missing."

"Yes. Did the sheriff call you?"

"No," Sonny groaned. My dream calls me.

"We talked to the sheriff. He told us it's just a case of a young girl staying with her friends. Or maybe she ran off with her boyfriend. She's not like that, Mr. Baca. We need help."

"Tell me what happened," Sonny said calmly.

"Last night our daughter went out with our church group. Every year we do *Las Posadas* here at Ranchos. You know, the story of Joseph and Mary going around the neighborhood asking for a place to sleep. She was playing the part of la Virgen. We also went, right here in our placita. There's never been any danger here. When *Las Posadas* were done, she stayed with her friends there at my compadre Horacio's. We came home and went to bed. A little later I heard her come in, go to bed. This morning she wasn't in her room. We called all her friends. Then I called the sheriff. It's not right, Mr. Baca, it's not right. Something bad has happened. The sheriff gave us your name. Can you help us?"

"What's your daughter's name?" Sonny asked.

"Catalina," the man answered.

9

Sonny, Taos is a three-hour drive. Yesterday you could have gotten killed. I can still hear the cold in your voice. Say you won't go."

Sonny sensed Rita's concern even on the phone.

"I feel better, amor, de veras. I got up, ate the great breakfast you left me, talked to don Eliseo, feel strong, and the weather's settled—"

"It's not settled. There's a storm coming in, and Taos will get snow. And you need to do your therapy."

"I walked to the bathroom," he said lamely. "The legs feel strong, really."

"Please stay home."

"I can't," he replied. He had told her last night's nightmare. He had to stop Raven. "There's a missing girl in Taos."

"But it's you he wants," Rita said, her voice tremulous for a moment, then in anger she cursed Raven. "Damn that man! I wish he had never come into our lives!"

"Maybe your curse will stop him." Sonny tried to smile.

"It won't."

"So it's up to me."

"How did he get from Bandelier to Taos?"

"Raven flies, remember. Anyway, he's out of the net they set around Los Alamos."

"Come by here. I'll send a lunch with you."

"Amor, you're too good to me. Don't worry, we can grab something there."

"How long will you be gone?"

"To Taos and back, that's all."

"Take care of yourself. I love you, cabrón."

"I'll take care. You take care. See you this afternoon. Un beso." He blew a kiss into the phone.

"Un beso," she replied.

Am I doing the right thing? Sonny wondered as he clicked off the phone. Chasing after missing virgins. Raven's picking sixteen-year-olds. But where in the hell is he taking them? He needs transportation and a place to hide. He needs help, like the crazies who worked for him in the past, and those kinds of locos don't work for free.

He got hold of enough money to buy the plutonium, and probably enough to pay the scientists he needs to assemble a bomb. Even ex–nuclear physicists from the former Soviet Union came with a price tag.

Money, he needs lots of money, and if Matt Paiz was right, the funds were coming from the extremists who wanted to create a nuclear "accident" to discredit the government.

This is not the kind of case where I hit the streets and dig for information, Sonny thought. I need to get into Los Alamos Labs, learn about the equipment they buy when they put a bomb together, find the names of scientists. Who is who in New Mexico nuclear technology? How come we never hear about these people? A computer! I need to get on to the Internet.

His thoughts were interrupted by Lorenza's arrival. She honked the van's horn once, then came inside. In jeans, a dark turtleneck, and black leather jacket, she looked ready for business.

"Buenos días." She smiled and kissed him lightly on the cheek. "How do you feel today?"

"Great. And you look de aquellas."

"Thank you. If I'm going to be chauffeuring number one private investigator around, I'd better look decent."

"I don't feel so number one. There's another girl missing."

He told her about the dream and the phone call.

"Somehow the girls are part of a much bigger game Raven is playing. Why take the girls at the same time he's trying to build a bomb? And why call the press and tell them something's rotten at the Los Alamos Labs? Doesn't jibe."

"It's his style. His trickster nature is to play games," Lorenza replied. "The four girls he wants to kidnap have something to do with his grand design."

"Four queens for his new universe. I think he's crazy!"

"He wants all of us to think that."

"Yeah, you're right. Anyway, I have to move around a lot. I can't ask you to keep driving me—"

She interrupted. "Hey, I volunteered, so if I can help, I will. Rita can't—" She stopped short, moved her finger around the lip of the cup.

"Something's troubling her."

"She's tired."

"No wonder, taking care of me these past three months, and trying to run the café. I know it's been hard on her."

"She needs rest. She promised to take off an hour every afternoon and go home and rest. I have her on some vitamins, a few herbs . . ."

Lorenza's voice trailed. Sonny didn't like the sound of it. Rita *was* tired, he had seen it in her eyes.

"She should see a doctor."

"She has."

"She didn't say anything—"

"She doesn't want to worry you. She's fine. She just needs to take it easy."

"I just talked to her. I'll call her back—"

Lorenza touched his hand. "Sonny, I promised her not to tell you about the doctor's visit. It will only upset her."

Sonny nodded. "Lord, I appreciate everything you do. I feel haunted. Like I don't know which way to turn. Now Rita—"

"Rita understands you have to take care of this. It's a matter of life and death, for the girls and for you. Let's stick to that."

"I know, but Rita's not well—"

"You don't have a choice. You stay put and Raven will get at you. You don't have much time."

Yeah, Sonny knew that. "The question is how? Can I stop him before he kidnaps another girl? Or do I just stay awake and quit dreaming? No dreams, no Raven kidnapping the grandmothers of my past."

"You have to dream," she said, her dark brown eyes staring at him over the lip of her coffee cup.

"Why?"

"The shaman dreams. That's his role—"

Sonny laughed. "Look, I'm no shaman, no brujo. I'm just me, Sonny Baca, your normal thirty-something Chicano who just wants to do his own thing. I—" He stopped short, looked intensely into Lorenza's eyes, the eyes that always fascinated because they held the knowledge of the owl.

"I keep resisting what I'm becoming," he whispered, and

cradled his head in his hands on the table. "I just want to be normal. Whatever that is."

She gently touched his shoulder. "You are normal, but you also have a gift. It's the same gift don Eliseo has, and he's led a normal life. He married, he had children, he has neighbors, like the rest. But he also has the gift."

Sonny looked up at her, arching an eyebrow. "His gift? He can fly?" Don Eliseo had never told him that, not in so many words.

"Yes, he can enter the dream world. That's how he helps people. By bringing harmony to fragmented souls."

"Men who can fly, curanderos, brujos. . . . When did it start? Where did this power come from?"

"It's been here all along. For our healers it started when the Spaniards were about to arrive in the New World. Moctezuma, the ruler of Tenochtitlán, had many dreams. He saw houses sailing on the Gulf. He couldn't figure out what they were, so he asked his priests to gather. The priests also had the same dream. Perhaps we should say nightmares, for they knew the coming of the strangers meant an end to their way of life."

"But the dream couldn't stop the course of history."

"No. Moctezuma had his priests killed because they had bad dreams."

"Like the messenger who brings bad news is killed. But I'm the messenger of my own dream. I am the dreamer. I have to be an actor in my dream, not just an observer."

"It's what we all have to learn," Lorenza said. "Owl Woman came to you for a reason. She is the Bearer of Dreams. Your dream, your destiny. Yours is the dream of your ancestors, the greater communal dream, the dream of humankind."

"Bearer of Dreams. I like that."

"Yes. Each of us has a spirit within that comes to reveal the pattern of our life, the reason for being—"

"Whoa, whoa." Sonny smiled. "You're losing me. Bearer of Dreams, dream of mankind. I need to do a little research into this. Maybe some books on dreams."

Lorenza looked at him in a strange way, shrugged, and Sonny knew he had taken a wrong turn.

"Not good?"

"Books can help, but the dream, or song line as it's called in some parts of the world, is specific for each sacred region."

"What do you mean?"

"Each region is a sacred place on earth for the ancestors. For the Pueblo Indians, our ancestors, it's here. Their myths and dream world is connected to this place. The song line of the Maori is in New Zealand. It has to do with their place. The earth is the Mother Earth because she holds the dreams of all the tribes."

"And there are sacred regions everywhere. The Holy Land, Stonehenge, Machu Picchu, the mountains of Tibet. Each of these regions holds the dream for the people of the place. But why so much conflict in these places?"

"Both the negative and the positive are attracted to the sacred place. The Garden of Eden was a sacred place, and it attracted Satan. Good and evil exist side by side."

"And it's that way here in our homeland."

"The energy here is strong. The Spaniards who came with Oñate returned after the 1680 Indian revolt because they had felt the sacred in the earth. By that time they knew there was no gold, only the hard work of farming. But here, they realized, they could speak to God. Like the Pueblo Indians spoke to their gods. Here they had made a new covenant with the earth."

"That's what the Bowl of Dreams signifies," Sonny mused. "The new dream, a new awareness. And people still come for that. They come for the beauty of the landscape, desert, mountains, sunsets, sky, summer thunderstorms. The painters come, the poets. It attracts those who seek a spiritual way."

"Yes. But the books will tell you very little about the dream of the region. Don Eliseo goes to the pueblo, where they still keep the dream alive, and perhaps a few poets describe the dream."

Sonny sipped his coffee and listened.

"Dreams come from the spirit world. Raven can enter your dream because he's a sorcerer. Long ago everyone had the power to enter dreams, to create dreams. But there was so much power in the dream world that the sorcerers began to separate humans from their dreams. They began to tell people that the devil created dreams and frightened the people. People left their dreaming, forgot how to be masters of their dreams, and chaos came to the dream world. But dreams remained sacred, not evil. Dreams are the language of the soul, and they belong to the person who dreams. Each person had to take back his or her dreams from the sorcerer who was there in the heart. To become master of one's dreams means one exiles the sorcerer."

"There's a lot to think about," Sonny whispered.

Like all other New Mexicans, he was heir to the Calendar of Dreams. The covenant was formed on the banks of the Río Grande when the Españoles and Mexicanos came into the Pueblo world. Owl Woman greeted them and offered her body and spirit as mother. Owl Woman was Sonny's Bearer of Dreams. Complicated things that needed to be resolved if he was going to save his ass. Save the girls Raven was kidnapping.

"More coffee?" Lorenza offered.

"No, I'm buzzed," he replied. "No sense in just waiting around. Let's head out."

"Pues, vamos."

"I'll get my jacket."

He pushed his chair into the bedroom, Chica trailing him. He reached under the pillow and took out the Zia medallion, pulled the chain over his head, and tucked the medallion under his shirt. Then he reached for the Colt .45.

The northern country would be cold, so he put on his heavy jacket with the sheepskin collar. He turned to Chica.

"Too cold for you to go with us. I don't know what we'll get into, so stay home and guard the house."

Chica sat on her hind legs, barked, and scratched the air furiously with her front paws. She understood, but she wanted to go.

"I know you want to go, and I hate to leave you alone, but it's best you stay. You go keep don Eliseo company, okay?"

Sonny guided his chair outside, into the van, and they were on their way.

A cold wind swept across the valley as a new load of clouds scurried across the sky. The weather was still unpredictable as a new front moved in from the north.

The phone rang as they headed toward the interstate. Matt Paiz asked Sonny if he could come by the FBI office.

"I'm on my way out of town," Sonny answered.

"It's important," Paiz replied.

"Por qué no?" Sonny said. The man had some news, and the Federal Building was downtown, not far. And Sonny needed a favor from them.

"FBI," he said to Lorenza.

"What do they want?"

"Don't know, but let's see." Lorenza nodded and drove

downtown, which was brightly decorated with Christmas lights. She found a handicapped parking space near the building.

Paiz and two agents, Mike Stewart and Eddie Martínez, the two who had chased Raven that summer, were sitting in Paiz's office when Sonny and Lorenza entered.

"You know each other," Paiz said.

"Oh, yeah." Sonny shook hands with the agents and introduced Lorenza.

"Damned sorry about—" Stewart motioned to the chair. He and Martínez knew about Sonny's encounter with Dr. Stammer, but they hadn't seen him since. They looked at him with some admiration, remembering how he had found the cocaine shipment in Stammer's office when everybody else including the DEA said no such shipment had come into the city.

"This is temporary." Sonny smiled.

"You're not doing so bad," Stewart said, looking at Lorenza. Sonny Baca always had an attractive woman at his side.

"You talked to Eric?" Paiz asked.

"This morning."

"I see. I'll get to the point. We found Raven's four-by-four. We went over it with a fine-tooth comb. I'd like to share a few things we found with you." He paused and looked at Lorenza.

"She's with me," Sonny said. "You know that."

Whatever Paiz had to reveal, Lorenza could hear.

It was clear Paiz felt uneasy about the arrangement, but he proceeded. "I need your help. You know Raven, so anything you can do to help us find him before—" He stopped. "Let me tell you what we found. Two things. First, traces of coke."

Sonny nodded. He knew Raven used the stuff. For Raven it was just a plaything, something he used to draw his cult together.

"What else?" Sonny asked.

Again Paiz hesitated, briefly glancing at Lorenza. Then he reached into a desk drawer and took out a plastic baggie. Inside lay a crumpled note. Paiz removed it carefully and laid it on the desk in front of Sonny. On it was written a phone number.

"We traced the number," he said, glancing at Stewart and Martínez. "It's Leif Eric's home number."

Sonny drew a breath. Raven was carrying around the phone number of the director of Los Alamos Labs?

He shook his head to clear the thoughts. This was too easy, too obvious. "He put that there for you to find."

"We know that!" Stewart interrupted, his voice rising. He was the impetuous one, the one that didn't think PIs were worth a cent. Paiz held up his hand. "Okay, it's planted by Raven. But we have to follow up on it. So we checked Eric's phone records. There are calls to a Dr. Alexandr Chernenko at Sandia Labs."

Sonny shrugged. So Eric calls everyone at Sandia. It's his business.

"Who's Chernenko?"

"Chernenko is a top scientist at Arzamas-16, one of Russia's two top nuclear weapons laboratories."

"The nerds at Los Alamos call it Los Arzamas." Martínez smiled. "Get it?"

"I get it," Sonny replied. Arzamas-16, the little he knew, was the biggest nuclear facility the Russians had. Now one of their physicists was at Sandia Labs, working as part of the post–Cold War relationship, and he was in daily contact with Eric. What was Paiz driving at?

Paiz leaned forward. "Last year Eric took a team from Los Alamos to Arzamas to install a high-tech accounting system to keep track of the Russkies' nuclear materials. I mean, that's the reason they gave the Pentagon. We know that while they were there, they *bought* some of their scientists. One or two. We suspect they did another job on the computer system, but we don't know what."

"So Eric met Chernenko," Sonny filled in.

"They worked together. The CIA has a file on Chernenko. The most interesting thing I found is that Chernenko is Ukrainian. His parents were killed during one of Stalin's purges. He hates the Russians. He was a CIA operative at one time. It gets complicated. Do you follow?"

Yeah, Sonny thought. Without revealing what was in the FBI file, Paiz was laying out a case. Chernenko hates the Russians; he's recruited by the CIA, and just recently by Eric. Chernenko is in charge of the nuclear materials tracking system in Ukraine, and that's where Raven picked up the plutonium pit.

"Are you saying—"

"I'm not saying anything," Paiz interrupted. "We are now observing Chernenko's lab at Sandia. We have to move carefully, the man is protected by exchange protocols. Ostensibly, he's here to learn our expertise in dismantling nuclear warheads. But he brings a lot of *stuff* with him—"

"Russian warheads at Kirtland?" Even Sonny was surprised.

Paiz shook his head to indicate he hadn't said that. "I talked to Doyle, and he expressly said to keep our hands off Chernenko."

Doyle's protecting Chernenko, Sonny thought. Lord, but Paiz was developing a complex plot.

"We can't share any of this with Eric, not yet."

"Why me?" Sonny asked. The local FBI office was tapping Eric's phone line, and Paiz didn't trust Doyle as far as he could throw him, and still Paiz was revealing pieces of the puzzle.

"I told you, we need your help. You know Raven." Again he glanced at Stewart and Martínez. "We need to know if Raven and Chernenko are related. Are they working together?"

"But Chernenko's at Sandia Labs? He works in the open."

"Not really," Paiz replied. "He's been assigned a lab right near the nuclear reactor they have up there. The man is working in absolute secrecy."

"In other words," Stewart added, "he can come and go as he pleases. Without revealing anything, we talked to Jack Ward, director at Sandia. He didn't appear concerned about security. We'd need a court order to go in and look around."

"And of course we won't get that court order," Paiz finished. "We don't want to spook anyone, especially Raven. I have to clear everything I do with Doyle in Washington, and he said hands off. Chernenko is free to continue his work, and no one seems to know what in the hell he's up to."

"The question is, what do you know about the Raven/Chernenko connection?" Martínez asked.

"Nada. All this is new to me."

"We don't have much time," Paiz said.

"Me, either," Sonny said. "Look, I need to find Raven worse than you. In the meantime, I need protection for Rita."

Consuelo and Catalina had disappeared, and in some way they were connected to Sonny's dream, to a relationship he had to the families. Rita, too, was related to him: she was to become his wife. Raven had kidnapped her and Diego's girl in the fall, and there was no telling what he might try now. The FBI wanted his help—okay, they should guard Rita while he was out running around the state.

"The woman at the restaurant?" Paiz said, looking at Stewart and Martínez.

"*My* woman at the restaurant," Sonny corrected him.

"You think Raven might go after her again?"

"I don't want her exposed."

"Can't blame you. I can spare agent Martínez for a few days, until we get this cleared up. And I can put a tail on you."

"We're okay," Sonny said, and looked at Lorenza. "It's Rita I'm worried about. I'll call her and tell her you'll be showing up," he said to the agent Martínez. "I don't want her to be frightened."

Martínez nodded. "I've eaten at Rita's Cocina. Great food. I may be gaining weight in the next few days."

"Not if you stay out of the kitchen," Sonny said, his double entendre clear. "If something breaks on Chernenko, call me."

"I will," Paiz said, coming around the desk and shaking Sonny's hand. "And if you find anything, call me." He handed Sonny his card.

Sonny glanced at it. Beneath the address and phone number was scrawled a message: "*Trust no one.*"

10

Interesting," Lorenza said as they rode down the elevator.

"Very," Sonny agreed.

"Why can't they just bust into Chernenko's lab. Get a search warrant? Or have the director of the labs authorize a 'visit'?"

"Doyle is protecting Chernenko, and Paiz doesn't trust Doyle. They're walking on eggshells around each other. Paiz can't go over Doyle's head and authorize a search, and Doyle won't."

"Who do *we* trust?" Lorenza asked.

"No one," Sonny replied, memorizing the phone number on Paiz's card and then tearing it in pieces and dropping it in a trash can. "Chernenko has immunity, like a diplomat, so they can't just bust in his lab. After all, they invited him to do his magic, and his thing is dismantling bombs. Secondly, who could invent such a wild plot? Would he be building a bomb right inside the lab? I mean, they wouldn't be that dumb, would they?"

"Would they?" Lorenza repeated.

"Chingao!" Sonny exclaimed. "Building a bomb inside

Sandia Labs? Right under the tightest security in the world? What a blast, huh."

"Quite a blast," Lorenza agreed.

"If, *and only if,* people as highly placed as Eric are involved, would it be possible. It's ironic, but if terrorists really wanted to build a bomb, inside the labs would be the perfect place. Think of all the equipment available there. Raven's plutonium pit can be carried in by one person, the people they need can be brought in by Chernenko one at a time, then boom!"

"It would wipe out the city."

"More than that. It would create a chain reaction. It would blow up all the other nuclear cores they have stored there."

"A megabomb? That's fin del mundo."

"Yeah. Paiz needs to catch Raven before he delivers the pit. He knows that. It would be quite a feather in his cap if he does."

"But things don't sit too well with Chicanos in the FBI."

"Not really. A group of Hispanic agents sued the agency for discriminatory practices a few years back, and a judge ruled for the agents. Paiz was the instigator," Sonny said as they left the building.

"Do you trust him?"

Sonny thought a moment. The Bureau had been used as a political tool to destroy a lot of good people during the Hoover years, so had anything changed?

"Don't know. Come on, race you!" He pushed the button on his chair and sped down the sidewalk. Lorenza took up the chase. People on the walk jumped out of their way.

When they arrived at the van, she was breathing hard and Sonny was grinning. "You win, I buy lunch."

Lorenza drove them north on I-25 to Taos. Sonny used

the opportunity to read the book on top of the stack: Kearny's entry into New Mexico in 1846. What was called in some history books a peaceful invasion by the Army of the West had not been so peaceful. In various communities the Nuevos Mexicanos revolted against the new American rulers. One reason the Nuevos Mexicanos had been so poorly organized for resistance was that their governor, Manuel Armijo, ran out on them.

"Governor Manuel Armijo was the only turncoat the manitos of New Mexico ever produced," Sonny said, making a note. "Sold out and retreated to El Paso."

He was reading interesting passages aloud to Lorenza.

"Surrendered?"

"He didn't even surrender to the gringos, he just took the money and headed for México."

"Well, there are bad apples in every barrel. Think of all the Chicanos who have gotten medals for bravery in the wars since then."

"A lot," Sonny acknowledged.

The Hispanic population was one of the most decorated ethnic groups in the country. They had more than proven their loyalty to the U.S.A., and yet as late as World War II, a Mexican American soldier killed in combat could not be buried in a national cemetery in Three Rivers, Texas. You were good enough to die, but not good enough to share the earth you fought for.

"Maybe Governor Armijo had a point," Sonny said. "The New Mexicans were farmers, not soldiers. To have resisted Kearny would have been a bloodbath. A lot of manitos would have been killed."

He leaned over the counter and made a note: "The New Mexican army, what was left of it, did not confront the Army of the West, and Kearny was free to march through Las

Vegas, Tecolote, and San Miguél del Vado and into Santa Fé on August 18."

Then he laboriously added Kearny's route to the map he was drawing, a star for the capital, Santa Fé, La Villa Real de la Santa Fé.

Outside, the gray clouds of the storm front swept in from the west, their shadows mottling the landscape. The juniper-covered hills on the way to Santa Fé took on a deeper hue. The winter earth was the color of skin, pink fading into brown, a tawny color of the sere grass, the soft curves of the hills. Like the soft curves of a woman.

At La Bajada red Triassic sandstone and shale ran like a gash up the mesa. The same red rock stratum, Sonny guessed, which north of Jemez Pueblo formed a spectacular small canyon. He had often driven past Jemez Pueblo to the Red Cliffs, where pueblo women sold horno bread to hungry weekend tourists. There the red was crimson, not bright but imbued with light, a light emanating from within the earth. Bright in summer and snow splotched in winter. A sight that always took the breath away.

To the north the blue Sangre de Cristo Mountains loomed more massive and closer to the earth as the clouds hugged the tall peaks, especially snow-covered Baldy. Last night's storm had left a fresh coat of white on the side of the mountains, so the snowy outline of a greyhound was well defined.

They drove through Santa Fé without stopping and headed north to Española, where they turned toward Chimayó. Sonny knew the Jaramillos, a family that owned the Ranchos de Chimayó Restaurant, so they stopped to eat. The restaurant was gaily decorated for Christmas: a tree sat in the corner of the lobby, and under it a nacimiento. The owner pleasantly greeted Sonny and Lorenza and sat them at a table by the fireplace.

The aroma from the kitchen and the cedar burning in the fireplace created a feeling of well-being, a feeling of home. Sonny sniffed the pleasant food fragrances and thought of his mother. He had called her that morning, trying to assure her he was well, just busy. She worried about him. Armando had told her about the van and she wanted to know why he needed a van. You need to stay home and rest, she said. This Christmas I want all of us to be together. Sonny assured her it would be so, but he wondered if any Christmas would ever be the same again.

He tried to dispel the mood by drinking a beer and attacking the blue corn enchiladas simmering with cheese and red chile. He tore apart the hot, fluffy sopaipillas and scooped up the red chile, rice, and beans.

"Sabroso." Sonny smiled as he ate, feeling the need for energy. In his bones he still felt the cold from yesterday's dip in Frijoles Creek.

"It is delicious," Lorenza agreed.

"Panza llena, corazón contento," he sighed when they had finished eating.

"Y 'hora?"

"Feed the body, feed the soul," he replied. "You feel like stopping by the Santuario?"

"Why not," she replied.

The Santuario was timeless. It was the mecca of New Mexican Catholics, the Wailing Wall and the Temple on the Mount all rolled into one. A small, simple church constructed of adobe bricks made from the earth of the valley, it was a holy place of prayer and miracles. Pilgrimages to the Santuario were common. People in need promised a visit, and promesas made had to be kept. People came from all over the world to fulfill their promises.

Here, in the valley of Chimayó, the natives believed that

the Santo Niño de Atocha walked at night, caring for the old residents of the valley and ensuring the fertility of their fields. The women who took care of the church changed the shoes on the statue of the Santo Niño often, because they claimed he got his boots muddy in the fields.

The deities of the Indians who had lived in the hills before the Spaniards settled the valley also imbued the land. Yes, in these sacred places the kachinas and santos walked on the earth, as long ago the gods of the Greeks had walked in bowers near sacred springs.

In the valley of Chimayó the kachinas offered protection, bringing rain for the crops in summer.

Here one could feel harmonious with the land, restore one's energy, heal oneself. Beneath the surface of the Catholic faith ran the abiding belief in the spirits of the place.

Around them, the trees of the valley were winter bare. Cottonwoods along the ditches and the apple orchards rested under a thin winter blanket. A breeze stirred. A family of raucous magpies pecked at the stubble in a cornfield.

The earth lay fallow, resting, the village somnolent except for a boy who raced his horses down the dirt street toward Ortega's Trading Post. He gave a loud hello as he passed by, the clopping of the horse's hooves pounding the frozen earth, then all was quiet again.

Sonny guided his chair down the rough path and entered the church. They were alone in the cold, dimly lit building.

"When people get well, they leave a memento of their illness here. I'd like to leave my chair."

"Make a promise, and we'll come back."

"I'll settle for some of the holy earth. Take it home and rub it on my legs."

Lorenza entered the small room where long ago someone

had dug a hole in the earth floor. Thousands of pilgrims had taken a handful of the holy earth from here, and the hole was constantly replenished. Some said an underground river of earth refilled the hole. Others smiled and said a priest came at night with a bucket of earth to fill the hole.

Around her neck Lorenza wore a small, cloth bag on a string. It contained an amulet. She opened it and poured a pinch of earth into the bag, then pulled the strings shut.

"Done," she said when she returned to Sonny and slipped the bag around his neck. "If this isn't strong medicine, I don't know what is."

"Gracias, am—" He blushed. He had almost said "amor."

"Amiga," he corrected himself.

"De nada," she replied. She sensed the slip but said nothing. She walked behind his chair out into the bright sunlight that suddenly filled the valley. The brilliant winter sun-showers had broken through the clouds, filling the entire valley with light and warmth.

In this respite of light they continued to Taos. Sonny had written down the directions to the Garcías' home, a narrow road somewhere in front of the Ranchos de Taos church.

It was in Ranchos de Taos that the famous Padre Antonio José Martínez had set up his school for orphans, educated and trained young Hispanos for the priesthood, and set up the first printing press in the state. It was here, too, that he had his falling out with Bishop Jean Lamy, the Frenchman who arrived in 1851. The cold and distant French bishop had been sent by the Vatican to rule over the faithful of New Mexico.

The independent and well-educated Martínez would not easily bow to the new bishop's rule. Martínez knew his paisanos well, he knew the yoke of poverty under which they lived. He understood their deep faith, the faith in Cristo and His mother, and their faith in the earth. Padre Martínez also knew the penitentes, the brotherhood of men who assisted at funerals and burials, helped the poor, and conducted a ceremony reenacting the crucifixion of Christ on Good Friday.

Padre Martínez continued to serve the people, even after pressure from Bishop Lamy to collect fees on all church ceremonies Martínez performed. He went on marrying them without collecting fees, openly disobeying the French bishop.

Lamy replaced many of the native priests with Europeans, and so an old pattern repeated itself even within the church: the French colonization of the New Mexican church began, and the separation between the Indian pueblo and the Hispanic village grew. But Lamy could not easily break Padre Martínez. Martínez refused to collect the church tax on the poor who couldn't afford it, and in the end Lamy excommunicated him. Even that didn't stop the padre. He went on saying mass and running his school. The energy of the padre could not be contained, and in later years he would even serve in the New Mexico territorial legislature.

Always watching out for his flock, Sonny thought as he flipped a page and made notes. Padre Martínez was born in 1793 in Río Arriba, married, but both wife and child died, and he joined the priesthood. In 1822 he was given the church at Taos. Brilliant, energetic, often domineering, he believed in education for his paisanos. He brought the first press to Taos and printed a newspaper, *El Crepúsculo*.

Governor Charles Bent, the governor appointed after Kearny's entry to rule over the New Mexico territory, hated Martínez. Many a historian still wonders if Martínez had a hand in plotting the Taos revolt in which the governor was killed on a cold January night. Indians from Taos Pueblo and

Nuevos Mexicanos burst into the governor's house and murdered him in a bloody battle of resistance against the gringo colonizer.

Actually, many of the terrified citizens of Taos, thinking a widespread revolution and a bloodbath were about to ensue as Nuevos Mexicanos took up arms against American rule, took refuge in the padre's home that night. Still, some historians accused Padre Martínez of fomenting the revolt.

The Garcías need someone like Padre Martínez now, Sonny thought as he glanced out the window and pointed. "Aquí."

The García house sat back from the unpaved street. Two leafless apple trees stood in the sere lawn. The flowerbeds where hollyhocks had blossomed over the summer now lay brown and crumpled, the staffs of the flowers heavy with the dry, round pods that held the black seeds.

Alberto García, a man about forty years of age, came out to greet them. He thanked them for coming and invited them into the home.

"I'm glad to see you," he said, shaking their hands. "Lleguen, lleguen. Está bien frío," he said, looking up at the mountain where it was snowing.

Sonny and Lorenza were met at the door by Estella García. She greeted them warmly and ushered them into the small living room.

"We're so thankful you came," she said, and set about serving them coffee and biscochitos. Sonny studied the cozy living room. On the ledge of the beehive fireplace sat family photographs, and two small wood carvings Sonny recognized as the work of Patrociño Barela. In one corner of the room la Virgen de Guadalupe presided over a small altar.

Alberto stood by the woodstove and told them about

Catalina's disappearance. It was very similar to the story the
Romeros had told in Santa Fé.

"We do *Las Posadas* every year," Alberto explained.
"We've been doing them since I can remember. The people
get together and go out every night. This year Catalina was
the Virgin Mary. My compadre Horacio has a burro, so my
daughter rode the burro. San José, my compadre Cayetano,
led the burro down the street."

"Last night was so beautiful," Estella said. "There was a
light snow. There was a real feeling of Christmas. But I
wasn't feeling well, so we came home early."

Tears filled her eyes.

"Nothing like this has ever happened," Estella said. "Yes,
some of the kids are wild, some use dope. They go out in
their lowrider cars and drink. But that happens everywhere."

Alberto looked at her helplessly and nodded.

"Did you find anything in her room, any clues?" Sonny
asked.

"No, nothing," Estella replied.

"Had she slept in her bed?"

"No."

"Are you sure she came in?"

"Yes, I stayed up till I heard the door," Alberto said. "I
figured she didn't want to wake her mother, and just went to
bed."

Estella wrung her hands. "We talked to her friends, and
to our compadres. She came home alone."

"It was below freezing last night," Alberto said. "If she
was alone out there—" He didn't finish his thought, he didn't
have to. The temperature last night had fallen into the teens,
and without shelter a body would freeze.

"May I see her room?" Sonny asked, dreading what he
would find.

"Seguro," Alberto said, and led him down a narrow hallway to the girl's room.

Sonny looked around. No sign of a struggle. No sign of Raven.

"Is there a back door?" he asked.

"Sí, the kitchen has a door to the back." He led Sonny and Lorenza to the kitchen.

Sonny opened the kitchen door. There on the threshold lay four dark feathers. Sonny glanced at Lorenza, and she bent to pick them up.

"What does it mean?" Alberto asked, looking at the glistening black feathers.

"Una maldición," his wife gasped behind him.

A curse.

11

Sonny's next stop was the sheriff's office. Sheriff Bernabé Montoya, who became famous in the Milagro Beanfield War many years ago, was now the Taos County sheriff. Sonny hardly recognized the old lawman. He looked beaten, the ghost of the active young man who had played such an important role in the water rights battle in Milagro.

"Sonny, Sonny, cómo 'stás?" he greeted Sonny, drawing himself up, smoothing the front of his somewhat creased shirt, which was spotted with red chile stains.

Sonny had met the sheriff a couple of years back, during a state lawmen's convention. Manuel López, who was then still alive, introduced Sonny, and it turned out Sheriff Montoya knew a lot of stories about Sonny's bisabuelo, the famous Elfego Baca from Socorro County. "Your great-grandfather is one of my heroes," Bernabé told Sonny.

Sonny introduced Lorenza. "Pleased to meet you, señorita," the sheriff said gallantly, inviting them to sit and asking if they wanted coffee.

"You're here because of the girl," the sheriff said when they were settled. "Beto's daughter."

"I just talked to them," Sonny replied.

"I was over there all morning. I've been talking to her friends, pero nada. No clues," the sheriff said, resignation ringing in his husky voice. "The girl's not the type to run away. No reason. And the kids she knows are good kids. Seems like she just disappeared off the face of the earth."

"Any strangers in the neighborhood? Strange cars, tracks?"

"Nope." The sheriff shook his head. "The ground is frozen, and even if it weren't, the dirt road is full of tracks and half covered with snow. I called the state cops and they're bringing in dogs." He paused, looking shriveled in his uniform.

"But we won't find anything," he said sadly.

"Why?"

The sheriff looked from Sonny to Lorenza. "I've been here a long time, probably be here until the Republicans kick me out." He laughed. "You want me to tell you what I think?"

"Sure," Sonny replied. He felt a story coming. The place was alive with stories.

"I think it's a curse. Spirits," he whispered.

"And they took Catalina," Sonny said. The girl's mother had intimated the same thing.

"I won't tell this to the papers," the old sheriff said. "But I know what I feel. There's enough ghosts around here to fill a novel."

Sonny looked around. Yes, no doubt many dissatisfied spirits wandered through the streets of Taos, gathered in the plaza to curse their fate.

Taos Pueblo loomed as guardian over the area, sitting at the foot of the mountains. Its history was palpable. So was the history of the Taoseños, the Españoles and Mexicanos who had lived for centuries at the edge of the pueblo. These people died and gave their ghosts back to the land. Later the Americanos came, Mabel Dodge Luhan, Dorothy Brett, D. H. Lawrence, the Taos art colony. Later, in the sixties, a new migration, hippies and Hollywood celebrities who moved to Taos seeking communion with the earth and the cosmos.

Taos drew those who sought beauty in the land, an Indian mysticism to guide their lives. But beneath the veneer of the Taos art colony and its descendants, another history existed. As sure as the kachinas of Blue Lake blessed the land and brought rain, the souls of many departed filled the files of the sheriff's office.

"What do you mean by 'curse'?" Sonny asked.

"Well, the way I heard the story, a lot of people believe it was some of Alberto's ancestors, you know, one of his bis-abuelos from way back, who was with the rebels who killed Governor Bent."

"Governor Bent?" Sonny interrupted, and glanced at Lorenza. "But that was in—"

"Eighteen forty-six," Bernabé nodded, "not too long ago."

No, of course not, Sonny checked a smile. For the sheriff, as well as for other Taoseños steeped in the tea of history, one hundred years was only yesterday. One hundred fifty years was but a sigh in the memory of the people. History did not happen and then go away for the people of the Sangre de Cristo Mountains, it festered and grew into the bones, blood, and soul. It stayed to inhabit the memory, and so the people learned to accommodate the ghosts of the past. People here lived and breathed history. It was all around them. In the mountains, around the plaza, in the adobes of old haciendas, like the Hacienda Martínez. Here the ghosts of the ancient past still walked, appeared, spoke, did mischievous things like the duendes of the forest.

"Anyway, the ghost of Governor Bent is like the ghost of Kit Carson, esos cabrones won't die. The way the folks around here figure is that el Viejo Bent, that's what we call him, wants his revenge. So he's been hounding that familia ever since. Now he's stolen Alberto's girl."

"That's what you think," Sonny said after a long pause.

The sheriff winked. "Like I said, I wouldn't tell it to the newspaper."

"I need a drink," Sonny said. He felt a fever beginning to bubble in his bones. In his nightmare Raven had taken Caridad, but there was no way he could explain that to the sheriff. Let the sheriff think it was the ghost of Governor Bent who had now kidnapped Catalina. One theory was as good as the other, and he wouldn't tell his to the media, either.

He turned to Lorenza. It was time to leave.

"Me, too," the sheriff said, rubbing his forehead and rising with them. "But I've got to go over and meet the state cops. You know La Cantina de los Pícaros," he said as he saw them out into the street, pointing down the plaza, where people moved like bundled ghosts in the cold.

Last night's dusting of snow was gone, but the day was chilly. A breeze whipped the blankets the Taos Pueblo men wore as they walked across the plaza. The trees around the plaza huddled like withered old men, raising bare branches to the gray sky and dreaming of sap and buds.

An old dilapidated truck, muddy red, a four-wheeler loaded with firewood, moved around the plaza looking for a parking place and, finding none, disappeared. A homeboy or a ranchero out making a living.

"Gracias," Sonny said, and shook hands with the sheriff. He knew La Cantina de los Pícaros.

"Wish I could join you." The sheriff tipped the brim of his hat, smiling at Lorenza. "But duty calls. Watch out for black widow spiders," he said in parting, and hobbled toward his old '57 Chevy, a prop left from one of the movies filmed in Taos.

"Is he real?" Lorenza asked, waving as the sheriff's car pulled away.

"Is anything here real?" Sonny replied. "Qué dices we get an Irish coffee to brace us for the trip?" What he really wanted was to hear what the locals at the cantina had to say about the case.

They entered the dark and dreary bar. It was packed with a wild assortment of local characters who were smart enough to come in out of the cold. Taos artists, writers, and wannabes in one corner, and raza in the other. Sonny recognized some old campers, vatos from the area who spent a lot of time digging up local folklore. A lot of stories were told in the cantina, so the denizens didn't have to go far to gather material.

Sonny headed his chair toward the group. The boisterous conversation grew as quiet as day-old tortillas as those seated around the table turned to greet him and Lorenza. A "quién chingao es este" look crossed their faces, meaning, "Who in the hell are you and what do you want?"

Then one of the revelers, Gonidas, recognized Sonny. He grinned, stepped forward, bowed to Lorenza, and whispered, "Wanna dance?"

"Ask me Saturday night," she replied, raising a smile of expectation in the old man.

"Quíhubole," Sonny greeted him.

"Pues mira quien llegó!" he exclaimed. "The president of Río Abajo—" He looked mischievously at Sonny. "I forgot your name, Mr. President?"

"Sonny Baca."

"Sonny," Gonidas embraced Sonny as if he were a long-lost brother, blowing wine-laden breath on him.

Those at the table smiled, and Sonny recognized Cleofes Vigil, the master musician and storyteller of the area. Cleofes sang the songs of the penitentes so mournfully, they said, he could make stones cry.

Next to him sat Estevan, an artist who belonged to a group that had done a lot of work preserving the agricultural techniques of the old Nuevos Mexicanos. One could see his piñon and cedar sculptures at his gallery along the Embudo road.

Others Sonny didn't know sat at the table.

"Este es Sonny, el detective de 'Burque," Gonidas said. "Y su linda—"

"Amiga," Sonny said. "Lorenza."

They all stood to greet her and to make a place at the round table, la mesa de los pícaros as it was called.

"¿Qué haces por aquí?" Estevan asked when the greetings were completed and drinks ordered.

"Pues, bad news," Sonny said.

"Oh, Beto's girl?"

"¿Qué 'stá pasando?" Sonny asked, thinking he should jump in right away and ask what they knew, because the sheriff was at a dead end, and both knew the state police dogs would sniff nothing out.

Besides, the smoky haze of the short day was settling over the Taos valley. It was two days till solstice, and Sonny didn't have much time left.

The men around the table shrugged and stiffened slightly. They didn't appreciate strangers asking questions, but the minute Sonny and Lorenza drove into the Garcías' place the entire neighborhood knew they had come to help. The gossip had reached the cantina before Sonny and Lorenza entered.

"Pues, es una desgracia—" Estevan began slowly, but Gonidas took over.

"Es el pinche Viejo Bent," he blurted out.

Sonny sipped his Irish coffee. It helped to clear his sinuses.

"El Viejo Bent?"

"Ese sanamagón!" Gonidas continued. "Mira, en 1846, más o menos, el Kearny came to Taos."

"Santa Fé," someone corrected.

"Okay, he landed at Santa Fé in his boats. La Niña, la Pinta, y la Santa María."

The others shook their heads, downed their beers, and called for another round. It was going to be a long afternoon if Gonidas got to recite the Viejo Bent history. Gonidas paid no attention, plowing ahead with his story.

"He told all the Taoseños that he was going to kick their ass if they didn't behave. 'I'm putting Governor Bent in charge while I go surfing in California and check out the beach,' he told our abuelos. 'Oh, please, Mr. Kearny, we'll be good boys,' la plebe said. Un bonche de marijuanos, how could they behave? They went and got together with the indios y colgaron al Governor Bent."

Sonny looked at Lorenza, who was listening patiently and sipping her coffee. She seemed to understand this was history told from the point of view of los paisanos.

"The Taos Pueblo Revolt," Sonny murmured, hoping the spiked coffee would clear his head. He felt a cold in his bones.

"The Chicaspatas Revolt," Gonidas grinned. "La plebe and the indios fought the GIs at La Cañada, El Embudo, at

Mora, all over the place. Kicking ass with Kearny. Muy ocupados, como dice el Morgan."

"What does it have to do with the kidnapped girl?" Sonny reminded Gonidas.

"Don't you see, hermano," Gonidas leaned forward, "el Viejo Bent was a real bad dude. He wanted to take over the whole enchilada. He wanted to be president. So when la raza and the indios killed him, he cursed the manito in charge. And that was Beto's great-great-great—uuu—*muy* great-grandfather. Entiendes. They say when el Viejo Bent was dying, les echó una maldición."

"He cursed them."

"Simón, cara limón. He told all the chicaspatas, especialmente a Beto's bisabuelo, he was going to get even. That means you, too, bro."

"Me?" Sonny looked puzzled.

"Sure, you, too."

"But I'm not related to Alberto—"

"Oh, yes, you are, primo," Gonidas cut him off. "We're all primos. You may be a detective and have a college degree y todo ese pedo, but under the skin you're just a manito. So way, way, way back your familia was probably related to Beto's familia."

Sonny glanced at those sitting around the table. Listen to him, their faces read. Sooner or later he makes sense.

Damn! Sonny thought. Don Eliseo's theory on the mark. I am related! In the dream Caridad de Anaya was going to marry Hernán López! How in the hell did Gonidas know?

Sonny nodded. "Yeah, I'm related."

"Pues, hay 'sta! So watch out for ese pinche Bent, he can get you, too. Póngote la cruz," he said, and made the sign of the cross over Sonny, as if to ward off Bent's curse. The curse that had hung in the air since 1846. "Now that will be twenty-five cents." He laughed and held out his hand.

Sonny smiled and gave Gonidas a high five.

"Thank you, father."

"Padre de cinco," he answered, and the others chuckled.

Sonny knew once a curse was laid there'd be no rest until it was lifted. Meanwhile, the ghost of Governor Bent haunted the roads and alleys of Taos, creating problems for the families of those who killed him long ago.

"Mira," Gonidas said. "Alberto García's grandparents were the Nuñezes, el viejito Escolástico, and the grand-mother doña Eulalia, who came from the familia Marquez in Río Seco, de mi compadre Alonso, and from the Aguilar family from Hondo, el difunto Escribano Velarde, and they came from the Archuletas, de allá de Tecolote, de los Sánchez, who married a woman from Taos Pueblo, la Tonita, way back to the Seguras y Salas, de Pecos y de Taos, way back in 1846. . . ."

He went on and on, naming families, their villages, and how they were related, and who had married who, and who had killed who, and who slept around, and the family feuds and jealousies, la envidia, and the quarrels of one small town against another, until he laid out the history of Río Arriba, connecting all the families.

Sonny had just browsed through *Sabino's Map,* and that's what the author had done for Chimayó. Naming the families until all the relationships came out.

But Gonidas didn't need to write it in a book, the history was in his head, even tying the bloodlines down to Río Abajo, southern New Mexico, extending la familia of Nuevos Mexicanos down to the Bacas from Socorro County, Sonny's father's family, and the Jaramillos from La Joya, his mother's family, and when he was done, he had proved they were all related.

"We're all primos," he finished. "Everybody has the same raices." He laughed. "Como dice la Biblia, they beget y beget. And every thirty years, el 'spíritu del Viejo Bent viene a chingarlos. Especially en Halloweenie."

"I guess." Sonny could only nod, dumbfounded by the man who seemed to know the genealogy of the entire state.

So, since 1846 the ancestors of those paisanos who had murdered Governor Bent, Gonidas said, "even if you were just driving the getaway car," had been blaming the ghost of the vengeful governor when they lost a cow or a sheep, or someone cut their pasture fences, or wells went dry, or husbands beat their wives, or kids took up smoking dope, or the death of a loved son occurred on a foreign battlefield.

It made sense. As much sense as any other explanation. The taking of the northern Mexican territories by the U.S. Army in 1846 was a violent affair. Manifest Destiny at its worst. The powerful forces swept across New Mexico, Arizona, and California, expanding the rule from Washington, securing a southern route to the California coast and all the lands, mines, and resources thereof.

Lorenza touched Sonny's arm. It was time to go. He looked pale and tired, and he was sneezing into the bar napkin. Enough history for one day.

"Gracias," Sonny said weakly, putting some money on the table to cover their drinks.

"Take it easy, greasy." Gonidas grinned.

"Tómala suave," the others said.

They withdrew, and the plática around the table went on as if they had never been there. In the smoky bar the exchange of ideas, idle talk, philosophy, and the constant recreating and reanalyzing of history would go on. The oral tradition exposed truth as a knife exposes the heart seeds of a watermelon when it's cleanly sliced.

Some of the plebe would get up to go home to cut firewood, home to eat, to milk cows, and as they drove, their eyes would keep darting to the side of the road, the ditches, the forest if they drove up toward Questa, searching for Beto's daughter.

Others just off from work would drop in for a beer and take their places at the round, well-worn table, the table of the pícaros, each lending his insight to the continuing story.

Sonny stopped at the bathroom. His legs were weak when he stood, his body trembled from the effort. He felt old, tired. He needed sleep, he needed something. He washed his face in cold water, splashing it on roughly to revive himself.

The ghost of Governor Bent, he thought. El Viejo Bent. Perhaps Raven had inhabited the governor's spirit to do his evil. Raven using the ghosts of history to enter the dream and destroy it. With the murder of the governor the full force of the American army came down on the paisanos, and enmity was strewn in the path of future relations. The split would be *we* versus *them: we* the Mexicanos and our way of life threatened by *them* the Americanos. In the middle were the once-great Indian pueblos of the Río Grande, which had seen the arrival of both great tides of immigrants onto their land. They cast a pox on both houses.

"How do you feel?" Lorenza asked when Sonny reappeared.

"The death of Governor Bent was a battle against an occupying force," he replied, glancing at the table of los pícaros. "There would be others. The battle at Embudo, and Vicente Silva and las Gorras Blancas in Las Vegas, a resistance movement that turned in on itself, and Reies López Tijerina's raid on the Tierra Amarilla courthouse . . ." He paused. "But for all practical purposes, the time of the gringo had come."

"Yes." She noted his pallid color and the dark around his eyes and knew it was time to get him home.

"Well," she said, guiding him outside and into the van, "there's more than one way to make a revolution." She started the engine to get the heater going.

Yeah, Sonny thought, as long as the memory was kept alive the way of the ancestors, los antepasados, would be known, and the lessons learned would serve as guideposts for the future. Most important, the people would know that Raven worked in many ways.

"Raven is everywhere."

Lorenza nodded.

"And he has many names."

"Wherever the dream is destroyed, you find his prints."

Footprints. Paiz had said the same thing.

They sped out of Taos, south, along the Río Grande Gorge while behind them spectacular clouds formed over the mountains, bringing snow to the peaks while Taos bathed in the slanting rays of mellow afternoon light, sunshowers that glowed on the sage. A magical setting. The light was biblical, spreading across the chamisa plain and infusing the foothills of the mountains, touching the clouds with burnt orange and soft mauves.

"You cold?" Lorenza asked.

"A little." He covered himself with the serape and snuggled back into his chair. He was tired. "I'm okay. I'll just read awhile. How about you?"

"I'm okay," Lorenza said. "You rest."

"Gracias," he whispered, knowing he was in good hands,

and thankful for it. Lorenza had been patient throughout the trip, a source of strength.

He opened a book and put the notepad in front of him. "The History of New Mexico," he wrote. "June 1846, Colonel Stephen W. Kearny began his march against New Mexico."

But the fatigue and the rocking of the van made the pencil slip from his fingers. He closed his eyes and planned the dream he would enter. You prepare the stage, don Eliseo had told him.

Prepare the setting of the dream, like a play or the movies.

Thinking this, Sonny faced the door of intense light, shading his eyes. This is about Kearny, he thought. I can compose the dream. Let me go to the Las Vegas, New Mexico, plaza on that day that changed history. He walked through the door and looked around.

A very hot mid-August day enveloped the foothills east of the Sangre de Cristo Mountains, and in the little hamlet of Las Vegas the people were busy making preparations to resist the Army of the West. Col. Stephen W. Kearny had left Fort Bent, the Alamo of the Nuevos Mexicanos, in southeastern Colorado and was marching on New Mexico.

Reconnaissance parties, the best and bravest young men from Taos and Las Vegas, had been sent to the eastern plain to keep track of Kearny's slow march. Kearny's two divisions were mostly volunteers, a green and ragtail army. With it Kearny planned to march all the way to California and wrest away México's northern territory. New Mexico stood in the way, but only momentarily. The gringo entrepreneurs who already had a foothold in the Santa Fé Trail trade had bought out Governor Armijo.

In Las Vegas the wedding of Epifana Aragón to Lisandro

Jaramillo had been interrupted by the preparations for war. Near noontime the last scout came riding into town, urging his pony at breakneck speed to bring the news that Kearny was in sight.

Epifana Aragón, a lovely young woman of sixteen, stepped out of her parents' home into the excitement on the plaza.

The gringos are coming! The gringos are coming! the young scout shouted as he rode around the plaza, like a Paul Revere of another time and place. It was Epifana's fiancé, Lisandro.

Lisandro! she called, and he pulled his horse to a smart stop in front of her and dismounted.

Epifana! He gathered her in his arms.

You're safe! she cried.

Epifana's father appeared at her side.

You're a brave man, son, he said to Lisandro.

Of all the young men in Las Vegas, none was braver than Lisandro, none a better horseman or more respectful to the elders. He was a shining example. Because of his family's wealth he could have excused himself from the preparations for war; instead, he had volunteered to scout.

I will go into the very heart of the enemy camp if I have to, he had vowed in front of the council of elders who were organizing the resistance.

Epifana's heart glowed with love at the bravery of her beloved.

They will be here soon, don José, Lisandro reported smartly, saluting his soon-to-be father-in-law and the other men gathered in the plaza.

A solemn don Jóse turned and mounted the small stage in the middle of the plaza. He spoke slowly, thoughtfully.

As you know, Governor Armijo has retreated to El Paso.

The rumors from Santa Fé are mixed. Some say he sold out to Santiago Magoffin, and Santa Fé is now helpless to resist the invaders.

But we're not, brave Lisandro shouted, holding up his buffalo rifle. Other young men around him cheered and also waved their pistols and rifles. Some only waved pitchforks or sticks, for as herders and farmers, they had only these weapons.

Let the Yankees come, one shouted, and we'll give them a taste of lead!

Go home, Yankees! another young man shouted, and the crowd took up the refrain. Go home, Yankees!

They come to ruin our way of life! Why can't they stay where they belong! a farmer shouted.

We should build a fence to keep them out, his vecino added.

For years the mountain men and traders from the United States had worked their way into the land of the northern Río Grande, and the people reluctantly accepted the intrusion. New goods appeared, farm implements, better rifles, iron pots for the kitchen, steel axes, all useful instruments in the daily life of the paisanos. But still the people feared being overrun by the Americanos, and now that war had been declared against México, their fears were about to be realized.

The shouts for war grew, and only don José could quiet down the young men who were ready to take on the Army of the West.

As you know, he said, the American colonel brings two divisions. Thousands of infantry. He has artillery, and we do not. Kearny has a thousand mules carrying their ammunition and supplies. And what do we have to meet such a force?

The men looked at their weapons. A few wore pistols,

and some carried the buffalo rifles that they used to hunt the bison in the eastern plains in the fall, but compared to the army described by the scouts, they would be like wheat before the scythe.

What can we do? one of the elders asked.

We must protect our families, our homes, another said. For many years now we have seen the Yankees come to our land. They speak a different language. They refuse to learn Spanish. Soon they will want us all to speak only English. And . . . they are Protestants.

A gasp went up from the women, who crossed their foreheads and muttered a prayer at the mention of the word.

So we must fight! the young Lisandro cried out, and again the young men cheered him.

Don José raised his arms. Wait! Sometimes the better part of valor is to listen and to learn, he said. Let us listen to the Americano colonel. Let us see what terms he offers. To resist will mean our young men will die. I do not want to be responsible for so many deaths, for the burning of our fields and homes, nor for the widows left in the wake of war.

The older men around him nodded. Perhaps the Americanos would be kind and show mercy. Don José was correct, the inhabitants of Las Vegas just didn't have the men or armaments to resist. Many would die if they opposed the huge army that even now was at their door. There would be carnage on the grasslands of the land they loved so well.

Don José put his arm around his daughter. If I want peace and time to grow into old age, he said, some will say it is because I am a coward. I am not! If you vote to fight, then I will march alongside you. But you know, and I know, that our armed resistance is useless. We will die. Who will care for my family when I am dead? Who will teach my grandchildren the ways of our ancestors? It is for my family that

I vote for peace with the Americanos. We must trust that this occupation of our land will be short-lived and that finding no gold, they will move on to California.

Or go back where they came from! a man shouted, and the crowd applauded.

The older men agreed, but the hot tempers of the young men were not so easily cooled.

If we don't resist now, they will take our land! Lisandro insisted.

Listen to my father, mi amor, Epifana whispered to Lisandro. He wants what is best for us.

I will listen to you, amor, he replied, and turned to the assembly. I will abide by what don José thinks is right, he said, and the people cheered. The young men reluctantly gathered around to slap him on the back and tell him they were with him.

They are speaking as though in a movie, Sonny thought. I am directing my dream! He looked for Coyote, but he wasn't around. It's me, I can do it! Sonny laughed.

I must finish my preparations, Epifana said to Lisandro as she withdrew. Be careful, he replied as the young men lifted him on their shoulders and paraded him around the plaza.

What am I doing? Sonny wondered. Am I really in charge here? What about Kearny?

The scene shifted and for a moment Sonny was caught off guard. He saw the long column of Kearny's army marching across the llano. Dust rose into the hot June day, horses and mules strained at their harnesses. The land of the Nuevos Mexicanos had seen many changes sweep across it, but none was to be as momentous as the coming of the Americanos. Military occupation, a new Code of Laws, a different language, and loss of their original land grants were to follow. The bones of history rattled and ached at the thought.

Sonny grew sad. Should the people of Las Vegas have resisted? No, of course not. Don José was right. A bloody battle would have inflicted casualties on both sides, but the losers would have been the people of Las Vegas. Farmers and sheepmen were no match for an army trained for war.

In the plaza fear turned to curiosity as the assembled people looked at the weary and thirsty volunteers who straggled in. Their faces were covered with dust, their lips cracked from the sun, and their blond hair matted from days on the trail. They were young men far away from home, and they were hungry and thirsty.

A woman took pity on the soldiers. From her pail of water she offered a soldier a drink. He smiled and said in his strange tongue, Thank you, ma'am.

Tanque Mam, she repeated. Se llama Tanque Mam, she said to her neighbors.

Tanque Mam, they said in greeting. The seventeen-year-old from Missouri didn't appear to be much of an enemy at all. He was thirsty and hungry and as appreciative of the drink of water as if his own mother had handed it to him.

Tanque Mam was the first Yankee to receive the hospitality of the Nuevos Mexicanos. While Colonel Kearny gave his famous "I'm taking over this territory" speech in the plaza, laying down the new American law, the soldiers wandered among the people, receiving gifts of cool water, meat rolled in tortillas, combs for their hair. They hadn't laid eyes on a woman for months, and now their eyes flirted with the young Mexican women.

But there was another enemy who dismounted. In the periphery of the dream Sonny spied a shadow. A lone soldier moving down a back alley, in and out of the stables and animal pens. The man, dressed in an army uniform, moved stealthily but quickly in the direction of Epifana's house.

Sonny waited, unable to will himself forward. He had fallen into the dream, but he wasn't constructing it! The image began to shift, as a dream shifts at will.

"No," Sonny mumbled, knowing he was losing the dream, trying to concentrate. Deep in the recesses of the dream he knew the U.S. soldier sneaking toward Epifana's home was Raven, but Sonny felt mired in a denseness he couldn't break. The denseness itself was the dream, it held the images, but Sonny couldn't order the sequence, he couldn't cast light on the images.

The man reappeared, this time carrying a bundle he lifted on to his horse. Epifana! Sonny gasped.

Raven mounted and turned his horse. He looked at Sonny and held him with eyes so dark and penetrating Sonny felt their chill.

She will give birth to Lisandro's children, your mother's Jaramillo ancestors, Raven shouted. Now she's mine!

He spurred his horse, and the horse's cry shook the ground, the blood from its flanks swirled into a dark whirlwind that swept all the images of the dream away.

"No!" Sonny cried, awakening, flailing out, grabbing at Lorenza, and the van went flying off the road, thumping along the shoulder of the highway until she brought it to a stop.

Lorenza turned to Sonny. "Qué pasa?"

Sonny opened his eyes, gasping for air.

"I was dreaming."

"Raven?"

"Yes." Sonny rubbed his eyes, his neck. The dream had been very real. He had smelled the horse lather, the sweat of the soldiers. The cigarette smoke of the men in the plaza. He had heard the flies buzzing in the hot air, the bark of a dog, the lowing of cows in the distant meadows.

"I couldn't get into the dream. Raven took the girl. A young woman, Epifana. She was to marry Lisandro Jaramillo."

"Isn't your mother a Jaramillo?"

Sonny nodded. "The family was originally from the Las Vegas area."

"Did Raven see you?"

"Yes."

"At least he knows you're watching!"

"To really stop him, I had to get *into* the dream."

"Yes."

"Where are we?" Sonny glanced out the window. In the dusk the Sandia Mountains loomed over him, wearing a thick scarf of low-lying clouds.

"We're nearly home," Lorenza replied, and started the van.

12

They sat at Sonny's table in Rita's Cocina and talked about what they had learned in Taos. Sonny wiped clean his plate, scooping up the last of the carne adovada with a piece of tortilla. He had looked pale and tired when they entered the restaurant, but the meal revived him.

He studied Rita surreptitiously, noting the shadows around her eyes. She looked tired. Running the restaurant and taking care of him hadn't been easy. But tonight he sensed a quietness, something stirring deeper in her.

"And you, amor?" he said, reaching out to hold her hands. "How are you?"

"I'm fine, just fine. When the weather changes, people eat more. We've been swamped."

"You're working too hard. You look tired."

She caressed his hand. "It's just a cold. Everyone seems to be coming in with the flu. Nothing to worry about." She glanced at Lorenza.

"You should see a doctor," Sonny said.

"I did," Rita replied. "I had a checkup today. I'm healthy as a horse."

"Who did you see?" Sonny asked.

"Dr. Sanchez. She's with a new group near Osuna."

"Good." Lorenza smiled.

"She's wonderful. We talked for an hour. You know, women doctors *really* listen to you. I like that. Anyway, let's not talk about me."

"I'm concerned," Sonny replied.

"Thank you, amor, but I'm fine. You're worried because I'm never sick. I haven't had a cold since I was in the sixth grade."

"I wish I had the time to be here more—"

"Hey, it's the missing girls we have to worry about. If Raven has them—" She shivered.

"He's loose and he's dangerous," Sonny said. "By the way, did Eddie Martínez, the FBI agent, come by?"

"Yes. Said he'd hang around the restaurant during the day. I told him I didn't need protection, I can take care of myself, but he insisted."

"I insisted. You have to be careful."

"Careful? It's you two that have to be careful. I'm fine, really, I am. I keep thinking about the girls."

One of the waitresses brought hot sopaipillas, and they ate them with honey for dessert.

"Me, too," Sonny said. "And I don't have a damned clue to go on. I'm sure they're here in the city, but where?" He looked out the window. It was dark outside; few cars moved on Fourth Street.

"When Raven's woman, Veronica, murdered Gloria Dominic, there were four women in his cult. What happened to them?" Rita asked.

"They scattered."

"Or he couldn't use them against you," Lorenza suggested. "So he needs four young women to initiate into his new cult."

"That frightens me," Rita said. "He's liable to . . ." Her words hung in the air. Then: "What if the girls won't obey him?"

"He has ways to control them," Lorenza said.

Sonny agreed. "He isolates them from their families, takes away their orientation to reality. Takes away that center don Eliseo calls the here and now."

"But the girls you've described have strong values," Rita said. "They'll resist him."

Sonny had thought of that. Yes, the girls came from families with strong values. If they resisted Raven, they would be useless to him. How far would Raven go? How much did he need them? The girls represented Sonny's grandmothers, would he kill them and thus symbolically kill Sonny's grandmothers?

He looked at Lorenza, knowing she was thinking along the same line.

"Maybe he wants to distract me. Have me looking for the girls while he works the bomb angle."

"Yes, you're right," Lorenza agreed. "He's working here, so his hideaway is here. You have to keep on his track. When you find him, you'll find the girls."

Sonny nodded.

"Both girls came from families that are related to yours," she continued. "It's a distant relation, but it's there. And both were participating in Christmas pageants. Consuelo was in *Los Pastores,* and Catalina was in *Las Posadas.*"

"And both were about to be married."

"The girls were playing the role of the Virgin Mary in the Christmas pageants. The Virgin is about to give birth . . ." Lorenza added.

"The birth of Christ comes four days after the winter solstice," Rita whispered. "Raven doesn't want the sun to return after the solstice, he can't stand for Christ the Light to be born. He is the Destroyer of Light."

"And he'll use the girls to carry out his plan," Lorenza finished.

These strands of the plot they knew, but the details escaped them. Sonny shivered, trying to shrug off the feeling of despair.

"Maybe Paiz will find something. Or we have to find a new way of tracing Raven," Sonny said.

"Like?"

"What is needed to put a nuclear bomb together? People and materials, I mean really specialized materials. Can someone like Raven buy those materials? And couldn't those purchases be traced? We need information on how to build a nuclear bomb."

"Will Eric help?" Rita asked.

Sonny shook his head. Right now he didn't trust Eric.

"He either won't tell us anything because of security, or he'll lead us down a wrong alley. There must be a way to break into his system."

"Break into Los Alamos Labs?" Rita exclaimed. "Whoa! I will draw the line at that. That's a lot of years in jail, Sonny Baca. Or they'll kill you. Like they electrocuted Ethel and Julius Rosenberg."

"Ethel and Julius Rosenberg?" He looked puzzled.

"It was one of the books you had in the van. I read most of it last night. The way the book tells it, the whole thing was Harry Gold's fault."

Sonny vaguely remembered the names in the famous spy case. Harry Gold had passed atomic bomb secrets to the Russians, or something like that.

"The spy?" he asked.

"Yes. Harry Gold got the atomic bomb secrets from

Klaus Fuchs, who had managed to get the information out of Los Alamos. Gold gave the secrets to the Russians. And part of the secrets he got from Greenglass. It happened right here in Alburquerque. Two-oh-nine High Street. I drove by there today. Can you imagine, all that happened right here in the 1940s. Now you want to break into Los Alamos. I don't think so."

Sonny smiled. "Looks like you've done your research. I had forgotten about the Rosenbergs."

"They took the rap," Rita reminded them. "They catch you breaking into their top-secret buildings, you will take a *big* rap."

"I don't mean break into Los Alamos Labs buildings," Sonny said. "I just need to find what is needed to put a bomb together. Begin to trace materials, see if suppliers lead to Raven."

"You mean break into their computer system," Lorenza suggested.

"Yeah, that's it. And for that I need a computer expert. PIs no longer chase credit card thieves or guys not paying alimony. Now they can all be traced with computers. It's all on the Internet!"

He smiled, uneasily. The technology was there, and he needed it, but what the hell did he know about it.

"In the meantime, Raven will come for another girl," Rita said solemnly.

"I'm sure. The question is where?"

"At another Christmas pageant," Rita said.

Sonny arched an eyebrow. She was on to something.

"If he came back here, because his plans for building the bomb are here, and he's hiding the girls somewhere in the city— They're having *Posadas* in Barelas!" she blurted.

"When?" Sonny asked, sitting up and paying attention.

"Tonight. They have the *Posadas* every night for a week before Christmas."

"It's just possible—"

"—that he'll be there," Lorenza finished.

"What else do we have to go on? Let's go!"

"Sonny." Rita reached across. "You've been out all day, your cold is getting worse. You have to rest."

Yeah, Sonny thought. He felt the cold building inside, the aches, the sniffling in his nose, the strange low-level fever clinging to him. But he couldn't rest, he couldn't sleep. Sleep meant dreams, and that meant, somehow, opening a channel into his past, a way for Raven to travel to the grand-mothers.

"I have no choice," he said.

Rita looked at Lorenza.

Lorenza understood Rita's concern, it was hers, too. She had seen the day take its toll on Sonny, but Raven wasn't resting. To rest meant death for Sonny. Raven was taking a girl a day, and there were only two to go. That meant Raven had to strike again, tonight.

"I'm all right, really." Sonny said, squeezing her hands, trying to allay her fear. "I just had a good meal, I'll stay warm, we'll go just to look around. It's probably nothing. But if you don't feel well—"

"I'm fine," Rita replied. "Remember we were there last year."

"That's right." Sonny smiled, the memory suddenly flashing like the scene from a movie in his mind. This is the way the past had been returning since his brain had been buzzed by Stammer. A word, a phrase, a sound would suddenly bring forth an image from the past, and the memory would be clear. He remembered the crisp December air at nightfall, the procession of people holding candles as they followed Joseph and Mary from house to house, the smell of wax, the songs.

"So let's do it," Rita said. "The fresh air will do me good. I'll pray Raven *isn't* there. Let me get my coat and tell Marta to close up."

"You sure?" Sonny asked.

"I'm sure." She kissed him and walked away.

"She looks tired," Sonny said to Lorenza. "Not her old self . . ."

"She works too hard. But the fresh air will be good for her," Lorenza said.

"What can I do? I feel I'm running in circles, neglecting Rita, neglecting everybody—"

"Rita knows your predicament: She knows you have to find Raven and get the girls back."

Ah, how the gusano turns, Sonny thought. It was a week before Christmas, and he and Rita should be doing the things they liked to do. Shopping for gifts. He needed to buy presents for his mom, Rita, Lorenza, all of them. Last year shopping with Rita had been a wonderful experience. Now they hadn't even had the time to visit friends. When's the last time he had seen his mother? He didn't remember; he had lost track of time.

He should be going to his therapy sessions, walking the parallel bars, strengthening his legs, willing them to listen to commands from his brain, maybe going to the Jemez Springs Bath House and sitting in a tub full of hot mineral water. Having his legs massaged. Lorenza had told him of a healer who worked there, Cosima, who knew how to free the body's blocked energy. He should be taking care of himself and Rita, but he was too busy chasing Raven.

He needed the time to rest, to get things straight. Winter was for kicking back, eating piñon, sitting in front of a stove burning sweet cedar, listening to don Eliseo's stories, reading, visiting with friends in the evenings, going to Lobo basketball games, watching football games on TV, and looking forward to the Super Bowl, or just helping Rita at the café. Time for doing ordinary things. Instead, he was looking for the grandmothers of his dreams, the two girls, and an insane Raven whom the FBI believed could build a nuclear bomb.

"Ready," Rita said, appearing in a black leather coat. She had freshened her makeup. Sonny looked at her and smiled. Suddenly she looked radiant, ready to go. He should be making love to her, not chasing after wild impossibilities.

"You look lovely, amor."

"Gracias," she replied.

"I—" He wanted to say something more, something about the love he felt that moment, some acknowledgment of the joy he found in her and how grateful he was for the time she spent nursing him. But his voice caught, and he was afraid if he continued his voice would crack.

"You don't have to say anything," she said, brushing his lips with hers. "It's something we have to do for now. When this is over, spring will come. Then we'll get married. You haven't changed your mind, have you?" She smiled.

"Did I say something while I was under?" Sonny grinned.

"Yes, you did." Rita winked at Lorenza. "Didn't he say he was going to make a decent woman out of me?"

"He sure did," Lorenza said, and both looked at him.

"Ah, come on," Sonny kidded, "you can't hold a dying man to his word. I was out of it."

"You still are, amor," Rita said, and took his wheelchair and pointed it at the door.

"Fever," Lorenza added. "Men are like that. They make promises, then blame it on their fever."

They laughed as they boarded the van and headed toward Barelas. For the moment, the joy of friendship and the joy of the season had returned.

Fourth Street south of Central was decorated for the season but nearly deserted. A few cars moved down toward Bridge Street and then on to the South Valley. The city was renovating the street, sprucing up the old barrio. Just past Bridge Street the Hispanic Cultural Center rose, a center where the art and culture of the old Hispanos and Mexicanos could be kept alive.

Don Eliseo had warned him: Lose the language, the threads of history, and the traditions, and the ways of your ancestors will disappear from the earth of la Nueva México.

Sonny shivered. The barrio, bathed by streetlights, was hanging on to its inheritance. A cold breeze blew across the mesa, over the sluggish Río Grande, crying as it swept past the bare alamos and elm trees and through barrio streets. The cold, mournful whisper forced many a barrio denizen to hurry home.

One bright spot filled the void. At Barelas Road they spotted the procession. Lorenza parked in a side street.

"Pacific," Sonny murmured, looking up at the street sign. Ben Chávez territory. Should I take my pistol? he thought, and decided yes. He stuffed the pistol under the blanket Rita had placed over his legs.

"We're in time," Rita said as they made their way toward the small but enthusiastic crowd gathered around the actors playing the roles of Joseph and Mary.

Sonny sniffed the air. Like a coyote coming into new territory, he had the habit of sniffing for scents. Smells revealed the place, and often revealed danger. But tonight his sinuses were stuffed, and this heightened sense he trusted revealed very little.

The barrio lay huddled under the cold. The darkness was punctuated by the flashlights and candles held by those in the procession.

A TV-4 van was parked nearby. Carla Aragón and her cameraman were shooting the pageant for the ten o'clock news.

Sonny turned his attention to the actors, paying special attention to the girl playing the Virgin Mary. The girl sat quietly on a burro while the man playing Joseph tugged at the halter. If Raven was here, he would go after the girl.

"Do you know her?" Sonny whispered. Rita had been raised in Barelas, and she knew a lot of the families, but she answered no.

A man next to Sonny drew close and whispered, "She's a substitute for Carmen Abeyta. Carmen got sick. She's at the last house of the *Posadas,* with her parents."

"Thanks," Sonny replied. The man was bundled for the cold, a scarf pulled up around his chin. The black hat he wore was pulled low so Sonny couldn't make out the face.

He turned his attention to the procession.

The man playing Joseph pulled the burro toward the gate of the first house. The chorus of neighbors following Mary and Joseph broke out with the first song, the plea for a room at the inn, their voices rising joyfully into the night:

> El Señor de bondad nos proteja,
> Nos bendiga y nos colme de amor;
> Su Sagrada Pasión nos defienda,
> Y nos libre de mal y dolor.

St. Joseph stepped up to the gate of the first house and knocked. The door opened and he asked for a room for the night, explaining to the innkeeper that he and his pregnant wife had traveled very far and needed to rest:

> Venimos de muy lejos
> Y llegamos cansados,
> Ahora les pedimos
> Posada esta noche.

The man who opened the door, playing the role of an annoyed innkeeper, answered:

> Quién viene a nuestra puerta,
> En esta noche de hielo?
> Quién se arrima con impudencia
> A molestar nuestro sueño?

"Váyanse de aquí," he finished, closing the door in their faces. St. Joseph and the Virgin Mary moved to the next house, followed by the carolers who now sang along with St. Joseph.

> Quién le da posada
> A nostros los peregrinos?
> Llegamos muy cansados
> De andar tantos caminos.

The person who answered the door in the second home was no friendlier than the first. He accused Joseph and Mary of being robbers and slammed the door shut. Again the patient Joseph took the burro's reins and moved slowly to the next house, where again he asked for a place to rest. Even a corner in the kitchen would suffice.

He was refused again by the man at the door. There was

no corner to spare. "Go out into the fields, there's plenty of room there!" he shouted, slamming the door shut.

Leading the burro with the young Virgin Mary solemnly perched on its back, Joseph moved on to the next house. The patient crowd moved with him, lighted candles casting a bright glow on faces.

At the next house Joseph explained his wife was pregnant, but the woman inside the house, yawning, accused them of robbing her sleep.

By the time they arrived at the fifth house, St. Joseph was irritated. "My wife is freezing," he pleaded, but again he was turned away.

As they moved along, the crowd parted, allowing Sonny to move to the front. Lorenza and Rita politely held back. When Sonny glanced back, he couldn't see them.

"My young wife is cold," St. Joseph sang at the next house.

"Too bad," came the response from within. "Move on!"

The procession moved to the seventh house. Here St. Joseph finally revealed that the woman with him was the Virgin Mary, Queen of Heaven. The unbelieving innkeeper shouted back, "There's lots of room out in the desert."

Sonny's attention had been on the young girl playing the Virgin, but the mood of the entreaties and the responses enveloped him in the story. Suddenly he was startled as someone behind him took hold of the handles of his chair.

"Hace frío," the man in the black hat whispered.

"Sí," Sonny replied.

"You'll catch cold," the man said.

"I'm okay."

The man remained standing behind Sonny's chair.

Sonny turned his attention back to St. Joseph, who was

knocking on one more door and pleading for a room. "I'm Joseph and this is my wife, Mary," he sang in Spanish verse.

"So what!" the people in the house sang back. "We don't know a Joseph and Mary. Go away, it's late and we're not going to open for you!"

Late arrivals had joined the swelling procession, pressing slowly toward the ninth house, where St. Joseph revealed once again that Mary was the mother of God.

This was the turning point of the drama. The innkeeper recognized Mary, the Queen of Heaven, and threw open the door, singing loudly:

> Ábranse las puertas!
> Rómpanse los velos!
> Aquí viene a posar,
> La Reina del Cielo!

"Thank you, thank you," St. Joseph cried out, the chorus around him joining in the revelation. "For the kindness you have shown us, yours is the kingdom of heaven."

The doors of the house were thrown wide open, becoming the church that will embrace the child about to be born. St. Joseph and Mary entered and were jubilantly greeted:

> Entren santos peregrinos,
> Reciban este rincón,
> No de mi pobre morada,
> Sino de mi corazón.

Those at the front of the procession eagerly pressed forward to get into the house. Hot coffee, tamales, posole, biscochitos awaited them, a welcome treat on a cold night.

"You want to go in?" the man in the black hat asked Sonny.

"Yes," Sonny replied, looking for Rita and Lorenza but not spotting them. He wanted to see Carmen Abeyta for himself.

"The Abeytas are friends," the man said. "We can go around the side of the house. It's easier for your chair. We can go right into the kitchen."

"What did you say is the girl's name?" Sonny asked as the man pushed.

"Carmen," the man answered.

Consuelo, Catalina, now Carmen. The hair along the back of Sonny's neck stood on edge.

"You said the girl is with her parents," Sonny said.

"Yes, inside," the man said. "This way."

The man guided the chair around the side of the house. The path was level but dark. Sonny glanced back to try to let Lorenza and Rita know where he was headed, but they were lost in the crowd.

Faint sounds of celebration echoed from the front of the house.

"Wait," Sonny said, and at the same time he felt a stab to the back of his neck, a needle entering, something warm oozing. He reached for the needle, but a thick canvas tarp dropped over him. Barely conscious, he felt ropes quickly securing the smothering tarp.

He felt two men lifting him, then he was dumped on a hard surface. A second thud told him they had thrown in his chair. The door banged, and through the numbness of the injection he heard the screeching of tires, felt a careering movement that told him he was in the back of a van or truck, heading out of the barrio.

Oh, please, he thought, let me stay awake.

13

He struggled to remain conscious, to keep the nightmare at bay. Whoever injected him and wrapped him in the tarp had worked fast. Two, Sonny figured, and strong enough to lift him.

Now he was on the floor of a van, heading, he could only guess, to a rendezvous with Raven. But *now* he knew why Raven played games, why he just didn't come out in the open and kill him.

The numbness remained, but his head cleared and Sonny could sense one man sitting next to him. The other drove. Where were they heading? He couldn't tell anything about the direction, bundled as he was.

Under the tarp he gasped for air and struggled to stay awake. Half an hour later, he guessed, they drew to a stop. Someone asked the driver for identification. They were entering a restricted area. Where?

Sonny thought of shouting for help, but thought better of it when he felt the muzzle of a pistol on his head. "Not a word out of you," the man whispered.

Outside, the guard said okay, and they were allowed to proceed.

Minutes later the van stopped again, and the back door opened. The two men silently carried Sonny into a building. He heard the door lock behind them as they carried him a short distance and set him in a chair. Someone with a very thick Russian accent protested.

"Why have you brought him here? Are you crazy? This is not good. There are guards!"

"Pipe down, Doc," one of the men replied. "We got orders."

"You are mad!" the man shouted. "I have not agreed to this!"

Another voice sounded in the room. "You don't give the orders around here, Chernenko. I do!"

Even through the tarp Sonny recognized Raven's voice. Sonny heard him moving to his side. The ropes around the tarp came loose and the canvas was lifted. Sonny blinked.

Raven stood in front of him. Behind him stood a very nervous Dr. Alexander Chernenko, the Ukrainian nuclear physicist. On either side stood his abductors. One was lean and tall, the other short and muscular. Sonny recognized Sweatband and Tallboy, the same two who had helped Raven at the Juárez warehouse where they had tried to burn Sonny to a cinder.

"Awake?" Raven scowled. "I thought you would be dreaming."

"The rough ride woke me up." Sonny grinned.

"Let's kill the sonofabitch and be done!" Sweatband cursed.

"We owe him one," Tallboy seconded him.

"That's exactly what I have in mind. But I have a far better way of doing it." He leaned over Sonny. The entire left side of Raven's face was an ugly scar.

"It's time, Baca," he whispered. "Solstice time."

Sonny knew Raven's plan wasn't to kill him in the flesh, it was his ancestral soul he wanted to destroy. So he had something in mind other than slicing his throat. Anyway, when really behind in the struggle, goad your tormentor.

"Why don't you kill me and get it over with?" Sonny taunted. "Come on." He turned to Sweatband. "Get it over with! You chicken? Afraid of a man who can't walk!"

Sonny reached out, inviting the man to a fight. Four men in the room and he couldn't even stand on his feet, but he wasn't going without a fight.

Sweatband jumped forward and hit Sonny full across the face. "I'll kill you!" he cursed, drawing a knife.

"Come on, try it!" Sonny taunted again. "You can't kill me!"

Sonny looked past Sweatband to Raven. Raven couldn't kill him! Not here, not in this world.

"Not even Raven can kill me!" he shouted, and laughed. His boldness made Sweatband hesitate.

"I can kill you anytime I want!" Raven retorted. "Or I let them do it. And it won't be pretty."

"Yeah," Sweatband said, gathering his bravado and brandishing the knife. "I'll carve you up real good."

He grabbed Sonny's hair and pushed his head back. Holding the sharp blade at Sonny's throat, he grinned and looked at Raven. "Come on, let me do it now!"

"No!" Raven pushed him away. "I've got better plans for Sonny Baca. Wait outside."

A hesitant Sweatband looked from Raven to his buddy, then slowly drew back. "I hope what you got planned for him is good," he spit. " 'Cause I owe him!" He motioned to Tallboy, and they both went out of the room. Chernenko started to follow, but Raven stopped him with an abrupt command.

"You stay! Prepare the second injection!"

"I don't like this," Chernenko mumbled. Sonny watched him walk to a small stand on which rested a syringe, a small bottle.

"Nobody's asked you to like it," Raven replied. "You do as you're told and you get paid. Leave the rest to me."

When Chernenko moved, Sonny got a clear view of the apparatus that rested in the middle of the large laboratory. A huge, round, barrel-like machine. Sonny recognized a crude device that was similar to pictures he had seen of the first atom bomb the Los Alamos scientists had built in 1945.

I'm in Chernenko's lab, right in the Sandia Labs' nuclear reactor area, Sonny thought, and this is the bomb he's building!

"Yeah, that's it." Raven smiled, following Sonny's gaze to the device. "Built right under their noses. Chernenko's a genius, building the Gadget was a breeze. He calls it the Gadget, after the first bomb detonated at Trinity. I call this beauty the Avenger." He looked at Chernenko. "Our man was once a top nuclear physicist in Ukraine."

"I only want to finish and get paid," Chernenko muttered. "Then I leave this place."

"Patience, Doctor, patience," Raven teased. "We have a little dream inducement yet to do. A shot of Valium for our boy. To make him ease into sleep nice and mellow."

Dream inducement? Sonny thought. So that was the plan. He looked at Chernenko as he inserted the syringe needle into the vial.

"Won't work," Sonny said. "The FBI knows about your little project."

Sonny watched Chernenko cock his head. Mention of the FBI made him nervous.

Raven sneered. "The FBI knows nothing! They think they're dealing with crazies, but we're not, are we, Doctor?"

Chernenko nodded. "With the right materials and expert assistance, I can build a bomb blindfolded. All I need is the plutonium pit, and the right price. My colleagues here think I'm disarming old bombs. But what a wonderful used-junk place this is." He chuckled. "I have everything I need!"

"Used junk. I like that." Raven gloated. "It may be crude, but it works. Once everything's in place, we can ask any ransom," Raven said.

Sandia Labs! Sonny thought. A nuclear explosion would not only wipe out the city of Alburquerque with the initial blast, it might also set off the missiles they were disarming. There were probably hundreds of plutonium pits stored on the base or in the nearby Manzano Mountains. Raven was planning an unparalleled catastrophe, and he had found the perfect place to pull it off. The chain reaction would be unimaginable.

"What's the price?" Sonny asked, knowing for sure that by now Lorenza and Rita had called the cops. But the cops had no lead; they wouldn't know where he was.

What kind of strength do I have in my legs? he thought. Can I lunge and take Raven down with me? No, Raven was too strong, and his two cronies were just outside the room. The odds were against him.

Raven drew close and whispered. "For the Russkie, it means money. Can you imagine that? He actually trades his talent for money?"

"And you've sold yourself to the Avengers!"

Raven laughed. "I sell myself to no one. But to carry out my plan, it helps to have people in high places. How else do you think we could have gotten in here?"

The look in his dark eyes made Sonny wince. Paiz had

been right; the Avengers were fronting Raven. Through the group he got access to Chernenko. Maybe Eric helped. The bomb would be ready in time for the winter solstice, when the Avengers would strike. They would have created the ultimate threat, and with it they could take over or impose a military dictatorship. And Raven would sit at the head of the table.

"The girls?" Sonny asked.

"Part of my plan," Raven replied.

"Let's make a deal. You've got me, so let them go."

Raven shook his head. "No deal, Baca. The Sun King needs women to attend his ceremonies."

"And if they don't, you kill them!" He turned to Chernenko, who had finished filling the syringe. "You hear that, Dr. Chernenko? When your friend's done using people, he gets rid of them! And you're next!" Sonny taunted.

Chernenko looked at Raven.

Raven backhanded Sonny, the slap jerking Sonny's head back.

"You're the one I'm getting rid of," he spit out, reaching forward and tearing open Sonny's shirt, exposing the Zia medallion. His eyes glowed and his lips twisted in a satisfied smile as he roughly pulled the medallion from around Sonny's neck.

"Thanks for taking care of it," he whispered. "Now it's mine!" He held the medallion up so that the light shone on the gold, and whispered, "The medallion of the god Ra. The Egyptian priests knew the Zia sun, but they called him by other names. They knew that he who wears the medallion is invincible."

Pausing, he looked down at Sonny and said, "It's been a long struggle, in different places, as different men and women, through the centuries—me against you. Now I hold the balance of power. And while you sleep, I will haunt your dreams and destroy your past. So you will never return, I will destroy your soul. Only in your dream time can I do that."

He turned and walked to the bomb and hung the medallion on it.

"See. The power of the sun has come to rest here."

"Not the power of the sun," Sonny replied. "Your power of darkness."

Raven scowled.

"We will return to chaos," he said. "Return to the original time. Destroy this age, and rule in the next. It's the only way."

"Do you really think you can bring the end of the world?"

Raven nodded. "I know it."

"The plutonium pits in the lab are too well packaged. You won't set off a chain reaction."

Raven looked surprised. "So you've been doing some reading. And you believe we can't create a chain reaction. Hear that, Chernenko, no chain reaction!"

Chernenko chuckled. "Who cares," he replied.

"We don't need a chain reaction here. When this baby goes off, the Russkies respond with their missiles. Your government has lulled people into thinking the end of the Cold War meant an end to the Russian missiles pointed at the U.S. Oh, no, hundreds of their warheads are still programmed to hit every city here."

Precipitate a nuclear war? Sonny thought. The Avengers had hired Raven to build the bomb they would use to take control, but they had underestimated him. Raven's purpose wasn't just to take over the government, he wanted to destroy the world!

"Why would Russia respond to a bomb going off *here?*"

"This baby is going to set off their alarm system." Raven grinned. He turned to Chernenko. "You see, my friend Dr. Chernenko, with the help of a few Los Alamos scientists, designed the Russian system. The Russkie computers are programmed to read a bomb exploding here as a *real* attack. When we explode our Gadget, a computer in Russia orders retaliation. The final world war will start."

Sonny shook his head. "There are telephones. The president would call Russia and explain—"

"Explain nothing!" Raven cut in. "It's programmed into a computer! It's failsafe! Nobody can stop it!"

Chernenko, too, had underestimated Raven. He, like the Avengers, thought that Raven worked for them to create a crisis that would allow them to take over.

For the first time he stepped forward and spoke. "Of course we won't need the final phase. Once the actual bomb is armed, we ask for ransom. Your government will pay. And we will be in South America, with enough money to buy our own country!"

"Don't you see," Sonny implored. "Raven doesn't want the money! He wants to blow up the world!"

Chernenko looked from Sonny to Raven but shook his head.

"He doesn't get it," Raven said to Sonny. "It's beyond his imagination. But long ago we concluded that the only way to bring down the world was to destroy it."

"Get rid of those who dream harmony and peace."

"Precisely. We have already made a mockery of your so-called morality. Some of you go on believing there is a good purpose in the universe? You persist in your belief because you have no choice. Written into your cells and memory is a dream of internal harmony and order. Since man first came to consciousness, it's been there."

"And I stand in the way," Sonny said.

"You always stood in the way," Raven scowled. "You and your other forms in prior lives. Time is a continuum, a cycle repeating itself, like the snake swallowing its own tail. We've fought each other in the past, and sooner or later one would have to destroy the other. Good and evil, the priests call it." His face turned dark. "How simplistic, how stupid!"

"You can kill the body, but not my soul," Sonny said.

That was why he didn't let Sweatband kill him, because the soul kept returning, as he said, in one form or another. The dream was continuous, as each soul was continuous.

"You have died many times before," Raven said. "But your spirit keeps returning to plague me! Tonight I destroy your soul!"

"By killing the souls of my grandmothers, their dreams."

"I found the points in your history when your soul entered a new state of consciousness. The coming of the Spaniards and the Mexicans to New Mexico was such a time. A great leap was about to take place, a new people would be born. Peace would reign. 'Peace,' how I hate the word! I came to bring the curse of destruction! I came to curse all the houses of New Mexico! With this bomb I can do it!"

"But you can't kill the dream," Sonny replied.

"Oh, yes, I can. Owl Woman is a messenger, a dream-keeper. Like the goddess of the Mexican Indians was a dream-keeper in her time. At certain times in the history of mankind they appear."

"Dream-keepers," Sonny repeated. The Bearers of Dreams of don Eliseo.

"Yes," Raven scoffed. "In the old days the shaman kept the Calendar of the Days, and each day had its power. But the Calendar of Dreams was more powerful. It was kept by the women. In the dream lies the power of the soul."

Sonny shook his head. In dreams he could know the past. But something clouded his dreams. Even as the mind evolved into a higher consciousness, it forgot the dreams. Was it simply forgetfulness that kept each generation repeating its karma, without memory of the past? Or was it Raven's power in the universe that closed off the knowledge of dreams?

"I curse all sides," Raven said. "I am the power inherent in the chaos."

God, Raven wanted to be a deity of chaos.

"You've got Consuelo, Catalina, and Carmen, but you need four young women," Sonny said.

"I'll get them," Raven replied arrogantly. "This thing with the bomb was only to get you here. But you can't even walk. How can I play games with a crippled man? I need a worthy opponent." He laughed and looked at Chernenko, who was holding the syringe.

"Drugs, our present gods of sleep." Raven smiled. "That rest so deep it allows the dreams to visit, to reveal the soul. Dreams are your salvation, Baca, and your end. Now it's time for you to sleep, and dream."

He took the syringe and tested it. A small stream of clear liquid shot into the air.

Sonny heaved, and using the strength in his arms, he pushed and stood up. He had to make a fight of it.

"Ah," Raven said in surprise. "He can stand."

"Shoot him!" the excited Chernenko said behind him. "Shoot him!"

Sonny took a wobbly step forward. He was used to pushing the wheelchair in front of him for balance. Now he had nothing to hold on to.

"Calm down, Doctor." Raven smiled, moving to the side, circling Sonny very slowly. "He's making it more interesting for me. Come on," he taunted, motioning to Sonny. "Come and get it."

Sonny turned slowly, facing Raven. Damn, he thought, it wasn't any good. His legs were already trembling. He had one burst of energy in them, so he grabbed a chair, lifted it, and took a giant step toward Raven, swinging the wooden chair as he toppled over.

Raven sidestepped and the chair splintered on the floor. Raven was instantly on Sonny's back, pinning him to the floor and stabbing the needle into the back of his neck.

14

Sonny reached for the needle dangling in his neck. He tore it away and tossed it at Raven, who had leaped to his feet.

"It's too late, Baca!" Raven shouted. "Too late."

Sonny rubbed the back of his neck where the needle had entered. Already he could feel the drug oozing into his nerves and bloodstream. Raven had picked something that would put him to sleep slowly, not a morphine knockout punch.

"Kill him!" Chernenko shouted, leaping forward and holding a curved sword.

Raven snatched the weapon and stood over Sonny. One blow could slice a man in half. Sonny had seen the effects of the sharp dark steel on the Los Alamos guards.

"No," Raven said mockingly. "I want him to dream."

Outside a shot cracked in the cold air, followed by another in rapid succession. Raven cocked an ear. "Ah, your friends have arrived."

"Police!" Chernenko cried in fear.

"Yes, Baca's friends."

"You knew," Chernenko said, fear mixing with surprise. "You knew they were coming."

"They've been watching you," Raven gloated.

Again the shots rang out, an automatic weapon, then silence.

"Our guards are dead," Raven said.

"The tunnel!" Chernenko shouted, pointing.

"Yes," Raven agreed. "But first let me pay you for your work, Doctor," he said, and raised the Saracen blade.

"No!" Chernenko cried as he crossed his arms to ward off the blow, but it came so quickly he could not fend it off. The scythe caught him just below the chin at the Adam's apple, cut open his throat, and sliced downward to split his chest, cutting through the sternum and stomach. A startled Chernenko reached down to hold in his guts, as if by stuffing them back into the cavity, he could ward off death. Blood spurted; he uttered a curse and fell.

"Consider yourself well paid," Raven whispered, and turned to Sonny. "Your friends are earlier than I expected," he said. "But it doesn't matter. We will meet shortly, in your next nightmare."

Through the numbness already spreading through his body, Sonny saw him disappear into the floor. A trapdoor, he thought, probably leading to a sewer. Raven always planned his escape routes well.

Sonny struggled to sit up, rubbing at his neck. The shooting outside had stopped; now he heard banging at the door. Three blows and the door splintered and in rushed Matt Paiz and four SWAT agents.

Never thought I'd be happy to see the FBI, Sonny thought with a smile. Just like the movies.

"You okay?" Paiz asked, leaning over Sonny, pistol raised and eyes searching the lab.

The other agents, pistols drawn, spread across the room.

One pointed at the Gadget, the bomb, and swore as he slowly circled it.

"Shot," Sonny mumbled, holding the back of his neck.

Paiz looked, and finding no blood, he couldn't understand what Sonny meant by shot. "Raven?"

"Yes."

"He used the tunnel," Paiz said, looking at the opening in the floor.

Sonny nodded.

"In there!" he shouted, and two SWAT men disappeared into the tunnel. "Any way to cut off the tunnel?" Paiz shouted at the man in jeans and a blue parka standing at the door.

The man turned and shouted something to the SWAT leader, and he ran out, followed by the FBI agents. Paiz holstered his pistol. By now Raven was probably at the lab's perimeter, leaping over a fence and driving away.

"All clear," Paiz said, and Rita entered, followed by Lorenza.

"Sonny, Sonny!" Rita rushed to him and held him in her arms. "Are you okay? Gracias a Dios you're alive," she said, glancing at Chernenko's disemboweled body.

"God, what happened here?" Paiz asked of no one in particular as he knelt near Chernenko and felt for a pulse that was no longer there. Then, removing his overcoat, he covered the dead man.

Sonny pointed at the syringe on the floor. "He gave me a shot."

Paiz picked up the syringe and smelled. "We'd better test this right away." He covered the syringe in his handkerchief and handed it to an agent.

"Something to sleep?" Lorenza asked, looking at Sonny's eyes.

Sonny nodded. Raven didn't want him dead just yet, he wanted him to sleep. His eyelids felt heavy, drowsy. The drug and the fatigue of the day worked together, lulling him into a warm, inviting darkness.

"How'ju find me?" he asked.

"Eddie Martínez, the FBI agent, was at *Las Posadas*," Rita explained. "When we couldn't find you, he called Paiz. He stayed to look for the girl—"

"The girl? Did he get Carmen?"

"Yes," Paiz answered. "She's reported missing. Apparently she took sick just before the procession started. She told the others she was going home, but she never got there."

Sonny cursed himself. They had gotten there too late. By the time the man in the black hat had lured him to the back of the house, Raven had already picked up Carmen. Now he had three girls.

With Paiz's help they lifted him into a chair.

"We got a description of the van," Paiz said. "We had spotted the same van here at the labs. I figured they were bringing you here."

"Ruined your stakeout?" Sonny said and yawned.

"You have to stay awake!" Lorenza said. "Can we get some coffee, ice?"

"Jack?" Paiz said.

The man in the blue parka nodded and punched his mobile phone. Sonny recognized him. Jack Ward, Sandia Labs CEO. The man had been in the news since the Cold War ended, trying to convince the public that the new mission for the labs was to help develop projects for private industry. He worked hand-in-hand with Eric at Los Alamos.

"Sleepy," Sonny moaned.

"You know why he wants you asleep?" Lorenza asked.

"Try to stay awake. Rub his shoulders," she said to Rita. "Hard. Get his circulation going."

Other men now entered the room, technicians. One, a man dressed in protective gear, carried a portable scintillation detector.

Ward, whose attention had been on the device in the middle of the room, pointed the man with the detector toward it. "I don't believe it," he whispered over and over. "I fucking don't believe it. This is something out of the past, a copy of the first atomic bomb."

All turned to watch the man with the detector sweep over the Gadget. He walked slowly around Chernenko's bomb. Two of them opened a panel and shone lights inside the Gadget. When they were done, they took off their protective headgear and looked at Jack Ward.

"Nothing," one of them said. "It's safe. There's no radioactivity at all. He's got a lot of wiring in place, but no pit."

"We got here in time." Paiz breathed a sigh of relief.

"Looks like it," the technician replied. "Wow. What about this?" He lifted the Zia medallion from where Raven had hung it and admired it.

"It belongs to Sonny," Rita said.

The man stepped across the room and handed it to her. She slipped it around Sonny's neck.

"I don't believe it!" Ward said. "We gave this man the run of the labs, complete secrecy, and he's building a fucking bomb! In my lab!" He looked at the coat-covered body of Chernenko on the floor. "He deserves what he got! He could have—" He shook his head and looked helplessly at Paiz. "All he needed was a pit. If they put one in there, they can blow the whole thing—" He didn't finish. He cursed silently.

"Yeah," Paiz agreed, "all he needed was the core." He turned to Sonny.

Sonny mumbled, "Raven knew Chernenko was being watched. He knew you would make a move as soon as you thought the pit was brought in. He's building another bomb somewhere in the city. . . ."

Someone arrived with Styrofoam cups of dark coffee. "Drink," he heard Rita say, and felt the hot liquid on his heavy tongue, the coffee dripping down the sides of his mouth.

It tasted good, something heaven-sent to his dry mouth. But he really couldn't fight the effects of the drug for long, and he didn't want to go to the hospital and get shot full of uppers. That would only postpone the meeting with Raven in the dream. Why not do it now and get it done with? Now or never. Turn the tables on Raven.

"Let me sleep," he whispered.

"He wants to sleep," Rita said to Lorenza.

"Sleep?" Lorenza asked.

"Yes."

"You're going to try to stop him in the dream?"

Sonny nodded. Come what may, the struggle had to take place in the dream world. Sonny would not be a bystander, he would actually be a participant in the dream.

"Coyote," he managed to say. Both Rita and Lorenza leaned close to listen.

"Yes," Lorenza agreed. "Coyote knows the world of dreams. Find Coyote." She turned to Rita. "Maybe he's found a way! We need to get him home!"

"You're taking him home?" Paiz asked. "Don't you think we should get him to a doctor?"

"We have a clinic—" Ward said, but Rita cut in.

"No, home is best," she insisted.

"Okay. Hope you know what you're doing. I'll call anyway, soon as we find out what's in the syringe."

"It's just something to make him sleep," Lorenza said.

Yes, Sonny thought, and felt himself being lifted. Someone had brought in his wheelchair. The wheels creaked as the chair moved, out into the cold night, past the bodies of Tallboy and Sweatband, past a swarm of SWAT figures looking like shadows from the underworld in the dark.

Somewhere a Christmas carol wafted through the cold night. It was probably nine o'clock, and somewhere a radio was playing carols. How nice, Sonny thought as he was lifted into the van. Rita put the serape around him. Around him the books he had collected had spilled on the floor of the van.

"We ran a few red lights," Lorenza explained as she swept the books aside.

"I'll clear you with the gate," Sonny heard Jack Ward say, his voice ringing from faraway.

He felt the van moving. "We're going home," Rita whispered, holding him in her arms. He was shivering. The night was cold, clear and frozen. The streetlights overhead seemed enveloped in fuzzy auras of light. Through the window a tile-covered Chevy appeared, riding high on a pedestal, then disappeared.

"A flying Chevy? Am I dreaming?" he asked.

"Not yet," Rita answered.

"Do you know where you are?" Lorenza asked.

Where I am? The same question don Eliseo had asked him right after Stammer juiced him. Knowing the here and now was something he knew he had to keep in mind. It centered his consciousness, his soul. It focused his identity in this world.

But the world was breaking apart, the seams were ripping open. The sacred regions were all plowed under or controlled by the feds.

"Novo Mexic," he answered sleepily, slurring the words. "Novo-Mesh-ic."

The ancestors of the Aztecs of Mexico, Owl Woman's people, had called this place Aztlán. The original homeland, the place of birth, place of covenant with the gods. Land of the pueblos. They named the sacred mountains, the rivers, the mesas. The Spaniards came to map it. Called it la Nueva México. Landscapes renamed, map overlaid previous maps, sometimes peacefully, most often violently. Que chinga, why was violence part of the naming ceremony? Why did the newcomers always have to rename, remap? The old people had kept the promise of the dream in their hearts, and waited. They knew the land was sacred. Sacred mountains, north, west, south, east. Sacred sun. Sacred food of the gods: corn, squash, beans, chile. Meat from the brother deer who gave his breath of life so the brothers and sisters might have sustenance. Bountiful summer rains of the spirits.

"We will keep it always," Sonny muttered.

"Yes," Rita answered as she and Lorenza got him down from the van and guided his chair into the house. Together they helped him into the bed.

"What does he need?" Rita asked.

"He needs to find Coyote," Lorenza answered. "Sonny, can you hear me?"

"Yeah, okay . . . feel dopey."

"Follow don Eliseo's instructions. Call Coyote. He can help. You need to set the stage. Do you understand?"

"Yes," Sonny mumbled.

Coyotes. He had first seen the coyotes when as a child he played along the Río Grande on visits to his grandparents in Socorro. He spent hours by the river, watching the coyotes play, and this most wily animal of the llano, the river, the hills, and forest had grown to trust him.

"Los coyotes," his grandparents whispered as they sat up late into the summer night, talking, discussing the day, the work, the growth of crops, animals, the neighbors, marriages and deaths, the weather, the acequia water flooding the fields under the moonlight of the Río Grande night, the crickets chirping away, filling the night with their love song.

"Habla la idioma de los coyotes," the grandfather said. The boy spoke the language of the coyotes.

How long had it been since a child who could speak to the animals had come to the pueblos south of Belén? They didn't remember. A few stories lingered. Los antepasados had told stories of those who spoke to animals. Now this boy, Francisco Elfego Baca, Sonny as he was called in school, spoke to the coyotes.

The voices of his grandparents grew hushed, and Sonny, who slept in a rollaway bed on the screened porch, caught only wisps of words.

They say his bisabuelo could also speak to animals. Those old vaqueros, him and Billy the Kid, they roamed the llano like coyotes.

Words with smiles turned to words of tragedy. It was a blessing, and it was a curse. The child who spoke to the coyotes would always have a strong guardian spirit to watch over him, but with it came a responsibility. A vortex of evil would gather around him to curse his footsteps. It had always been so.

"He's asleep," Rita whispered.

No, Sonny replied, not asleep. I'm preparing my dream.

Where to go? To my bisabuelo, Elfego Baca, and his adventures with Billy the Kid. Just now I heard my grandparents speak of them. For a reason. Maybe el bisabuelo and Billy have come to help me.

I will open the door, set the stage, call his name.

"Billy?"

A young man appeared. He was about five foot seven, with a slight build, brown hair, and blue eyes that sparkled. It was his friend, William Bonney.

Billy? Is that you, Billy?

Quién es? the Kid answered.

Sonny Baca. Hijo de Polonio Baca, nieto de Lorenzo Baca, bisnieto de Elfego Baca, tu amigo del condado de Socorro.

There, Sonny thought. I've described myself in my dream. That's a start.

Sonny, I've been waiting for you. The bucktoothed kid with wavy brown hair stepped out of the shadows and smiled. Lordy, Lordy, Sonny, am I glad to see you.

The Kid, twenty or so, held a Winchester rifle in one hand. A pistol hung easily on the belt around his waist. A wide-brimmed, dusty hat shaded his smiling eyes.

Where you going, Billy?

I'm going to Fort Sumner, Sonny. Come with me.

What's in Fort Sumner?

Didn't you know? I'm gonna marry Rosa, the prettiest flower on the Llano Estacado. I told you about Rosa. I'm going to marry her, settle down, raise children instead of raising hell.

Billy the Kid laughed good-naturedly, as was his manner. He looked happy.

Rosa!

Yeah, Paco's sister. You know that Mares/Luna clan from Puerto de Luna. She's related to María Luna, who was the daughter of Liborio Mares. Big family, lots of pretty daughters.

Billy continued speaking the names of the llano, the names of the Pecos River valley, and Sonny thought, Ah, so this is why I entered this time. Rosa is a grandmother! Billy is going to marry, give up his violent ways. Peace can come to Lincoln County and to the Llano Estacado.

Say you'll come, Billy pleaded. I want you to be my best man.

Rosa is a grandmother of the llano, that bloody land of the Nuevos Mexicanos cibolleros and comancheros who went from the villages of the Río Grande to hunt buffalo, to trade with the Comanches. Mexicanos from Taos, Mora, Pecos, Ranchos de Taos, Córdova, Truchas, Picuris Pueblo, Santa Clara Pueblo, and San Juan Pueblo.

They settled along the Río Pecos, founded the farming villages from Anton Chico to Puerto de Luna, and another dream was born. They grew corn, chile, and squash in the fertile valleys. Small adobe villages sprouted as the Nuevos Mexicanos claimed the eastern Llano Estacado. They sought the dream of peace.

But east of the llano in the land of the Santa Fé Trail, east in the place called Kansas, St. Louis, east in the land of the Americanos, the Civil War had just ended, years of bloody rage and murder had finally come to an end, and the war-weary soldiers of the South returned home to find devastation. Their homes were burned and their slaves were gone. Antebellum life had been turned upside down during the four long years of struggle. Many moved west, into Texas, across Texas and into New Mexico. New Mexico, they said in their southern drawl, a slang flavored with the Cajun tongue of Louisiana.

They moved west in search of a dream, and they brought with them the memory of violence from the killing fields of Gettysburg, Appomatox, Shiloh, and all the other battles where violence swelled and grew fat with the blood of men.

Cattle barons appeared on the stage, men eager to run the

Mexicans and Indians out of those plains, men who claimed the land and mapped it with barbed wire and a new language. Cowboys like Billy appeared, young men who learned horsemanship from the Mexican vaqueros and hired out to cattle rustlers.

Rosa belonged to Sonny's past. Part of his family had moved out of the Río Grande valley, spilling over the Sangre de Cristo Mountains onto the eastern plains, where the fat buffalo provided meat and hides. Families from Atrisco near Alburquerque, families from as far south as Socorro, finding the mountain passes to the old Abo and Quarai missions, and into the llanos of Mountainair, Vaughn, Roswell, Portales, Lincoln, Alamogordo, Carrizozo.

The U.S. Army constructed Fort Sumner on the banks of the Pecos, a fort in which to imprison the Navajos.

The tragedy never ceased. The Diné Nation was defeated by Kit Carson and the U.S. Army, and a once proud people were herded into concentration camps long before the world used such terms to describe the atrocity.

Now Billy was going to Fort Sumner, for Rosa, his love.

He's waiting for you, Billy.

Billy smiled. Hey, I've got my pistol handy. I can take care of myself. Besides, Pat Garrett may be sheriff of Lincoln County, but he's not going to come up to Fort Sumner.

I don't mean Pat Garrett, I mean Raven, Sonny replied. He had to go with Billy. He had chosen the dream.

I fear no man, Billy replied.

Pues, vamos, Sonny said.

That's what I like to hear! Billy smiled and put his arm around him. He slapped him on the back. You watch, we're going to have a grand time. Imagine me, Billy the Kid—el Desperado, as the eastern newspapers call me—married. Settled down and married. I'm giving up the gun.

They mounted their ponies and slapped leather, spurring and turning the horses east, rising a cloud of dust on the back trails to Fort Sumner, on the trail to meet their destinies.

Just like a movie, set the stage! Sonny shouted. Coyote, are you with us?

Ajua! The vaquero Coyote shouted, full of tequila and an urge to ride with those close to his soul.

Vamos! he, too, cried, following on his flaming steed.

15

Don Eliseo's here," Rita whispers.

Sonny thinks it's Rosa talking to Billy. His mouth is dry as cotton. He senses don Eliseo entering the room. Chica is nearby, whining. She understands he is caught in some sort of web; she wants to help him.

Sonny smiles. He can sense their presence, smell their perfumes. The sheets on the bed smell fresh, crinkly. They brought him here, to his bed, to sleep. He feels Rita's hands, ministering to him, and he feels the urge to make love to her.

Outside, a winter storm rages. Snow falls, driven by a cold wind. Sonny can feel the fury of nature around him, the fury that reflects the turmoil within. He feels hot, but Rita won't let him toss away the blankets that cover him.

He has only to say the word and they will awaken him, shower him in cold water, and fill him with coffee, take him to a truckstop where he can get enough uppers to keep him awake into the next century, but he doesn't want to be awakened. He must face Raven. Can't let him take Rosa.

"Where are you, Sonny?" It is the old man's voice.

Sonny struggles to open his eyes. "With Billy the Kid. Billy's girl in danger . . ."

"What's her name?"

"Rosa," he manages. "Fort Sumner."

"Who is Rosa?" Don Eliseo asks.

"A grandmother. . . ."

"What did the family tree say about families in the llano?" Don Eliseo asks Lorenza and Rita.

Lorenza answers. "Yes, there is a Mares/Luna branch. They settled in the Pecos River valley. Don Jesús had two children, Rosa and Paco."

Don Eliseo shouts in Sonny's ear. "She is your grandmother! Raven will be there! You must act in your dream! Understand? Act!"

Sonny knows this.

There is silence in the room, silence in Sonny's dream. He crosses the threshold of the luminous door, returning to the dream he is creating. Like an old Western movie. Keep hold of the story. Become the actor in your dream!

On the other side of the door he is greeted by Coyote. He is dressed in a shiny purple cowboy shirt, Mexican leather vest, a cheap one, the kind one buys in Juárez mercados, and jeans. A red handkerchief adorns his neck, and two low-slung pistols hang at his sides. He peers at Sonny. His nose twitches, smelling for Raven-danger, but he says nothing. His honey-colored eyes continue to stare at Sonny.

Coyote?

Yes.

You're here?

Been here all along, Coyote replies. His pistols are two Colt .45s in well-worn leather holsters.

Can you help me, pardner?

You want to find Billy?

Yes. Billy and Rosa.

You think you're ready, pardner?

Now or never.

Pues, vamos! Coyote calls, like an old Indian scout ready to lead Sonny into the underworld. He mounts his horse, a red stallion that rears and paws the air. He turns it smartly and skids down the slope of the mesa into a wide arroyo, leaving a cloud of red dust behind him. The cloud boils and becomes dark. Sonny follows on a skittish paint pony.

Can I reenter my dream? Can I find Billy? Can I be there to protect Rosa? For a moment he feels lost, a hot panic engulfs him. He can't see Coyote in the darkness.

Coyote, help me! he calls.

Spur that sombitch! Coyote shouts. Full speed ahead and damn the torpedoes!

He laughs, a wild Coyote laughter that echoes in the labyrinth they're entering. A wild howl of the West, for Coyote is the spirit of the West, the guardian animal of even those who hate him and poison him. His laughter echoes all the way from the Rocky Mountains to the Sierra Nevada of California. From the frozen reaches of Alaska to the Sonoran Desert. Even in the eastern cities he haunts dark alleys.

Vamos! he shouts like the old vaquero he is.

Sonny follows. As usual, Coyote is right on target. When Sonny reins in his horse, Billy appears.

Sonny! Billy calls. I'm darn pleased you came back. Boy, you missed the action. Tom and me and Charley Bowdre just rustled us up some cattle.

The cowboys around Billy laugh and disappear in a cyclone.

Life in the dream is no easier than in the other reality, Sonny thinks. In fact, it's damn harder! No matter what he says, he can't seem to control the dream.

You've got to get deep into the dream, Coyote urges. His

horse rears up. Coyote is an expert vaquero! A trickster! A carrier of the dreams!

Anda! Vamos! Sonny shouts, gathering his courage and mounting his pony. Let's find Billy! Let's see how deep I can go!

With purpose and gusto he rides into the rustling, gambling, and hard life of the New Mexico territory. From Tularosa to the Texas panhandle, Billy's boys are wanted men, and Sonny follows.

Folks, a reporter for the *Las Vegas Optic* writes, a dangerous drama is being played out in our territory. Down in Lincoln County a bunch of wild outlaws threatens our civilization. These murderous bullies have had their way with the law long enough. We, the law-abiding citizens, call upon the governor to stop this bloodshed once and for all.

Pat Garrett enters from the back of the stage. Azariah Wild has just made him a U.S. marshal, and Governor Wallace has just posted a five-hundred-dollar reward for William Bonney, alias Billy the Kid.

If no one else can stop Bill Bonney, I can, Pat Garrett vows, his words as dangerous as a rattlesnake bite, his eyes gleaming with determination. I know Billy from a long time ago. I know how he thinks, where he goes. I can be there waiting for him.

Sonny rides into Fort Sumner, hoping to catch up with Billy. He reins in, ties up, and enters the saloon. The fallen doves of the cantina are putting on a play. They take Sonny's arms and direct him to a seat.

I don't want to sit, I want to be on the stage, Sonny replies.

Oh, but this is not your play, a young whore with flaming red hair chides him. This is Billy's play. You just watch and clap in all the right places. Remember, life is but a waking shadow, and we the petty players that strut and fret our hour upon the stage and then are heard no more.

She goes off laughing.

Sonny watches Billy enter and meet his old friend, Paco Anaya. Paco embraces Billy. Oye, Bilito, que gusto me da verte. Anda, vamos a mi casa.

They move to center stage where don Jesús, his wife, and Rosa wait. They greet Billy with open arms. Anda, vieja, dales de comer a estos vaqueros.

Billy takes Rosa's hand and they walk on the open llano. They look at each other with deep attraction.

You've been riding hard.

Riding hard to see you. I hear there's a baile tonight in Fort Sumner.

Yes. Don Pedro Maxwell is having a fiesta. Are you going to the baile?

Only if the girl of my dreams will accompany me.

She must be very brave.

Why?

Because you're a bandido.

Bandido? I only draw my pistol when I have to protect myself.

They say you killed Sheriff Brady.

Brady killed John Tunstall. I was just settling the score.

We don't want the violence of Lincoln to come here. We want to live in peace—

Yeah. Live and let live. . . . But down the Pecos the Dolan vaqueros don't think like that.

And you?

Some of those vaqueros want my hide. . . . So I keep my pistol handy.

A person can change.

I've thought about that. Thought about getting myself a

ranch, minding my business, running a few head of cattle. Pero no es posible.

Por qué?

The territory changed after the war. All those southern soldiers and Tejanos returning home found nothing but ruin. So this has become the new battlefield, and the man who isn't armed gets pushed out.

My father isn't armed.

Yeah, but the Mexicanos down in Lincoln County carry rifles. A man needs to protect his family.

A man can change.

Become a sheepherder on the llano?

We are happy, we are content. We have our families, the vecinos who help, the fiestas of the church.

There's a U.S. warrant for my arrest. Somebody would come looking for me. Every time I try to change, someone starts a new fight.

So it is your destino.

You are my destino. He kisses her. Now, let's go dancing.

The cantina doves change the set. A wild dance full of polkas and rancheras. Billy and Rosa spin around the dance floor while a jealous Josefina watches. Josefina is Pedro Maxwell's daughter, and one of Billy's old girlfriends.

Sonny tries to rise but the young barmaid pushes him down. Shh. Just watch and listen.

They're in danger! Sonny protests, to no avail. He looks around for Coyote, but the trickster has gotten roaring drunk and is useless.

That moment of distraction is all the dream needs to fast-forward. Sonny hears Billy's plaintive cry, but he can't move.

Where are you? Sonny calls.

He peers into the dream stuff and sees Billy escaping

from the old Dolan store in Lincoln, shooting the deputies Bell and Ollinger on the way out.

Billy slaps leather for Fort Sumner. The Mexicanos, who realize that Billy is being used as the scapegoat for the crimes of the rich ranchers and politicians, help him.

As Sonny watches helplessly, he sees a cowboy dressed in black appear.

Raven, Sonny gasps.

I hear you're looking for Billy the Kid, Raven says to Pat Garrett.

The Kid is fast as a rattler, Garrett replies.

Ambush him, Raven whispers.

It ain't right, Garrett replies.

Billy ambushed Brady. An eye for an eye. Josefina Maxwell, the woman Billy spurned, will help.

No! Sonny shouts. Or thinks he shouts. In the dream he has no voice.

On the stage, Josefina approaches: Buenas noches, Sheriff Garrett.

Buenas noches. You're up late.

I can't sleep, Sheriff. I walk around the lonely streets at night . . . the people call me la Llorona. In my heart I am crying.

I'm looking for Billy. Where is he?

With his querida.

I've got a warrant for his arrest. I aim to take him, dead or alive.

If I cannot have him, no one can.

Do you know where he is?

Yes. Go to my father's bedroom. Wait there.

Garrett moves across the stage to wait.

A light shines on Billy and Rosa as they enter. Sonny attempts to rise to warn him, but he is a mere spectator in the dream.

Espera aquí, Billy says to Rosa, kissing her.

No. Voy contigo.

We have plenty of time to be together, querida. Tomorrow we leave for México.

A new life.

Don Pedro wants to see me.

Why so late?

He owes me some money. Josefina said he's ready to pay.

Josefina? No, Billy, don't go!

Why are you trembling?

There's no light in his room.

The old cheapskate doesn't like to burn his oil. Wait. Billy.

Qué?

Te amo.

Y yo te amo a tí. They embrace warmly, then Billy turns and softly enters don Pedro's bedroom. He senses Garrett.

Quién es? Quién es?

That's him!

Garrett?

Garrett fires once, Billy grabs at his gut in pain, steps forward, reaching for Garrett. Pat . . . You got me coldblooded.

Garrett fires again. Billy winces, stumbles. He falls and the figure of la Muerte stands over him.

There is a scream, and Rosa rushes in to gather Billy in her arms. Billy! Billy! Oh, Bilito.

I love you, Rosa. . . .

Amor, amor. . . . She rocks the bleeding Billy in her arms.

Sonny can no longer hold back the tears. Convulsive sobs

shake his body as the grief he feels comes pouring out. The cantina ladies have put on a great play, but it wasn't meant to be this way! Sonny knew he was supposed to take a part, to direct the dream play!

The bed shakes with Sonny's sobs, and a worried Rita is instantly at his side. She touches a wet cloth to his forehead and can only guess why tears flow from his eyes.

16

Outside, the storm intensifies. Pre-Christmas snowstorms don't often drop as far south as Alburquerque. Taos, Santa Fé, and the villages of the Sangre de Cristo Mountains receive the snows of early winter. From Chama to Questa to Raton, the same storms that sweep across Colorado strike with cold and snow, but the Duke City is most often spared.

At 5,280 feet above sea level, 'Burque lies at the foot of the Sandia Mountains, protected from the cold fronts that drop down from Canada when the jet stream dips south. Those cold masses of air slip down as far as the Texas panhandle. The arctic fronts freeze the eastern part of the state, as anyone raised in Clayton, Tucumcari, or Santa Rosa knows.

Such blizzards have been described by those raised in that eastern llano, those whose ancestors traveled there to hunt buffalos. Los cibolleros, comancheros, tough, hardy Nuevos Mexicanos who learned Comanche ways. When the going was good, they sat around and smoked the pipe with the tribes of the southern plains, traded goods, drank rotgut whiskey, mula, the New Mexicans called it. When the going was tough, there were skirmishes on the plains, and those who the prior year had called each other amigos now scalped each other. In the end the Comanches lost, not to the presence of the Nuevos Mexicanos, but to the presence of the Tejanos. The Texans wiped them out.

The Comanches were the Vikings of the plains, Sonny remembers reading in a book. It filters through his dream.

When things got dull fighting the Osages, or after a long, cold winter, they would swoop down to México for horses, women, and kids to work like slaves. They rode south to just plain kick ass with the Mexicanos. And of course, México was warmer than the plains in the winter. There were pretty Mexicanitas there, women to capture and bring north as slaves, to bring to the teepee as wives.

And the pulque, the drink of the Aztec gods, distilled from maguey, the liquid that burned the intestines also burned the mind, and visions came in drunken stupors. One could get roaring drunk and wasted on pulque. A man could go wild, fuck forever, become invincible. There was nothing like it on the plains. So what if the headaches came after days and nights of drinking. The Mexicanos had menudo, a rich stew made from the tripe of sheep. Spiced with hot chile, menudo cured the stomach and cleared the head.

While the young warriors attacked the Mexicanos, the old men, the shamans of the tribe, went out into the desert to collect the peyote buttons. Cactus medicine. Peyote god. Yes, they called him el Señor Peyote, because he deserved their respect and because he brought the visions that were far sharper and more sacred than those of pulque. Don Peyote, el Mero Chingón, un diosito who took you into another world—why, he was worthy of a new religion, a new faith, new followers.

Some of those same Comanches were captured by the Nuevos Mexicanos and brought back to the Río Grande settlements. They became farmers and began to dream of corn, give thanks to the Corn Mothers. They began to pray to the kachinas for rain for their dusty fields.

La Nueva México was becoming the crossroads of the southern belly of the continent, the womb. Here all could mix, produce the mestizaje, and here all could make war against each other. To the northern Río Grande came the Comanches, Navajos, Utes, Apaches, Mexicanos, farmers and hunters, Catholics and converted Jews, peninsular Spaniards and criollos, mestizos and genizaros, all came to the land of the Pueblos. Then arrived the Americanos, the Anglos, the gringos, gringos salados, gabachos, gueros, los Americanos de los estados unidos, speaking a strange tongue, praying to the Christ in the Bible, not the bloody Cristo on the penitente cross. There were the Yankee traders from St. Louis, and there were the mountain men, French fur trappers, too. This mixed bag began to call themselves New Mexicans.

"What's he saying?"

"He seems to be telling stories about the people of the llano."

"Sonny, get to Rosa. Where is Rosa?"

It is don Eliseo telling him to get on the stage. Billy is dead, and Raven will now go after Rosa.

Sonny groans deeply and returns to the dream.

Please be seated. The second act of our play is about to start, the cantina lady with the red hair announces. (Is she doña Loneliness, la puta who comes to sing the blues in the hearts of lonely men?)

It's July 14, 1881, and Billy is dead, she says in a sad voice. A grieving Rosa walks the dusty street to the church. A dry, hot wind moans across the flat landscape, sweeping up dust and tumbleweeds, whispering as it stirs the sere grass of the scorching summer.

The cantina lady withdraws, and everyone in the bar turns to look at the stage.

Rosa appears, dressed in black, and a lovelier Mexicana never walked that road to the church. The young men take their hats off as she passes, partly in grieving and partly in lust. Oh, what a beauty had given her heart to Billy. Her red lips once so full and warm with the fire of love, now whisper only prayers. Her dark eyes shine with tears. Her black hair is tied in a bun and covered by a black veil. There isn't a vaquero in Fort Sumner who wouldn't give his best horse to console the grieving Rosa.

Raven has other plans. He steps out of the saloon where he has been celebrating Billy's death. He has plans for Rosa. He walks out into the middle of the street in front of her. He, too, is dressed in black. Black hat, black shirt, black kerchief around his neck, black pants. Even his holster and pistol are black.

The villagers see Raven step out into the street, and they scurry for cover. The young men know they are no match for Raven's fast gun.

Billy's dead, he tells Rosa, a thin smirk on his face. Now you're mine.

Rosa looks at him, unflinching. Murderer! she replies. I will never belong to you! You are evil!

Evil is as evil does, Raven answers coldly. It's time to come with me.

Now! Coyote nudges Sonny. It's now or never!

Yes, it's time to act. With Coyote at his side he knows he has the will to direct his dream. He can stop Raven!

No! Sonny shouts from where he sits. Rosa and Raven turn to look as Sonny struggles to stand. They are surprised to see him on his feet.

Sonny!

You don't belong here! Raven shouts. Stay out of this!

Is he worried that I've found a way to face him in my dream? Sonny thinks, and looks down at his legs. They have been numb for so long, but now they seem to be holding him up. He takes a step and tests their strength.

He turns to Coyote. Help me.

Coyote nods. He understands the soul of this young man, understands the goodness within, and there stands Raven, an old enemy from long ago. Raven can move back and forth into the dream world because evil sorcerers taught him how. But this is not the trickster bird of many an Indian legend. This Raven is a sorcerer in the guise of the forest bird.

The world of the spirits is bound to the world of the flesh, Coyote says, twirling a rope. The flesh dreams, the dreams yearn for flesh, both are one. In the heart.

Sonny shakes his head. He doesn't understand. He only knows Raven will not wait forever. He is ready to take Rosa.

Can I play the main role in my dream? His words stumble, one upon the other.

Yes. There are not two worlds. Dream and waking, it's all the same. Raven and the sorcerers separated the worlds. They set themselves up as the priests who could take you into the dreams to interpret them. But the road of symbols is clear to anyone who wills to see.

This is what Owl Woman taught us.

That and many other things, Coyote replies. The Calendar of Dreams holds your dreams.

Sonny feels the hot July breeze cool the sweat on his neck. He steps forward, slowly, feeling the blinding sun overhead, the shadow of two turkey vultures circling overhead. There's something rotten on the road to Tucumcari.

He feels the Colt .45 strapped to his side, the pistol of his bisabuelo, Elfego Baca. He has never used the pistol. Can he use it now?

You can't have her, Raven! Sonny calls. She belongs to my history. She's one of my grandmothers.

Raven turns and hurls his curse into the wind: I will erase your memory forever!

The townspeople shrink from his words, words that can destroy many of them if Sonny's history is unraveled. All scurry to hide.

This is *my* dream! Sonny replies. If you're going to take her, it's over my dead body.

Raven's birdlike eyes narrow. There is concern there. Has Sonny learned to *act* in his dream?

He curses Coyote: May your name be erased from the legends of all people, Coyote! You meddlesome freak!

Coyote merely laughs. His twirling rope becomes a whirlwind. Hats, tumbleweeds, trash are swept up in the roaring wind.

You belong to me, Sonny says to Rosa. You are my history.

Sonny! Rosa cries and starts toward him.

A young man who would one day be her grandson has come to rescue her from the anonymity with which Raven threatens her. Even Billy the Kid, the young man she had truly loved, had not been able to do this. Billy was too caught up in his karma, too much of the world of the flesh. He did not truly know that to love is to dream. He had been caught up in the violence created by Raven, too trusting in his gun.

But Sonny is different. Sonny knows how to fight Raven, and now he has found her in the dream world. He had come to make sure her life is lived out. He knows generations must issue from her womb, and the blood of birth bathe her loins. Yes, she will people the llano, and from her sons and daughters will come one of the families of Sonny's past.

No! Raven shouts, and grabs her arm. She's mine!

Let her go! Sonny cries, his fingers resting lightly on his pistol.

You haven't found the way! Raven tests him. You're not here! You're not in the dream! Your grandfather's pistol is worthless.

Sonny hesitates, looks at Coyote.

You need not be the victim of your dreams, Coyote assures him. The dream is yours, it's part of the memory of many generations. It's the blood speaking. The dream is the dream of your ancestors.

Yes. Sonny knows. He turns to face Raven.

I'm here all right, Sonny replies. Make your move.

He glances out of the corners of his eyes. The people of the adobe village have taken cover. Eyes peers from dark windows, from behind parted curtains.

Damn you! Raven cries, flinging Rosa aside and drawing his pistol. The report of his pistol echoes across the dry land, startling men and beast alike. The bullet strikes Sonny in the chest, its force like a fist. Sonny reels from the impact, but does not fall. There is no blood: Raven has met a man who cannot die!

The people step outside and cheer. Raven cannot stop Sonny.

Raven looks surprised. Yes, he knew Sonny would be strong, guided as he was by Coyote, his old enemy, but not this strong. He has withstood the force of the bullet.

I underestimated you, he says with a smile, drawing back.

Sonny advances, walking slowly. According to the rules

of the Old West, he now has the right to draw his pistol and fire at Raven.

I'm in control now, Sonny replies with confidence. I claim Rosa, my grandmother.

So you've learned to enter the dream, Raven sneers, hate contorting his scarred face. Coyote helped you! He and the meddlesome don Eliseo! And la bruja Lorenza!

Yes, Sonny replies. I can enter my dreams, so can every man, woman, and child. You and your sorcerers have separated us from our dreams for too long. Now we return. Your power is failing you, Raven.

Raven grits his teeth, his voice is strident. We'll see about that! I promise you, we will meet again! He turns, mounts his horse, and rides out of the village.

Rosa rushes into Sonny's arms. My son, my son, she cries. You saved me.

You got him! Paco slaps Sonny on the back.

The townspeople rush forward to surround Sonny, smiling, cheering.

The mayor steps forward to place a sheriff's badge on Sonny. Young man, you have saved our town, and our women, from that scoundrel. Please stay and be our sheriff. We're tired of the violence and murder that sweeps across our territory.

I can't stay, Sonny replies, looking at the sun setting in the west. Raven is still out there, in the night.

He feels under his shirt and touches the gold Zia medallion. Raven's bullet struck the medal, and it saved his life.

He mounts his horse. The villagers look up with sadness, the women touch hankies to their eyes, the men take off their hats and hold them over their chests. In respect.

A little boy runs up to Sonny. Don't leave, Sonny, please don't leave. He is crying.

We'll never forget you, Paco says, his voice hoarse with emotion.

Sorry I couldn't save Billy, Sonny says.

It was his fate, Paco says. You know, el destino. It was meant to be.

Our dreams affect our destiny, Rosa adds. Thanks to you, we can go on dreaming. She reaches up and takes Sonny's hand. Adiós, mi hijo. Cuídate.

Adiós, Abuela, Sonny replies.

His nervous pony rears up, then Sonny turns it smartly and rides into the sunset.

Tears dampen Sonny's eyes as he sees himself riding into the brilliant sunset. A private investigator shouldn't be crying, he chides himself.

"Sonny," Rita whispers.

Sonny opens his eyes and smiles.

Part III

The Shaman's Guide

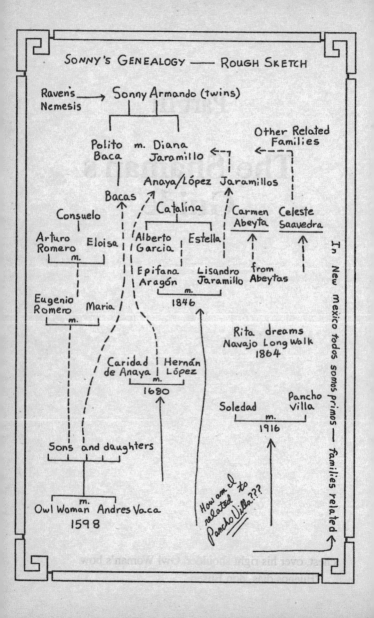

17

Sonny opened his eyes. He could sense dawn breaking outside, the first flush of morning light filling the valley. Rita opened the curtains and came to his side.

"How do you feel?"

"He didn't get Rosa, . . ." Sonny said hoarsely, and added, "Thirsty."

She held a straw to his lips and he sipped the water. Chica jumped in bed with him, wagging her tail eagerly, licking him.

"Chica, how are you?" He rubbed her and she responded by turning belly up to have her stomach scratched.

"Can you eat something?" Rita asked.

"No, gracias. I feel like I'm still floating. Lorenza?"

"She was here most of the night, but I sent her home to get some sleep," Rita answered.

"Don Eliseo?"

Rita nodded in the direction of Sonny's wheelchair, where the old man sat drinking coffee. Behind him on the chest, over his right shoulder, Owl Woman's bowl.

"Buenos días, don Eliseo."

"Buenos días, Sonny." The old man didn't stand. He looked exhausted. "Did you get him?"

"I scared him off," Sonny replied, sitting up, then leaning on the pillows Rita offered. Bit by bit he related the dream.

When he was done, don Eliseo seemed pleased. "You learned to follow Coyote into the dream. And you set the stage. A play in a dance hall, you said. Not bad. How were the dancing ladies?" He chuckled.

"Actually one with red hair tried to keep me sitting down and watching for a while," Sonny remembered.

"Probably one of Raven's helpers," don Eliseo noted. "But you got there. Most people *see* their dreams from a distance, and when they report the dream, they talk about what happened to them. They are never active participants in the dream. Sure, they learn a little more about themselves, but not much. Why? Because the dream acts on them. What you're learning is to enter a great source of energy."

"Why me?" Sonny asked.

The old man sipped his coffee.

"You were chosen," don Eliseo said simply. "It goes back to when the earth was a turtle swimming in the blue sky around the sun. Man and Woman lived in the womb of the turtle. It was very dark. There was no light, little air to breathe. In the dark they heard the frightening sounds of evil sorcerers who also lived with them in the womb of the turtle. Man and Woman wanted to get away from the sorcerers.

"They sent scouts through an opening to the surface. The scouts came back and said there were green forests, mountains with deer, streams with fish on the turtle shell. But Man and Woman didn't know how to break through the shell. They remained in the dark underworld.

"In those times Coyote and Raven were brothers, they were tricksters. That's what they were born to be. Anyway, one time Coyote and Raven were walking near a cave where water came up from the ground, and they heard the people beneath the shell calling to them.

" 'Get us out of here,' the people said, 'and we will reward you.'

"Coyote and Raven ran to Owl, one of the wisest creatures in the forest.

" 'We heard the voices of those who live beneath the earth,' they told Owl. 'We must help them come and live on the shell of the turtle with us. How can we do that?'

" 'Climb on my wings,' Owl said, 'and I will take you there. But be prepared. There are many dangers when one travels to the underworld.'

"So Coyote climbed on one wing and Raven climbed on the other wing, and Owl flew down the cavern where they had heard the voices.

"They went through many adventures on the way down. The heart of the earth pounded so loud that they had to cover their ears with wax. That is why we have wax in our ears. They had to cross a river of fire and fight off the burning boulders that pelted them. Anyway, they came to the center where the people lived.

" 'Help us break through the turtle shell, and you will be our heroes. We will tell our grandchildren stories about you,' the people told Raven and Coyote.

" 'Raven,' Owl said, 'with your beak you peck at the shell and make a hole on the crust.' Raven pecked and made a hole.

" 'Coyote, stick your tail into the hole, and Man and Woman will grab it. When you feel their tug, pull.'

"Coyote stuck his shiny tail down the hole and soon he felt Man and Woman grab his tail. He pulled, and Man and Woman came through the hole to the surface of the earth.

"Unfortunately, the evil sorcerers also grabbed Coyote's tail, and so they, too, came to live on the earth.

" 'You will always be our brothers,' Man and Woman said. 'We will honor you by telling many stories about you.'

"Coyote and Raven continued to help Man and Woman. They taught them to hunt and fish and gather grains and nuts. They taught them to respect life, from the smallest to the greatest.

"But the evil sorcerers who had sneaked up from the underworld didn't like the stories about Coyote and Raven. 'We want the people to desire more than they will ever need,' the sorcerers said. 'Let us turn Coyote and Raven against each other. This way we can take their place.'

"So they devised a contest. The idea was to return to the center of the earth to retrieve the dreams that Man and Woman had left there. It seems that in their haste to climb Coyote's tail, they had left their dreams behind.

" 'No problem,' Raven said and he flew down the hole he had pecked in the turtle's shell and brought up all the dreams he could carry in his beak. During his return there was a loud explosion in the river of fire. The dreams fell to the ground, and when he gathered them up, they were all jumbled. That's why our dreams often are mixed up.

" 'I can go down for the dreams he left behind,' Coyote said, and wrapped his long tail around a tree and climbed down. He picked up the remaining dreams and was climbing up when the sorcerers cut his tail. That's why coyotes now have shorter tails. He fell and dropped the dreams, so what he brought up was also very jumbled.

"Man and Woman, who were an old grandfather and grandmother by now, gathered the dreams as best they could and gave a dream to each nation. But the dreams were all mixed up, and it took a great deal of preparation and fasting for each person to have a true vision of the original dream.

" 'This is not easy,' Man and Woman said to Coyote and Raven. 'We expected our dreams would be easy to understand.' They chased off Coyote and Raven. Never again would the two live in the human houses. Raven and Coyote each thought he was the king of the tricksters, so they went on arguing and pulling tricks on each other to this day."

Don Eliseo paused.

"Interesting," Sonny said. "You should publish your stories."

The old man laughed. "A trickster has special powers. In the story they not only help Man and Woman come to earth, they return for the dreams they left behind. But a trickster is also very proud. He thinks he's numero uno. The sorcerers use that pride to create conflict."

"So Coyote and Raven, the old tricksters, represent our nature," Sonny said. "They're two sides of the same coin."

"Yes," don Eliseo replied. He stood slowly and went to the bed. "Bueno. I better get some sleep. Rest well, Hijo." He leaned and pressed his forehead to Sonny's.

"Gracias," Sonny said, thanking the old man for his blessing.

"What would I do without him?" he said to Rita when they heard don Eliseo shut the front door behind him.

"He loves you like a son," Rita said.

"And you?"

"I love you like my lover, mi alma."

"Come here," he said, and drew her to him. "Did I ever tell you how much I love you."

"You sure it's not just my cooking?" She smiled and pressed close, her body fitting his.

"Your cooking, your body, everything," he whispered, nibbling on her ear.

"Last night you could have been killed, and you still want to make love."

"I came back for you, Rosa."

"Rita."

"Rosa, Rita, I want you."

"And I want you."

"Escaping death gave me the ganas."

"I dig ganas."

"Tengo ganas."

"Yo también."

He kissed her, a deep satisfying kiss. She responded.

"Take off your robe."

"First we bathe you, amorcito. I like my man to smell like piñon, like sage, like the wind that whispers across the mesa."

"And I don't?"

"You smell raunchy," she teased, "like you've been riding a horse on the dusty llano." She disappeared into the kitchen, returned with a cup of fresh coffee and a washbasin full of hot water.

She pulled the sheets back. Chica looked up. "Sorry, Chica, but we need a little privacy for this." Rita lifted Chica up and put her in her basket on the floor; then she dipped a washcloth in the basin and began to bathe Sonny.

"Your fever's gone," she said as she scrubbed.

"I have fever for you," he said, lying back and enjoying the coffee and her sensuous touch.

Outside the storm had abated. The raging winds moved east, over the Sandias and across the eastern llano toward the Texas panhandle.

"So, part of your family tree comes from the llano," she said as she sponged him.

"Yeah. My dad used to take us to Santa Rosa when he was alive. He knew people there, primos. The Campos brothers, George González, the Chávez family. Soon as I get better, I'm going to start looking up my primos."

"They're probably spread all over the state."

"Probably."

"When you called Billy and Rosa's names, don Eliseo knew where you were."

"He's taken Owl Woman, Caridad de Anaya, and Epifana Aragón. If he had taken Rosa last night, that's four. No more Sonny Baca."

"And those three correspond in some way to the girls he's kidnapped: Consuelo, Catalina, and Carmen," Rita said. "But if you were actually in the dream, now you can stop him."

"Not really. I could face him and frighten him off, but there's another level. Raven has a circle of evil in this world, so he must have one in the world of spirits."

"And he's safe there?"

"Yes."

"Everywhere you turn, there's danger." She sighed.

He heard her sigh, knew she worried. He touched her arm and said, "Gracias."

"For what?"

"Taking care of me."

"I love you," she said, rubbing him vigorously with a towel. His chest, stomach, arms, legs.

"Feels good."

"Brings the circulation back. Now for the anointing."

"Ah," he smiled, "the oil of love."

She had a special oil, a base of almond oil, which carried

the fragrance of pine or piñon, sage, the scent of roses, a faint sting of menthol.

Sonny loved it. Nothing took out the soreness like her balm and the magic of her fingers.

"Anoint my head," Sonny whispered.

"Malcriado," she whispered as she caressed the length of his body, playing with him and arousing him. He closed his eyes and listened to her, her words purring in the soft morning light. "Mi niño, pobre huerfano que no tiene papá, tu eres m'ijito."

He took a deep breath and whispered back, "Estoy en la gloria."

"No Gloria, Rita."

She laughed and slipped out of her robe. For a moment she stood naked in the early morning light that shone through the windows.

"Dios mío." He reached up, placed his hand on her stomach, caressed her hip. "Te amo."

"Y yo te amo a tí," she said, and slipped in beside him, covering them with the sheet and blanket.

"But you're tired. Maybe—"

"No," she said. "I'm fine."

He turned to face her, fitting perfectly into her body. "You're sweet and warm. Like pan dulce."

"Are you hungry?"

"Yes."

"You want breakfast first?"

"You are my breakfast."

He pulled her toward him, moving his hands along her curves, the soft mounds and recesses he knew so well.

Something like the breath of life, a deep gratitude for the beauty she brought to him, quickened in him. It flowed like a hot river of love through him, creating a hunger, a need, a yearning in his stomach, his groin.

"You feel good."

"So do you."

The sweetness of apricot blossoms touched his nostrils.

"My sinus is clearing up. Feels like spring."

"Yes."

"Little green apples."

"You can eat . . ."

"Here?"

"Yes," she said, guiding him. "Nibble, don't bite!"

"You're sensitive?"

"No, feels good."

Yes, maybe he had pressed too hard. He felt something different in her.

"What is it?"

"A secret."

"Do you want to stop?" he asked, afraid of asking her to reveal her secret.

She moaned and pulled him tighter to her. "Oh, no . . ."

She was ready for loving, as ready as he.

"I want you, I'm hungry."

"Huevos rancheros?"

"Uuuum." He made a slurping sound.

"I'll fix you some as soon as—" she said, snuggling closer. She closed her eyes, enjoying the way he satisfied her, enjoying his tongue on her skin.

She did taste different, he thought. Not the Rita of summer. Something had changed her. The season. Winter has come to grace her, and I will worship her on this altar, our bed.

"Better," he said.

"Butter?"

"Yes. I'd like to cover your skin with butter and—"

"I'll get it—" She started to pull away, teasing him.

He drew her back to him. "You stay. I'll eat you without butter, this time."

She closed her eyes and smiled, her hands like warm doves over his body.

"Oh, you're going to make me—"

"I want to."

"I had fever, remember."

Her hands like butterflies, hovering over his sex.

"I'll take away the fever."

He laughed softly. "Oh, you're naughty. I love it. A curandera who goes all the way!"

"Only with you, amor."

The image of an apple orchard in bloom appeared around her.

"We don't have to—" He would be content to lie with her, explore the beauty of her body, with her wrapped in his arms, warm, safe.

"Te quiero." Her voice was so soft, her hands guiding him again, the dove's feathers wet, the perfume like the aroma of the earth after a summer rain.

"Te quiero con todo mi corazón."

She slipped over him. The bed creaked. She pressed on him, her body dissolving into his. Her lips teased him, her tongue like a hummingbird's, gathering nectar from a dark flower.

She whispered words. "Ay, que calientito . . ."

"Como pan dulce."

"You're still hungry . . ."

"No, don't stop."

Her motion was thrusting now, their bodies moving to the pleasure of touch, smell, sweet breath, the warm kisses, the heart of hers melting into his, his sweat mixing with the oil, releasing a new fragrance, the oil of love.

His hands moved over her.

"I want to."

"Yes . . ."

The bed creaked harder, the rhythm increasing in anticipation, he thrusting upward, and she meeting him.

"Cariño!"

"Ay, amor!"

"Please don't stop!"

"I never want to stop!"

A moan sounded, soft at first, then more frantic as it grew into a release, a primal sound coming from deep within her. Time exploded in brilliant colors as she grew taut, breathing hard until she collapsed, and both were consumed in sweat.

"Ahhhh . . ." He breathed for air.

"I love you, amor. Me haces loca."

"I love you, morenita. Por siempre."

Then, wrapped in each other's arms, they slept.

18

He moved his arms and felt the stiffness in his legs. He stretched, feeling like a lion stretching, taking pleasure in the cracking of his spine and joints, feeling his muscles ripple.

"Ah, good," he groaned. He smiled, felt the bed beside him. Rita was gone, but her fragrance lingered. His nostrils twitched, like a male coyote smelling the air for his female. Ah, even his sense of smell was returning.

"Damn my tired bones!" he shouted. "I'm getting better!"

He looked out the window and gave thanks. "Santo día."

The storm had powdered the valley with a thin, white blanket. Sandia Crest wore a white scarf. The sun shone brightly on the snow, and Sonny whispered a prayer, the morning blessing for life don Eliseo had taught him. "Bless Rita. Bless this woman that brings love into my life. Bless all of life. Bless my mother, Lorenza, Armando, don Eliseo, don Toto, Concha, Diego and his familia, Howard, all the lowriders, the cholos, los pintos, los enfermos, the trees and plants that sleep. Bring clarity to my soul."

Lord, I need it, he thought.

In the kitchen he heard voices. He sniffed the air. Posole. Someone was cooking a pot of posole with pig's feet. Tortillas on the comal. Damn, only *real* women cooked tortillas on the comal these days. The spicy aroma of red chile. His stomach growled.

On the chest of drawers sat the bowl, the Calendar of Dreams. Even from his bed he could make out the symbols that delicately wound their way around the outside of the bowl. Would their meaning be revealed in a dream, in a future meeting with Owl Woman, the grandmother from the south, the woman who would have delivered the dreams to la Nueva México?

El Norte. Once the region had been part of México, and the Indians from the Río Grande valley had traded far to the south, as far as the western coast, as far as la perla del Pacífico, Mazatlán, place of the deer, seashells, abalone, and mother of pearl for necklaces. South into the jungles of Chiapas, home of the Maya, where they traded for the brightly colored feathers of macaws, parrots, the quetzal bird. The colorful feathers of the birds who spoke to the sun.

Once there was no border between nations, only trade routes, roads like those at Chaco used for ceremonial purposes.

Once there were only the natives, visiting their vecinos. They needed roads, trade routes. Once it was all sacred land.

That is what the bowl said.

Next to the bowl Rita had hung the Zia medallion. It had saved his life last night. More important, he realized that the medal now belonged to him.

He felt the pressure of his bladder, sat on the side of the bed, and stood slowly. He tested the strength of his legs, reached for the chair, and pushed it ahead of him into the bathroom.

He had finished showering and dressing when Rita knocked at the door. "Buenos días, amor. How do you feel?"

"Feel great," Sonny replied, opening the bathroom door. Chica came rushing in.

"You look a lot better," Rita said, kissing him.

"Glad to be back in the world of the living," he said, caressing her back. "Gracias por tu amor."

"Mi placer."

"As the old people used to say, el amor fixes everything."

"They were right, you know. Don Eliseo and Lorenza are here, breakfast's ready."

"No time for a quickie?"

"Míralo," she teased him. "What a man."

"Gracias." He smiled back. "You look great," he said, admiring her.

"Thank you. You look great, too."

"I'm hungry," he replied. "Feel like I haven't eaten in weeks."

"We've got a feast for you," she said.

"I can smell it. Shouldn't you be at work?"

"I went by earlier. Everything's fine. Marta is working full-time now, and she's a great manager."

He slipped into the wheelchair, picked up Chica, put her on his lap, and followed Rita into the kitchen. Don Eliseo and Lorenza sat around the small table.

"Hey, Sonny, you're just in time for some huevos rancheros," don Eliseo said.

"Buenos días," Sonny replied. "I'm ready. Hi, Lore."

"Hi to you. How do you feel?"

"Like a new man. Thanks for saving my ass last night."

"De nada." She smiled.

"I feel like James Bond getting rescued by two lovely

women," Sonny said, taking a hot tortilla from the plate and slapping butter on it.

"James Bond doesn't hold a candle to you," Rita said, placing a plate of huevos rancheros in front of him.

The taste of eggs, potatoes, and beans smothered with green chile was like manna from heaven. He tore into the warm tortillas, the breaking of bread for the new day, and devoured them. He was alive, not fully recovered, but alive. And he had friends watching over him. He was thankful.

"That's a good sign," Rita said, pleased he was eating. She filled big bowls with posole for everyone, garnishing it with oregano, freshly diced onions, red chile.

"Um, posole. It's beginning to feel like Christmas." Sonny dug into the corn and pig's feet stew.

But even the renewed energy and the food could not completely dispel Sonny's anxiety about how little time was left to find Raven, and the impending doom of the consequences if he didn't.

While he ate, he told the dream. When he finished, he burped and sat back in his chair. He had eaten a huge plate of huevos rancheros, a big bowl of posole, and a dozen tortillas. Now he reached for the biscochitos, the Christmas cookies Rita baked for her restaurant, munching as he drank coffee.

"It's a good sign," Lorenza said. "You stopped him from taking Rosa."

"If I know Raven, he'll try something else," Sonny said.

"Yes," don Eliseo said. "Never forget, Raven plays games. He recognizes you as an old soul, an old enemy. You stand in his way, and he doesn't like that. He won't rest until he gets you. Once and for all."

Sonny paid attention; the old man's words were ominous. "Once and for all," he had said. They had come to this point in history. Their struggle had to come to an end.

Stopping Raven in the dream was one thing, but in the real world he held three young girls captive, and he had the capacity to construct a bomb.

"I've got to find him," Sonny said.

"Don't start thinking about going out again," Rita said, rubbing his shoulders. "You need to rest."

Sonny took her hand and kissed it. "I feel better, really. But I have to find the girls."

"How?" she asked. There were no clues.

Sonny looked for help at Lorenza and don Eliseo.

"There is a pattern," Lorenza said. "You figured out he would strike at *Las Posadas*."

"Yeah. What's next?"

"He organizes around the winter solstice," don Eliseo said. "December twenty-first."

"Tomorrow," Sonny said.

"Yes. The shortest day of the year, the sun is at its weakest point. This time of the year we are aware of the dying light. We *feel* the season ending, the cold, short days, so like our ancestors of long ago we respond. Our spiritual life needs to be renewed. Some put up Christmas trees, lights, reminders of days when we prayed to the sun. The Aztecs used to sacrifice butterflies and lizards on the winter solstice. Offer the beauty of the small creatures to the weak sun so it would return north to warm the land. To grow corn, squash, chile. In the pueblos the people hold dances. The deer come down from the hills. Without the sun there is no life. Raven knows this. At this point in the sun's journey he will try to destroy it."

"Blow up the bomb?"

"Yes."

"The sonofabitch has everything on his side," Sonny swore.

"Not yet. He needs four of these young women for his kingdom," don Eliseo said. "Until he has four, the girls are safe. After that—" He shrugged. No one knew. "Well, I better be on my way," he said, sipping the last of his coffee. "Gracias por el almuerzo, Rita. Bien sabroso."

"De nada, don Eliseo. Thank you for everything."

"Ah, I feel I've done so little. In my bones I feel the time of the sun standing still. I keep thinking of the messages in the bowl. You know, being human, we have so many limitations. Just about the time we figure out what life is all about, we die."

"You're not going to die," Sonny said, and took the old man's hand. "You're as healthy as— What is it Concha said?"

"She says I'm as healthy as her grandfather's mule," don Eliseo said, smiling. "I remember don Liborio riding that mule from here all the way to Bernalillo. Don Liborio used to go there to drink wine with his friends and gamble at the cockfights. Late at night he would get on his mule and fall asleep. The mule brought him back home. The old man died, the mule lived on for many years."

"I agree with Concha," Sonny said, "you'll live as long as the mule." But something in the old man's tone caught his attention.

"Oh, my health is good," don Eliseo agreed, glancing at Lorenza. "But sooner or later we begin to see death in our dreams. Just as you did last night. Raven is your death waiting to happen. Sooner or later we have to enter that dream . . ." His words hung in the air with an illuminating certainty.

Sonny cleared his throat. "So where are you headed today?"

"Up to Sandia Pueblo, to say prayers with the medicine men."

"Are they performing *Las Posadas* there?"

"No, but they have a Matachines dance on Christmas Eve."

"Doesn't la Malinche play the part of the Virgin in the dance?"

"Yes."

Sonny looked from Rita to Lorenza. "Another dance with a virgin in it. If we follow this line of thinking, there are just too many bases to cover. Christians are celebrating the birth of Christ—" He paused. "The Virgen de Guadalupe was a new dream of peace after the Spanish conquest. Is that it?" He asked in frustration.

"You're close," don Eliseo said. "But you have to extend the meaning of birth. The birth of every child represents a new dream, a new possibility. A child will come to lead us from war to peace. That's the hope. Owl Woman was to marry the capitàn and give birth to a new community, a new possibility. There's a clue there."

"A child shall lead us," Sonny said, "but Raven doesn't want the child of peace to be born."

He looked up at the old man. He was in his eighties and still going to the pueblo to join in the prayers. Walking out in the predawn cold to pray to the sun. His prayers, and those of many like him, were what kept the sun going. They believed that, and so it was.

He held the old man's arms. "Gracias," he said.

"Que los Señores y las Señoras de la Luz iluminen tu vereda," don Eliseo replied, leaning to touch his forehead to Sonny's. "Y que el Tata Sol, los santos, y las kachinas te cuiden."

He blessed Sonny. He believed in the young man. He knew the ordeal Sonny was going through, and only he fully knew the import of Sonny's struggle with Raven.

"I am going to make you a dream catcher," he said. "Some of the men from the pueblo brought down some juniper branches. It is one more piece of medicine in your fight against Raven."

"I catch him with the dream catcher?" Sonny asked.

"No, you make him pass through the hole in the middle, and like a bad dream he disappears. You will see." He turned and went out the kitchen door, into the cold morning. Chica scampered after him.

"I love that old man," Sonny said. "Imagine, going to the pueblo to join in the ceremony. At his age he ought to be content to stay in front of his warm stove."

"He needs to be at the pueblo with his vecinos. They consider him a war chief—" Lorenza began.

"War chief?" Sonny interrupted. "I never knew—"

"Those involved in the ceremony don't talk about their roles. But he's been around the pueblo so long they consider him one of them. He's fought the big battles in his time," Lorenza said as she started clearing the dishes.

"Against Raven?" Sonny asked.

"Those like him," she replied.

Yes, Sonny thought, in his youth don Eliseo had been like Sonny, tempted and pursued by the evil sorcerers who had always plagued humanity. Now he was instructing Sonny. Last night he had figured where Sonny was in the dream, and it helped Sonny face Raven.

"And the dream catcher?"

"We'll see."

"One thing compounds to another, and I don't even have the time to—"

Rita put her arms around his neck. "Time to enjoy life. I know, amor. But what you have to do will save a lot of lives. I called your mom this morning. Told her you're fine. Didn't mention what happened. She sends her love, wants us to come and eat Christmas dinner with her."

He kissed her hands. "Gracias."

"And Chief Garcia called last night, just after we got here. To congratulate you on exposing Raven's lab. He was complaining that the FBI hadn't shared any of the information with him until last night."

"They look down their noses on the local cops," Sonny said. "But something like a nuclear threat will bring them together."

The phone rang. Sonny frowned, looked at Rita and Lorenza, then picked it up. "Hello," he said, crossing his fingers that it was not another report of a girl missing.

"Sonny, good morning, Leif Eric here. Talked to Matt Paiz last night, heard the good news. Thought I'd wait till you were up to call you. I can't tell you how much we appreciate what you've done."

"I didn't do anything," Sonny interrupted, "except nearly get myself killed. Paiz and his agents did the work."

"Don't be modest, young man. Paiz told me how hairy things got. Too bad about Chernenko, but he played with fire, and he got burned. We brought that man in, gave him clearances here and at Sandia, never suspecting what he was up to. I suppose it's too cruel to say, but he got what he deserved."

Yeah, Sonny thought. You brought him in and now that he's dead, he can't divulge information.

"Raven's still got the plutonium," Sonny reminded him.

"Yes, but he no longer has Chernenko. Without him the bomb can't be put together. There's no one of that caliber willing to sell out. It's only a matter of time before the plutonium is found. But any media exposure of what happened at Sandia can hurt our credibility."

"Does the media know?" Sonny asked.

He heard Eric hesitate, clear his throat. "No, not yet. You understand we have to keep it under wraps, for the time being. We're not releasing any information yet. That's why I'm calling you. Paiz should not have allowed the two women, your friends, into the labs. You know that. They called him, he met them at the lab gate, and he let them follow him in. Lab security thought they were with him. But they shouldn't have been inside the labs. We need to keep this quiet. Do you understand."

"So my two friends are not supposed to talk to anyone, is that it?"

"That's it. We need to get Raven first. We get him and the plutonium, then we can clear up this whole bloody mess."

Sure, Sonny thought, keep it under wraps. Don't let the public know there have been murders committed at Los Alamos and at Sandia Labs. Damn! Didn't Eric know Raven could hire others to put the bomb together! Lord, there were a hundred ways to import specialists without U.S. Customs, the CIA, or the FBI knowing. With the kind of money Raven was getting from the Avengers, it was easy as logging on to the Internet.

"Anyway, Doyle's satisfied the plutonium will be found shortly. By the way, any luck on reading the glyphs on the bowl?"

"No," Sonny replied.

"If you need an expert in decoding, I can send it up to Washington. Let some of our men see it."

"How do you know I have the bowl?"

Eric paused. "I think Paiz, or someone, mentioned it. I just assumed you had recovered it. Did you?"

"Yes—"

"Good. Remember, our deal was to let you keep it, hoping you could read the glyphs, decode it so to speak. What we're learning about this Raven character leads Doyle to believe that the glyphs on the bowl might contain information on him. He wants the bowl examined at the FBI lab."

"I can't let it go," Sonny replied.

Sonny felt Eric's irritation in the pause. "As you say. Remember, no statements to the press. Nada. Any questions from the press are directed to me. That's got to be absolutely clear." The phone line went dead.

"Yeah," Sonny grunted. They weren't leveling with him, he knew that. Paiz had saved his ass last night, and he was thankful, but could he trust the Bureau?

"Eric," he said to Rita and Lorenza.

"What did he say?"

"For us to keep quiet about what happened last night."

"Okay, so what's next?" Lorenza asked.

"Used to be a good detective would hit the streets, go listen to los de abajo. People on the streets, those who know who's scoring what in the city."

"Used to be?" Rita asked. "Now?"

"Now we surf the Internet." Sonny smiled.

"The Internet?"

"Raven can smuggle in the materials he needs, but he needs the help of the Avengers. They, maybe working with Eric and Doyle, got Chernenko the kind of security clearance he had, and Eric and Doyle are connected to e-systems."

"E-systems?"

"The whole nuclear enchilada, the defense department, all the labs, the CIA, it's all connected. The truth is stranger than fiction, as they say. And how do they communicate? Computers."

"You think you can find the names of these disgruntled, out-of-work bomb builders from Ukraine on the Internet?" Lorenza asked.

"I don't know. I don't know a damn thing about the system, except what I read. But Los Alamos and Sandia labs have databases. Information I need. I need to look for materials, names of people or companies who buy machined explosives. Who are the experts who can put bombs together? What kind of stuff does he need to make the 'Gadget'? There must be very few specialized corporations, subcontractors that make those kinds of things for Los Alamos."

"Don't you think the FBI is looking into that?" Rita asked.

"They would if they were really interested."

"What do you mean 'interested'? They've got a madman on the loose threatening to build a nuclear bomb. You mean—"

"I mean—" Sonny said, looking from the window where he had been watching the sun glistening on the snow, quickly melting it so it would be gone by noon. "I mean, why did they wait so long to bust into Chernenko's lab?"

The phone rang again and Sonny picked it up.

"Sonny, Matt Paiz here. You okay?"

"Fine."

There was a pause.

"Just thought you'd like to know we've been at Chernenko's lab all night. My men have gone over it with a fine-tooth comb. What we found ain't pretty."

"What?"

"Seems like Raven isn't only into building a bomb, he's into other poisons."

"What?" Sonny asked.

"We found a few vials filled with viruses—"

"What do you mean?" Sonny exclaimed.

"We've sent the vials to the CDC in Atlanta, but initial indications are it's the Ebola virus."

"Hijo de su chingada!" Sonny cursed, a shiver racing

down his spine. He felt his neck where Raven had stuck the needle. Yeah, that was Raven. He always had a backup plan. The Ebola virus in a vial in this country would scare a lot of people.

"It doesn't look good, Sonny. If he can't build a bomb, he's got the viruses. I just got through talking to the director at Atlanta. This stuff is extremely dangerous."

"How much did you find?"

"Only a few vials. It's as if Raven wanted us to find them. He's alerting us to what he has."

"Yeah," Sonny whispered. "That's Raven's way. He wants us to know he holds the aces."

"You think he has more?" Paiz asked, seeking confirmation.

"Yes," Sonny replied.

"We've got a couple of epidemiologists working on this," Paiz continued. "Apparently the syringe he used on you was Valium, a mild antidepressant. Lord knows why. Anyway, just to be on the safe side, our doctors suggested that you get yourself checked."

Sonny felt something cold in his bloodstream. What if Raven had slipped a virus into the injection he gave him last night. He looked up at Rita. Had he underestimated Raven?

"We need to have you checked right away. We have a doctor working on this at Lovelace." He read Sonny the doctor's name. "In the meantime he says try not to be in close contact with anyone."

Sonny frowned as he clicked the phone off. He looked at Rita and Lorenza. His stomach churned with a wave of fear. "Damn!" he cursed. What if?

19

"I can drive," Sonny said to Rita. He wanted to go alone, to shrink from the contact with her and Lorenza. He had told them Paiz's story and read the concern in their faces.

"You're not strong enough to drive," Rita said.

"Oh, yeah, wacha." He maneuvered his wheelchair up to the van's door, pulled himself to a standing position, and with some effort hoisted himself into the driver's seat. The van wasn't refitted with hand controls or foot pedals, so he could turn the ignition easily enough, but his right foot pressed clumsily on the gas. His legs trembled.

"Damn!" he cursed.

Rita rested her hand on his. "It takes time. Let Lorenza drive."

Yes, he thought, he wasn't ready. Something in his brain still wasn't connecting with his legs, and the effort only tired him.

Lorenza should drive. He was grateful for all Rita and Lorenza were doing for him, but dammit! He was just too used to being independent. He wanted his legs to move the way they used to. And he didn't like having to go to the lab to be checked for the possibility that a virus planted by

Raven was even now growing and multiplying in his blood-stream.

"What if I have something?" he said, looking at Rita.

"You don't," she assured him.

"And I haven't gotten a ticket yet," Lorenza said. "So unless you want to fire me, I'm ready."

"Okay," he said, and slid out of the van and into his chair. "Besides, you're the better driver."

He scooted around the side of the van, opened the door, and lowered the lift. Books spilled out.

"Rough ride last night," Rita explained, picking them up. "You want me to take some out?"

"No. I want to keep on reading. Maybe I just haven't found the right one."

"Cuídense," Rita said, and leaned forward to kiss him. Instinctively he drew back.

"The doctor said no contact—"

"You're okay," she said, "you're just fine." She kissed his cheek. "Call me."

"I will."

She stood back and waved as they pulled away.

"What a woman," Sonny said.

"She is quite a woman," Lorenza agreed.

After a pause Sonny asked. "What do you think?"

"I think you're okay."

Good, he thought, and settled back for the drive to Lovelace. It took all morning, with the doctor in charge personally drawing the samples of blood she needed, but when it was over she gave a thumbs-up sign and smiled.

"Negative for now," she said, "but it's a little early for the antibodies to build up. I need you to come back in a few days."

"More tests?"

"Just to make sure. Okay?"

"Okay," Sonny replied. "What about the stuff Matt Paiz brought in?"

"We're sure it's Ebola virus. Potent stuff, extremely dangerous. We sealed everything, sent it to Atlanta for confirmation. Do you know where it came from?"

The doctor was inquisitive, and obviously Paiz and his boys had given no information. Sonny shook his head.

"Well, we knew Iraq used chemicals during the Persian Gulf War, and we know the superpowers have anthrax and nerve-destroying chemicals aimed at each other, but now someone has the Ebola virus in our own backyard. I mean, what kind of an insane person would do this? Why here? We're not a threat to anyone, are we?" She shrugged in exasperation.

"Maybe we are," Sonny replied. He thanked the doctor and they went out. "South Broadway library," he said to Lorenza as they boarded the van.

"More books?"

"No, I need a computer expert."

He dialed Rita and told her the good news. He could hear her sigh of relief turn to a sob of thanks.

"Cuidado," she said. "I love you."

"Y yo te amo a tí," Sonny replied.

Clicking off the phone, he looked at Lorenza watching him in the rearview mirror. He blushed and picked up the book on the counter. *Interpreting Your Dreams in Five Easy Steps.* He laughed. "What will they think of next?"

"What?" Lorenza asked.

"How simple some people want to make the world."

"Some people just want to sell books, and those who don't want to go any deeper than a fast analysis buy them.

Anyway, how come you don't trust Eric?" she asked as she turned from Lead onto Broadway.

"He knows I have the bowl. Claims Paiz told him. Bullshit. And I don't buy the story about the cop near Raton intercepting the plutonium shipment. What if the core was already inside the labs—"

"You mean they manufactured it there?"

"Or someone brought it in," Sonny suggested.

"Eric?"

"Or one of his boys."

"Not possible, is it?"

"Anything is possible," he replied. "You think I'm paranoid?"

"No, but wouldn't it be very difficult for someone to sneak something like that into the labs?"

"Maybe. But what if there's a small group *inside* Los Alamos? What if they can buy the plutonium and bring it in? And they don't have to go to Ukraine, they get it from Pantex, where all the cores are being stored. Or they get it from Kirtland, where some are being dismantled."

"Wait a minute. You're talking *big* conspiracy."

"I smell it."

"But as far as I know, nobody's ever bribed a U.S. scientist of that caliber before. I mean the guys who can actually put bombs together."

"They bought the guy that was selling CIA secrets, what's his name?"

"So you believe Paiz's theory?"

"Given the course of events, it makes sense. The more I think of it, the more I believe the Avengers exist."

"Can it happen here?"

"There are signs in the air," Sonny said. "They've created a race war in this country. Whites are afraid of dark-skinned people, and the Blacks don't trust the whites. Now it's a population war, fed by fear of a mass migration from Latin America. In twenty years the majority population of this country is going to be colored, not white. But there's a check on the people promoting race war. The system they despise so much still works. They want to bring down the government, but democracy still works. People are smart enough to know they don't want white supremacists running the country. The Avengers tried using drugs to destroy this country, turning people into addicts. That fed into the class war they created. Now it's the bomb, viruses."

"Sounds like the Apocalypse," Lorenza said.

"If Raven can get into my dreams, he can get into other people's dreams. You bring the downfall by making people doubt themselves, doubt their dreams. Once we doubt ourselves, we turn on each other."

"That's an old controlling tactic, the *us versus them.*"

"Yeah, but it's working too slowly for their purposes. They want control now. Howard has a theory like that. Speaking of Howard," he said, and pushed Howard's number. Howard answered.

"Howie."

"Hey, compadre, como 'stás? How are you feeling? Got word you're cruising around the country."

"I'm getting there," Sonny replied. "You heard about last night?"

"A couple of our boys were on the perimeter when the bust came down. What they heard is unbelievable. Does the man *actually* have the stuff to build a—you know?"

"That's what the big boys say."

"You okay?"

"Yeah. Lorenza's driving me around."

"Lucky dude," Howard said. "Anyway, Paiz called Garcia. I figure he told Garcia only the skim off the top. Just what the hell *is* going on?"

"The end of the world, my friend," Sonny said, and told him about the virus.

"Garcia didn't tell us that."

"They don't want a leak to the media. Anyway, do you have files on militia groups?"

"I'm in forensics, not the library. But I hear you. Anything specific?"

"Have any of the big guns at Sandia or Los Alamos been linked to any of the militia groups in the state?"

"Hey, bro, you're not suggesting—" Howard caught himself. "Yes, you are. I know a chicanita in the computer room who can run a computer check."

"Thanks."

"De nada. Anything else?"

"Keep your gunpowder dry."

Howard laughed. "Ten-four."

Sonny called his mother. He couldn't remember when he talked to her last, and the irritation in her voice told him she couldn't either. "Hi, Mamacita—"

She stopped him short. "Don't 'mamacita' me! Sinvergüenza, malcriado, vagamundo. I just talked to Rita. Why are you running around all over the place? Que no sabes que tienes que descansar? I was going to come over this afternoon, bring some ungüente to sobar your legs. And why are you not home? It's cold outside. Not good for your legs. Have you lost your mind?"

"I love you, Mom," Sonny said with a smile.

"Ay, Sonny Francisco Elfego Baca, you always did know how to twist me around your little finger. I love you, too, but please stay warm. Where are you?"

"With Lorenza. South Broadway."

"Ay, Hijo, please be careful."

"I will, jefa. How's Max?"

Max was the first man his mother had taken as a friend since Sonny's father died twelve years ago. Nice solid man. Sonny liked him, although he hadn't had a chance to really get to know him.

"He's fine, except for the flu. I made some chicken caldo for him, with plenty of cilantro. And lots of hot chile. I finally convinced him to stay over here—"

"Stay with you?" Sonny asked. Max was staying at his mother's house?

"Well, only till he gets over the flu. And don't worry, he's sleeping in your and Mando's room. Poor man, he's all alone. His family is like my family, they're too busy to visit us. So we have to take care of each other."

Sonny gulped. She spoke the truth. So now Max was staying over and she was doctoring him, and Sonny knew he needed to get back in touch with her, with his brother, take care of familia again.

"Come for Christmas Eve," she said. "I want you and Mando here. Bring Rita, don Eliseo, Lorenza. We need to have the familia together."

"Have you seen Mando?"

"No, that brother of yours is worse than you. You have an excuse m'ijito, you're sick. But Mando is as healthy as a horse. He called last night. Has a new office, he said. He meant a new bar. And a new *lady friend.*"

"You mean Marlene?"

"Yes. Pobrecita, she's a tejana. He picks them because they have big—you know what. This woman is better fixed than Dolly Parton. And does her hair like Dolly."

"He always had a passion for chichi," Sonny joked.

"I spoiled you two," his mother replied. "I used to hold

you, one to each breast. Armando would hurry up and finish to get yours. Ay, que mi hijo. I swear, I don't know where he finds these women. Yes, I do. He went down to El Paso. A used-car dealers' convention, he said. He gets a little money together and he goes to Sunland to bet on the horses. I swear, they should never have legalized gambling in this state. The poor gamble, and they can't afford it. Armando likes to show off. Wants to prove he can compete with his buddies, used-car salesmen. Pendejos. Will he ever learn?"

"He enjoys life, jefa" was all Sonny could say.

"Then he shows up with Marlene. Broke. Wants to borrow a hundred till payday. He's not working, how can there be a payday! Get a job, Mando, I tell him. Find a nice woman. You're thirty-one and not getting younger. He keeps winding up with these broken-down Texan women that look like those women in bad movies. They wear their hair in beehive hairdos. Pobrecitas, they're so nice. They really like Armando. Now it's Marlene, and she's got two kids. Nice-looking mocositos."

"So he might make you a grandma—"

"Don't even think it! Ah, what's a mother to do. They're nice kids. I would do anything if it helped Armando get settled."

"I'll call him," Sonny promised.

"Promise you'll come for Christmas Eve."

"I promise."

Then in a whisper. "I think Max is going to propose."

"Propose?" The word shocked Sonny.

"Yes. He's been leading up to it. Then he caught the flu. But he keeps telling me he's got a secret Christmas present for me. I think it's a ring. Oh, he's such a good man. And I want all of you here. So we can celebrate. You and Armando need to get to know him better."

"Yes, yes we do," Sonny agreed. "I'll be there. And I'll drag Mando if I have to. Adiós, Mamá."

"Bye, m'ijo. Cuídate. Don't get cold."

"I won't. Un abrazo," he said, and turned off the phone. "Propose, humph," he said to himself, and dialed the library. He was going to have to get used to the fact that his mother had found a man she was interested in, a man who treated her with kindness and respect. Ah, she deserved some happiness. He and Mando hadn't been exactly easy to raise after their father died. And now? They didn't see her often enough. She was lonely, she had a life of her own. Yes, it was best for his mother, and he would have to get used to it.

"South Broadway Center Library. May I help you?" the voice on the phone said.

"Hi, Vangie, this is Sonny Baca."

"Oh, hi, Sonny. How are you?"

"Vangie, I need some help."

"Okay."

"I need to get on the Internet. Do you have a computer?"

"We've got a doozy. Sandia Labs donated one to the library."

"I don't know how to use one. Do you have someone who can help me?"

"I've got one kid who sits at that computer all day long. I swear, I have to chase him to school. He's a little, you know—"

"What?"

"Weird. Oh, I mean that in a nice way. A geek way. The other kids from Albuquerque High come here to use the computers to do their research. They look up the encyclopedias, but Cyber is into stuff I don't even know."

"Cyber?"

"That's what the kids call him. Short for cyberspace. He's in it, Sonny. He can surf anywhere with the Avenger."

"The Avenger?" Sonny leaned forward to make sure he had heard correctly.

"That's what he calls the software. A code name he found. I don't know anything about it. Only that he is a genius, and it makes him happy. He hangs around all day, won't go to school."

"Just who I need." Sonny smiled. "Is he there now?"

"Yup. He's good, but I warn you, he makes up strange stories."

"Like?"

"Yesterday he was sitting here saying there's something fishy going on at Los Alamos. At the labs. So I said, 'Cyber, how do you know?' "

"So what was fishy?" Sonny asked, feeling the hair rise along the back of his neck.

"Said there's a bomb missing. Can you imagine that. I told him, 'Cyber, they don't make bombs at Los Alamos.' 'I know, I know,' he said, 'but that's what the signals are saying.' "

Sonny gulped. "Hold on to him, Vangie. I'll be right over."

20

Vangie was there to greet Sonny and Lorenza as they entered the South Broadway library.

"Sawnee," she said with a wide smile, taking his hand in hers. "It's good to see you. Híjola, look at you. You're looking well. You know what they say, you can't keep a good man down. How's Rita?" she asked.

"She's fine, just fine. The restaurant keeps her busy. She said to say hello."

"Hi, Lorenza, good to see you. So welcome. Come in, come in. Cyber's dying to meet you. I told him you were a private investigator. You're looking for the missing girls, aren't you?" she whispered conspiratorially.

Sonny knew she loved mysteries, and more so if they had local color. She stocked Tony Hillerman novels for her patrons.

"Yes, that's part of it," Sonny acknowledged. The news media had carried the stories of the missing girls, and people in the city were very concerned about the disappearance of Carmen Abeyta from Barelas.

"That poor girl. It's awful, and so near Christmas. I hope they find her," Vangie said.

"You're busy," Sonny said, glancing around. The library was full.

"It's our busiest season. People come in to get out of the cold, to read Christmas stories," Vangie explained. "The kids aren't in school, so if they're not hanging out in the streets, they come in here. Which is where I'd rather have them. Here instead of out spraying graffiti. Anyway, I told Cyber about you," she continued, leading them past the main room toward the back.

"Good. I need a hacker, or a surfer, or whatever they call themselves."

Vangie laughed. "Cyber's the best."

"Good," Sonny repeated.

"We're here to help. Just tell us what you need," Vangie said, and led them into a space reserved for computers. In the back of the narrow cubbyhole Sonny spotted a teenager, fifteen or so, hunched over a keyboard, mouse in hand as if he were hunting lions in deep Africa. Cyber was hunting on the network.

Vangie paused, and in a soft voice she called his name, "Cyber."

She had to call three times before the boy turned to look at them. His dark shining eyes looked as if he were just awakening.

"Hi," he murmured.

The thin boy wore a scruffy pair of Adidas, holes in the knees of his baggy jeans, a tattered cotton shirt, and a Cowboys football cap backward. His likewise tattered backpack and parka lay on the floor by his chair. His round glasses fell down on his flat nose. Sonny guessed Cyber was Chinese. But his complexion was dark.

"Cyber, this is Mr. Baca," Vangie said, approaching.

"Call me Sonny." Sonny held out his hand.

Cyber smiled. "Sonny," he said. "Wow. I've heard about you. I never met a PI. You kinda look like that detective I see on the late, late shows. Perry Mason."

"Oh, the chair." Sonny smiled.

"Yeah, but you're not as fat as that dude."

"And this is my friend, Lorenza," Vangie introduced Lorenza.

"Hi," Cyber said shyly.

"Mr. Baca needs help."

"Sure," Cyber nodded eagerly.

Sonny nodded. "I need a guide. I've never been on the Internet."

"Never?" Cyber asked, incredulous. "Don't you have a computer?"

"Yeah, a small one. For a while I couldn't talk, so my friends bought me a computer with a large keyboard. I could type in messages."

"You couldn't talk—" Cyber's expression grew worried.

Vangie cleared her throat. "Well, here he is. I'll leave you to get acquainted. You help Mr. Baca, okay." She smiled and turned to leave. "Call me if I can help. There's coffee and cookies in my office. Help yourselves."

"Thanks for everything," Sonny called after her. He turned back to Cyber. "I'm better now. But I'm kind of computer illiterate. So I need help."

"You're a detective, so you look for people, right?"

"Right."

"That's where they are." Cyber pointed at the computer in front of him.

"In there?"

"Well, the information on just about everyone is in there."

"You can find people in there?"

"Yes."

"You're an investigator, too, huh?"

"Kind of. The Net is just a bunch of networks tied together with telephone lines, cables, fiber-optic lines. If you have a modem and a computer, you can access it, buy stuff, talk to people. It's awesome. I go in there and I feel I'm going to another reality. Sometimes I fall asleep and dream. Right here."

Lorenza had pulled up a chair next to Sonny. They both looked at Cyber like willing students.

"What do you dream?" Lorenza asked.

"Scary stuff. There are body snatchers in the Net."

"Body snatchers in cyberland?"

"Oh, yes," Cyber said seriously. "The teachers keep telling us we're in a new age. The cyber age. Techo-knowledge. Plug in, be in touch, know everything. What they forget to tell us is that sooner or later the body snatchers get you."

"How do they get you?" Lorenza asked.

"They erase your file," Cyber replied. "I suppose if there were good cybercops, they could take care of the body snatchers. But all the cops in cyberspace want to do is censor stuff. See, being on the Internet is like an addiction. I don't do drugs on the streets like some of the kids, but I'm addicted all right. To this. When cyberspace crashes, the whole world will crash. Be like Adam and Eve getting tossed out of the garden and starting all over again."

"Whoa," Sonny said. "You're going too fast for me. How can we start over?"

Cyber shrugged. "If we don't have the technology, we won't know what to do. We become like cavemen."

"I see," Sonny mused. He looked at Lorenza. "I could use some of that coffee Vangie promised," he said.

"Me, too." She rose and went out.

"So, you live here?" Sonny asked while Lorenza went for coffee.

"Here? In the library?" Cyber laughed. "Just about. My mom's got an apartment on Broadway, but—" He paused. "She has to support us, so she spends a lot of time making jewelry. She sells at Old Town, maybe you've seen her?"

"Maybe."

"Merlinda Chen. She's the best-looking vendor there." Cyber beamed. He described his mother, the kind of jewelry she created, the place under the portal in Old Town where she sold. Then with a worried expression he finished: "I worry about her. It's been hard since my dad disappeared."

"What do you mean, disappeared?" Sonny asked, taking the cup of coffee Lorenza offered. "Gracias," he said. She placed a plate of Christmas cookies on the floor and sat. Cyber reached for one.

"He just disappeared. He was working at Sandia Labs, for Phillips really. One day he just didn't come home. The lab director said he was drinking on the job, and things just got too hard so he split. But I know it ain't true, 'cause he really loved me and my mom. He wouldn't have gone without us. My mom took it so hard."

"I see," Sonny said, and sipped the strong coffee. He glanced at the monitor. Cyber found people on the Net; he was looking for his missing father.

"I'm looking for him." Cyber nodded, biting into the biscochito. "I don't believe the cops. I know he wouldn't leave us."

"Found anything?"

Cyber shook his head. "Not yet, but I found out other people have disappeared. They're there, in the government files, then they just disappear. Deleted."

"Deleted?"

"Yeah, like they fall off the edge. Like there's a portion in the hard drive we don't know is there. Like empty space. There's weird things going on in the government. Things I don't understand."

"Yeah," Sonny acknowledged. "Maybe I can help."

"Would you?" Cyber said, his voice rising with hope.

"Well, that seems to be my current specialty, looking for missing persons." Sonny nodded. "Yeah, I'll help."

"You don't believe my dad just dropped out?"

"No."

"You're the first one to say that. Thanks." Cyber smiled. "I got into the Mormons' mainframe up in Salt Lake," he continued, munching on his cookie and turning to pat the computer on the table, as a boy would pat a dog. "They have the family tree of everyone who ever lived on earth. Just about. My dad's Chen. He's Chinese from Shanghai, so he's not listed in the Mormon file. But they have my mother's family name in there. We're Navajo. Diné. My great-grandfather had married a Mexican lady from Seboyeta. That was in the eighteen forties. So I'm part Navajo, part Mexican, part Chinese. One of these days I want to go back to the res. Soon as I find my dad. My mom wants to stay here. She keeps hoping some news of my father will turn up."

So that's it, Sonny thought. The kid was using the computer to look for his father, and in the process he ran into part of his family tree. He got into the Mormon genealogy files. Had he also gotten into the Sandia Labs files?

"Don't lose hope," Sonny said. "But tell me, if you know people have been deleted from government files, does that mean you've gotten into those files?"

Cyber remained silent, chewing slowly on his cookie.

"Look," Sonny said softly. "I'm not here to find out what

you're doing. I need information on missing girls. Just like you need it on your father. I need help."

"I can get into almost anything," Cyber smiled. "But there's some government stuff that's so coded, and if you *happen* to break the code, they set a cyberdetective on you. I have to go slow."

"You're what they call a hacker?" Sonny asked.

Cyber smiled. "I don't mess with anyone's files. I just want info on my dad."

"That's fair." Sonny nodded. "But how do you do all this?"

"Easy." Cyber smiled. "I've got a directory, a modem, and Circe." Again he patted the computer.

"Circe?"

"That's the name somebody scratched on the back of the computer. I found it when I was hooking up the phone line. I looked it up. Circe was a witch who lived on an island during Greek times. She turned Odysseus' men into pigs."

"Yeah." Sonny nodded, recalling the story in *The Odyssey*. Odysseus landed on Circe's island, and the seductive witch turned his men into beasts while he loitered with her. *The Odyssey* was everyman's journey. Too much loitering on the island of desire turned one into a pig. One had to remember the goal: get home. Penelope was waiting. The son—what was his name?—was waiting. Cyber's father was on an odyssey.

"Maybe a scientist who reads books named the computer," Sonny suggested.

"I guess," Cyber nodded. "Circe was a witch who could tell the future. People went to her for answers. Now they go to the Internet. They surf all day long, all night." He shivered.

"Cyber escape," Lorenza said.

"Yeah." Cyber nodded. "In cyberspace you can be anything you want to be."

"You get sucked in," Sonny added.

"It's easy. Too easy."

"But you've got to be connected. Who pays the phone bill?" Lorenza asked.

Cyber gulped. Crumbs of the cookie hung on his lower lip. His wide dark eyes looked from one to the other.

"Well?" Sonny asked.

"You going to tell?" Cyber whispered.

"What's there to tell?" Sonny asked.

"I ain't got no money. Vangie ain't got no money. So I—"

"What?"

"I kind of just charge the fee and the phone bill."

"Charge the phone bill?"

"You know," Cyber said softly. "To the labs."

Damn. Sonny smiled. The kid was charging the phone bill to Sandia Labs. Looking for his father meant taking chances.

"Well," Sonny leaned forward and whispered, "I heard the lab has a program that encourages kids like you to learn about computers. It's kind of an investment they're making in the future."

Cyber smiled. "That's what I figure," he said, and gave Sonny a high five. He turned to Lorenza. "Is it okay?"

"I didn't hear a thing." She smiled, and Cyber gave her a high five.

"You've got a cool lady, Mr. Sonny," Cyber said.

"I think so," Sonny agreed.

"She drive you around?"

"Yup."

"You been in a chair a long time?"

"A couple of months."

"You hurt your legs?"

"Ran into some bad guys," Sonny said.

"Same guys you want to catch on the Internet?"

"Yup."

"I'll help."

"Good."

"I look into some of this stuff on the Net, and I see how people are using it. Some of the deals coming down are worse than the crime on the street."

"True." Sonny nodded. Cyberspace had already become the territory of the criminal. The Cyberspace Mafia was making deals, shaking down the world. *Anything* could be ordered over the wires. Money could be laundered and moved so fast that the IRS couldn't keep up with it. Deals to buy countries, or to bring down countries, all at the touch of a few keys. Virtual criminals were *real* criminals, and Cyber was beginning to run into them. Now there were missing persons, and cyberspace was beginning to look like any other dictatorship in the world. The dictatorship of cyberspace was coming. The disappeared. Deleted files. Cyber's missing dad. Others.

"How come you can do so much with Circe? Don't you need special programs?" Lorenza asked.

"Sandia Labs donated this baby to the library," Cyber replied.

"So?"

"So," he whispered, "they left their programs in the hard drive."

"Programs from Sandia Labs?"

"Yeah. I was surprised, too. I figured it was a mistake, a typical government snafu."

"What's the program?"

"It's called Avenger 2000," Cyber replied. "And it's bad, believe me."

"How?" Sonny asked.

"For one thing, the government seems to be fighting itself. There are groups carrying on a war. Like war-simulation games, but not with tanks and airplanes. It's like a plot. People disappear. There are codes in here you wouldn't believe. That's how I found my dad's record."

"But you said files are deleted."

"The payroll and classification files are deleted, so he's not in the active file. He just never showed up for work, they told my mom. But I found his 'deleted file' in their mainframe. It shows he was working one day and gone the next. His file just got pushed into the *disappeared.*"

"How can you get into their mainframe?"

Cyber smiled. "They have an internal fiber-optic system. Nobody can crash in from the outside, but I figured a way."

"How?"

Cyber hesitated. "I work at the labs."

"I don't get it," Sonny replied.

"I composed a person, gave myself identification, classification, a code number, everything. They think I'm there, so I can access their system."

"Too much," Sonny whispered.

"For sure," Lorenza said. She, too, was amused, and startled, by Cyber's revelation.

"Almost anything's possible on the Net," Cyber replied.

"Including people disappearing," Sonny mused.

"Where are they?" Cyber asked. "Where's my dad? That's what I want to find out."

"And you're the only one using this computer?" Lorenza asked.

"It's too complicated for the other kids. When the lab

guys delivered Circe a few months ago, the kids couldn't get into the programs, so they couldn't play games on it. Even Vangie couldn't use it. She tried to get someone from the labs to come and fix it, but they never showed up. I began to fiddle with it, and I got in. That made her happy, so now I've got my own personal weapon. I just happened to hook into a phone line, and Vangie gets no bills, so that's cool."

"And the rest is history," Sonny said, glancing at Lorenza. They had come to the right place. The kid had the software to navigate the Net. How far could he go?

"So whatchu wanna look for?" Cyber beamed.

"I need to learn a lot about nuclear weapons, and I need to learn it today. I also have a list of people I need to research, but I don't want to get you into trouble."

"Look, Sonny, I'm already in trouble. I got into the Sandia and Los Alamos systems. If they catch me, so what. I don't disturb files, I just look for info on my dad."

"You've already been in the Los Alamos computers?" The kid kept astounding Sonny.

Cyber bowed his head. "Yes," he said softly, then looked up. "Only because the work my dad was doing at Sandia had something to do with a project up there."

"I need info from those computers," Sonny thought aloud, weighing the possibility of getting Cyber into trouble against the alternative: Raven constructing the bomb, Raven killing the three missing girls, Raven *disappearing* Sonny. "It could be dangerous."

"I'll help," Cyber insisted.

Sonny took out the list he had written. "This man. Leif Eric. He's director of Los Alamos Labs. I need to know all I can about him. Everything. And I need to know how to build a nuclear bomb."

Cyber whistled. "You wanna build a bomb? That's cool."

"Can you keep a secret?" Sonny asked.

"You bet," Cyber nodded eagerly.

"I want to know *how* to build a nuclear bomb, I'm not really going to build one. If I had the plutonium pit ready to go, what other materials would I need? Where does Los Alamos buy such materials? Who are the suppliers? Do they manufacture components there, or do they buy from the outside? Are there names attached? And this guy."

He wrote "Raven."

"This man is known as Raven, but he has a dozen aliases. Anthony Pájaro, Antonio Cuervo, John Worthy, Worthy John, all these combinations." He pointed at the list. "His name might be involved with a nuclear bomb project. He's probably in FBI and CIA files—" Sonny stopped and looked at Cyber. "But tell me, you haven't gotten into FBI files, have you?"

Cyber beamed.

"Lordy, Lordy," Sonny chuckled. What could this kid not crack?

"Okay, Raven is being sought by the FBI. Where is he? I want to know anything about him that might be in—there." He nodded at the computer.

He gave Cyber the names of the missing girls, the names of their parents, and where they worked. Anything at all that might show up in the files Cyber could access. Anything that might create a pattern.

"I'll get right on it," Cyber said when Sonny was done. Something about Sonny's urgency told him the task was not a game. Sonny was looking into government stuff, and that meant going into mainframes that had codes, encrypted stuff. There where the surf could turn ugly and drag a surfer down. Circe's pit, the black hole of cyberspace that surfers feared. You cracked a code, and security could trace you if you didn't move fast enough.

"When I find something, do I e-mail you?"

"I don't have e-mail," Sonny replied.

"You don't have e-mail?" Cyber said in astonishment. Then as if apologizing, he added, "That's okay, probably be read by others."

"Call me," Sonny replied, writing down his phone number.

"Your phone's probably tapped."

"I don't think so. I've checked for bugs, so we'll take a chance. You see, Cyber, I have to have all this figured out today."

"Today? Today's all the time we have?"

"Yes."

"Okay," Cyber said eagerly. "I'll go to work right away, call you if I find anything."

"Thanks, Cyber. You're a real trooper."

Cyber smiled and gave Sonny a high five.

21

While Lorenza drove, Sonny read and made notes. Set the stage, don Eliseo had said. That's exactly what the red-haired woman in the cantina had done. She set the stage for Billy's play, and it was on that stage that Sonny finally faced Raven. But she made Sonny sit, she didn't want him to be an actor. She was Raven's helper.

The three missing girls had been in Christmas plays.

To enter your own dream, you had to set the stage, like in a movie or a play. Make yourself the principal actor. And it didn't have to be Shakespeare, any damned stage would do.

"Ah, here," he murmured, and found the entry on plays.

The Oñate colonists brought many plays to la Nueva México, he read, dramas put on by talented soldiers and friars to entertain the troops in the field. One such play, still reenacted in some of the small villages of the state, was *Los Moros y los cristianos*. It illustrated the ferocity of the Spanish knights defeating the Moors in Spain.

Shouting their battle cry, "Santiago," the Spanish forces called on St. James to defeat the enemy, sweeping the Moors south, out of Granada, and finally back to Africa. Winning against the entrenched Moorish civilization and its warriors convinced the Spaniards that God and St. James were on their side, for many a story was told of miraculous appearances of the patron saint on the field of battle. Santiago rode alongside them as a shining knight, riding a white stallion, encouraging the knights of Aragón in their struggle against the infidel. When this happened, the Spanish troops responded and the battle was won.

The appearance of the saint in battle regalia was also documented in the legends of la Nueva México, during the early battles against the Pueblo Indians.

Good odds to have in your corner, Sonny thought. A saint on horseback dropping from the clouds in armor, charging and cleaving the enemy as a scythe cuts down wheat. It emboldened the faithful, made them courageous and ferocious. A ferocity and faith that helped them conquer the New World. Faith and ferocity. A terrible combination.

But in 1492 not all the Jewish and Muslim outcasts from the Iberian peninsula disappeared into thin air. Some made the sign of the cross and journeyed to México; newly converted into the Catholic fold, the conversos joined others in the dream of the New World. Of course the civil and church authorities knew who these conversos were, marranos they were called, and as more and more of México was conquered, the marranos were often pushed to the more dangerous northern frontier. Rich men like Oñate paid for the outfitting of the expedition, but the common people who were recruited were those who had nothing, and so a few of the crypto Jews and Moors joined the Oñate expedition.

Centuries later, in a few of the adobe hovels of New Mexico, the prayers the children heard were not the Hail Marys of the rosary, but chants in a foreign language. Jewish and Muslim prayers on days that had nothing to do with the calendar of saints' days.

Sonny paused. You had to read the fine print in the history books to find things like this. For example, Tlaxcalan Indians, over five hundred strong, the backbone of the expedition, those who would build the first chapel in Santa Fé, also came with Oñate. History barely noted the contribution of the Tlaxcalans, and their progeny hardly remembered them.

Ah, Sonny thought, history glorifies those who write it.

We need to arm ourselves with computers and write our history, our punto de vista. Why not curanderas armed with computers? They would explain the healing process don Eliseo knew so well. Lorenza taught Sonny to enter the world of spirits by finding his nagual. Assuming the power of the coyote, he was able to meet Raven in his circle of evil.

Coyote spirit. Who would believe? It meant not only that he no longer feared the coyote, it meant acquiring the power of the coyote. When he returned from becoming Coyote, he understood the message in the old cuentos, the folktales of the people.

The ancestors had learned how to acquire the power inherent in the natural world, the energy of animals. People could enter the spirit of the animal to travel, to fly. Those with the power could penetrate the world of spirits, a reality that was as close as the outstretched hand.

Now a parallel reality was coming into being. Cyberspace and its cyberdream. Reality, like DNA, twisted and took new forms, and dreams sometimes became nightmares. Either way, he had to learn how to enter his dreams.

But to enter dreams one needed a guide. Was Cyber to be his new guide? A child would lead him?

"We're home," Lorenza said.

Sonny looked up. "Ah, yes, I was thinking," he said, putting aside his books and notes. "If I had known how to use the computer when I was composing my family tree, it would have taken me half the time."

"True," Lorenza replied, "but the books you took to bed are a warm comfort. A keyboard and a blue monitor? I don't know."

They laughed and went inside, where Rita was waiting. Over lunch they told Rita about Cyber. They were just finishing when Cyber called.

"Mr. Baca, Cyber here. I've got some stuff. I 'visited' the Los Alamos parallel system. There's a mountain of info on the nuclear stuff. I don't have time to break it down. So I looked into your man, Leif Eric. I found out where he lives, how much his salary is, where he buys his toilet paper, when and where he flies out of here, transfers to other places from Albuquerque, et cetera. He flies a lot to Washington, D.C. I thought I should look for a pattern, as you told me. He fights with his wife. Police were called to a family fight one time. Other people in some of the offices gossip about him, and I found some of their e-mail messages. Not nice. He's a tyrant, they say. Some call him crazy. Imagine, a man in charge of a place that makes bombs and all sorts of other weapons, like laser guns, is crazy. By the way, did you know that recently a very bad accident has happened? Someone was killed at the labs, and they're trying to hide it. I can dig into that if you like."

This kid's for real, Sonny thought. "Later, right now focus on Eric."

"I pulled up his phone calls and made a complete list. One number is at the top. Fine, I thought. He calls the generals at the Pentagon. Oh, no, the number he calls the most is Intel in Rio Rancho. Not a general or the CIA." He paused, and Sonny knew he was teasing.

"Who?"

"He calls a woman. Mona Vandergriff. She runs Intel, did you know that?"

No, Sonny thought, I don't know who in the hell runs Intel.

"No reason for you to know," Cyber continued. "I suppose the labs use a lot of Intel chips. Anyway, the second number he calls is her home phone. Unlisted of course, but I hacked Intel. They are really lax on their stuff. Even you could hack in." Cyber laughed. "Just kidding, just kidding. So why does he call her at work and at home? I checked all his flights out of the Albuquerque airport. He stays overnight. He rents cars. As I compute it, he drives to Rio Rancho. Does he go to her office, or to her home. All visits are late in the day or at night. He's regular as a scientist. Why did I spend the time on this? Because the FBI has Mona Vandergriff under surveillance. Does this help?"

"It sure does." Sonny breathed a sigh of relief. Was Leif Eric having an affair with the Intel CEO? If yes, what did it mean? And why would the FBI be tracking her?

"What else, Cyber?"

"I checked into Mona Vandergriff's file. I've got her address if you want it?"

"Shoot."

"Sixty sixty-nine Doña Catarina Court. Rio Rancho. And get this. She's an expert marksman, and she's met with the leaders of a militia group. That information was hard to get, but I guess she's a member. I dug deep, but it's a dead end. I also found something on the man Raven—"

"Wait a minute. What about this militia group Vandergriff meets with?"

"There's very little on it. It has a code name: Doomsday. That's all so far, but I can look some more."

"Be careful," Sonny replied.

"I will. Anyway, this Raven has many aliases. But who is he? And why does he appear in the Los Alamos files? Because he was working there—"

"Repeat that," Sonny said.

"Raven worked in the Los Alamos Labs. He used the name John Worthy. He was a courier. You know? A guy who delivers messages."

"Worked for Eric?" Sonny whistled softly. It didn't make sense. Cyber had run into the wrong name, he was confusing people. "Are you sure?"

"Positive. He had security clearance. He went all over the world before he was deleted. He was working in Russia on what seems to be a high-level mission, a big project between the Russians and scientists from Los Alamos. Raven, alias John Worthy, carried messages. Then he was deleted, which means his file is now in confidential files closed to everyone. They got rid of him a year ago."

"Hold on." Sonny put his hand on the phone and turned to Rita and Lorenza. "Raven was working at Los Alamos up to a year ago. Can you believe that? **He** was a courier, so he was at the right places at the right time. When the Cold War ended, bombs were being dismantled all over the place. Last summer he appears as Anthony Pájaro, an antinuke activist. A Save the Earth eco-terrorist. We thought the truck he tried to bomb was just carrying low-level nuclear waste, but what if it was carrying something more dangerous? What if that was really the Avengers' first try to create the catastrophe they're looking for?"

"So the Zia cult was just a cover-up," Lorenza said. "He was using the women, using Tamara Dubronsky."

"The question is," Sonny pondered, "why was he kicked out? Was there a parting of the ways? Raven has his own agenda, and that doesn't include taking anyone's orders."

"Or is it just another cover-up, and they're still in it together," Rita said.

"Perhaps." Sonny nodded. "Go on, Cyber."

"I also have something on the missing girls. But it doesn't make sense. Their names appear in lab files."

"How?" Sonny asked.

"Well, when I looked into Raven's file, the names of the girls appeared. In Raven's files he lists one as his first wife. There it is, 'Consuelo Romero, wife.' That's the name of one of the girls you said was missing, right?"

"Right," Sonny replied, frowning. Just what in the hell was going on? Raven listing a Consuelo Romero as his wife?

"I checked the Social Security numbers. They match. So I kept digging. Six months later there's a memo. His first wife, this Consuelo Romero, dies. Raven, this John Worthy, remarries. He lists the name of the second girl as wife, Catalina García. He even gives the addresses you gave me. So what does this mean?"

Sonny shook his head and sagged into his chair. It just didn't make sense. He felt Rita's hand on his shoulder.

"Qué pasa?" she asked.

"I don't know. I just don't know—"

Cyber continued. "He listed Consuelo's name when his name first pops up at Los Alamos, summer 1992. That means that he knew *then* that he would later kidnap Consuelo. How could he know that? I don't think so, so the other possibility is that he is *now* accessing the computer files and putting in information. But why? And Los Alamos has the best encryption and the best Net detectives around. I'm good enough to get through their codes, but so can Raven? I figure he's playing cat and mouse—and you're the mouse."

"Yeah," Sonny replied. Cyber had just put his finger on it. Raven knew what Sonny was doing. So he was playing games back, going into the Los Alamos files and entering data to shock Sonny, to throw him off guard.

"Okay, that's all I got for now."

"That's a lot. Thanks, Cyber, you've been really helpful."

"I'll keep digging."

"Be careful," Sonny cautioned. He hung up the phone and related Cyber's findings to Lorenza and Rita.

"It doesn't surprise me," Lorenza said. "Raven the trickster loves games. He wants you to know he's one step ahead of you. You decide to look into his past, and he plants clues to surprise you."

"So he knows about Cyber. Is Cyber in danger?"

Lorenza shook her head. "I don't think so. Raven is focusing on the girls, on your dreams. The worst he can do is turn Cyber in for hacking, but that's not his interest. Right now he needs one more girl."

"What about Eric and the woman?" Rita suggested. "He has family problems and he sleeps with his alter ego, a woman scientist who speaks his language. Does it mean anything?"

"It does if she meets with the Doomsday group," Sonny replied. "But why FBI surveillance? Does Paiz know?"

"Raven can play games around the FBI," Lorenza cautioned. "Just like he did up at Los Alamos."

"Yes," Sonny agreed. "Raven is playing games with me, and playing games with his own bosses, the Avengers. And there's not a damn thing Eric can do about it."

"They created a monster, and now the monster is loose," Rita said.

"Maybe Eric is an Avenger," Lorenza said. "He hired

Raven not knowing who he really is. Now Raven is using them."

"What now?" Rita asked.

"Got to visit Mona Vandergriff," Sonny replied, and picked up the phone.

22

Sonny called Mona Vandergriff's office and tried his best to imitate Leif Eric's voice when the secretary answered.

"Good morning, this is Dr. Eric. May I speak to Ms. Vandergriff? I've developed a cold and I have to break our engagement."

"But Dr. Eric," the secretary said sweetly, "you *know* Ms. Vandergriff has a D.C. appointment on her calendar. In fact, she told me she would meet you there."

"Ah, yes," Sonny stammered. "My cold has wrecked my calendar. Thank you, thank you very much." He turned to Rita and Lorenza. "She's in Washington. Time to check out her place."

"What do you expect to find?" Rita asked.

"A link to a militia group, then a link to Eric. Anything I can use to make Eric confess what he really knows about Raven."

Sonny really didn't know what he would find, but if Raven was playing cat and mouse in the lab computers, and Eric was courting Mona Vandergriff, then he was sure there was a connection. Slim, but the only thing he had to go on.

"Sonny, you're playing with fire," Rita cautioned him, touching him.

"So's Raven," Sonny replied. "And we don't have much time left."

Rita leaned to kiss him and take Chica from his lap, resigned to what he had to do. They went outside into a cool wind. Overhead, gray, driven clouds carried no moisture, but they presaged another storm.

"Ten cúidate."

"You, too, amor."

"I've got Eddie Martínez protecting me," she replied. She motioned to the red and muddied Jeep parked two houses down on La Paz Lane. Agent Martínez waved.

Sonny acknowledged the greeting. "Good to see the Bureau is finally doing something right."

"He follows me like a dog. Comes into the café to eat, and does he eat."

Sonny looked at Rita. She was feeding agent Martínez? "Don't feed him too well," he mumbled.

Rita winked at Lorenza. "Don't be jealous, amorcito. It's bad for your stomach." She leaned and whispered in his ear, "You're the only man in my life." She kissed him.

Sonny blushed. "Yeah, okay, let's get the show on the road." He drove his chair onto the lift and into the van. In moments they were headed toward Río Grande Boulevard.

They passed Sondra's stables, where he had once stabled his mare. Keeping the mare had gotten too expensive, so he sold her and bought a gelding to use in bull wrestling in the local rodeos. All of that seemed so far away, another time and place.

He thought of don Eliseo praying with the medicine men, bending green juniper branches to make the hoop for a dream catcher. Meanwhile, somewhere in his hideaway,

Raven played with vials full of deadly viruses and prayed to the destructive energy in the plutonium pit.

Sonny wondered if the ending of an age meant a return to the cave and the club. Along the street Christmas lights decorated homes, hung from front-yard trees, eaves, fences. A few homes already had electric farolitos lining driveways. It was the season of light, but Sonny felt no mood of celebration.

"Not much time," he said.

"No," Lorenza agreed.

"A lot depends on Cyber. Imagine our future hanging on a teenager."

Lorenza turned west and over the Alameda Bridge. Out the window the bare branches of the huge cottonwoods rose like specters into the somber afternoon. A thin, gray overcast covered the North Valley. Below them the sluggish Río Grande was a thin slate of brown; it did not look so grand at all. The river bosque was bare and gray. A large flock of crows swung across the sky to roost in the trees. In the west the sun was waning, leaving a lingering nostalgia on the mauve cirrus clouds.

Time and the river, Sonny thought. As a boy he played on the playas in the summer. The huge sandbars spread for miles along the South Valley where he grew up. Time and the river were innocent then. Who could have guessed that he would, at age thirty-one, be chasing a man bent on destroying the world? Who could have guessed he would be an apprentice to a kind old man who knew more about the soul and its ways than any psychiatrist he had ever interviewed? Apprentice to a curandera who had taken him so deep into his nature that he learned the power of Coyote, his shadow in the animal world.

"El destino," he whispered. El destino is the tradition and

custom that can trap a man. But it's more than that. It's the soul's connection to the universal destiny, a road map we do not yet know. A fate unfolding itself before our eyes. That's one reason he liked to read. The poets spoke of fate, karma, a kind of inexorable working of the universe where all the souls wound toward their destiny.

He wished he could recall something appropriate about time and the river. "Oh, lost and by the wind grieved" . . . or "The fault, dear Caesar, lies not in our stars, but in the river of our birth." Life is like a river. The Río Grande had been the river of his ancestors for hundreds of years, and so the bones and blood had seeped into the water.

A four-by-four boss truck riding high cut Lorenza off. The young cowboy in it grinned. Lorenza started to flip him off, then shook her head.

"Pendejo," she said. "He bought a truck, lifted it ten feet off the ground, now he goes around threatening people."

"Macho guys," Sonny added. It was happening. Young men with tough cars and trucks and guns. They blew each other off, and more and more they turned their anger on strangers. Road rage. Rage against life.

The traffic going toward Rio Rancho moved slowly. Commuters plugged the road. The new Cottonwood Mall seemed to be thriving with last-minute Christmas business. On the hill, the Intel building rose like a giant behemoth, a dangerous whale beached on the sands of the West Mesa.

Half the computers in the world ran on Intel chips, Sonny knew. The biggest corporation in the state, Mona Vandergriff's playground. So how did she and Eric figure into the bigger picture?

"We'll soon know," Lorenza said, turning down Doña Catarina Court. "Sixty sixty-nine, right? This should be it."

Mona Vandergriff's brick house sat on a quiet street.

Sonny looked out the window. The ranch-style house was landscaped in gravel, cactus, a few juniper bushes. Neat xeriscape, a desert landscape for those into water conservation.

Three houses down Lorenza drove up to the curb and parked.

"What now?"

"Take a look inside."

"Break in? Hey, this isn't 'Burque," she reminded him. "This is Rio Rancho, the all-American city. If these cops find you in the house of the woman who runs Intel, you will spend Christmas, and probably the entire new year, in jail."

"It's the only lead we have."

He was studying the quiet, residential street. He knew he could be in the house quickly. His first break-in in a wheelchair. And the secretary had said Mona was in D.C.

"Pretend we're soliciting for Goodwill if someone gets snoopy," he said as he let down the lift. "I shouldn't be gone long."

"Cuidado," Lorenza whispered.

He let himself down the lift and rolled to the front door. There was no time to scope the backyard. Thankfully, the front door of Mona Vandergriff's home was handicapped accessible.

Just in case, he rang the doorbell three times and waited. No answer, no dogs barking, so he jimmied the door and checked for a security system. Nada. He wheeled in, turned, and shut the door behind him.

A small rose-colored divan and a vanity graced the anteroom. He wheeled himself into a spacious living room. Spotless, new furniture, trendy. Rio Rancho chic, Sonny figured.

No children. He wheeled to the patio door, checked for

backyard dogs. Nada. The woman lives alone. He made his way down a hallway toward the bedroom area. Pictures adorned the wall. One from "your friend" Ronald Reagan. Other top government officials, including the FBI's Doyle. A shot of her at NASA, one in Russia standing next to Yeltsin. The photo that made Sonny pause was Mona at the beach. Next to her stood a tanned, muscular Leif Eric. "Mona my love, thanks for a week in heaven." Signed, "Leif."

"Lordy," he whispered. Mona Vandergriff was quite a beauty. Dark short hair, a pleasing smile, a wrinkle or two beginning to appear around the eyes, but those only lent her a mature, aggressive look. She was smiling, apparently happy with the week in heaven.

The fun-loving twosome didn't exactly conjure up militia-outfitted Avengers. Not the kind of people who would blow up a bomb to take over the government.

Three huge mirrors adorned the bedroom walls, all reflecting the king-size bed. The carpet so plush the wheelchair almost stalled. Sonny chugged to the closet and opened the door. What he saw made him gasp.

Neatly hung behind Mona's business suits were two camouflage military uniforms. Militia wear. Cyber was right. On the floor, mountain boots. On the shelf above, where women normally kept shoes, sweaters, and purses, were stacked two AK-47s. High-powered stuff.

"So she loves the outdoors," Sonny said sarcastically. "Doesn't prove a thing. I bet she also has hand grenades stored somewhere, all come in handy during a weekend stroll in the mountains."

Two huge files sat to the back of the very spacious closet. Sonny pulled a handle and the drawer slid out. He riffled through the files. Lots of Intel material. The second and the third were all the same, but in the bottom drawer was the thing he was looking for. The Doomsday file, thin but full of encrypted codes he couldn't begin to read.

He was flipping through it for names when he heard the front door open, and a happy but muffled voice. "There's wine in the fridge. I'm going to take a shower."

Eric and Mona? She's supposed to be in D.C.

"Chingao," Sonny cursed. Could he race to the patio door and make a quick escape in the wheelchair?

No, the voice was already in the hallway, heading for the bedroom. He was trapped! He slid quickly into the closet and closed the door behind him. He turned the chair and pushed back against the wall, away from her gowns, covering himself with the business suits.

He didn't hear her footsteps on the carpet. The closet door opened and Mona Vandergriff quickly pulled a silk gown down from its hanger. She closed the door and headed for the shower.

Sonny breathed relief, then peered through the slats. He saw her enter the bathroom, heard the water running.

Make a run now, he thought, and was about to push out when a tall, assured Leif Eric entered the bedroom, two glasses in one hand, a bottle of New Mexico chardonnay in the other. Had Eric sensed his movement? Sonny held his breath as Eric looked toward the closet, approached, then shook his head and returned to the bed table.

He poured the wine, sat at the edge of the bed, slipped off his shoes, and drank. He finished the glass of wine and stood to remove his jacket and tie.

Mona, draped in the silk gown, entered from the bathroom, towel-drying her hair. "Lord, it was a tough week," she muttered.

"Tell me about it," Eric replied. He handed her a glass of wine.

"I'm glad to see you." She lifted the glass in a toast.

"I'm glad to see you." He returned the toast.

"This makes it all worthwhile. . . ."

He held and kissed her. "I would go insane if I didn't have you."

The gown opened and he pressed his hands against her breasts. She moaned, then drew back.

"Raven?" she asked.

Eric frowned. "Not dead yet, but he soon will be. But let's not talk about it."

"What do you mean 'soon'? You know how dangerous he is. Why haven't they caught him?"

"Not that easy," Eric replied. "Look, let's not discuss Raven. I only have a few hours. Let's relax. . . ."

He ran his hands down her hips.

"Yes," she murmured.

"God, I need you." He kissed her hard, taking her breath.

"And I need you. I am so fucking tired of the nerds I work with."

"I've got the thing for all that tension."

"I need it," she moaned, "oh, I need it. I'm still cold."

"I can warm you up."

"Promise, laserlick," she said, lifting the glass to drink.

He laughed and pulled her down on the bed.

Sonny leaned forward, slightly moving a suit on a hanger. The squeak was barely perceptible, but Eric heard it.

"Do you have mice?" he asked, and stood, facing the closet.

"No," she replied, drawing her gown around her and reaching into the nightstand by her bed. When she turned, she was pointing a .38 toward the closet.

"Raven?" She asked, glancing at Eric.

"Sonofabitch!" he swore, stepped to the closet, and threw the door open.

Sonny pressed the forward button on his chair and sped forward.

"Baca!" Eric cried.

"Who?" Mona exclaimed, a hair's breadth away from pulling the trigger.

"This is Sonny Baca, the private investigator!" Eric explained. "What the hell are you doing here!"

"Looking for the plutonium," Sonny replied, staring from the barrel of the pistol into Mona's eyes. As long as he kept eye contact, she might not fire. He smiled. Most people didn't shoot at a smiling person. But then, Mona Vandergriff wasn't most people.

"So this is the great Sonny Baca." She smiled, and her trigger finger eased. "I should kill you for breaking and entering."

"Ruin your carpet," Sonny replied, still staring at her.

Her smile broadened. "You're probably right." She glanced at Eric. "Should I?"

Sonny cleared his throat. "Uh, I've got someone outside waiting for me. A shot would bring them in—"

"I don't give a shit who you've got," the undaunted Mona replied. "This is a break-in. You threatened us. I have a right to defend myself."

"You've got a point," Sonny said, widening his smile. Lord, she had a point.

Eric raised his arm, hesitated. His voice grew icy.

"Who's waiting for you?"

"One of Matt Paiz's boys—"

"I don't believe you! What the hell are you doing here?"

"I told you, looking for the plutonium," Sonny replied.

"Why here? Oh, you think we have it?" He laughed.

"You set me up," Sonny replied, "so you became a suspect."

"What do you mean set you up?"

"You didn't tell me about Raven's past. That he was a courier for the labs. That you've used him in the past."

Eric nodded, his shoulders sagged. "Put the gun away," he whispered. Mona let her arm drop to her side. Sonny let a sigh of relief escape softly.

"That was the past," Eric said. "We didn't know he would go crazy."

"Is that why you're trying to kill him?"

"He needs to be killed for a lot of reasons," Eric replied.

"Doyle has a contract on him?" Sonny asked.

"I don't inquire into Doyle's business," Eric shot back. "All I know is the man has a plutonium pit, he's running around the country, and he has already hired one greedy Ukrainian! If Doyle takes him out, so much the better."

"He *also* knows a lot," Sonny said.

"What do you mean?"

"He knows about the Avengers."

Eric glanced at Mona, who was coldly watching the exchange, as if measuring the two. She picked up her glass of wine to sip, shrugged.

"I don't know what you're talking about," Eric said.

Mona stepped forward, raising the pistol again. "Yes, I can say I shot in self-defense."

"A man in a wheelchair is not much of a threat," Sonny said.

"You know too much," she replied.

"Don't let him rile you," Eric said, stepping in front of her. "A lot of people in government know about the

Avengers," he said, looking at Sonny. "The FBI has a file on them. So what's it to us?"

"*Very few* people in government know about them," Sonny replied. "The real question is, what do *you* know about them?"

"Nothing," Eric replied. "The FBI says it's a hotheaded militia group. Saturday soldiers pissed off at the government. I don't understand what you're getting at."

"You hired me to find Raven and never told me he had worked for the labs!" Sonny exploded. "That's what I'm getting at. And the military uniforms in the closet! What about the Doomsday group?" Sonny asked, motioning to the closet.

"Oh, I get it," Mona replied. "You're trying to tie me to a militia group." She laughed softly. "You're way off track. I've been a sharpshooter since I was in college. Saturdays when I get a chance to go out, I go to the range and shoot. I dress up for the part. There's a group of us—ladies. Mostly professional women. We call ourselves Doomsday. If it proves anything, you're welcome to join us sometime. I assure you, we're quite harmless, perhaps that's why we use the name Doomsday. Some of the nicest women in town belong."

Eric nodded, confirming her story. Alibis thick as flies, Sonny thought. Where did the truth lie?

"You haven't done your research, Mr. Baca," Mona continued. "Or should I call you Sonny. You should know our security receives briefings from the FBI. We keep files on terrorist groups. Actually, we keep files on any nation, corporation, or individual who might threaten our firm. That's no secret."

"Same at the labs. The FBI helps us, so we supply them with information," Eric said.

"Why didn't you tell me about Raven?"

"Not relevant," Eric responded. "The only thing you have to know is that he's got the plutonium. If you can help Paiz, fine. If not—"

"It's not fine," Sonny raised his voice. "Not if I put my life on the line!"

Mona raised an eyebrow, smiled. "You mean like being shot for being in the wrong woman's bedroom?"

"You're making too much of the Avenger thing," Eric said. "The truth is there are groups like them all over the country."

"None so well placed," Sonny replied.

"I think you should leave now," Mona said. She had kept her eyes on him the entire time, measuring him. She had come close to killing him, and the excitement shone in her eyes.

"You need a security system," he said.

"I know," she replied, "or take my chances with whoever breaks in."

Eric looked at her, frowned. "Just get out of here."

"Sure," Sonny replied.

"And you'd better tell your hacker that we've got his number. Tell him it's a federal offense tapping into our computers."

"Don't know what you're talking about," Sonny replied. "It's been a pleasure. Enjoy the rest of the evening."

"I'm sure I will," Mona answered, glancing at Eric. "Not even your break-in can ruin that."

Sonny scooted his chair out of the room, followed by Eric.

"You know she could have killed you," he said at the front door.

"I thought of that," Sonny replied.

"I don't want your blood on my hands. I think it best you forget about playing a role in finding the plutonium. I'm calling Paiz. As of now, our relationship is ended. We never met you, do you understand?"

"You mean you're firing me?" Sonny said sarcastically.

"I never hired you. Your role was to help Paiz. It's over."

"Yeah," Sonny replied. "Except I was being used, and I don't like that. Look, I don't mind you folks playing your games and blowing yourselves to pieces, but there's a lot of good people that shouldn't get hurt. People who still think a democracy suits them fine."

Eric laughed. "Think what you want. I'm only saying this for your own good."

Sonny's anger rose to the surface, but he kept it in check. They had used him, but he was on their turf, and this was no time to blow his top.

"Sure," he said, and scooted down the walk to the van.

A very concerned Lorenza greeted him. "Thank God you're safe. I saw them drive in, but there was no way to warn you. We've got to hurry. Rita's in the hospital!"

"Hospital?"

"Don Eliseo just called. She had a miscarriage!"

23

She never told me," he whispered, shaking his head. Don Eliseo's message had hit him like a ton of bricks.

"She didn't want to worry you," Lorenza replied, gunning the van down the hill. "What's going on with you is a matter of life and death. Finding the kidnapped girls means a lot to her. She wanted you to concentrate on them."

"You knew."

She nodded. "That's why I suggested she see a doctor. She made me promise not to tell you."

"Not to worry me," Sonny said. "She should have told me."

Nothing was more important than Rita. But she was thinking of him and the girls, and so she kept her pregnancy a secret.

"Hurry," he urged Lorenza, realizing she was already driving as fast as she dared. He wanted to go faster, to fly to Rita's side. Concern for Rita's safety pumped through him, mixing with self-anger. Why hadn't he been more aware of the change in Rita?

At Pres Hospital they headed for the maternity ward, and Sonny pushed his chair to the limit down the corridor, whizzing past startled nurses and patients. Lorenza ran beside him. He turned the corner and careered into the nurses' station.

"Rita López! What room is Rita López in?"

The heavyset black nurse peered over her glasses. "Hold on, young man—"

"I need to see Rita!" Sonny shouted. Behind him Lorenza put her hands on his shoulders.

"Easy," she whispered.

"Rita López? She just came in." The nurse flipped through her charts.

"Yes," Sonny nodded. "Where is she? Is she all right?"

"You the husband?" the nurse asked.

"No," Sonny shook his head. "Yes, she's my—"

"Uh-huh," the nurse said, flipping again through the charts on the clipboard. "Sonny Baca?"

"Yes."

"Husband. She just came out of the operating room—"

"Operating room! Is she okay?"

"She's fine," the nurse said, putting aside her chart, turning to Lorenza. "It was a standard procedure. Went just fine. The miscarriage began at home. She's resting—"

"I've got to see her," Sonny interjected.

"Humm," the nurse puckered her lips. "If she's awake, you can visit awhile."

"Yes, please—"

"Follow me," she said, and led them down the hallway.

"Does she need anything?" Lorenza asked the nurse.

"She did ask for lipstick and a comb. By tomorrow she'll be up and around, so she'll need a robe." She opened the door to the room. "Rita, honey, you got some company. You up for a little company?"

"You go on in," Lorenza whispered to Sonny. "I'll drive to the house and pick up some of her things."

"We can do that later—"

"There's things I know she needs. Be back as soon as I can."

"Okay. And flowers. She loves roses." He fumbled for his wallet.

"I'll get them," Lorenza said. "Go on."

Sonny nodded and guided his chair into the room.

"She's resting," the nurse said to Sonny. "Bed number two." She pointed at the bed by the window.

The pregnant woman in bed number one, swollen stomach covered by a white sheet, lay staring at the television. She glanced at Sonny, then turned her gaze back to the set. The TV's light flickered in the room as a soap opera played itself out on the small screen.

"You got company, honey," she said to Rita. Sonny pushed around the curtain to Rita's bedside.

"Sonny," she greeted him, her voice weak, her face pale and drawn. Sonny drew close and took her hands.

"Oh, Sonny," she cried.

He kissed her. "Rita . . ."

"I'll pull the curtain so you can have some privacy," the nurse said. "Now don't go tiring yourself out. And you call me if you need anything," she whispered to Sonny, patting his shoulder as she walked out.

"Yes, thank you."

"I'm sorry, I'm sorry," Rita cried. "It came so suddenly. There was nothing I could do."

"Shuu," Sonny whispered, his voice choking. "You're all right. That's what matters."

"I tried to stop it, but suddenly it started letting loose. There was nothing I could do."

Her words came in soft sobs, her eyes brimming with tears.

"Don't cry, don't cry," Sonny tried to comfort her, holding her hands, reaching up to touch her face, handing her a tissue from the box on the bedstand.

"I don't know why," she sniffed, trying to control her sobs. "Our baby—"

"Don't think about it," Sonny said, searching for comforting words. "Whatever happened, you're safe. That's what matters, amor. You're all right."

"After you and Lorenza left, I went to take a nap. I felt tired. I must have fallen asleep, because I remember the dream. It wasn't a dream, it was a horrible nightmare. Where is Lorenza?"

"She went to the house to pick up some things for you."

"God bless her. She thinks of everything. I have to tell you my dream—"

"The nurse said you have to rest—not to worry yourself."

"No, I have to. It was so vivid, I actually felt I was living it. I finally understand what you've been trying to tell us about your dreams. You said you were *actually* in the dream. That's how I felt."

Sonny felt a shiver. "Yes, tell me your dream."

"I could see everything so clear. I was a Navajo woman, and the red cliffs around me were home. I was in a hogan, about to give birth. Yes, women were there, taking care of me. Then there was shooting and fires, and the army was killing the men and burning the hogans and the peach orchards. You know what it was? It was the time Kit Carson drove the Navajos out of Canyon de Chelly. The men cried his name, like a curse. They shouted for us to run into the hills and hide, but it was too late. It was an army of wolves.

We were rounded up like sheep and made to march many miles."

She stopped to blow her nose and wipe her eyes.

"Don't tire yourself," Sonny pleaded, knowing what was coming.

"No, I want to," Rita whispered. "I want to tell you. Something about the terrible nightmare was so real. I was there, pregnant, and there was no rest. No food. No protection from the cold wind. I began to bleed. I looked around me, and all the women were bleeding. All the strong Navajo women were bleeding to death as they walked, and the blood was staining the earth. No children could be born. We were all strong women, but we were slaves, leaving our land. The babies in our wombs drained out and became the blood marking that trail of tears."

She clutched Sonny's hand. "What does it mean?"

Bile seeped through Sonny's veins. He knew what it meant. He had lost his child, perhaps a son who would carry his name, perhaps a daughter whose beauty would fill their home— Rita had lost her child. That loss was cause enough for the anger he felt, but a new emotion swept over him that was far stronger. Something boiling in his blood, something he tried to control as he held Rita's hand. Vengeance.

"The Long Walk," he whispered. "The Navajos were taken to Bosque Redondo, where the land was so poor it couldn't be farmed. There was no rain. The smallpox nearly finished them. They learned to drink whiskey. The U.S. Army wanted to bring them to their knees."

"Why so much suffering?" Rita questioned.

Because Raven, in many guises, came to bring death and destruction, Sonny thought, but said nothing.

"It's just like you said. We planted corn," Rita continued. "The women were skeletons of death, planting corn, and the plants sprouted, but there was no rain. We prayed, but it wouldn't rain. There wasn't enough food for the people. There was hunger. It was a nightmare. It was so real I must have Navajo blood in me."

"That's what makes you so beautiful, morenita." Sonny kissed her hands.

"My father used to tell stories about the Nuevos Mexicanos who went west, past Jemez Pueblo over to Seboyeta to trade with the Navajos. When they weren't trading, they were fighting each other and taking slaves. Navajo women brought here as slaves. Not one or two, but hundreds. Maybe my ancestors were some of those who went to bring Navajo women to the Río Grande."

"Yes," he whispered. It was so.

"I let you down—"

"Don't say that!" he said. "You didn't let me down. We'll get over this."

"Do you think so?"

"Yes, we can. I love you."

"But everything seems so bleak." She looked out the window. The afternoon had darkened; a cold wind scratched at the window. "The girls? Is there any word of the girls?"

He shook his head.

"Feels like the world is coming to an end," she said sadly. "I don't think we can ever have a child again."

"Shh. Don't think that way."

"You're right. We can get over this. I'll be all right. A little weak, but you're right. I can't let it get me down."

Her eyes filled with tears again.

"You've never seen me cry."

"No."

"God, it's left me empty. Inside."

"You'll be home in no time. Then it's my turn to take care of you."

She smiled. "Oh, sí, you in your chair."

"I feel strong. Really I do. Mira."

He lifted himself forward and stood up, holding the bed.

"See. I'll be walking in no time."

He stood straight, then leaned over and kissed her.

"I'll be able to take care of you."

"Gracias a Dios," she whispered, holding his hands tight for a moment, then letting go as he sat back down.

"I've got new energy. De veras, we'll be okay."

"Yes." She tightened her hold on his hand again.

He leaned his head on the bed.

"Yes, we'll be okay," Rita said, running her fingers through his hair. "I feel a lot better now that you're here."

"Rest," he said, and wiped her tears. He knew he couldn't really feel what she was going through, her loss, but she was safe and that's what mattered to him. They had lost the child, but she was well.

Sonny thought of her nightmare, the torturous journey of the Navajo women. The history of the Navajos, like that of the other New Mexican tribes, was written in blood. Was it only a coincidence that that morning on their way to Mona Vandergriff's, he had been reading about the Diné, the Navajo nation of the Four Corners area?

In the summer of 1863 Kit Carson from Taos had been hired by Brig. Gen. James H. Carleton of the Department of New Mexico to round up the Navajos. The U.S. Army vowed to put an end to their raids once and for all.

Kit Carson, a man who couldn't even write his name, gathered together a New Mexico regiment of volunteers, men who would fight the Indians for any excuse and a few dollars a day. All summer Carson waged war against the

Navajos, killing hundreds, burning fields of corn, scattering sheep, burning hogans, requiring unconditional surrender of those who survived.

By early 1864 he had trapped what was left of the resisters in Canyon de Chelly, the ancient home of the Diné. He stripped them of everything they owned, then marched them across the state to a place near Fort Sumner, a reservation called Bosque Redondo. The Navajos remembered the forced march as the Long Walk. They still told stories of their exile. Hundreds died on the march. Men killed themselves rather than leave their homeland behind. Women and children froze to death in the February cold.

Bosque Redondo became the place of death.

"Qué piensas?" Rita asked.

"Nada," he replied.

"You're probably as tired as I am," she said. "Rest."

Yes, rest. He had been with Billy the Kid in Fort Sumner in the previous dream. Did Rita's nightmare have anything to do with his? Did he have to go back into the dreamworld to find Billy, or Coyote, or someone who would help him understand the tragedy?

He closed his eyes, feeling the warmth of Rita's body by him, secure in her aroma, a scent he knew so well. He was surprised to see the luminous door in front of him, and just before he passed through it, he thought he must be entering the world of Rita's dream. He had never entered someone else's dream. Why now? To return to the Fort Sumner of 1863, find Rita among the Navajo women? Maybe with Billy's and Coyote's help he could rescue her! Maybe he could still reverse what had happened to her in her dream!

You construct the dream, set the stage, he heard don Eliseo's instructions.

He tried to direct the dream toward the bleak and desolate Bosque Redondo where hundreds of Navajos lay dying from hunger, disease—and the worst sickness, the separation they felt from their homeland. To be out of the circle of their homeland was to be separated from their guardian spirits.

Billy? Sonny called in the web of dream.

A shadow came toward him, a stout man holding a carbine in one hand. Behind him his sorrel stallion pawed the ground.

Billy? Is that you?

No, Hijo, soy tu bisabuelo.

Sonny twitched, startled. His bisabuelo? Elfego Baca? Yes, it was him, his great-grandfather, the famed lawman of Socorro County.

Bisabuelo? Is it you?

In flesh and blood, Elfego Baca replied, wiping his thick mustache with his hand.

I can't believe I'm really talking to you.

Pues, here I am. Carne y hueso y un nervio en el pescuezo. Time to ride.

To Fort Sumner?

No, south.

But Rita's dream. The Navajos are in Fort Sumner, and Raven is there! The Bringer of Curses is killing the babies. I gotta go see if I can help Rita.

Hijo, Elfego said, don't you know that sonomabiche Raven doesn't stay in one dream for long. He's gone down to Columbus, New Mexico. Pancho Villa is threatening to cross the border and attack a town on this side. If I know Raven, he's going to try something. We have to warn Pancho!

Why attack Columbus?

They goaded him into doing something by putting

Soledad, his querida, in jail. She was coming over the frontera to work for the gringos, and the army figured if they arrested her and put her in jail, Pancho will come for her. Don't you see, they want him to cross the border! The U.S. will use it as an excuse to take more of México's territory. They'll send Black Jack Pershing after him, and the general will take over México's northern mines.

But I thought Pancho Villa was your enemy? Sonny said.

Pancho my enemy? That's just a story the newspapers made up. Look, in the New Mexico territory a man has to learn to play both sides. In the spring of 1911 Madero's army, with Villa's help, defeated the Díaz forces at Ciudad Juárez. That toppled the Díaz regime, and Díaz fled to France. Madero became president of México. Anyway, I was in El Paso, and right after the battle Pancho asked me to deliver some rifles to him. The border blocked, I couldn't get across, so Pancho thought I let him down. After that he claimed I stole one of his prized Mauser rifles.

Elfego laughed and held up the rifle. Well, I did keep one of the Mausers—as pay. But Pancho got so mad that he offered a reward for me. But that's in the past. We've been good friends ever since. Now he's as mad as a castrated bull, and he wants to do this pendejada. He's only going to get himself killed. Vamos! Let's ride!

The stocky Elfego Baca was surprisingly swift on his feet. In one leap he mounted the sorrel stallion, calling for Sonny to mount the red mare.

Viva Villa! he cried, and they slapped leather and rode south, along the Río Grande, past Belén, Socorro—where they stopped to eat and rest, and then on to Hot Springs and south.

On March 9, 1916, a very weary and hungry Elfego Baca and his great-grandson Sonny Baca rode into the small

desert town of Columbus, New Mexico, a stone's throw
from the Mexican border. From the distance they had seen
the smoke rising into the clear blue sky. Gunshots echoed as
Villa's ragged army rode up and down the main street, firing
on anything that moved. Eight citizens of the United States
lay dead or dying in the streets.

We're too late, Elfego Baca cried. Pancho's here! I'll
check the cantina, you look around!

The tattered remnants of Villa's Mexican troops rode up
and down the main street, firing into the air, laying torches
to buildings, venting their anger on the quiet border town.
The U.S. had aided Carranza's army and defeated Villa in
the battle of Agua Prieta at Hermoso, and a defeated and
brooding Villa had retreated to the Sierra Madre to lick his
wounds. Hunger stalked the camp, and so the women
sneaked across the border, seeking work to feed their families.

Sonny spurred his horse down the street and reared to a
halt in front of the jail. The man entering the jailhouse was
none other than Francisco "Pancho" Villa, the great general
of the Mexican revolution. Sonny jumped off his horse and
followed him in.

The deputy in charge fired at Villa, missed, and Villa
fired back, hitting him in the arm. He grabbed the deputy's
pistol and the jail keys and rushed to open the cell door.

The woman who rushed into Pancho's arms was Soledad.

Amor, she hugged and kissed him. Gracias a Dios que
has venido. Por qué me tratan como criminal los Americanos?

Los pinche bolillos no quieren al Mexicano, Pancho
replied. Then, sensing Sonny behind him, he turned and
aimed his rifle.

Sonny held up his hands. No despare! Soy amigo!

Quién eres?

Francisco Elfego Baca, bisnieto de Elfego Baca.

Bisnieto de Elfego Baca, my old compañero. Villa smiled. Well I'll be a sonomagón. How is old Elfego?

He's fine. Right now he's looking for you, trying to stop you from this pendejada—I mean, from this raid.

Ah, this is nothing, Villa motioned with his rifle, his other hand still around Soledad's waist. To get my woman back, I would take on the entire United States Army! Maybe I will anyway, and get our land back from the gringos!

He looked out the jailhouse window at the burning town. Maybe it's no longer up to us to take it back. Maybe you Chicanos will have to do the thing. He was contemplative only for a second, then looked at Soledad. Forgive my manners. This is my beloved, Soledad. I came for her.

Soledad smiled. Con mucho gusto.

El gusto es mío, Sonny replied.

We can no longer support our women in las montañas, Villa explained. There is nothing to eat. The traitors who sold México banished us to the mountains. Soledad and other women come here to work, and the law—if that's what we can call it—threw her in jail for being illegal. Can you imagine that? They say she crossed the border illegally. What is illegal? That border is illegal, because it was bought and sold by thieves! Politicians made that border, not la gente! He spit. I do not respect the border of scoundrels! And if they threaten my woman, then I will make a revolution!

Sonny agreed. To protect one's woman and familia was to be macho, and Pancho Villa had just earned his respect. He was about to speak when he felt someone enter. He felt the hair along the back of his neck rise. He turned and faced Raven.

Raven!

Raven's evil smile spread across his thin lips. He venido por Soledad, he said.

Pájaro desgraciado! Villa cursed and stepped in front of Soledad. Before he could reach his pistol, Raven fired.

The bullet hit Pancho's shoulder and spun him around. He fell to the floor, a curse of "hijo de la chingada" on his lips, blood streaming from the wound. Soledad screamed and knelt at his side.

Sonny jumped to face Raven.

Do you think you can stop me? Raven said. You can't even order your dreams. I create them! And I have brought you here to see me take your Mexican grandmother. Now I have the four: Indian, Spanish, Mexican, and—

No! Sonny shouted, struggling forward to stop Raven. I stopped you in Fort Sumner, I can stop you here!

Raven laughed. Do you *really* think you've learned to play a role in your dreams? You have no guide to help you. He struck and Sonny fell to the edge of his dream, a world half-light, half-shade.

"Bisabuelo," Sonny whispered, clinging to the dream he felt slipping away, knowing if he didn't face Raven now, he would take Soledad.

Outside, a roaring wind whipped dust and smoke into the brazen sky, and Sonny couldn't tell if the storm blew in the dream or outside the hospital wall.

He's dead! All your ancestors are dead!

No, Sonny sobbed.

And your child is dead!

My child!

Yes! Where was your don Eliseo when you needed him? He grasped Soledad's arm and pulled her away, she resisting and screaming but no match for Raven. On the floor a bleeding Pancho Villa struggled to rise to his feet, but he, too, was no match for Raven's power.

In the wind Sonny heard Raven's final words. Don Eliseo's the only one who could help you. Now you will die, Sonny Baca!

"No!" Sonny shouted with a start.

"Amor, amor," Rita said, reaching for him. "You fell asleep."

He blinked and looked around to remind himself he was in the hospital room with Rita.

"Raven?" Rita asked.

Sonny nodded. The images of the dream were still clear. Raven had stolen the fourth grandmother, and as Raven taunted in the dream, it meant Sonny's death.

That meant another girl was missing!

"I have to call Lorenza," Sonny said, making an excuse. He took the phone from the nightstand, dialed his number, and pushed the number of his answering machine.

As he feared, the frightened voice of a woman sounded on the tape. "Mr. Baca, my name is Dolores Saavedra. You don't know me, but your name and number were given to us by the police chief. Mr. Sam Garcia. We hate to bother you, but we want to hire you. Our daughter Celeste . . . We have read about the missing girls, and we're afraid for her. We're turning to you for help. She's in a play. . . . We're with her every night . . . at the Kimo Theater—"

A harsh screeching sound interrupted the message as the tape ground to a halt.

24

What is it?" Rita asked. Sonny looked pale.

"Lorenza's probably on her way, she didn't answer." He had to lie, and he was saved from further explanation by Lorenza entering the room.

"Buenas noches," she said, coming around the curtain to greet Rita. She held Rita, and Rita sobbed on her shoulder.

"Oh, Lore, I'm so glad to see you. Both of you. I didn't mean for this—"

"Sh," Lorenza comforted her. "It's going to be all right. Look, I went by your place and brought your robe, a few other things. And I called the restaurant and talked to Marta. She'll close up. She sent her prayers."

"Thanks, thanks for everything. I feel helpless—"

"You've been through a lot."

"And you need to rest," the nurse said, entering the room. "This young lady is under strict doctor's orders to get a lot of rest. We have a lounge down the hall where you can wait—"

"When can she go home?" Sonny asked.

The nurse shrugged. "Doctor sees her tomorrow. I think after that."

"I'll be ready to go."

"And we'll be here for you," Sonny promised, kissing her.

"I wish you didn't have to go."

"Hey, you got me for life. But you have to rest, nurse's orders. We'll be here first thing in the morning. The important thing is for you to rest. Get a good night's sleep. Okay."

Rita nodded. "I love you. . . ."

"And I love you, amor." Sonny kissed her again; she smiled, then closed her eyes.

"She's going to be all right," Lorenza said on the way down the empty hall.

"She looks pale," he replied, trying to keep his composure, keeping a lid on the anger he felt inside.

They went out into the December night and into a cold wind gusting down from the West Mesa, driving all but the homeless off the streets. On Central Avenue, around Jack's Cantina and the Blood Donor Center a few shivering figures in shaggy overcoats hurried down the avenue.

Rita was right, Sonny thought as he zippered his jacket. The world had gone cold and dreary. There was misery in the streets, misery in their hearts. The child, their child, seed of their love, was gone, blood flushed away, and Rita had been alone during the frightening experience.

It was cold inside the van. Sonny lifted a few books off the floor and placed them on the counter. In the dim light he read one title: *History of the Navajo.*

Fate or destiny or whatever the uninitiated called the great force of the energy that swept around the world had long ago settled in his soul. It stretched from battles in past times with Raven to Rita's nightmare of the Navajos' Long March.

Lorenza started the van, and as they waited for it to warm

up, Sonny told her Rita's nightmare. "Then I dozed off and ran into Raven again." He told her his nightmare and the abduction of Soledad and the call he had placed to his answering machine.

"He has Owl Woman, Caridad de Anaya, Epifana, and Soledad," Lorenza said. "And your child," she whispered.

"And in this life, Consuelo, Catalina, and Carmen. Now he's going after Celeste." Sonny shivered, not from the cold but from the foreboding sense of time ending that settled in his blood.

"I thought I was learning how to be in the dream and turn him back. Why was I so helpless tonight? He hit me and knocked me out of my dream."

"He used the strength of the child he just took," Lorenza whispered.

"How?" he asked. He had guessed as much, but how did Lorenza know?

"Raven is everywhere now, moving freely. The minute I heard about Rita, I suspected—anyway, I really went to Rita's to check the place. I found four black feathers."

"Damn him!" Sonny cursed, and slammed his fist into the counter. "Damn the sonofabitch! He taunted me in the dream! He couldn't get me, so he went after Rita! God Almighty, what's there left for me to do?"

He lay his head on the counter and sobbed, his pain palpable in the van, the pain of a man who has just lost a child. Lorenza reached out and held him. "There is nothing you could do, Sonny. Once evil works its way into the dream, the only way to stop it is to enter the world of the sorcerer."

He looked up at her, wiped his eyes. "What do you mean enter his world?"

"You have to go to his dream."

"How? Tell me how. I'll follow him to hell and make him pay!"

"Only don Eliseo has the power to enter Raven's world. Only he can take you there."

"Don Eliseo?" Sonny looked closely into Lorenza's eyes. All along she had revealed the world of spirits in parts, as he needed them; now she had said the old man could enter Raven's dark world.

"Yes," Lorenza said.

"He never said anything—"

"He's been fighting the Bringer of Curses longer than anyone."

"Why now?"

"Now is the time for you to know. Don Eliseo knew I would take you along the path as far as I could. To fight someone like Raven takes strength."

"Me. That's why I was chosen?"

"Don Eliseo is old. It could be very dangerous for him."

"There isn't much time left, is there?" Sonny asked, looking into her eyes, fearing the truth in them.

"No," she said. "Tomorrow is the solstice. Raven has the four grandmothers. He only needs one more girl. . . ."

"What now?" Sonny asked.

"We go to don Eliseo."

"To ask him for help? But you said he is old, and it could be dangerous for him."

Lorenza's eyes gathered the dim light in the van, and they reflected sadness. "It's the only way," she said, pulling back to the driver's seat.

The old man was his guide, his mentor, they were kindred souls. Don Eliseo had passed on the learning and the struggle to Sonny. When Sonny first began to realize this was his destiny, he had resisted. First he didn't want to go to

Lorenza for the cleansing ceremony, then he doubted her, and just days ago he had even doubted don Eliseo. But now he had seen too many things. He had been to the spirit world. He had been initiated, the power to fight Raven had been given to him, as he knew he must someday pass it to someone else.

"Bueno," he said, resigned. "Let's go see don Eliseo." He felt drained, from the day and the emotion.

Lorenza drove out of the hospital parking lot.

"How do you kill someone who has no history?"

"He has a history," Lorenza replied. "Evil has a history."

"I enter myself to find him," Sonny said.

"Yes. But now you need the medicine that don Eliseo has been preparing."

"The dream catcher?"

"Yes. Dreams are only one way into the world of spirits. Some shamans meditate. If you can take the medicine of a shaman with you, you can control the evil that comes in the dream. Make it disappear. Don Eliseo will teach you this cleansing of the soul."

Cleansing of the soul? Now it became clear. It wasn't just about cleansing away spirits that attached to the soul, it was about going within. Going deep to the root of the soul and cleansing the evil that came inherent in human nature, the impulse toward destruction. Lorenza was telling him there was more yet to be revealed. The old man had an ace up his sleeve, there was hope. Sonny listened.

"Raven found your strong suit. You are a dreamer. You make an excellent brujo, but you are lighthearted. Sangre liviana, as the old people say. You love the joys of this world too much."

She's right, Sonny thought. Wine, women, and dance. That's all he ever wanted, to be a regular guy, one of la plebe, one of the vatos, doing the things most men his age did. Thirty was a time to enjoy life, to be alive, to take Rita dancing on Saturday nights, to make love, to marry her and have children.

Then his soul had been revealed, and his life had acquired a very serious edge. The apprenticeship took on meaning. He has been chosen to be a shaman. A winter shaman.

"Nothing wrong with having a good time," Sonny protested weakly.

"No," Lorenza smiled. "There isn't. It's part of what women love in you. You love life, your sensuality flows freely and naturally. But the Calendar of Dreams is also your inheritance. The time was right for it to be revealed to you, so Owl Woman appeared in your dream. She *is* your grandmother. Raven recognized this, but you didn't."

"Ah," Sonny nodded. She was right. Even after Lorenza helped him find his coyote nagual to fight Raven, he had doubted. He had not taken seriously the power latent in her teachings. He had resisted. He could blame the electric shock he got from Stammer and these last months of recuperation, but that was only an excuse. The truth was that when he fought Raven on the mountain, he had seen a vision of the world of spirits, and its awesome power had frightened him.

"I was afraid." There. He dared to say it.

"I know," she said, studying him in the rearview mirror. "We feel fearful when we learn we have a gift. We doubt it, try to get rid of it, run from it, and in the end we recognize its goodness. With the gift we can clarify not only our own path, we can help others. So we join the battle."

"Like don Eliseo," Sonny said. "He's spent a lifetime learning about his power, using it to help people."

"Yes. Now it's you. You are a Dream Bringer."

"A Dream Bringer," Sonny repeated. Oh. Lord, why me? Why me?

As if reading his thoughts, Lorenza replied: "You can go in and out of the world of spirits so easily, so vividly. To tell the truth, I've never met anyone with this ability. Sometimes to probe the dream we need to hypnotize the person, go into meditation, do a night of drumming and chanting. We need to pay a lot of attention to ceremony, and sometimes even the ceremony can get in the way. But you seem to zap in and out. Once you learn to be the actor in your dream, the world will become complete. One."

"And Raven, too, has this power?"

"Yes. It comes from the same source."

"The same source?"

"You are the dream," she answered.

"He can enter mine, so I can enter his."

"Yes."

"How?"

"That's where don Eliseo comes in."

"Ah," Sonny mused. Yes, he had to meet Raven head-on. It was time.

"I saved Rosa. I can do it again!"

"Yes. The power is in you."

Sonny looked out the window. A lone Christmas decoration, a plastic candle hanging from a lightpost, swung in the cold wind. In the awesome dark of the night someone had hung a candle. Someone believed in the light. He wasn't alone.

La Paz Lane was quiet when Lorenza drove into Sonny's driveway. It was cold and it was dinnertime; no neighbors stirred in the street. Across the way a light shone in don

Eliseo's kitchen window. The old man had returned from the pueblo.

Chica's barking greeted them at the door, and when Sonny entered and flipped on the light, she scooted around in circles as fast as she could go, then leaped up into Sonny's lap.

"Chica, how are you, girl? Sorry we've been gone so long. Did you visit don Eliseo?"

Chica barked.

"You hungry?" Sonny guided his chair into the kitchen. "I hate to leave her alone all day. I don't think dogs are for bachelors. They need family."

He paused and looked into the small dog's eyes. Yes, she needed family, someone around the house, children to play with, to go on walks with. Family, he thought, and the word stuck in his throat. He thought of Rita in the hospital and he shivered.

"Cold," he said.

"I'll turn up the thermostat," Lorenza offered, touching his shoulder as she walked by, "and I'll get Chica some food. Come on, Chica. Food for you, coffee for us."

"Thanks," Sonny said, and guided his chair to his answering machine.

Dolores Saavedra's voice played again, there was a pause, then a garbled "she's in a play. . . . We're with her every night . . . at the Kimo Theater—"

But no phone number to call.

"Damn, I've got to replace the tape," he muttered, "or fix the machine."

He picked up the phone and called the South Broadway library.

"Feliz Navidad," Vangie answered.

"Vangie, this is Sonny—"

"Sonny, cómo 'stás?"

"Bien," Sonny replied. "Is Cyber around?"

"He's always here, at the computer as usual. We're having a Christmas party for the neighborhood kids, showing them the new *Christmas Carol* movie, popcorn and hot chocolate, and Cyber's at his post. Hold on."

After a wait Cyber answered: "Sonny, am I glad to hear from you. We got trouble."

"What kind of trouble?" Sonny asked.

"Lab security is hot on my trail. They've hired a Net detective. Right now I'm playing tag with him, but I don't know how much longer I can hide."

"Eric mentioned their detectives were on to you. Get out. I don't want you to get in trouble because of me."

"I can't get out, Sonny. And don't feel guilty. Remember, I was a mole before I met you. I'm getting close to a lot of caca."

"Like?"

"Like I'm getting close to finding my dad. There's a government file. Really encrypted. Top secret. Code name: Roswell—The Apocalypse. My dad used to read everything that had to do with the Roswell Incident. He told me what happened there. You know the story. A flying saucer crashed near Roswell in 1947. The air force found aliens from outer space. They have a very encrypted file on the whole thing. There's a small group of generals in the air force who really believe there are flying saucers out there. You wouldn't believe the incidents they have listed. Anyway, a spaceship crashed in Roswell, and they actually found bodies. Not human bodies. The air force investigated and told the press it was a weather balloon that crashed. But they took the bodies from the wrecked flying saucer."

"Took the bodies? What the hell are you saying, Cyber?"
Has the kid flipped, Sonny wondered, or am I not tuning in?

"About the same time the Russians are threatening the
U.S. with atomic bombs. They're building all sorts of secret
weapons, including airplanes that can carry a nuclear bomb
but can't be spotted by radar. Now they call it the stealth
bomber."

Sonny grew irritated. "What does Roswell have to do
with anything?"

"The group in the military who took the alien bodies and
hushed up everything are in charge of the Roswell file. Now
they call themselves the Avengers."

The hair along the back of Sonny's neck prickled.

"Why in the hell would they be interested in something
that took place forty years ago? Something that's science
fiction?"

"It's not science fiction," Cyber's voice rose defensively.

"What is it?" Sonny asked calmly.

"They took aliens from that UFO, Sonny. And they're
still alive."

"I don't—"

"You don't believe. Okay with me. But that's what I gathered from the files I could read. This group called the
Avengers, they've kept those aliens alive all these years!"

"You can't prove—"

"No, I can't prove anything. But if I crack their files, I
can!"

"Why would they keep the secret all these years?"

"Because they didn't know how to use the aliens. Now
they do. There's something in those alien bodies they can
use!"

Sonny rubbed his forehead. He was losing it.

"This group uses government money and experts, but

they don't answer to anyone. They're government people, but they're not even listed in Pentagon files. It's scary."

"Could be loonies, a wild militia group," Sonny suggested. "They're using computers now, communicating with each other."

"No. These guys are too smart. What they've set up is impossible to get into. They must have their own fiber-optic lines. It's sophisticated, Sonny, believe me."

"And you think your dad came across them?"

"That's right. He probably tripped into their network by accident. He was a Roswell Incident freak, always looking for stuff about it, so he found the Avengers. He broke their code. He found the Avengers, reported to his superior, and that same day he disappeared. Does the name Jack Ward ring a bell?"

"CEO of Sandia Labs," Sonny said.

"My dad's supervisor," Cyber replied.

No, Sonny thought. Jack Ward wasn't into disappearing people. Cyber had gone overboard.

"He stumbled into Avenger territory and got murdered."

"You think they killed your dad?"

"Yes."

"Whoa. Wait a minute—"

Cyber's gone off the edge, Sonny thought. Accusing the labs of murdering his father. Had Cyber been in cyberspace too long? Lost it? The whole thing smacked of science fiction. Cyber had gone loco in his eagerness to find his father.

"You don't believe me," Cyber said. "You think I've coasted into cyberdream? You think I'm making this up?"

"I don't know what to believe," Sonny replied. The headache that had been forming in the back of his skull pressed down on him. He wanted to help Cyber, but the information was jumbled, Cyber had his own agenda, and yeah, maybe he was falling into cyberdream. The fatigue and Rita's loss weighed heavy on Sonny.

"How do the aliens figure into all this?"

"A superior intelligence, Sonny. Don't you get it! If they can build a machine to fly to earth from outer space, they are smart! Maybe the Avengers have the aliens building a spaceship. For sure they're milking them about a communication system. Maybe telepathic, I don't know."

"Telepathic?" Sonny shook his head. "That's great stuff, Cyber. For a *Star Trek* episode. What I need is *real* information."

"Like what?"

"Like Mona Vandergriff's favorite pastime! Her hobby!" Sonny asked.

"Target shooting," came Cyber's reply. "She's a sharpshooter. Goes out once a month. That's in her file."

"You told me, and her secretary told me, that she and Eric were supposed to meet in D.C.! I broke into her home and they caught me. They weren't in D.C.!"

"D.C. as in Doña Catarina Street. I gave you her address. The secretary probably covers for her."

Sonny groaned. Yeah, Cyber had given him the info. He had just been too dense to break it down.

"I screwed up," Sonny admitted. "But I need info on Raven, not the Roswell aliens!"

"I checked through Chernenko's records, the scientist on the list of names you gave me. The man was getting e-mail messages from the Avengers."

"Chernenko was working with the Avengers?"

"Yup," Cyber replied. "The messages are coded, it would take an expert to break them. In the ones I could read, they gave Chernenko instructions to pass on to Raven. They called him Ke-mo-sab-ay."

"Kimo Sabi?" Sonny interrupted. "What Tonto used to call the Lone Ranger."

"Yeah, that's it. It's not a word from the Pueblo languages, I checked that. I think it's a name taken from the northern tribes. I can do a search—"

"No, no, I don't have time," Sonny said. "Kimo Sabi," he repeated the word. "Kimo sabe. Kimo knows something. What?"

"You tell me" came Cyber's reply, irritating Sonny more, because on top of the headache he felt a numbness spreading over his body, entangling his mind so he could barely think. The Avengers used both Raven and Chernenko, then played them against each other, and Raven used everyone.

"Kimo Sabi is Raven?"

"Yes," Cyber replied.

"Thanks, Cyber, you've been a great help. Now get out."

"What are you going to do, Sonny?"

"Go see a play," Sonny replied, and clicked off the phone.

Dolores Saavedra, Celeste's mother, had said she was in a play at the Kimo. He opened the Sunday paper on the table and flipped through it until he came to the Arts section. There it was: a Christmas play at the Kimo Theater downtown.

He looked at his watch. If they hurried, they might catch Raven before he took Celeste!

25

The Kimo downtown!" Sonny said, grabbing his jacket and turning to Chica. "Stay, Chica. Sorry to leave you again, but this is an emergency!"

He told Lorenza what Cyber had found as they sped downtown.

"According to Cyber, the Avengers were using both Chernenko and Raven."

"They thought they were using Raven to bring in the plutonium—" Lorenza said. "Nobody *uses* him."

"Celeste is in the play at the Kimo. She's Raven's last target!" Sonny said. "Consuelo, Catalina, Carmen. Celeste is number four."

They reached downtown in record time. Lorenza took the red light at Fourth and Marquette, scooted to Sixth Street, then to Central. There were no parking spaces near the Kimo.

"Park in front!" Sonny cried out.

Lorenza made a wild U-turn on Central and climbed the sidewalk to stop the van right in front of the box office.

There were no city cops in sight, but an angry, dark-haired Chicana came running out as Sonny let his chair out of the van. "Hey! You can't park here! It's against the law!"

"Who are you?" Sonny asked.

"I'm CC, the director, that's who. And who are you?"

"Police," Sonny said with authority, taking out his wallet and flashing his great-grandfather's sheriff's badge. "I need to get in there."

"That's a cheap way to see the play," she complained. "I would have sent complimentary tickets."

"Is Celeste here tonight?"

"Celeste? You mean Gila. Yes, but the play's already started."

"Get us in," Sonny said. "It's a matter of life and death."

CC grimaced. "Spare me the bad lines."

"Step aside," Sonny said, and plowed his wheelchair into the lobby.

"No need to interrupt the play," she cried, rushing after him.

Inside, the lobby was warm and deserted, except for a dark-haired woman who stood behind the punchbowl.

"I need to get in there!" Sonny insisted.

"Okay, okay, but try to be quiet."

She led them into the darkened theater. On stage the confrontation scene between San Miguel and el Diablo was just starting.

"Who's the Devil?" Sonny asked.

"Vic Silva. He's great. Did you see him in *Billy the Kid?*"

"The play? No." But where's Raven?

The actors, a motley crew that made up the cast of shepherds, had just stepped back to allow the Devil to take center stage. Sonny spotted Celeste, playing the role of the shepherd girl, Gila, the only woman in the group.

Vic wore the mask of a devil, a resplendent red cape, two

horns, and a pitchfork. Speaking lines in old, archaic New Mexican Spanish, he angrily stepped forward, lifted his pitchfork, and looking out at the audience as he called for war and destruction:

O, Miguel, suspende tus dulzuras.
Lo primero que tengo que borrar es el mundo.
Yo mando el sol, mando la luna,
mando ese cielo estrellado.
El sol se verá eclipsado solo porque
yo lo mando. Yo haría todo un infierno.

An appreciative audience applauded the poetic delivery.

Now San Miguel, dressed in white with feathery wings flapping behind him and a wooden sword in one hand, stepped forward and answered the Devil's challenge, declaring that Christ, the Messiah, had been born and that the shepherds would adore him as king of the universe.

San Miguel's speech was not convincing nor as poetic as the Devil's, but he struck at the Devil with his sword and the Devil stumbled backward. A second figure appeared and pushed both San Miguel and the Devil out of the way.

"That's not in the script," CC whispered to Sonny.

The flash of a fireball exploded in front of the actor who had suddenly taken center stage. Dark smoke swirled around him. The audience held up their hands to shield their eyes from the bright flash. A ripple of *oohs* and *ahhs* swept through the theater. The stage effects were great.

Nervous theatergoers jumped into the aisles, unsure of what was happening.

"Raven!" Lorenza exclaimed.

Raven in black, the stagelights shining off his silk outfit, raised his cape and looked fiercely at the audience, and those in the front rows, seeing his hideous face, drew back in horror.

"It's just a mask," said a boy in the front row.

"The play's ended!" Raven shouted. "Gila's mine!" He grabbed the unsuspecting Gila by the wrist.

"No!" she cried in pain.

Raven's piercing eyes found Sonny. "Mine!" he repeated. He had come to kidnap Celeste in front of Sonny, left him the clues to follow, daring him, as always, to stop him.

"Get off the stage!" CC shouted, pushing her way through those crowding the aisle. "Where's José Rodríguez when we need him!"

Others in the audience began to shout: "Get off the stage! We want the old Devil."

"Is this for real?" somebody asked. The play was quickly falling apart.

"Let me go!" a confounded Gila cried, struggling to get loose. The other actors on stage also appeared confused. This was not the play they knew.

Raven turned to the audience. "There will be no birth of Christ," he said scornfully. "The land of Canaan shall remain barren, and your women will remain barren. You must turn to me and pray that I relent. Pray to me as your king!"

A few, believing the scene was part of the play, nodded in agreement.

"Gila!" Sonny shouted, his cry echoing through the theater. "Don't go with him! Fight him!"

"She's mine!" Raven shouted. "Number four! You lose!"

He pulled Gila away, and the audience, hearing her cries, sensed something wrong. This is not the way the play should end. San Miguel the archangel was supposed to beat the Devil and drive him away.

A couple of the actors started forward to help Gila, but a

second flash filled the stage, and Raven and the girl were gone.

"Back alley!" Sonny cried, and he and Lorenza turned to push their way through the crowd.

Outside, Lorenza started the van, and as soon as Sonny boarded, she stepped on the gas. The van lurched forward, leaping off the sidewalk and just barely missing the stoplight on the corner. She turned right onto the street, then into the alley behind the theater. Ahead of them a black van was just squealing away, leaving a cloud of burned rubber in the dark alley.

"That's him!" Sonny shouted.

Now it was onto the streets of Alburquerque, with Lorenza pursuing a reckless Raven, who loved the game he played.

He tried to lose them by driving around downtown streets, in and out of alleys, but Lorenza clung to him. Then he raced up Central Avenue, not stopping at the red lights. The late hour and the cold meant there was little or no traffic. Raven gunned his van up Central, and by the time they drove past Jack's Cantina, they were doing ninety.

"Don't lose him," Sonny whispered, peering intently at the taillights they were following. If they lost Raven, they had nothing. Nada. The clock would quit ticking for Sonny and his grandmothers.

At University Avenue, Raven made a wild left turn, sped to Martin Luther King Avenue, and hung another left. Then he gunned it down the hill toward the center of town.

The van's speed attracted a siren, a red light flashed. They had picked up a city cop, one who quickly got on Lorenza's tail. A bullhorn sounded but the words weren't recognizable.

"We've got help," Lorenza said.

"We need it," Sonny replied, glancing out the window at the car with the flashing light. The men in blue sometimes did come in time. Sonny took the phone, dialed 911, and asked for Police Chief Garcia.

At Broadway an old 1950s veterano in a customized Olds was creeping home toward Sanjo after sharing some mota with some compas in Martineztown. He started across the street, then stopped to stare blindly into the lights of Raven's van pressing down on him. The black van appeared as Doña Sebastiana's death cart. The old pachuco swore, made the sign of the cross, and closed his weary eyes. La Muerte had come for him this night.

Raven's van swerved, hung on two wheels as it went around the Olds, then sped up the overpass.

The old lowrider breathed a sigh of relief and thanked the Virgin. Then he saw Lorenza's van. "Chingao," he whispered, and closed his eyes again. Muerte number one had spared him, but number two was bearing down on him.

Lorenza clipped the front end of the lowriding Olds and spun it around, metal tearing into metal. She swerved and straightened out the van. A ball of fire exploded in the back of the van as the ruptured gas tank caught fire.

"We're on fire!" she cursed, and gunned it up the overpass, Raven's lights were now barely visible, and a second police car was tailing them.

"Stay with him!" Sonny shouted. Raven turned right on Second Street and headed north. Now three police cars had joined the chase.

A police dispatcher came on the line, and Sonny tried to explain the situation, shouting into the phone. "I don't have time to explain! This is an emergency. Call Chief Garcia! This is Sonny Baca! Tell him I'm heading north on Second toward Alameda. I'm chasing Raven! Repeat, Raven! Tell him I've got Raven!"

At that moment a rear tire blew and pulled the van to the left. Lorenza struggled to hold the van straight as it bounced across the median, scooted a hundred yards up the wrong lane, then leaped over the curb onto the wide dirt path along the irrigation ditch.

"Can't hold it!" Lorenza cried, fighting the steering wheel.

She hit the brakes, but the tires couldn't grip the frozen dirt along the deep ditch. The van, trailing flames, skidded and flipped over.

Sonny grabbed the counter, but it tore loose and the books came crashing down on him. On the van's first roll the rear door opened and Sonny and wheelchair flew out. He went sliding down the slope of the ten-foot ditch, then the chair went out from under him and he hit the ground.

He was aware of the bouncing and rolling, then a brilliant light, like phosphorus burning, exploded in his brain, an explosion of lovely colors creating a luminous door through which he entered.

"I have entered the dream." He heard his voice.

The pyrotechnic display coalesced into a rainbow, then the rainbow became a shower of bright butterflies, iridescent, many-colored butterflies that danced in front of him, then slowly fluttered away.

He heard a voice call his name.

A muddy hand reached out and touched his face.

I'm alive, he thought, his eyes fluttering open, feeling the frozen, damp earth of the ditch. His face was covered with dirt and mud, as were his hands and arms. He kicked and felt his feet strike the brittle grass and weeds of the ditch. He didn't know how long he'd been out. Down the ditch the burning van lit up the night.

Lorenza, he thought, and cried her name.

"I'm here," he heard her response. She appeared, hovering over him, kneeling beside him.

"Are you all right?" he asked.

"Just roughed up. You?"

"I can't tell."

"Any pain?"

"No."

"Can you move?"

"Yeah."

"I lost him . . ."

"Those lights . . ."

"Cops," she said. "Do you feel any broken bones?"

"No."

"God, you just flew out—I hit the air bag. Don't move, the cops will help. Luckily the gas tank didn't explode—"

The police cars that had been chasing them had skidded to a stop, their lights illuminating Lorenza and Sonny sitting in the ditch. Several police officers with pistols and shotguns drawn stood behind their cars.

"Don't nobody move!" one shouted.

"I can't, cabrón!" Sonny cursed.

"Hands above your heads!" the second officer shouted.

Lorenza stood, held her hands in the air. "We need an ambulance! We need help!"

"My books," Sonny groaned. The books were burning to ash.

"Sonofabitch was doin' a hundred," one of the officers said, approaching them cautiously.

"It's a wonder anyone's alive." Two drew close, a third ran toward the van with a fire extinguisher in hand.

"The chief just radioed in. He knows the guy."

"Are you hurt?" one of the officers who drew near asked.

"No," Lorenza replied. "We need help. He was in the wheelchair when we went over."

The cop shone his light on the wrecked wheelchair that stood twenty feet away. "He won't be using that again."

"Help me up," Sonny said, holding out his hand. "I'm okay."

"You're not supposed to move," the officer said, shining his light on Sonny's muddied face. "Ambulance will be here soon. Chief Garcia called. He's on his way, too."

"Never mind the ambulance," Sonny complained. "Did you guys stop the black van we were chasing?"

"No," the cops answered. "We didn't see a black van. We were following you."

"Damn!" Sonny cursed. He pushed his leg to brace himself and felt it respond. For the first time in months the leg had actually responded to a command to move. He tried again and his leg moved, a surge of energy filling the muscles.

"I think I can—"

"Best not to move. We've got an ambulance coming," the officer that knelt by him repeated. He shone his flashlight in Sonny's eyes. The guy didn't appear to be drunk or on dope, and he had just escaped uninjured from the wreck, but his eyes seemed happy, juiced up, maybe the adrenaline.

Somewhere in the excitement an angry Chief Garcia appeared at the top of the ditch, then scooted down.

"Sonny! You sonofabitch! You could've gotten yourself killed!"

"He wasn't driving," Lorenza explained. She had taken off her coat and covered Sonny. The night was freezing.

"Was it Raven?" Garcia asked, scowling.

"Yes," Lorenza replied, and turned her attention to Sonny. "Can you feel anything?" She squeezed his hands.

"I'm okay," Sonny groaned. He was fully conscious now, and the first thought that crossed his mind was that they had lost Raven and the girl.

"You're bleeding," Lorenza said. Blood was dripping from a scrape on his cheek.

"You were chasing Raven?" Garcia asked.

"Till your boys got on our tail," Sonny said.

"This van was doing over a hundred on this stretch," the cop who had knelt by Sonny said to the chief. "We had a report that someone driving a van had just kidnapped a girl at the Kimo Theater. These two were running fast."

"Raven took a girl?" Garcia asked Sonny.

Sonny nodded. "Help me up."

"No, stay on your back," Lorenza ordered.

"An ambulance will be here any minute," the officer said again.

"No, help me up," Sonny insisted.

"You sure?" Garcia asked. "The ambulance is here. It's best if they strap you down and take you in."

"Dammit! Help me up!" Sonny repeated.

Garcia and the cop lent a hand, and Sonny stood up, unsure of his strength for a moment but aware that a change had taken place during the crash. His legs, which till now had felt so numb and useless, felt strong. He tested them by taking a step forward.

"Sonny? You sure you can—" A worried Lorenza spoke to him.

Sonny smiled, wiped mud away from his lips, and took another step. "I can walk! Help me out of here."

Garcia and the cop helped him up the steep side of the ditch, and when he stood at the top, Sonny was breathing hard, but there was no doubt about it, his legs were responding. He pushed the two aside and took a step forward.

"I can walk!" he shouted into the glare of the police car lights.

A clanging firetruck from Ranchitos drove up, followed by an emergency rescue vehicle. Two attendants jumped out.

"You the injured party?" one asked, looking at Sonny.

"Do I look injured!" Sonny shouted. "I can walk!"

26

Sonny rested in his bed. A hot shower and aspirin had eased some of the soreness, but what had really buoyed his spirits was knowing he could walk again. Some of the despair he felt over Rita's miscarriage lifted.

"The shock must have cleared up the circuit board," Lorenza said as she bandaged the cut above his left eye. "Your brain finally can get messages to the legs."

"The blow to the head?" he asked.

"Probably. We'll see what your neurologist says."

"Yeah," Sonny whispered. He stroked the sleeping Chica.

Chief Garcia had given them a ride home. Sonny had not only been able to walk to the police car, he had walked from the car into the house. Whatever had happened was miraculous, and he kept reaching down, rubbing his thighs, checking their strength. The numbness was gone. His brain said flex, and the correct muscle grew taut to do his will.

Still, the feeling of elation alternated with blame for losing the girl.

Garcia contacted the Saavedras, and after he spoke to them, he let Sonny talk to the distraught mother. It turned out that Sonny was distantly related. These Saavedras were from Tomé, near Belén, and that family was related to the Jaramillos, Sonny's mother's side of the family.

"Distant relations," he murmured as he hung up the phone.

"Todos somos primos," Lorenza said.

"Including Raven and me," Sonny mused. Raven was his alter ego, his other self, the dream of chaos in the memory. He was sitting there now, in the middle of his evil circle, gloating over his conquest.

"I've got an officer at the Saavedras'," Garcia said. "I'll go over there myself. Damn Raven!"

Yeah, damn Raven, Sonny thought. If Garcia only knew how much he wanted to damn Raven to hell! And now it might be too late. Four girls and four grandmothers were in his clutches. Sonny's time on earth could be measured by hours. Tomorrow was the solstice. Raven would use his sorcery on the grandmothers at the exact solstice moment, when the sun hung in a balance, and Sonny would disappear from the face of the earth.

"Is there time?" Sonny asked as he looked at Lorenza making preparations.

"Yes. You have a few hours left before the solstice. Don Eliseo will be here any minute now."

"Is there another way? Not to involve don Eliseo?"

"No," she replied.

"He has to help," Sonny whispered.

"Yes," she said, and disappeared. A short time later the aroma of sweet grass filled the house. She was cleansing the house, preparing for the ceremony. Still later he heard the shower running.

Yes, dangerous or not, it was time to meet Raven. He lay back on the bed, trying to relax, trying to find the power of Coyote and draw it into his soul. He was about to enter the most important dream—nightmare really—of his life.

On the way home he had tried to explain some of the details to Garcia, as much as he dared.

"I knew Paiz was after Raven. Hell, I've been chasing him, too!" the chief had retorted. "But God Almighty, Sonny. This is science fiction! Plutonium? Raven has a ball of plutonium? And he's running around 'Burque? I don't believe it. But I do know he's got this girl, and I'm going to nail him! I've got the city shut tight."

Sonny told him about the other girls. He didn't tell him about Rita's miscarriage. Long before he dreamed of being a father, he had thought if he had a girl he would name her Cristina, after his great-grandmother.

Now the daughter would not be, Cristina would not carry his dream. Raven had killed the most innocent, the weakest, and the girls he held were next.

"What the hell does it mean?" the chief had asked in a subdued voice.

"It means that Raven can hold the city, and the state, hostage," Sonny replied. "At best. At worst, it means he actually is connected to a group that wants to take over the government."

"Damn, why here?" the chief moaned. "Why here?"

"We are a spiritual center," Sonny replied, speaking almost to himself because he knew the chief really didn't understand the nature of Sonny's struggle. "Now we're a center of technology. A center where the fire of the gods has been created. Los Alamos, Sandia Labs, Intel, Phillips, the research at the university, that's why. Raven wants to take over that center of fire. Destroy the dream, destroy the world."

"He can't get away with that," the exasperated chief mumbled.

"Has so far," Sonny said, and shrugged.

It didn't matter what the chief believed. It didn't matter if Raven was connected to the Avengers or not. Raven had his own reason for blowing the world apart.

"There's more," Sonny said simply.

"You goddamned right there's more!" Chief Garcia said loudly. "I'm calling Paiz! I'm going to rake him over the coals for not letting me know what he knew! My job is to protect this city! Damn, where do those pinche FBI boys get off!"

Garcia's parting words rang empty. He was on a linear track; the dream was circular. From where he lay, Sonny glanced at the dresser where Owl Woman's bowl rested.

A rustling sound made him turn toward the door. Lorenza appeared, dressed in a white embroidered cotton skirt and huipil. Her long black hair fell over her shoulders. It was glossy, like silk. He felt like touching it, running his fingers through it, like he did so often with Rita. Rita always loosened her hair when they made love. He loved the way it fell over him.

"You look—" He started to say "beautiful," but any compliment would fall short. She had been with him through thick and thin, and for a moment he wondered if he had fallen in love with her. Was she still only a guide, or much more?

"Gracias," she said, accepting his thoughts. "And you? How do you feel?" she asked, sitting on the chair by the side of the bed. Her eyes were clear, almost radiant. A sweet fragrance clung to her, a faint trace of herbs or the aroma of the sweet grass she burned when she performed her cleansing ceremonies.

"I want to thank you for everything you've done," he said, and taking her hand, he kissed it.

"You don't have to—"

"Hey, you've taken a chunk out of your life. Nearly gotten killed. And I have nothing to give to you."

"Maybe in the future," she whispered. Her eyes shone in the dim light. She was looking into him, and the strong attraction they had always felt for each other rose like a pleasant wave.

For a moment he wanted to reach out and draw her down beside him, make love to her, let go of the blame and anger he felt inside. Entering her flesh would erase the pain and loss he felt. He needed some measure of peace and stability right then, and dissolving into Lorenza was one way to get it. But no, Lorenza meant much more to him than a quick fix.

"Right now we have to attend to your journey," she said. "Are you ready?"

"Yes."

"Don Eliseo," she said, turning.

Sonny heard the kitchen door open and close; he sniffed the air. Chica looked up and let out a friendly whine. She, too, recognized the old man's sounds.

"Why?" Sonny asked, still afraid to get the old man involved.

"I need his help," Lorenza replied.

"You mean *I* need his help," Sonny said.

"Yes."

"But you said it could be dangerous for him. His age—"

"He insisted—" Lorenza said, and Sonny turned to see don Eliseo enter the room. Dressed in well-worn, soft buckskin pants and shirt, the old man looked like one of his vecinos at Sandia Pueblo, a medicine man in prayer garb.

Sonny had never seen don Eliseo dressed so regally. A feather clung to his white hair. He was holding a small drum.

He didn't look like a withered old man of eighty, he looked like a young warrior.

"Don Eliseo?"

The old man bowed. "At your service." He lay a large object at the foot of the bed and solemnly looked at Sonny. "I am sorry Rita got caught up in this—"

Sonny nodded. "Thank you for calling us."

Don Eliseo shook his head. "When she called, I knew what had happened. Now it is up to us." He paused. "Lorenza told me you have your legs back."

"Yes."

"Good. You need strong legs where we're going."

"After Raven?"

"Yes."

"I have to go alone, don Eliseo. I can't let you do this," Sonny said, starting to rise from the bed. Lorenza's touch told him to stay put.

"It's after midnight," the old man said, motioning to the window where the fading crescent moon provided little light. "The sun will rise and the hour of the winter solstice is not far away. At that moment when the sun stands still, Raven will act."

Lorenza and don Eliseo knew what lay ahead; Sonny could only guess. But he did know it was dangerous for the old man.

In the darkness, Lorenza lit a candle.

"Raven will kill the girls and take their spirits," don Eliseo said, his voice a whisper that drew a whine from Chica. "For his evil reasons he will offer their blood to bring down the sun. For a few moments the sun hangs in a balance. We pray it will return north on its normal cycle. The days will get longer, spring will come, we will plant again. Mother Earth will nurture us."

Kill the girls, Sonny thought, and wed their souls to his. In each evil quadrant of his dark world, he'll keep a spirit captive.

Lorenza moved to the foot of the bed. Sonny looked at don Eliseo. So this was the final lesson of the old man's way of life. He had taught Sonny about the Path of the Sun, now he would walk with him into the underworld.

"Raven can fly," the old man had cautioned Sonny, and it wasn't until Lorenza helped Sonny find his coyote guardian spirit and fly into Raven's circle of evil that Sonny began to grasp what flight meant.

Now as don Eliseo peered at Sonny, his face was the face of a child, his eyes filled with light.

Ah, Sonny thought, he can fly. The old man can fly! He truly is a shaman. He can fly.

Sonny looked at Lorenza. She nodded. Yes, don Eliseo was a shaman. Not an evil brujo, but a good one, a man devoted to the path of light.

Don Eliseo had spent his life studying the essence of the old Nuevos Mexicanos and of the Pueblo Indians. He had filled his spirit with light, until there was perfect clarity. He had become the spirit of light. He could fly.

Chica whined, rose, and went to the edge of the bed, sniffed don Eliseo's hand.

"Yes, Chica, you will go with us," don Eliseo said.

Sonny shook his head. He didn't understand. "Chica?"

"Yes," the old man nodded, rubbing Chica. "Maybe that's why she came to stay with you. She's not too old to nip at Raven's heels."

Sonny wasn't understanding the old man at all. Don Eliseo was preparing to go into Raven's circle and face possible death, and still he was kidding. He was talking of taking Chica with them, as if they were going on a walk. It didn't make sense.

"Long ago, one of my compadres at Sandia told me, the people kept dogs around the village to keep away Raven. This is when he was pulling a lot of bad tricks on the people."

"Is it dangerous for her?" Sonny asked.

"Everything has an inherent danger in it," don Eliseo said. "If the thing is not used properly, according to our instructions from the ancestors, then even an ear of corn can cause injury. Time itself can be dangerous. Time flows this way, then that way, and the sorcerers of evil mount it like a wild stallion to trample us. Each day has a face, a mask that can be good or evil. But it is not the fault of time that this last day of the cycle of the sun has a dark face. It is Raven who clouds the face of the solstice. When the face of the day grows troubled like this, the old people say prayers. It is important for the sun to rest in peace, to be gathered in the arms of the great ocean where it rests at night. In the womb of mother ocean it can sleep, dream, and in the morning it rises renewed, as a man rises renewed from peaceful dreams."

"Gracias a Dios," Lorenza whispered.

"Sí, gracias a Tata Dios, a las kachinas, a los espíritos de nuestros antepasados. The day about to be born is not only the beginning of a new season, it is the beginning of a new age on earth. We have come to the edge of a great cycle of time enveloping the earth, like a river coming to a waterfall. There ahead of us is the abyss where Raven lies waiting, ready to destroy the mother. We, the old warriors, must do battle with the forces of evil. It has always been dangerous, but we are prepared."

He took the Zia medallion from Lorenza and slipped it over Sonny's head.

"The sign of the sun has been blessed by a woman," the old man said, acknowledging Lorenza's role as Sonny's guide. "Now you will wear it to meet Raven. Do not let go of it. He will come for it, but do not let go. He was wearing it during the Zia summer, but he possessed it only because in a prior age he took it from us. This gold of the sun has been with us since before the pyramids were built. It is timeless. It does not belong to Raven, it belongs to us."

Us, the old man said. The Zia medallion didn't just come into play a few months ago, it was the symbol of prior ages. People had been passing it down through the ages.

"A long time ago, the people knew how to catch dreams. Well, they screwed up and lost the ability," don Eliseo said, a mischievous look in his eyes. "So they began to make dream catchers to catch the good dreams. So I have made you one."

He held up the large dream catcher he had placed at the foot of the bed when he entered. The dream catcher hoop was made from a juniper branch. Perfectly round, it was almost two feet in diameter, and the web was made of thin strips of deer leather. Painted in different colors so that even in the candlelight the colors glowed. Four eagle feathers hung at the bottom.

"Rainbow colors," Sonny muttered, taking the dream catcher.

He remembered Rita had bought him a small one at the arts and crafts show at the State Fairgrounds when they first met. It hung on the ceiling over his bed, but he was so accustomed to it, he had forgotten about it. Now he looked up at the dream catcher that had gathered dust. It paled in comparison to the vibrant one don Eliseo had made for him.

At the center of the dream catcher's web, there was a round empty space. Good dreams would catch on the webbing and belong to the dreamer, but bad dreams would slip through the hole and be gone.

"My vecinos at the pueblo say it's strong medicine. I believe it. It carries the colors of the rainbow, and so the good spirits are in it. It will be your shield."

"Shield?"

"Pues, look at it this way," don Eliseo said. "I put some leather straps on each side. So when you strap it to your arm, it's a shield. You know, like the knights used to wear."

Sonny smiled. Even now, after all he had been through, it seemed every time he entered the world of the spirits, the world of dreams and nightmares, there was a new twist. And often it verged on the ludicrous. But that was only before he understood the proper role of rules and objects associated with the journey.

"I'm supposed to hold this up and Raven's sword won't cut through it?"

"If you hold it right," don Eliseo said, "like this." He showed Sonny how to wave the dream catcher like a shield, how to turn it, how to approach Raven. "Turn like this when he strikes. He cannot touch you. When you catch him off guard, turn it like this and he will pass through the hole in the middle. That's what you want to do," he said, his voice rising. "Make him pass through the hole."

"He will pass away like a bad nightmare?" Sonny said. "Will he die?"

Don Eliseo looked at Lorenza. Would this man never learn, his look seemed to say.

"Raven cannot die," Lorenza whispered.

"Let me continue," don Eliseo said. "Pay close attention. Your life will depend on it. Raven is holding the young women he kidnapped. They will appear in their spirit form. So we will catch them like this." Again he showed Sonny how to turn the dream catcher. "In this way we capture their spirits and bring them back from the underworld."

He peered at Sonny. "You got it?"

"I got it," Sonny replied. He had to trust the old man, he knew that. He and Lorenza hadn't been wrong yet. But did he have the courage to meet Raven's scimitar charge with only a few dance steps and the dream catcher? Shouldn't I be thinking of my pistol? Or Coyote? Yes, the guardian spirit would help. But a fragile dream catcher?

"What if I can't get Raven to pass through the hole?" he asked.

"Then you die," don Eliseo responded.

Die, Sonny thought, die in the dream I create.

"Follow his instructions," Lorenza said, and handed Sonny the small leather pouch that contained the coyote hair she had gathered by the river. The string was knotted, like the old quipus cords of the Incas. The knots had been undone, one by one, until only one remained.

Tonight the sun was tethered to the Sun Post at Machu Picchu, tonight the sun grew pregnant, desiring to rise over the pyramids of Teotihuacán. If Sonny could overcome Raven, it would rise again. If not—

"Maybe I should have a drink," Sonny said, half in jest, half serious. His anxiety was mounting. He was expected to bring back the girls and conquer Raven with a dream catcher?

"No, no drink," don Eliseo said. "We go with clear heads."

"Not even a little of that peyote you chew with your vecinos at the pueblo?" Sonny smiled.

"We are going beyond the realm of Señor Peyote," the

old man replied. "Señor Peyote can lead us into one vision, but the world you are about to enter is deeper and more powerful. It is so true and real that it will attract Raven. He will come sniffing around, like the trickster that he is. He may transform himself into an animal, perhaps a beautiful woman, or he may come as a friend. You must recognize him. He wants the sacred sign of the Zia sun, the medallion you wear around your neck. If he gets that, he gets your soul."

"Listen to don Eliseo," Lorenza said. "He has been there. He knows the ways of the Raven."

Yes, the old man fought Raven and his cohorts long before I came into the picture. He taught me the way, and so I must trust him.

"I understand," Sonny said.

"Raven knows you're coming," don Eliseo continued. "He knows how strong your dreams have become. He will take chances. He is very crafty. Perhaps he will offer you one or two of the girls. Or he might offer to sit and talk with you, perhaps play cards, winner take all. You must be as crafty as Coyote. Do not let him trick you."

"And when I find him?" Sonny asked.

"It is a battle to the death," don Eliseo said solemnly.

27

Are you ready?" don Eliseo asked.

"Yes."

"You dream your own dream, entiendes?"

Sonny nodded.

"It's your show, your stage. He's got his circle, and he's going to try to get you in there. You stay in your dream. You bring him to you, to your power."

Yes, Sonny thought. Maybe a cantina. I could have Billy there, and Coyote. Maybe even my bisabuelo could show up, and Pancho Villa. Like the Old West dreams I've been having.

No, he was sleepy, he wasn't thinking straight. He needed a stage that had to do with the kidnapped girls.

"The girls he took had something to do with a play about the birth of Christ. . . ."

"You choose," don Eliseo said. "I will be the drummer tonight. I will carry the drum into the dream world. You follow with the dream catcher. Pay close attention. Don't step into Raven's circle. Don't let Raven trick you, and don't take anything he offers you."

The old man went to the window and looked out. A thin

moon shone on a cold earth. In the dim light his cornfield stood sere and withered. Among the frozen cornstalks a shadow moved.

"He's here," don Eliseo whispered.

"Here?" Sonny started to get up. "Where's my pistol?" He had forgotten where he put his pistol.

Lorenza's touch told him to remain still. "The pistol is useless. Follow don Eliseo!" she commanded, her voice harsh.

Don Eliseo stood at the window a long time, Sonny watched. The old man began a steady drumming, which he kept up for a long time.

Sonny grew sleepy. We're supposed to be chasing Raven, he thought, but don Eliseo didn't appear to be in a hurry. The drumming grew hypnotic, the minutes stretched out.

Sonny felt Lorenza get up, take the Bowl of Dreams from the bureau, and place it on the nightstand next to him.

"Follow don Eliseo," she whispered. "Enter your dream. Walk upright. Be confident, be in *control* of your dream, for it belongs to you. It is your dream, no one else's. Raven will envy the power and clarity of your dream, and he will come to you. Do you understand?"

Sonny mumbled yes. His eyelids felt heavy. The dream catcher strapped to his arm grew heavy and uncomfortable.

"Remember to sing your song. . . ."

Sonny uttered the words to his song, composing as he went, fitting the sounds to the rhythm of the drum. "I walk the Path of the Sun. . . . I ask a blessing from the Lords and Ladies of the Light. . . . My soul so clear, it flies to my grandmothers. . . . I am their dream. . . ."

He kept repeating the lines, adding to them, calling the dream that was his, and even as the trance of dream began to take hold, his questioning mind wondered how he would enter the dream.

"Chica!" he called, and she answered with a bark.

The short, fat candles sitting next to the Bowl of Dreams cast a flickering bronze light on the bowl. Lorenza was burning copal in the bowl. The smoke rose in wisps, like thin white feathers rising in still air, like clouds whispering in the New Mexican blue sky.

Sonny heard don Eliseo's voice.

"On the first rung of the bowl is written the dream of creation," the old man said softly, his words in rhythm to the drumming.

"The many stars are the children. They fly across the heavens into the farthest reaches. Our Zia sun, too, is born, and the voice of the creation expands throughout the universe. In the cosmic wind, our souls wait to be dressed in flesh, the flesh of the earth. . . ."

Don Eliseo knows the secret of the glyphs!

"Here are signs for the oceans, for the continents, for the mountain chains, for great rivers. There is a sign for each tribe that has walked the earth and dreamed of peace. . . ."

Sonny was mesmerized by the bowl. It seemed to turn slowly in the candlelight, revealing the trail of glyphs that wound their way around the outside to the lip at the top. The bowl can't turn by itself, he thought. Lorenza must be turning the bowl so I can follow don Eliseo's explanation.

He looked for her in the dark.

"The bowl contains your dream. Enter the bowl. To enter the bowl is to enter the dream of the earth. Do not be afraid to enter your dream. The glyphs are keys to your dream."

"Yes," Sonny whispered in acceptance.

Don't look for answers in this world. My task now is to enter the dream world, the world of spirits.

When he said this, he saw the shining door of prior dreams. At the door stood don Eliseo, ready to go to the cornfield to meet Raven. Sonny stood and held the dream catcher like a shield. He would meet Raven like a warrior.

He looked back. In former dreams he had observed himself dreaming, but he was no longer that person. Now he was the actor in his dream.

He turned and faced the web of the dream world that spread before him. Don Eliseo waited for him. Next to him waited a patient Chica.

"Grandmothers," Sonny whispered, "I come to claim your spirits. You belong to me and my dream, not to the sorcerer who holds you prisoners."

The bowl continued to turn, slowly. The glyphs began to blur.

Forms appeared. People—or ghosts—for they poured from the lip of the bowl and rose in the copal smoke. People from ancient civilizations, from the past. Statuesque African women, carrying bowls of water to the fields. Peruvian stone cutters from the Andes, strong and nimble, cutting and lifting great monoliths to build their cathedrals to the sun. Druid women from the plains of Stonehenge and Avesbury, shaman women so powerful their gaze alone was a communication across the earth's song line. Men with Asian wisdom from the steppes of Manchuria, monks from Tibetan mountains turning prayer wheels in sanctuaries worn by time, chanting to the one Buddha, chanting to the one spirit that was both earth and universe. The gods from the Egyptian pantheon appeared in the glyphs, then rose and walked on desert sands; light-footed, they stepped aboard boats that sailed the blue Nile, blessing the fields on either side of the great river, praising the sun god. Dark women bearing flowers in canoes cut from giant logs floated down the broad river of the Amazon. Medicine men and women from the Anasazi pueblos appeared, offering corn pollen to the new day, praying to the spirits for rain. Ancestors of the Maori walked in the deserts of the southern continent, stretching the song line across their land. Their melody passed through Sonny's heart, a humming sound like the sound of the earth turning. He could *see* the words of the song, shining like filaments of a spider web, spreading over the earth. He recognized the song. It was his own.

On and on the procession rose from the womb of the bowl, the Calendar of Dreams freeing itself so Sonny could peer into the past and see the dreams of those who dreamed of peace.

I asked for booze or a chew of peyote, to make the dream a little easier, but don Eliseo said no. Now I understand. I don't need hallucination, the dream is real. I am the dream!

"Yes, you are the dream," Lorenza's voice echoed.

He smiled, satisfied. So this is it. I don't need a shot of anything to get into this. I'm it.

The glyphs in front of him resonated to his soul, the dream of the Americas etched on volcanic rocks of the New Mexican desert that he knew so well. Carved thousands of years ago, by ancient wanderers on the land, those who carried the dream on their migrations. This was the covenant of the Americas! Carved into the sun calendar of the Aztecs! Each day had a name and a face, as did groups of days, as did centuries held together with golden cords of time. Each star, planet, and moon had a name. The sun had a name, Zia sun!

"There!" Sonny cried. The Zia sun hung in the sky, its glyph was carved into the bowl. Like the sun sign of the medallion hanging on his chest. This was it! Home! Bowl! Earth!

The bowl stopped turning. The drumming stopped. On the bowl's sensuous curve shone the round emblem of the Zia sun with its four radiating lines. Lines pointing north, west, south, east. The four sacred directions of the earth. The four quadrants of the universe.

From the sun symbol a stream of light shone on Sonny's medallion. A door of light.

Don Eliseo pointed. "Esta es la puerta de luz," he said. "La puerta de los sueños."

Door of light, the same door Andres Vaca had stepped through to continue his journey north to la Nueva México. Door of dreams, the same dream Hernán López had dreamed in 1680, his dream of home in New Mexico, his dream of Caridad de Anaya. Lisandro and Epifana's dream after the American invasion. Billy the Kid's dream to settle down with Rosa, to raise a family, and Pancho Villa's rescue of Soledad. Everything was before him. The door was there, the dream could continue.

The Bowl of Dreams was the door, chalice of love, vessel of the blood of the living earth.

Around don Eliseo stood the Lords and Ladies of the Light, the light of the blessing sun, the kachinas of the new millennium.

"Now you know," don Eliseo said.

Yes, now he knew. Only in moments of love with Rita had he known this power of transcendent flight, the commingling with pure light. Now he knew.

"Enter your dream," don Eliseo said as they passed through the door out to the cornfield where Raven waited.

Sonny waved his dream catcher and his stage appeared. A simple stable in a small New Mexico village bathed in starlight. A cold December night. In the distance, the villagers dressed as shepherds approached.

A bright star hanging in the frozen sky illuminated the manger. Four girls appeared, the young women Raven had kidnapped.

I've done it! Sonny cried. I set the stage and found the girls. Look!

He hurried forward. Lordy, Lordy, this is easier than I thought! There they were, sitting around the stage, each one occupying a sacred direction. He had called for the stage to appear and the kidnapped girls came with it! How much easier could it get?

Don't hurry, don Eliseo cautioned him. Chica whined nervously. Raven was near.

Sonny, the girls cried, save us. We came to witness the birth of the child and now we're prisoners!

I'll free you! Sonny cried, lunging forward, waving the dream catcher. Like this! I catch you in my web and return you home.

No! Don Eliseo cried. Even Chica tried to stop him by barking a warning, but Sonny didn't pay attention. He leaped forward without paying attention to the trap that lay between him and the girls.

Step back! Don Eliseo called sharply.

Sonny turned to look at don Eliseo, and at that moment he realized that he had stepped into Raven's circle. Around him a ring of black crows descended, flapping their wings angrily, encircling him. Chica barked and rushed into the evil circle to help her master. She snapped at the crows, but she was no match for their vicious beaks.

Step back! Don Eliseo cried again, but it was too late.

The crows rose angrily, striking at the spirit dog that bared her fangs. Then a larger shadow appeared in the circle, and Chica whined and retreated, seeking shelter between Sonny's legs.

Welcome, Raven cried as he stepped forward. Welcome to my world.

Get back into your dream! Sonny heard don Eliseo shout.

It's too late! a defiant Raven called. Tonight he dies! Death forever! Chaos forever!

He raised his curved sword and struck at Sonny, who raised the dream catcher to ward off the blow. The sword glanced off the dream catcher, but the force sent Sonny reeling. A second thunderous strike followed, this time knocking Sonny to his knees, exposing him for the final blow.

Time to die! Raven shouted, and raised his scimitar.

Only don Eliseo jumping into the circle and throwing himself at Raven saved Sonny. With what strength he had, the old man held Raven back.

For a moment they locked in combat, the old man straining against Raven, shouting to Sonny: Step back into your dream!

Fool! You entered my circle to die! Raven cursed.

Not yet! don Eliseo groaned, and raising the drum he struck a powerful blow that momentarily stunned Raven.

Don Eliseo turned, grabbed Sonny, and pushed him out of Raven's circle. His strength and magic allowed Sonny to tumble safely into the circle of his dream.

Stay in your dream! Don Eliseo shouted, and like a warrior, he turned to meet Raven's onslaught.

Raven struck, the sword cut through don Eliseo's chest into his heart.

Time to die, old man.

Don Eliseo put his hand to his bleeding chest. But we have come this far, he replied. He looked at Sonny. Stay . . . , he whispered, . . . in your dream. You are strong.

He offered his soul to the light glowing in the east, then slumped to the ground.

He died to save you, Raven said to Sonny.

A sob caught in Sonny's throat. Yes, the old man had sacrificed himself so Sonny might have a chance.

He was too old to continue the fight, Raven said. If he remained in his world, he would still be alive. He brought you here only to die.

I don't intend to die, Sonny replied, his gaze resting on don Eliseo.

Raven laughed. But no one has said you have to die. He smiled, his voice now beguiling. No, you don't have to die at all. You've been listening to the old man, and to Lorenza. She's a witch, you know that. Always warning you, always making things a matter of life or death. That's her way, but it's not mine.

Sonny looked from the crumpled figure of the old man to Raven. He looked invincible, resplendent in his black coat, glistening green and violet as the light shifted.

You know if I can kill the old man, I can kill you. But I don't want that. We can make a deal, Raven said solemnly.

Sonny looked around him. Huddled in the middle of Raven's circle lay the crumpled body of don Eliseo. Near the manger stood the girls he knew were Consuelo, Catalina, Carmen, and Celeste. Behind them hovered the four spirits of the great-grandmothers. And hovering over the crib, the aura of a young spirit.

Sonny heard himself moan, a pitiful low cry. The spirit was the soul of Rita's dead child, his child. No wonder Raven had grown so arrogant, in his circle he still held those most dear to Sonny. He had killed Rita's baby and don Eliseo, and he would kill again.

A quiver shook his body. He felt the weight of the dream catcher on his arm. Yes, this is what Raven intended, to show off his power and disarm Sonny. He had already killed don Eliseo, and now he was closing in on Sonny. If he was to survive, it was time to take on Coyote's trickster nature.

What kind of a deal? Sonny asked. Sheer force would not be what conquered Raven; Sonny had to get him through the dream catcher.

A truce. So we both can live side by side, Raven answered.

I agree, Sonny howled, the cry of Coyote rising like a whine when he and Raven argue over roadkill. But how can we deal when you stand in the middle of your circle. Step forward where I can hear you. You are very powerful now. You have won the right to enter my dream.

Raven grinned, his croak a cry of victory. Sonny Baca was beaten, willing to bargain, and those who bargained with darkness were already lost.

Very well, he said, stepping out of his circle into Sonny's dream. See, you have nothing to fear from me. I am willing to meet you in your own dream.

Sonny held the dream catcher ready, but Raven didn't attack. He was talking of making a deal. Don Eliseo and Lorenza had warned him, Raven would offer bargains, he would trade. He was hoping to get Sonny's guard down by stepping into Sonny's dream and pretending to be a friend, but Raven only had one purpose in mind. To kill Sonny.

What kind of deal do you want to make?

A haughty Raven chose his words carefully.

I have your grandmothers. If I kill them, you die. You understand that?

Sonny knew he had to be ready and crafty. Moments ago he had been caught off guard and sucked into Raven's trap, and it had cost don Eliseo his life. Now the same shadow of evil moved to control him in his dream.

Yes, I understand, Sonny replied. You have played a very

good game, Sorcerer. Learned to enter my dreams and steal my past. But I, too, have some power!

None as powerful as mine, Raven replied, lifting his curved sword to strike.

Sonny waved his dream catcher shield, and Raven jumped back, shielding himself from the strong pull of the hole in the middle of the dream catcher.

Ah, so the old man and his medicine men have given you a toy to threaten me! Why do you wave that thing at me? I came as a friend.

He's afraid of the dream catcher, Sonny thought. If he slips through the hole, it will suck him into the land that is the origin of dreams. Let's see what else he fears.

Sonny began to move slowly around Raven. I have the shield, the Zia medal, the coyote medicine, he said to Raven, all the while watching Raven's glistening eyes.

So let's make a deal. Take me, release the girls, Sonny said, realizing that the bargaining was part of an old game they played.

Oh, no, I need them, Raven replied cautiously, also circling, feinting with his sword as he talked, frowning when Sonny easily stepped away.

Why do you need them?

Let's say they are ransom for the future. As long as I have them, you cannot come after me. Besides, I need the women to serve me. In a few hours the fifth sun dies, and I will rule in the new era. The king of chaos needs ladies at his side.

Four women, one for each quadrant of the universe, Sonny said, all the while circling and positioning himself.

Raven looked surprised.

So you know. Yes, even in the universe of chaos the four quadrants remain. There are essentials even chaos cannot break down. I need a lady in each section, so as I travel across the heavens I have someone to visit.

Four feminine spirits to visit, Sonny thought. No, not just ladies to visit, but wombs in which to give birth to eternal chaos.

The thought made Sonny shiver. The outcome of the game had consequences far beyond the struggle tonight.

What else do you want?

Raven pointed his sword at Sonny's chest. The Zia medallion. And I will take the leather pouch the witch gave you. You must not have the coyote medicine.

Sonny touched the medal and pouch hanging around his neck.

What do you give me in exchange?

I spare you.

Ah, so Raven was willing to let him live. Good news. But if Raven kept the spirits of the young women, Sonny would have very little power in any future struggle. When the power of the winter shaman was gone, the edges of the universe would begin to crumble. The solstice sun would not return, or return so weakened that catastrophic weather would create havoc on the earth.

I want to live, Sonny said, playing the fearful part but constantly gauging Raven's movements.

Of course you want to live, Raven replied. And I offer you life. Why die here, in your dream? Why not return and enjoy what is left of your time in the arms of the witch?

Lorenza?

Yes, the bruja who taught you the coyote medicine has lust in her heart for you.

I have a woman, Sonny said.

True, but think what happened to the child she carried. You need a son to pass on your knowledge.

I can't accept your deal, Sonny said, waving the dream catcher, making Raven jump.

Why?

You killed my child!

I needed to show you my power! Raven said menacingly. I want you to know I can strike anywhere! I have taken your grandmothers from your dreams, the blood of your ancestors, and I have taken the blood from the womb of your woman. What more do I have to do to prove I am your master?

A soft moan escaped Sonny's lips. His child, Rita's child, sacrificed by Raven to prove his omnipotence. Damn the evil spirit! He would take him apart with his bare hands! But he must do it as Coyote, with craft and cunning.

I must fight you, and yet I feel your strength.

He clutched his side as if in pain, began to limp as he backed away.

If you do not accept my bargain, I will kill you! Raven replied.

Kill me, Sonny thought, but it won't be as easy as killing don Eliseo.

Look at you, you can barely walk, Raven gloated. Your spirit is weak. Give me what I seek, and I'll leave you alone. Return to the witch or your woman, it doesn't matter. In a few hours I kill time, the sun will die. All is lost.

I should have known you were too strong, Sonny whispered, his voice pleading, drawing the arrogant Raven to him. Around the circle of his dream he saw the coyotes appear.

Time ends with a whimper, Raven said. I can wait no longer. Give me the medallion of the sun!

You win, Sonny said, lowering his shield and reaching

for the medallion and the pouch that hung around his neck. He held them out for Raven to take.

Yes, I win, Raven said, reaching forward.

As he did, Sonny struck Raven across the face with the dream catcher. Raven roared with pain and fell back. Sonny struck again, hitting Raven's leg, trying to position him so he could wave the dream catcher as don Eliseo had taught him.

But Raven would not be so easily vanquished. He struck back with his sword, making Sonny raise the dream catcher to protect himself. Again and again he struck, driving Sonny toward his circle. The crows cried and clawed at Sonny, and Chica barked and attacked to help her master.

Back and forth Sonny and Raven parried, the blows of Raven's sword landing like thunder on the dream catcher, and Sonny's slashes swirling with the force of a hurricane. The earth trembled as the battle continued, first one taking the lead, then the other. Both knew what was at stake.

As they fought, they shouted at each other, calling each other by ancient names, names from battles fought long ago.

Sorcerer of the Evil Ring! Sonny exclaimed.

Son of the Last Lord of Light! Raven answered.

As they drew near Raven's circle, they also drew near the manger and the light hovering over the crib. Slashing and swinging the dream catcher, Sonny turned Raven toward the light. When the brilliant light shone on Raven, he cried as if in pain.

I curse the light that blinds!

He raised his hands to cover his eyes and Sonny struck the fatal blow. Raven howled in pain and threw his sword down.

I'm blinded! Raven cried, sinking to his knees.

Sonny waved the dream catcher as don Eliseo had instructed, bringing it down over Raven's head, sucking him through the hole. The shadow that lurks in every dream disappeared, passing like a gigantic gushing wind through the dream catcher. A howl far more frightening than any la Llorona ever cried split the darkness as Raven passed into forgetfulness.

The powerful gush of wind knocked Sonny to the ground. He lay there, panting for breath, sweating from the nightmare, listening to the last curse of Raven as he disappeared. Then a calm settled over Sonny's dream.

A weak but triumphant Sonny rose. The first light of the rising sun shone in the east. The shepherds he had seen when he entered the dream were drawing near.

He put the medallion and the pouch over his neck and walked into Raven's circle. The crows rose threateningly, but Sonny waved his battered dream catcher and they fled, limping away like defeated scavengers. With Raven dead, their power was gone.

A limping Chica followed Sonny as he hurried to the four grandmothers.

You're free! he shouted. I set you free!

One by one the four grandmothers embraced him and thanked him. When he stood in front of Owl Woman, he bowed.

You have come a long way, Hijo, she said, smiling with pleasure at her son.

It has been a long journey, Sonny said. I am glad to see you.

Owl Woman nodded. I will go north with Andres Vaca and raise his children. We will take the Calendar of Dreams with us, and we will pass it to each new generation. The people of la Nueva México will suffer much. Great changes will come to the land. They will strike out against each other with enmity. But the bowl will be there, waiting for them to pour their dream of peace into it.

Thank you for this gift, great-grandmother, Sonny said.

He stood in awe as Owl Woman, Caridad, Epifana, and Soledad entered the bowl, disappearing back into their own time, returning to their memory, returning to their own dreams.

Sonny turned to the four girls Raven had kidnapped. Somewhere in the city he held them prisoner, but here he held their spirits. By waving the dream catcher over them and catching them in the web, he was returning them to safety. They would walk away from Raven's prison, not knowing what had happened to them, but they would return to their homes unharmed.

Go Consuelo, Catalina, Carmen, Celeste. Return home, he said.

Then he turned to the aura of light that was Rita's child, the light that had blinded Raven. Return with me, he said softly, but in his heart he knew the impossibility of such a thing. The spirit remained light, light shining on him, bathing him with the clarity of love.

In his heart he knew it wasn't possible. This spirit could not return. Not now. Maybe in the future it would find its way to earth. In another time, for another chosen man and woman.

Sonny felt tears wet his eyes. You will live in our hearts forever, he said, allowing the light that was the love between him and Rita to bathe him.

He turned to don Eliseo and gathered the crumpled body of the old man in his arms. The old man had become pure light, so his body weighed nothing.

Carrying the body, Sonny walked through the Door of

Light, calling to Chica, who limped after him. Two warriors returning home, returning to La Paz Lane.

The sun was rising over Sandia Crest when Sonny returned. He walked across the frozen cornfield, crunching the stubble beneath his feet, feeling a great sadness that came from knowing don Eliseo had died that night. Feeling a deep ache for Rita's child, who could not return.

But, as don Eliseo had taught, all grief was to be balanced with knowledge. The spirit never died. Don Eliseo would leave his body behind, but his soul was already flying into the morning light. The warm and joyous energy of the sun was returning. It was the day of the winter solstice, and the battle had been won. The sun was rising, returning north, and even as winter gripped the land, the days would begin to get longer. In a few months spring buds would soon proclaim the new season.

"Gracias, don Eliseo, for all you taught me," Sonny whispered as he laid don Eliseo softly on the ground. He pressed his forehead to the old man's. The kiss of life as the old man had taught him.

"Gracias por todo."

28

Sonny opened his eyes to Lorenza's clapping, leaving behind him the brilliant light of the door, stepping into the pearl light of dawn that suffused the room.

She sat by the side of the bed, her face drawn from the night's work.

"Don Eliseo's dead," were the first words he uttered.

She nodded. "I'm sorry . . ."

"Chica?"

"I bandaged her. There's a cut above her eye. She may lose it. But she's sleeping." She glanced in the direction of Chica's bed.

"God Almighty," Sonny whispered. He felt washed, full of the grief he had felt when he lay don Eliseo to rest, exhausted from the journey.

"Raven's gone."

"For now," she said. "The sun is rising. Don Eliseo's death has a meaning."

"I couldn't have done it without him. And Chica. How was it possible?"

"The power of the dream," Lorenza replied. "Just before

you returned, the bowl stopped turning, and a light seemed to fill it."

Sonny looked at the bowl. Now it contained the souls of his grandmothers, the soul of Rita's child. He smiled.

"Rita?" he asked.

Lorenza handed him the phone and he dialed her number. "Amor," he said. "How are you?"

"Sonny. I'm fine. I'm so glad to hear your voice. You made it."

"Yes, thanks to Lorenza and don Eliseo." He looked at Chica sleeping in her basket. "And Chica."

"I prayed all night. I knew it wouldn't be easy."

"I'm okay. It's you we're concerned about."

"I feel much better. I felt your dream last night. Somehow we, me and the child who couldn't be born, were there. With you."

"Yes." Sonny nodded. "I have something to do, then we're coming right over."

"I love you, Sonny."

"And I love you, amor."

He turned the phone off and looked at Lorenza.

"We can go see her as soon as you feel ready," she said.

There were shadows of fatigue around her eyes. The night had drained her energies.

On the dresser the candles by the Bowl of Dreams had burned out. Light entering from the window fell on the bowl. An aura of peacefulness filled the room.

Outside, the storm had passed. The winter solstice sun had just burst over the Sandia Mountains.

"The storm's over," he said.

"It will be a beautiful day," she replied. "Thanks to you."

Sonny thought a moment. The loss of don Eliseo lay heavy on his heart. Like losing a father. The old man had taught Sonny a path of life, and he had been there when Sonny entered Raven's circle.

So Raven was destroyed for now, and a new cycle of time could wrap itself around the earth. A new beginning. A beautiful day, Lorenza said, made possible by those like don Eliseo, those who said the daily prayers for peace and harmony. So it had always been, so it would be.

But it wasn't just prayers and chants the old people knew, they knew the way of evil and they fought it actively. They put their lives on the line so their children would know a better future. The dream of peace, after all, had to be forged by the hands of courageous men and women. It didn't come easy.

But one could learn to be the actor in one's dream, and once that was learned, the harmony of the soul could not be destroyed.

"I had good teachers," Sonny said.

"Yes," Lorenza said, "and now you're the teacher." She touched his forehead. "You have taken back your dream, Sonny. You have the knowledge. Now I have to tend to don Eliseo." She gestured toward the window.

"No," Sonny said. "I'll do it."

"I'll fix you something to eat."

Yes, he was hungry. He felt as if he had just come back from a long trip, exhausted and hungry, but filled inside with the revelation of the journey. He slipped off the side of the bed and tested his legs. They held him, obeying the simple automatic commands from his brain.

"A miracle," he whispered, pulling on his jeans, a sweatshirt, and his boots. He went to the window, and looked out. There in the middle of the winter-withered cornfield, in his old rocker, sat don Eliseo.

Sonny went out the front door, across the dirt road, and

through the brown and beaten field. The old man sat quietly, like a Buddha, facing east, face uplifted in prayer.

Sonny walked softly, aware of the crunching, frozen earth and the corn stubble beneath his feet, aware of the plumes of his icy breath in the cold morning. As he drew near the old man, he understood anew the power of dream. The center of the dream returned you home. Don Eliseo had come home to rest.

This valley of the Río Grande had been home to don Eliseo. The Romeros had been in the valley for centuries. They farmed and raised crops, they married and had children, they prayed the Catholic prayers their ancestors had brought to the valley. Some, like don Eliseo, also said the prayers they learned from the Pueblo Indians, their vecinos. Prayers to keep the sun on its path. Prayers from their inheritance.

"Don Eliseo," Sonny whispered, as if afraid to awaken the old man. Yes, perhaps don Eliseo had come out to greet the sun and pray, and he had fallen asleep. That was what Sonny wished as he touched the old man's shoulder.

The body was frozen. But his eyes were open, open to the sun that now rose over the crest of the mountain and bathed the face in radiant light. Now in this moment of stillness and magic, los Señores y las Señoras de la Luz came like a host of angels across the dark, cold space to bless the earth. Don Eliseo's Lords and Ladies of the Light came streaming down to create a halo around the body of the old man.

Don Eliseo's soul became light, became the light of the universe. For that was the purpose of life as don Eliseo taught, to fill the spirit with light, to become one with that cosmic light that flowed across the universe. To become God.

Sonny stood beside the old man for a moment. The old

man had been his mentor, his guide into the dream world. He had died so Sonny might live. He put his hand over don Eliseo's eyes, and they closed. He bent and picked up the old man, the temple of flesh that was left after the spirit departed. He turned and faced the rising sun.

"Señores y Señoras de la Luz," he prayed, the words choking in his throat, tears filling his eyes. "Receive the soul of this señor who honored you and honored life. Come and bless all of life. This was his prayer."

He stood with the old man in his arms, head bent, allowing the tears to flow. He wondered how it was the old man could weigh so little. So much of his substance had been soul, and that, once departed, left only the body.

If he had his way, he would bury the old man in the cornfield, right now as the morning sun made the valley brilliant with light. Dig into the frozen ground and return the flesh to earth. But don Eliseo had sons, and they would come and claim the body, and knowing little of the old man's way of life, they would want to deliver the body to a mortuary. A ceremony very different from don Eliseo's way would be performed. The sons had forgotten the ways of their father.

The old man should be buried here in the cornfield or under the old cottonwood where he sat on summer days. Buried where he could daily listen to the comings and goings of his neighbors, where he could hear the gurgling water of the acequia as the water was turned down the ditch to water the corn. Here in his garden the old man's body would dissolve back to the earth in peace.

The bones of don Eliseo's ancestors and the ancient bones of his vecinos from the pueblos lay beneath the earth of the valley. Construction workers digging foundations for homes or swimming pools in the North Valley often dug up the bones. Shards of pottery. Broken bowls in which women once cooked, stored seeds, stored the blood of life. But the old man's family, and the law, would have it otherwise.

"I will bury your ashes here," Sonny said. "I promise you that."

The old man had said that his ashes should be returned to the earth that nourished him. Sonny was sure the sons would see it his way.

He turned and carried the body back to don Eliseo's house. The front door was open, an old habit of don Eliseo. One's door was never locked. He laid the body on a bed and covered it with a sheet. Then he walked back across La Paz Lane.

The fragrance of coffee, eggs, chorizo, and tortillas filled the house. He entered the kitchen and Lorenza looked up.

"I laid him on his bed. I'll call his boys later. Right now I think don Toto and doña Concha should know."

He called doña Concha and told her don Eliseo was dead. "Ay, Dios mío," she cried, "mi viejito se murió. I'll get Toto. We'll be over right away. Don't worry, Sonny, we'll take care of everything."

Sonny thanked her. The two old friends knew what to do. They would bathe the body, dress him, and then sit with him. They would pray. Don Toto would sing alabados, songs for the dead. Catholic songs with the high pitch of a Moorish canto, songs from the old world.

Don Toto would also bring a bottle of his homemade wine, and between their prayers they would also drink. They would sip wine and remember all the good times they had with don Eliseo. They would talk to him as if he were still with them, sharing old memories with him, asking him if he remembered such and such an event. Memories of their life.

Later Concha would prepare a meal and they would eat.

The living had to eat. And so those hours would be their personal velorio, their wake for dead.

"It's going to be hard on them," Sonny said when he hung up. "They were always together."

Lorenza nodded. "But they understand the flesh must die. Don Eliseo's spirit is now their companion. Do you feel strong enough to drive to the hospital?"

"Yes."

"I'll stay with them. Take care of don Eliseo's things."

Sonny nodded. The old man had told him to take his Bible when he died, and the things the medicine men at the pueblo had given him over the years. A few simple things wrapped with prayer.

"Gracias," he replied. Yes, it was important Lorenza stay with doña Concha and don Toto.

"Now the good news about the girls."

"They were found."

"Yes. Chief Garcia just called. He's going to call right back. The girls were found downtown this morning. In a building believed to have been rented by Raven."

"Lord, I'm glad!" Sonny exclaimed. He sat and she handed him a cup of coffee.

"Is that the way it is?" he murmured. "We return from a dream."

"Yes," she said, and sipped her coffee.

"What a mysterious world" was all he could say.

The phone rang and Sonny picked it up.

"Sonny, you up?" Chief Garcia thundered. "Ah, the life of a PI. Sleep late, breakfast in bed. Us ordinary cops have to work twenty-four hours a day, and you guys drink coffee all morning. Work when you want, party at night. But today I'm the one breaking the good news." He laughed. "Did Lorenza tell you?"

"Yes."

"Damnedest thing," Garcia continued. "One minute they're bound, the next they're free. Got up and phoned the police. I got down there right away. Took them to St. Joe's to get checked. They're all right."

"Good," Sonny said. "And you called—"

"Yeah, I've notified the parents. The girls are tired, but they're safe and they weren't bothered. So we beat you to *two* catches this morning, Sonny."

"You found Raven."

There was a pause. "How in the hell did you know? Yeah, we found his body this morning."

Sonny was intrigued. "Where?"

"You won't believe this. Last night he broke into Sandia Labs, into a lab where they had some kind of laser experiment going. He got burned by the Z machine. Lab security figures he was back trying to steal plutonium, and he walked into a fusion machine. Fried him."

"How can you be sure it's Raven?" Sonny asked.

"You don't sound too goddamned excited," Garcia chortled. "I'm sure it's Raven. There wasn't much left of him. A black cape. You know he likes to dress like a vampire. There were feathers stuck to his body, like he was some kind of a bird!"

Garcia laughed again. "Dead Raven if you ask me. Dead as a chicharrón. The lab will check the prints out, but I'm confident they'll match. So, while you were sleeping safe in bed, we nailed the sonofabitch!"

"Did you get the plutonium?" Sonny asked.

"Well, no, but . . . We'll find it. It's only a matter of time. He's dead, and sooner or later the plutonium will show up."

"And the Ebola vials he was carrying?"

"Well, no, but the stuff is going to turn up. I'm sure."

"Yeah, let's just hope it doesn't turn up in the city's drinking water," Sonny replied.

"Dammit, Sonny! I've got my men working on it! FBI has their agents on it. Don't go talking scary stuff like that. Don't mention that to the press. You hear?"

"I understand," Sonny said. "I'm not going to mention anything to anybody. I'm confident you and Paiz are going to take care of things. We're in good hands, Chief."

"Yeah, well, thanks," Garcia grumbled.

"How did he get into the labs?" Sonny asked.

"How am I supposed to know!" Garcia replied. "He can break into Fort Knox! He had that damn Chernenko building a bomb right under their noses. Let the lab's security figure out how he got there, I'm on my way to a press conference. This is big, Sonny. Goddamned mayor is so happy he's taking me out to lunch."

"Have a good lunch, Chief."

"Yeah, thanks. Say hi to Rita for me. Tell her I'll be stopping by her restaurant for some of that carne adovada."

Sonny clicked the phone off. The chief didn't know Rita was in the hospital. The chief didn't know about dreams.

Sonny looked at Lorenza. She had freshened up while he was taking care of don Eliseo. Brightened her face. Like Rita in the morning, always showered and ready to face the day. What luck to have such beauty to gaze at early in the morning.

"You look very beautiful," he said.

"Gracias." She returned his smile.

Chica dragged herself into the kitchen, whining softly. Lorenza had bandaged the cut over her eye, and blood spotted the gauze.

"Poor Chica," Sonny crooned, picking her up softly.

"Next time you stay home. Human dreams can get dangerous. Even for a power dog like you."

He fed her pieces of buttered tortilla as he ate, surprised that even with the grief of losing don Eliseo he could eat.

It comes together, he thought, the loss and going on. Today he had to go to Rita. He needed the strength to walk, to drive, to bring her home.

As he finished, the phone rang.

"Buenos días," Paiz greeted Sonny. "I suppose you heard."

"Yeah, Garcia called."

Paiz chuckled. "He thinks he broke the case." Then his tone changed. "I don't think the body they found is Raven's."

Sonny waited. Of course the body burned by the laser at the labs wasn't Raven. But somebody had gone through great trouble to plant it there.

"Oh, I think the fingerprints will be a positive match. They will belong to the man who once was a courier up at Los Alamos. There are ways to make that stuff fit. That will satisfy Doyle and Eric."

"Yes." Sonny agreed. "What about the plutonium?"

"That's what worries me," Paiz continued. "Doyle is flying in from Washington. He and Eric are going to reveal the whole story to the press. Raven, the man found dead at Sandia Labs, will be identified as the person who killed the Los Alamos guards. Expert work by the FBI tracked the man down. There is no missing plutonium pit, no vials of Ebola virus floating around. Disinformation rules the day, case closed. The public won't be panicked."

"But the poison is still out there."

"Yup."

"In the hands of the Avengers," Sonny said.

There was a pause. "I'm calling from my office, Sonny. You know what I mean."

"Yeah," Sonny replied. His phone was tapped. He had to believe that there were still good men who couldn't be bought. He had to believe Paiz was not with the Avengers.

"So what do you do now?"

"I show up at the news conference. At Doyle's right hand. I nod and say 'Yes, that's the way it happened.' Then I turn in my badge. I'm retiring, getting out."

"Going fishing, huh."

"I'm tired of the game. I used to think we could beat the drug cartels, beat the crazies who want to destroy the world. I don't anymore."

"Sounds negative, bro."

"Not really. I'll have the time to do a little of my own investigating. Maybe give you a little competition. Become a PI."

He laughed.

"That's all the world needs." Sonny managed a chuckle. "One more Chicano PI. But, hey, with your training you can really make a difference."

"I don't know. I have a feeling you do all right."

"Let's say I work in another reality," Sonny said. "But the workplace is changing. Now we need computers. From now on I sit at home and do all my work on the Net. With a little help from an expert."

"Just be careful what your expert gets into," Paiz said.

He knew about Cyber.

"They're on to him?"

"Eric's pissed."

"And if they catch him?"

"He's okay for now. Pulled the plug and disappeared."

Good, Sonny thought.

"Anyway, soon as I give up my badge, I think I'll snoop around. Look for the plutonium," Paiz said.

"Take on Raven?"

"Somebody's got to do it. You know the score better than anyone, and computers aren't the only answer. A good PI knows the streets, the people. I'd like to work with you."

"Why not. But I'm taking time out to take care of my familia."

"Didn't know you had a family."

Sonny looked at Lorenza. "Oh, yeah, large family."

"Well, family comes first," Paiz said. "Take care."

"I will. Buena suerte."

"Yeah, you, too," Paiz replied.

29

He felt strong and renewed when he stepped outside. Above him the clear, blue New Mexican sky was a bowl holding the promise of clarity. Around him the neighborhood stirred. A red Ford Mustang moved down La Paz Lane, the driver waved. César and his wife, Bette, going to church. Sonny waved back.

People were going to work, preparing for Christmas, going about their daily work, unaware the hinge of time had turned one more time, the solstice sun was returning north. He breathed deep the life-giving element, then exhaled vapor plumes.

How beautiful the simple things of the earth appeared, how sublime the nature of ordinary things.

"Gracias a Dios," he whispered, closing his eyes and turning to face the warm sun. "Bless all of life."

The warm sunlight filled the valley with a dazzling dance. The million rays of light were the Lords and Ladies of the Light, as don Eliseo taught. They came streaming from the sun, source of light, representatives of the Universal Spirit, the transcendent. Lords and Ladies dressed as brightly feathered Aztec dancers, kachina warriors, souls of the departed, brilliant spears of light that returned promise to the earth, infusing everything with life.

The bare branches of the alamos and elms reached up and breathed through frozen pores the light that fed the sleeping sap, and in the cornfield sere plants grew golden. On the pot-holed road thin crusts of ice glistened, a flock of sparrows swooshed by, alighting to feed in the cornfield, somewhere a dog barked, a horse whinnied.

Sonny's nostrils quivered to the smell of a new day, the frigid air that carried traces of composted leaves, faint piñon smoke, the aroma of coffee, breakfast, lovers parting.

Everything participated in the light, became light.

Moments passed, there was no count, for time itself be-came an element of the light, a commingling of matter with spirit, earth and sky animated.

Then slowly he returned from the blessing the sun con-ferred, breathed deep again, felt the solid earth beneath his feet, looked across the street at don Eliseo's home. The old man was resting, but his spirit was here in the morning light, still blessing Sonny's path.

"Gracias, don Eliseo," Sonny said, as he had thanked the old man on many a morning. "Gracias por mi vida."

He walked to his truck, thanking the miracle that had re-turned his strength. Opening the door, he felt the cold inside the truck. He turned the ignition, feeling surprised when the motor turned and started. All was strange, yet all was as it should be.

He shivered. There were many worlds. Planes of reality. He touched the steering wheel, amazed at the simplicity of metal. It served a function, but it melted away in the time of dream, the time of the ancestors.

He drove down Fourth Street, deeply aware of people moving on the street, cars and trucks, children, stores opening for business, Christmas decorations glistening in the bright sunshine.

When he arrived at the hospital, he felt weak and thought he had attempted too much too soon. But he wanted to show Rita he could walk. It was important to him, and to her.

He walked slowly, bypassing the nurses' station and going directly to Rita's room. When he opened the door, Rita looked up in surprise. "Sonny! You're walking!"

He gathered her in a warm embrace. "I'm so happy, so happy," she kept repeating. "How did it happen?"

Sonny shrugged. "We had a little car accident last night. Something snapped when I got tossed around. I got up and I could walk."

"An accident? Are you all right? Your face is scratched."

"No, I'm fine. Can you believe, I drove here. Got in the troca and drove myself over."

"That's wonderful. Where's Lore?"

"She stayed with don Eliseo."

He didn't yet want to tell Rita that the old man was dead. He thought of the body of the old man resting in the cool shadows of his home, and doña Concha and don Toto praying over him, lighting candles, bathing the old man and dressing him in his Sunday suit. They would want him to look nice when his sons came.

He pulled up a chair and sat by the side of the bed.

"You look beautiful, amor," he whispered to her, gazing into her eyes. The clear brown eyes brimming with love for him.

"Gracias, señor. The nurse is wonderful. She came in before her shift was over, gave me a sponge bath, helped me with my makeup."

"You look like a rosa de Castilla on a bright summer morning."

"Oh, listen to the poetry." Rita smiled. "I like it, I like it."

She was being brave, he could tell. But the pain and loss of her ordeal still showed in her eyes, and he knew that would be with her for some time.

"Good news," Sonny said.

"You found the girls!"

"They're safe."

"Ay, gracias a Dios. I've been so worried, prayed for them. But I knew you'd find them."

Her eyes sparkled with admiration when she looked at Sonny.

"What about Raven?"

"He won't be hurting anyone for a while. It's a long story. I'll tell it to you as soon as we get you home. Can we take you today?"

A shadow crossed Rita's face. She shook her head.

"Qué pasa?"

Rita bit her lower lip. "The doctor wants to keep me another day."

"Why?" Sonny asked, holding her hands. The inflection in her voice told him all wasn't well.

"She wants me to rest, do some lab work." Her voice broke, tears filled her eyes, he handed her the tissue box. "I just wanted to go home—"

"It's all right," Sonny reassured her. "Don't worry. She probably wants to make sure you're strong enough to leave."

"I hope so."

"I'm sure that's it. I'll talk to her. I want you home where I can take care of you. I'm going to get you good and strong. Feed you."

"I like that."

"You just concentrate on getting well."

"I will."

"As soon as you're well enough, we're going to get married."

"Get married?"

"Yes. Just like we planned."

Rita shook her head. "We planned, but that was before this— You don't have to."

Sonny smiled. "Have to? Hey, this is no shotgun wedding. We made plans, remember? This thing with Raven slowed me down, but that's over. I'm walking, I'm well, and as soon as you feel better, we do it. I want to marry you."

"It's not right, Sonny, it's not right. What if I can't have children!" Her voice broke with emotion.

"I don't care about that. I love you, I want to live with you. That's what matters."

"You need children, Sonny. A man needs a family. It wouldn't be fair—"

"A man needs the woman he loves."

"Are you sure?"

"I'm positive. You're the woman in my life. Children? Hell, if we want children, we can adopt half a dozen. We'll have as many as you want. I just want to make you happy the rest of your life."

"And I want to be good for you." Rita smiled.

"You are."

He took Rita's hands and held them to his lips.

"Qué piensas?" Rita asked.

"I've been thinking about quitting this business."

"No more chasing bad guys," Rita said.

"Maybe go back to teaching."

"You're an excellent teacher, you have so much to share with the kids."

"That's what Mamá tells me." Sonny smiled. "Lord, I

have to call her. I have to call a lot of people. Mando, Diego, friends. I need to buy you a present for Christmas, buy everybody presents."

"You're a good man, Sonny."

"Ah, I'm not getting younger. Gotta settle down."

"Only if it's good for you, Sonny."

"It's good for me. I've learned a lot. I want to take time to digest it. Talk to people who understand the world of dreams, the world of our ancestors. Maybe understand how Raven comes to a new reincarnation."

"New reincarnation?"

"It's nothing," Sonny said.

"He's not dead?"

"Let's not talk about Raven. Let's just concentrate on you getting well. I want to sit still for a while, enjoy life. Have time to go for walks, read books, maybe go to the pueblo and listen to the old men, don Eliseo's friends. And spend a lot of time with you."

"That sounds lovely."

"You are lovely, amor," Sonny replied.

"There's hope."

"Amor y esperanza. And a new dream."

He looked into her eyes, and she saw the wisdom that had settled into his soul.

She drew him to her and whispered, "Yes, a new dream."